Wish Lists
& ROAD TRIPS

Lauren H. Mae is a romance author who loves a hard-earned happy-ever-after. She lives with her husband and two sons in beautiful Portland, Maine. When she's not writing, you can find her obsessing over fictional couples and letting the Red Sox break her heart.

To find out more, visit **www.laurenhmae.com**, or find her on Instagram **@laurenhmaeauthor**.

By Lauren H. Mae

Wish Lists & Road Trips

Summer Nights Series
The Catch
The Rules
The Exception

Wish Lists
&
ROAD TRIPS

LAUREN H. MAE

HEADLINE
ETERNAL

Copyright © 2023 Lauren H. Mae

The right of Lauren H. Mae to be identified as the Author of
the Work has been asserted by her in accordance with the
Copyright, Designs and Patents Act 1988.

First published in Great Britain in 2023
by HEADLINE ETERNAL
An imprint of HEADLINE PUBLISHING GROUP

1

Cataloguing in Publication Data is available from the British Library

ISBN 978 1 0354 0167 3

Typeset in 11/14pt Minion Pro by Jouve (UK), Milton Keynes

Printed and bound in Great Britain by Clays Ltd, Elcograf S.p.A.

HEADLINE PUBLISHING GROUP
An Hachette UK Company
Carmelite House
50 Victoria Embankment
London EC4Y 0DZ

www.headlineeternal.com
www.headline.co.uk
www.hachette.co.uk

To Cici:
For having high-concept friends
and for telling me a fun story, knowing I'd make it sad.

CHAPTER ONE

Pura Vida

Nick

"You're going to be late, *señor.*"

My driver leaned against the hood of his cab, chewing casually on a toothpick as he shouted his warning.

I peered over the edge of the wooden zip line platform, surveying the jungle canopy while gripping a flimsy-looking harness. I wasn't nervous about the ride. My brother Alex had been making me do shit like this since we were kids—rickety roller coasters, jumping into the lake from an old, fraying rope swing he'd found at our uncle's camp, the race car driving lessons he'd bought me for my twenty-first birthday. I wasn't exactly fond of near-death experiences, but I was used to them.

What had my blood pumping in my ears and my neck slick with sweat was the fact that I only had one shot to check "zip line over the rainforest" off of Alex's list. I still didn't know how I was going to pull off the most important part.

I'd made it all the way to the top of this tree, though, and I'd paid this local cabbie a hundred U.S. dollars to get me here. I wasn't about to fail.

"I'm going," I hollered to Javier. "Just . . . give me a minute." I stuck my hand in the cargo pocket of my shorts, turning over the little green tin in my fingers. This marked number eight of ten on Alex's list. Almost done.

My attention bounced from Javier's impatient *get the fuck on with it* face—translated across dialects by his wide eyes and his watch held above his head—to the three-hundred-foot drop ahead of me. *No kid's rides,* the letter had said. If I had kids, I wouldn't let them anywhere near this thing.

"Keep it running," I yelled. Javier only scrunched his face in reply. Our ability to converse was limited to snarky facial expressions.

Luckily, the guy who'd hooked me up to this thing translated my instruction. With an easy segue that my broken ninth-grade Spanish envied, the guide turned back to me and said in perfect English, "Now or never, dude."

Wasn't that the truth. This shit was a one-time deal. A promise—something I was going to complete, then consider myself un-indebted.

I checked the fit of my helmet one more time, then stepped to the ledge where the scent of permanently wet soil wafted around my face. *Shit.* Okay, maybe I was a little nervous. This wasn't a swing ride over the relatively shallow lake at my uncle's camp.

My stomach started to tighten. *Maybe I can just do it from here.*

No. I knew Alex. That was the easy way out. I unzipped my pocket and popped the top of the tin just enough so that I could tip it with one hand while hurtling over the treetops.

Now or never.

"Let's go." I nodded to the guide who motioned with his hand to another guy perched carelessly on a tree branch. Tree Guy took a casual glance down the line that didn't look to me to be all that thorough, then made a chopping motion.

The guide behind me slapped my shoulder. "*Buena suerte, chico*," he said. "Don't forget to get your picture code at the desk before you leave."

"Thanks." There's nothing like an upsell to make you feel a little less like an adventurer.

I ran my fingers through my sweaty, helmet-wrecked hair. I'd somehow managed to look like I was about to birth a toucan in the souvenir picture, so that was great. I clicked on the second digital file I'd received, but that one was just as bad. It really didn't matter what I looked like in the photographic evidence, but it annoyed me just the same.

I opened my texts, typing with one hand while Javier maneuvered the cab around a donkey pulling a cart full of bananas.

I finished number 8. It's getting harder.

I attached the picture and hit send.

Seventeen minutes passed before I got a response. Long enough for my mind to wander away from jungles and cabs that smelled vaguely like weed, and land in the world of job permits, unfinished budgets, winter build schedules . . . the way my dad had looked nervous and stressed when I told him I'd be away from the family business for two weeks to do this for Alex. My brain had been so far away from that zip line, that when the text had come in, I'd swiped it open carelessly, not even taking a breath to prepare myself.

Willow: It's getting harder for me too. You're amazing, Nick. I love you. XOXO.

The back of my throat tingled and I rubbed at my jaw, staring out the window at the thick green palms and vibrant red and yellow huts whizzing by. This place, Costa Rica, it was like a dream. I could hear Alex in my head, going on about the picturesque scenery, the rich culture. It made sense, him wanting to be here forever, but me, I needed to do this thing and get home.

I typed out a quick "love you too" to Willow and my gut squeezed like a fist, nagging at that little part of my brain that had been conditioned since childhood to think that any little twinge of pain was a death sentence. I could thank my mother for that.

Tossing my phone aside, I unzipped my pocket and pulled out the tin, carefully wrapping it in a bandana and securing it in my backpack between my *Spanish for Beginners* book and three extra pairs of boxers because it was hot as balls in this place.

I did it, I thought. *I'd better not miss my boat, asshole.* Satisfied, I zipped it up and settled the pack on my lap. Then Javier shouted something I couldn't understand and slammed on the brakes. My face bounced off of the seat in front of me and the cab banked to the right, the front tires landing in a ditch. "What the—?"

"*Señor,*" Javier said. "You're going to be late."

CHAPTER TWO

Watching the Ships That Go Sailing

Brit

Three-fifteen.

When I'd heard the reboarding time for today's port announced over the PA system in my cabin I'd thought: *What an absolutely craptastic coincidence.*

I dropped onto a wooden bench on the dock and fiddled with the new sleeve of colorful string bracelets wrapping my wrist while my mother aired an updated list of her grievances.

It had grown exponentially this week.

"This whole thing is a humiliating mess, Bridget." Her polished voice lilted through the phone. "It's the last time Cheryl Williams calls *me* in a favor with her personal florist, I'll tell you that much. My God, I'll have to find someone else for the Christmas party. And of course I ran into the owner of the Luxe. Did you know they couldn't fill the date? Imagine their embarrassment when people saw the ballroom empty on a Saturday night." She paused for a dramatic breath. "Bridget, are you listening?"

I muttered an obedient "of course" into the phone, but I was still stuck on this weird temporal event. *Three-fifteen. Three-fifteen.*

That number kept coming up over and over. The change from my ten-dollar bill when I'd bought a coffee and pastry at Penn Station before boarding the ship, the number on the cab I'd taken from my hotel. Oh! This was my favorite—the price of the colorful scarf tied in my ponytail. I'd just purchased it at a roadside shop and even with the exchange rate in Costa Rica, I couldn't escape it.

I knew it was a coincidence. A random fluke, or at the very worst, a mental manifestation of my guilt. There was only the slightest of chances that it was the result of a head game the universe was playing with me to remind me of the day I'd disappointed two hundred and fifty people in one fell swoop. A personal record, even for a professional disappointment like myself.

Three-fifteen. March fifteenth. Eight days ago. My wedding day.

At least it was supposed to be.

Just to avoid any bad luck, I'd decided I wasn't going *anywhere* at three-fifteen. After spending the afternoon taking a van tour of the Costa Rican rainforest and shopping artisan tents in the local village, I came back to the dock early. I'd been entertaining myself by watching bright white fishing boats bob on the crystal-clear turquoise water until this call came in.

"The money we've lost on deposits isn't even the worst of it," my mother continued. "Your father is furious at the way you treated Sean. And his parents! How are we going to look them in the eye? We go to the same *club*!" Her voice was a familiar melody of faux concern and genuine exasperation. I hated this song.

"I can't help you out of this one, Bridget."

"I'm not asking you for help," I said. "And there's nothing I need to get out of." *Because I wrenched myself free, thank you very much.* "Sean and I are done. Daddy has to accept it."

"Yes, well, that's not his strong suit. Though, leaving a mess certainly seems to be yours. You won't believe the trouble we've gone through to cancel this wedding."

"I'm sorry I caused you extra work." I wasn't. Neither of my parents had done any of that dirty work themselves. They had "people" for those things.

My mother let out a heavy sigh. "We forgave you when you squandered your education to start your silly makeup business, Bridget, but I really thought you'd started down a more responsible path being with Sean. I'm sorry, but I can't support this. You're on your own."

She hung up and I nearly laughed even as my eyes stung with tears. When had I ever been anything but?

My "silly makeup business" was a growing freelance gig and a beauty blog that got ten thousand hits last month. The money I made from paid partnerships helped put me through cosmetology school. Sure, I had to keep a part-time job for now, but I had big plans.

None of that mattered to my parents, though. To them, it would always be a hobby that wasted my potential. Potential for what, I'd never been clear on.

I wiggled the bare ring finger on my left hand. The decidedly un-bridal, pink manicure that I'd given myself for my Instagram series on cruise-ship-inspired makeup palettes glinted in the sun. It felt lighter, my finger. Though it was probably in my head. How much could a ring really weigh? Not enough to say, oh yeah, there's a difference there. It was a symbolic lightness. Free of Sean. Free of the version of me that I'd grown to hate. Free to be whoever I was supposed to become.

Free of a roof over my head.

I pushed that thought aside. It didn't matter that I was technically homeless until the check I was waiting on cleared. I'd been twenty-five for eleven weeks and counting, and after liquidating the last of the stocks and bonds where my grandfather had invested my trust, I was finally getting the first disbursement.

When I got home from this trip, I was going to use that money to buy myself a shelter from this storm. Working out of my car felt like amateur hour. I wanted square footage. I wanted salon chairs and styling cabinets. Mirrors and lighting. A sign on a post out front. Not to mention a place to live that wasn't my parents' house.

I had it all picked out, my new studio-slash-apartment. A place where I could build my own happy ending and set my dreams in motion. Dreams that were mine. Not my father's, not Sean's—mine.

I'd just closed my eyes to draw pictures of those dreams in my head when a guy in a black T-shirt plunked down his backpack, causing a flock of birds to screech and scatter and startle the bejesus out of me.

He dropped onto the bench across from me, pushing the brim of a well-worn baseball cap off his head, and buried his face in his palms. Before he hid it from me, I'd thought that his face looked vaguely familiar, like maybe I'd seen it in passing, but that was silly. I'd been on a boat for a week. Where would I have seen him?

It was a nice face, from what I could see: dark vacation-style stubble and a strong, square forehead and prominent nose. His profile looked chipped out of the side of a mountain, but the headlong view of his face was softer. His cheeks were round and boyish. It was a surprising contrast.

He rubbed circles into his temples with his thumbs, stretching the sleeve of his T-shirt with each tiny flex of his biceps. I should definitely stop staring, but somehow I'd forgotten all about the gorgeous ocean view surrounding me, and decided there was nothing else worthy of my attention while I waited for this ship. Besides, he couldn't see me.

Until his head popped up like one of those Whack-a-Mole games, and he looked straight at me. It wasn't being caught that made my heart do a frog jump in my chest. It was the way his pastel-colored, sea-foam green eyes looked alien against his tan skin and almost black hair. How did he walk around with eyes like that? Buy coffee, ask for directions? Were people constantly awestruck?

For God's sake, Bridget. You were engaged less than a month ago.

But it couldn't hurt to look. Emotionally, Sean and I had been done for a long time. And our relationship certainly hadn't stopped *him* from looking. Or touching.

I fought off the familiar wave of humiliation and loneliness that came with thoughts of Sean and went back to stealing looks at Alien Eyes. It wasn't just this guy's face that had my interest piqued. He looked like he was going to be sick. Even from here, I could see he'd sweat through the back of his T-shirt.

I watched him unzip his backpack and dig around. He huffed a sigh and turned to me. "Do you have a pen?"

I blinked at him for an awkward number of seconds before answering. I was wearing a sleeveless white handkerchief dress and lace-up wedge espadrilles. I didn't even have a purse with me. Where would I hide a pen? "Um . . . No. Sorry."

He nodded, his eyes shifting away. He seemed like he'd forgotten the pen dilemma altogether. Did he have sunstroke? Why was he acting so weird?

"I'm sure they have one at the ship agent's desk," I said, wanting to keep up the conversation for no other reason than I was half-infatuated with his face.

His shoulders slumped like the space between us and the desk could be measured in miles not feet. "Will you watch my backpack for a minute?"

My burgeoning crush wavered as a robotic-voiced warning from every airport and docking station that I'd been in on this trip played in my head: *If someone asks you to hold a bag for them, don't do it. Report it immediately.*

He was a little jumpy. His knee bounced furiously, and he was swallowing more than he should. Either he was going to be sick, or he had a couple of kilos of cocaine in that backpack.

I looked around the empty pier. Who was I supposed to report him to, though? The guys pulling in their fishing nets? It seemed dramatic.

His alien eyes took on a very human exhaustion while he waited for my answer.

"Of course," I said, feeling a little naive, not for the first time since I'd started this solo vacation.

He pulled his large frame up and walked stiffly to the desk like he might be in pain. I took note of his stuff, safely where he'd left it, then slipped my phone from my bra and sent my best friend Meri a picture of the ocean to keep from staring at his butt. He had a really nice butt. Like *he must spend all of his free time doing squats* nice. I blushed just looking at him.

Meri texted back. **Gorgeous. I hope you're enjoying every minute of your Sean-free vacation.**

Guilt kept a smile from blooming at her snarky response. I couldn't seem to shake it, especially with all of this three-fifteen nonsense.

Pen in hand, Alien Eyes dropped back into the seat and

nodded his thanks. He picked up the clipboard he'd left on the bench and began scribbling. His hand was too big for the pen, I noticed, and he was a lefty. He probably had terrible handwriting.

"Are you filling out a job application?" I asked cheekily.

He raised an eyebrow and I gestured to the clipboard.

"Yeah," he said. "Ship captain."

I snorted a laugh, and he ran a hand over his chin, scratching. "I missed my reboarding time," he said. "By an hour. Apparently, it's a paperwork nightmare."

"You were on a cruise? And they left you here?" My arm hair stood up, my mother's voice whispered in my ear: *See, Bridget! Dangerous!*

"Yup."

"They didn't wait? Or come looking?"

He huffed a laugh from his nose, his eyes on the clipboard. "It doesn't work like that."

"Wow. *That* sucks." I was suddenly ecstatic for that obnoxious three-fifteen reboarding time. Turned out, I was being responsible by showing up this early, not ridiculous. I could admit being responsible hadn't been high on my priority list thus far. At least not as high as working on my tan and proving something to everyone who'd ever known me.

He raised his head and peered at me, sea foam swirling. "What are you here for?"

"I'm on a cruise too. The ship is coming in an hour." I glanced at the phone I was still using to keep my hands occupied. "Actually, forty-five minutes."

He straightened, turning over his shoulder, and looked out to the water, then back at me. "What do you mean it's coming?"

"Here." I waved a hand at the dock where I'd disembarked

this morning for a day of exploring with just my phone, pass-port, and credit cards tucked in my bra.

He cocked his head, studying me like *I* was the one being weird. *What's this guy's deal?*

"It's a cruise ship?" he asked, even though I'd literally just said that it was.

"Uh, *yeah.*"

His thick, black lashes blinked at me and he licked his lips. "They don't leave and come back," he said slowly. "It's a hundred-and-fifty-thousand-ton ship, not an Uber."

Heat crept up my neck, but I wasn't sure if it was indigna-tion at his tone or the understanding that was starting to stir in the back of my head. "Well, this one must have," I said with my practiced *everything is fine* voice. "Because this is where I left it, and where they said to be back."

"And are you the only one on this cruise?"

"No." I followed his eyes around the dock and my heart dropped like a hundred-and fifty-thousand-ton rock. Then my breath started to come out all wiggly and uneven. *Oh God.*

"Seems there would be more people here if it leaves in forty-five minutes."

Okay, he had a very valid point, but I'd heard them say three-fifteen. I'd had an entire crisis over it.

"What cruise line?" he asked when I'd gone mute.

Now my forehead was starting to sweat. I swallowed a lump. "Festiva."

He shook his head. "Oh, sweetheart."

"They said three-fifteen." My heart thudded against my chest, but my voice sounded oddly calm even to my own ear. *Handle it, Bridget. Take a deep breath and handle it. Do* not *let everyone be right about this.*

"They said three-fifteen New York time," he was saying. "That's one-fifteen Costa Rica time. They said that. They even said it in military time. They said it three different ways."

I met his eyes, cursing under my breath. I'd been so distracted by that number that I must have missed the finer details. Suddenly the sound of the ocean lapping the side of the empty pier was amplified, ringing in my ears, screaming: *There's no ship here! Look at this big empty hole! Gone!*

Shoot. This is sooo bad. As my mother had just reminded me, I had a reputation for making a mess of things and this was a really big one. Which was exactly what they expected when I told them I was taking my honeymoon cruise alone.

"You're just not made for it, Bridget," my father said. "You can't go gallivanting around the world because you feel . . . stifled." He'd whispered that last part as if it was some shameful thing that would bring embarrassment upon our house if anyone had heard.

My bearer of bad news stared at me, obviously thinking the same. "Are you traveling alone?" he asked.

"Yes." *Double shoot.* Maybe I shouldn't have told him that. My eyes caught on his again. It was distracting, that color. I was trying to work this out and I kept seeing flashes of alien green out of the corner of my eye.

"How can you be traveling alone?"

I scrunched my nose. "You're traveling alone."

"Yeah, but I'm a guy."

"Oh, I see. I didn't realize your dick came with a compass."

He pinched the bridge of his nose the way my father did when the Red Sox were getting creamed. "You don't need a compass. You need a watch." He stood abruptly, yanking out the hat he'd stuffed in his pocket and popping it onto his head. "Come with me."

I most certainly would not. "You missed the boat too," I said, crossing my arms over my chest. The gesture felt childish and I imagined my mother's rolling eyes. I dropped them back down to my sides. "Why would I go with you?"

He took a deep breath through his nose, his eyes slipping closed for two beats. When he opened them again, they'd softened. "I'm Nick," he said, holding out his hand.

I blinked at him. This guy was all over the place. He'd just looked like he was going to toss his lunch over the railing, and now he was apparently going to save my day. I didn't need a White Knight.

"Bridget," I said, reluctant even to share as much. I shook his hand, trying not to have a physical reaction to how big it was. "I'll just go talk to the ship agent. That's what you did, right? They helped you?"

"I'll go with you."

I narrowed my eyes, trying to look fierce and capable. "Why?"

"I'm old-fashioned like that." He smiled, full lips pulling back to reveal bright white teeth, like a perfect picket fence except for the left incisor which turned ever-so-slightly inward. I stared at it for a moment before nodding my acceptance. It was ridiculous, but something about that tooth said trustworthy. If they'd all been perfect, I would have marched away.

CHAPTER THREE

Brown-eyed Girl

Nick

"Ah, Mr. Callaway. You're back." The ship agent, Marco, pasted on a smile when I stepped up to the counter. I knew he was swimming in a shitstorm because of my missing the boat and was trying his hardest to maintain the hospitable expression his job required. Though, his smile grew infinitely warmer when he saw Bridget.

"I've got your accommodations worked out. I'm sorry, I didn't realize you were traveling with someone." He turned to Bridget. "We'll need to fill out separate paperwork for your luggage, Ms.—"

"We're not traveling together," she declared like she might get it stamped on her passport. She stepped in front of me, squeezing up to the counter. "I did miss the ship, though. So, I guess I need some help."

She glanced over her shoulder, catching my eye in a quick, almost reflexive search for approval that surprised me.

I gave her a nod of encouragement, guilt warming the back of my neck. What I'd said before had sounded sexist. I didn't mean to imply women couldn't travel alone, of course. It was just that this particular woman had a sort of rare innocence about her. For Christ's sake, she thought the ship was just on a coffee run. Even in heels, she only made it to my chin, and now that we were close, I could see her hair was . . . various shades of dark pink? With some purple in there too. Not in a gaudy way—it was surprisingly pretty—but still, she had rainbow hair. Just the thought of her stranded alone here shot my blood pressure up. A million things could go wrong.

She was right, though, I'd missed the ship too, and I'd been kind of an asshole. I wanted to make up for it by helping her with this.

Bridget's colorful ponytail swished in front of me, sending the pleasant scent of grapefruit drifting my way. Suddenly aware that I did *not* smell like fruit after sweating my balls off on that zip line, I stepped back.

"Yes. Well, as I told Mr. Callaway, you'll have to fill out these forms. The luggage you have left on the ship will be transported to the final destination. You can pick it up there." Marco sighed at having found himself in front of another logistical night-mare. "Fill this out and I'll work on a place for you to stay. Would you like to be in the same hotel as Mr. Callaway?"

"Oh . . ." Bridget turned and looked up at me, her hip cocked to the side. For reasons I couldn't explain, I smiled like a puppy at the pound hoping to get adopted. *Jesus.*

"I guess we're friends now, Nick," she said. "We'll be sharing a ride somewhere tomorrow, anyway? To get to the airport?"

"Probably."

She seemed relieved by that. "Okay. Yes, please put us together."

"Splendid," said the ship agent. "Settle in. It will be a while until I get you a shuttle."

Fucking splendid.

The ride to the hotel was mostly quiet, me slumped into a sticky bench seat at the back of the van, Bridget in the seat in front of me, her knees tucked under her, staring out the window. We'd been traveling for forty-five minutes in the same direction as I'd come from. I'd wondered if I'd see the banana cart that stranded me here, still on the side of the road. Bridget hadn't said much, but she didn't seem overly bothered either. She'd doused that little flicker of fear I'd seen with a wide-eyed appreciation of the scenery.

Her head swiveled as we drove further inland, taking it all in—the fading view of the beach, the almost pervasive greens of the trees and plant-life. I watched her press her face against the window and thought about reminding her how many filthy hands had touched that glass. Then I mentally kicked myself for being so awkward with her even in my own thoughts.

She was uniquely gorgeous, I'd noticed in the hours we'd spent waiting for this van. In addition to pint-sized and feisty. Her high, sloping cheekbones were the kind I'd always associated with vampish Victoria's Secret models, but her eyes were huge and sweet, and her lips were permanently smiling. Just looking at her made my own mouth tip into a grin, which rarely happened these days.

We finally pulled into the circular, crushed-stone driveway of the hotel, and she tipped her head back, taking a deep breath. The sun was on its last legs now and the warm air from the window made the ends of her ponytail flit in the light from a line of tiki torches. This hotel wasn't cheap. The front facade was all teak, with warm light spilling from the tall, rectangular windows of the lobby. Sprawled as far as we could see on either side were thatch-roofed bungalows with brightly colored lounge chairs set in front of each door. I counted four pools just from my vantage. I had a feeling Marco hadn't picked this place for me.

"This is unbelievable," Bridget breathed. She swung in my direction, fixing me with amber eyes that reminded me of those tiger's eye marbles I had as a kid. "Did we just win the lottery?"

I stared back at her, flat-faced. We were stranded in a foreign country with just what we carried in our pockets. I'd hardly consider it a lucky-penny moment. Beautiful or not, there was something seriously wrong with this woman.

"The cruise company isn't covering this hotel," I said. "This place must cost a fortune. Not to mention the cost of getting back to the States." The shuttle rolled to a stop and I unbuckled. "Where are you from?"

"Boston." I could have guessed. She had the slightest accent, but it was more Kennedy than Southie. "You?"

"Philly."

She smiled. "We both boarded in New York, then?"

I stood and pulled the straps of my backpack over my shoulders. Bridget hadn't moved and it occurred to me for the first time that she didn't have any luggage. I at least had the extra underwear I'd packed in my backpack. I also had my phone charger, my wallet, and the little green tin.

"Yeah," I said. "My car's there. I guess that's where we have to get back to. The ship isn't stopping again for us to meet up with it."

"Oh." Her nose scrunched and in the dome light that had just switched on, I saw little freckles sprawled over the bridge. It seemed like she hadn't thought much about the logistics of this fiasco yet. I'd spent the entire ride considering the options—where I would have to fly into, if the cruise company would help me get a flight home once I got there or if I'd be on my own trying to book at the last minute. How many days this would add to my time away from work. I had projects to deal with; one in particular that was languishing on my dad's desk while I sailed around the Caribbean for Alex. Didn't she have somewhere to be?

"Welcome," the driver said in accented English as he opened the van door. He swept his arm out, revealing the property to us.

Bridget still hadn't moved.

"This is where we sleep and eat," I said, rolling my hand impatiently.

She blinked up at me and I caught another rush of guilt. She looked tired and unsure, like it was all hitting her. No doubt due to my harsh reminder.

"Come on. We'll go to the concierge together and I'll walk you to your room."

"Okay," she said, standing. "Thank you."

The front desk gave us our room keys and a little map of the property, not that we'd be here long enough to explore. Our rooms were side by side, it turned out, but when we turned down a gravel path to our block, Bridget seemed to forget how twenty minutes earlier she'd wanted my help. Now she was power walking ahead of me, though her shorter legs weren't taking her more than an arm's length.

When we got to her door, she fussed with the key, suddenly avoiding my eyes. I didn't know what I'd done to piss her off in the last five minutes, but I was too tired to try to dissect a woman's body language. "So, I guess I'll see you in the morning?"

Her eyes snapped to me, focused, intense. "I'm not stupid," she said.

"What?"

"Earlier. I just had some other stuff on my mind. It didn't occur to me that the ship wasn't there. Obviously, it doesn't leave . . . that was stupid. *I'm* not stupid."

I shook my head, surprised. "I didn't think you were stupid."

She looked away abruptly like she'd lost a game of chicken. "Okay."

Her expression jabbed at me. That was the furthest thing from what I thought. Crazy, maybe. Vulnerable, for sure. But never stupid.

"I didn't," I said, touching her elbow lightly. "I thought you looked at peace about the whole thing. I sort of envied it."

Her eyes were back on mine, burning gold and brown in the flame of the lantern sconces on the wall. She tilted her head and squinted, studying me. "Why aren't you at peace, Nick?"

He's finally at peace.

The infuriating refrain that people kept throwing at me burst through the enjoyment I was taking at Bridget's face—a little bud of happiness smashed like a seedling under a heavy boot. A solid lump formed in my throat.

I didn't answer and she didn't push. I had to go. I needed to eat something. I had to call Willow and let her know my plans had changed.

"Good night, Bridget." I let go of her arm, turning toward my door.

"It's Brit."

I looked over my shoulder.

"Only my parents call me Bridget. I go by Brit."

I nodded. It fit her better, with that rainbow hair and

spunky attitude. She didn't feel like a Bridget. "Okay. Good night, Brit."

"Good night, Nick."

The door clicked closed behind me and I didn't bother to turn on the lamp beside the bed. The curtains were open and the light from the outdoor walkway made the gaudy, tropical-print duvet glow orange in the middle of the dark room. I tossed my pack onto the mattress, then fell down beside it.

What a strange woman—Bridget, Brit, whatever her name was. She was like a glowing ball of light. I'd meant it when I said I envied it, though. I hadn't just said it because I couldn't stand to see her eyes flick away like that. Why did she do that? And why was she traveling alone? How could she seem completely unbothered by the fact that we were stranded, but somehow still look to me, a stranger, for reassurance?

Christ, I didn't even know her and now I was analyzing her secret tics.

It was none of my business. I had enough to worry about. I sat up and pulled my sweaty T-shirt over my head, tossing it onto the armchair across the room, then I unzipped my pack. The bag of peanuts I'd swiped from the minibar in my cabin sat forgotten on top, and I nearly cried tears of joy. Opening them and pouring a few into my mouth, I dove back in and found the bandana, unwrapping it carefully.

"You son of a bitch," I said. "Do you know what a pain in the ass this is going to be?" I pressed my lips to the top of the tin, noticing the air-conditioned room had already cooled the metal. I wished it would dry the sweat still pooling at my temples.

I set the tin on the bedside table and removed my watch, then pulled my wallet out of my pocket and laid them all side by side. "And is the lost girl part of your plan?" I asked. "If she turns out to be some psycho, dude, I'm going to kill you twice."

Shit. Something reached up and squeezed my throat shut. I'd said it without thinking—Alex's line. A memory flashed in my brain: My brother's arm around my neck, his fist burning my scalp. "*Come in my room again, Nick, and I'll kill you twice.*" Then the two of us sitting in his hospital room, pounding on Xbox controllers. "*Make me lose this level and I'm gonna kill you twice.*"

I couldn't believe I'd said it, but I guess it was strange that it hadn't slipped out of my mouth before now. Thank God I hadn't said it in front of my mother. She was barely hanging on these days and something like that would have sent her down one of two roads: lying in bed for hours, shades pulled, or pouring a bottle of wine down her throat before lunch just to get through the day.

That was her preferred choice when we were kids, when Alex was just sick instead of dead. As fucked up as it was, sometimes it soothed me to hear the glass clinking when I spoke to her on the phone. I knew how to deal with this version of her. The playing pretend, the perfect soccer mom suit she'd tried on in between these bouts, it was those times she felt like a stranger.

Still, to say she was a mess would be remembering a time when things were manageable. I hadn't seen her fully sober since the funeral.

I tossed the nuts aside, suddenly sick to my stomach, and kicked off my sneakers. The decor might leave something to be desired, but the bed was a cloud. My eyes crashed shut as soon as my head hit the pillow. I should shower. I should brush my teeth. I should get some fucking rest.

It was barely seven, though, and I had a hard enough time with sleep on a regular night, let alone with the stress of this weighing on me. Tomorrow would be a shit-show—no doubt about it. I could already feel the muscles in my neck tightening—the fender bender probably didn't help—and my brain didn't want to settle no matter how hard I tried to force it.

I lifted the silver Saint Christopher medallion around my neck and flipped it between my thumb and forefinger. I was a terrible Catholic, to my mother's endless disappointment, but there were certain things I still carried from my childhood. Things I did because they were so ingrained in me, they were like breathing.

Please let my mom sleep tonight, I thought dutifully. *I'm sorry for how much this change in plans is going to make her worry. Another fucking thing Alex could have taken into consideration.* I sighed out loud. *I'm sorry for that too. I'm sorry, Alex. For everything. I know I owe you and I'm not going to let you down.*

I crossed myself and flipped to my side, wishing I'd drawn the curtains, but too beat to do it now. It didn't matter anyway; I'd probably still be staring at this window when the sun came back around.

CHAPTER FOUR

Fight or Flight

Brit

I woke up to a flurry of frantic texts from Meri, all time-stamped the night before. After saying goodnight to Nick, I'd finally taken a minute to fill her voicemail in on the fact that I was stuck in Costa Rica with exactly one dress, my wallet, a forty-percent charge on my phone, and a cute guy who I really hoped was as confident in navigating international travel as I was pretending to be. Then I shut my phone off, hit up the gift shop at the hotel, and crashed for the night.

She wasn't pleased.

Meri: BRIT!!! Do I need to call the consulate??

I laughed into my pillow. She'd probably saved the number in her phone as soon as I booked the trip.

Sometimes I wondered if Meri and I were switched at birth. It would have made a lot more sense if I were the one who was spawned by hippy parents who gave me a name that belonged on a Christmas card. Instead, Will and Lyric Marcum ended up with a successful, happily married dental hygienist for a daughter, while stuck-up, country-club-going Marcia and Kevin Donovan got me—a college drop-out whose only real relationship ended with me running away from my wedding.

I skipped the texting back and forth and decided to call Meri back. The concierge had rung my room at six a.m. with an update from the cruise line. They'd fly us to Houston, the woman had said. She also said plane ride, not flight, and that little detail had stuck in my brain as potentially concerning. Maybe it was just a language difference, but I didn't think so. It sounded more like a propeller plane than a commercial jet.

Meri answered on the first ring. "Oh my God, Brit. Don't ever do that to me again. Are you okay?"

"I'm fine . . . I think."

"Tell me you're not sleeping on the dock."

I groaned. "Of course not." *Thanks to Nick.* "I'm at a gorgeous hotel. You should see this place. The bed has a fairy net, and the minibar is, like, full bottles of booze and exotic mixers. There's fresh pineapple juice in here!"

"It's called a *mosquito* net, and are you sampling the minibar for breakfast? What is wrong with you?"

Um. Rude. "I'm just enjoying the adventure."

Her sigh was so loud, I winced. "How did you manage to miss the reboarding time, Brit?"

"It's a super-long story." One that didn't make me look all that competent, so I was going to dance around it. "Look, everything is going to be fine. I'm flying into Houston this afternoon and then I'll get a flight back to New York. No biggie."

I'd never been to Texas. At least this detour would be interesting. Wasn't that what I'd wanted? Something more interesting?

A "plane ride" from Costa Rica to Houston sounded interesting.

"No *biggie*?" Meri repeated. "No biggie is packing the wrong jacket for the weather, not getting left behind in a foreign country alone."

"Actually, I'm not alone. I met a guy."

"Brit!" Meri shrieked. In the background, I heard her husband, Justin, startle over her outburst. I pictured him spilling coffee on his Armani tie and Meri jumping up to blot at it with a paper towel, her hair in a perfect blonde bun. They'd smile at each other and a pre-recorded studio audience track would *awww*.

"Not like that." I rolled my eyes, though she couldn't see me. "He missed the boat too."

"Oh, excellent. The two of you should be brilliant travel partners."

I could tell this was wearing on her. Meri and I met freshman year at Northeastern at the coffee shop she worked at, like every other first-year besides me. The tone of our relationship was set early: Meri was all checklists and responsibilities, and I . . . Well, I waited for her to be done with those things and provided the fun. Which I did! Until I dropped out senior year, leaving my parents grieving the loss of my degree as if it were another child. One I think they preferred over me.

I met Sean a year later, though, and all was forgiven.

In my previous life, when I used to wake up in an ivy-covered loft in Back Bay, Sean and I shoved to opposite corners of a California King, someone else's perfume wafting between us, Meri was the first one to notice when I started to lose myself. The only one, really.

I decided to ease her mind a little. "I promise I'll be really careful, Mer. This guy I met is super uptight, like you! And he seems to know what he's doing. I'll let him be my Buddy System or whatever until we get to the airport, and then I'll get on a direct flight home. I can handle a domestic flight, right?"

Meri groaned. "You're sure you'll make it back in time?"

A nervousness that I'd been ignoring since I realized I was stranded poked me. My entire plan hinged on being home by Friday when a gorgeous two-story Queen Anne Victorian with studio space on the first floor and a loft where I could live was going to a foreclosure auction. It was pure perfection.

Okay, that was being generous. It was dilapidated to the point where almost everything you could see needed to be replaced, but the "bones" were good. That was what the inspection report said, and I didn't underestimate the cosmic significance of the two of us going through a rebirth together—the house and me.

Missing the ship was bad luck, but it was only Tuesday. Of course I'd be home in time for the auction.

"Absolutely," I said. "And I'll call you if there's any chance I won't."

"Justin and I are on call." Justin was a contract lawyer. He'd been helping me with this from the start. "You know I have your back, Brit. Forever and always."

The corners of my eyes spilled with affection. If there was one person in this world I didn't have to hide the messy pieces of myself from, it was her. "I've always known, Mer. I love you and I'll see you soon."

I hung up with Meri and gathered my stuff. It didn't take long, since the list of things I had was less than most people's list of basic necessities. Nick probably got the same call this morning, I realized as I stuck my new toothbrush into my bralette for safekeeping. I should knock on his door. We could grab breakfast together.

How will that look? A reflexive stab of caution shuddered through me. Except that caution was out of date and I hadn't quite worked out how to live without it yet. It was like trying on a new pair of heels that were just a little higher, a little sexier than you were used to. I would eventually learn how to walk in them, but right now I was still wobbling around.

I supposed having breakfast with Nick would be the first step. It was just breakfast and we were partners in this little adventure now. Also, I hated eating alone. It reminded me of evenings watching the clock tick well past quitting time, with Sean not even bothering to call with an excuse as to why he wasn't home.

With that depressing thought on my mind, I opened the door to the already-scorching morning sun. The Panama Canal had its own brand of hot—the kind that made your pores damp and your hair curl as soon as you stepped outside. The thick jungle air smelled sweet and made my already sleep-teased hair wing into big waves. I grabbed a few, scrunching with my fingers and hoping I wasn't doing more damage. Meri's voice whispered to me: *For God's sakes, Brit. You don't need to look cute—you need to get home.*

"Right," I said out loud to Meri's spirit. "Home. Totally on it."

I knocked on Nick's door and the sun burned the backs of my arms as I prepared myself for those bizarrely green eyes. The door swung open and there was Nick, standing shirtless in a pair of athletic shorts slung low on his hips. I hadn't, however, quite prepared myself for this.

"Morning," he said. He sounded groggy, like I'd woken him from an accidental nap rather than a good night's sleep.

"Morning!" And I sounded like a chirping bird. *Awesome.*

He stretched his arms over his head and my gaze climbed the ladder of muscle on his stomach, locking on to his broad chest like I was trying to X-ray his heart. His body was athletic and defined, the kind of muscle that came from pushups and crunches, not heavy weights. I imagined him dropping to the ground and giving me fifty, that little half-smile cocking the corner of his mouth. It was a weird daydream even for me.

My mother had been accusing me of being boy crazy since I was eight. I liked to remind her that she was the one who sent me to a private, all-girls school, effectively sheltering me from a gradual introduction to the male species. When the only experiences you had with boys were perfectly safe ones on magazine covers and boy-band posters, it was hard not to be crazy about them. By the time I got to college and realized that real men were all hard lines, deep voices, and chest hair, I was equally terrified and obsessed.

"Did you get the call?" he asked. He had a T-shirt in his hand and to my utter devastation, he slipped it over his head.

"Mm-hmm." I ignored my burning cheeks and injected some confidence into my voice. "You want to grab some breakfast before we go?"

He looked over his shoulder at his bed and I snuck a peek into his little den. His clothes were on the chair, the comforter in a ball on the floor. His hair was fairly short on the sides, a little longer on top, and he had multiple cowlicks going on up there. Rough sleeper, I decided. I bet he was one of those guys who woke up wrapped like a mummy in the sheets.

He rubbed his fist into his eye. "Just let me get dressed."

"Okay. Yup! Totally." *Gawd, Brit.*

"Dressed" for Nick just meant a different pair of shorts and the Puma sneakers he had on the day before, so it didn't take long. By the time we were walking a path through white sand to an ocean-front cafe, a few gray clouds had settled over the sun. Costa Rica was stunning and a wisp of an idea traveled across my brain about staying, getting a job doing mud masks at the resort spa, living in a stucco bungalow. The beach would make a gorgeous backdrop for my Instagram.

"You're shorter," Nick said casually, his hands in his pockets. "I didn't think that was possible."

I paused and kicked a foot out from under the maxi-skirt I'd fashioned from my dress. "I bought these at the gift shop before I went to bed last night," I said, wiggling my toes in my new pink flip-flops. "And this." I pointed at my ribbed tank top where the words *Pura Vida* scrolled across my chest.

Nick's eyes bounced off the cursive, pink creeping up his neck. "Is that a toothbrush in your bra?"

I shrugged. "I don't have any pockets."

He slipped his backpack from his shoulders and held out a hand. "Let me take it. And your shoes."

"Thanks." I handed him my espadrilles and used my newly free hands to wipe moisture from my forehead.

"So, Houston," he said. We took a rattan table, and he pulled my chair out for me. "We should be able to get a direct flight from there back to New York."

"Perfect," I said in my new bird voice. Then I'd drive back to Boston to my old bedroom in my parents' house, a broken engagement and a new tank top to show for it. It was enough to kill the buzz of my morning in paradise. "And this flight—"

"Plane ride," he corrected.

"You noticed that too?"

Nick rested a hand on his flat stomach, and I watched it rise and fall with rapt attention.

"I couldn't get back to sleep after I heard it. I was hoping it was just semantics but—" he looked over his shoulder at the thick jungle canopy "—I think that's wishful thinking."

"Are you afraid to fly? Is that why you were traveling by boat?"

"No." He picked up his menu and it was clear we weren't going to swap origin stories. Though he was filling in like a pencil sketch with each little thing he declined to share with me.

I was what some people call an empath. I wasn't psychic or anything, although I did go to one of those palm readers on Revere Beach once and she told me that I probably could be if I'd learned to harness my power. Whatever that meant.

I didn't have any power, I was just acutely aware of other people's emotions. Sometimes painfully so. I felt little shifts in their mood, tiny micro-movements that gave them away. It wasn't supernatural, it was just like super-smellers or people with creepy good hearing. I took in more of what people naturally put out.

What Nick was putting out was heavy. The way his upper lip had curled last night when I'd asked him why he wasn't at peace had made me hungry to read him more, but the way he'd taken an unconscious step backward had told me it wasn't happening. Not yet at least.

I pretended to read my own menu. "Will you miss much work?"

"We'll probably be back around the same time we would have if we were on the ship," he said.

"What do you do?"

"I'm a real estate developer."

"Oh. So, you're like a millionaire." I snorted. Maybe I should propose, get back in my parents' good graces. My dad had an affinity for what he called "self-made men" like himself. As if my grandfather hadn't died and willed him the capital to start his investment firm at the age of thirty. The same will that was going to allow me to buy my studio.

Still, Sean had instantly endeared himself to my family with his snobbish affection for top-shelf bourbon and tailored suits. Apparently, that was more important than loyalty and kindness in the man who'd proposed to their daughter.

Nick laughed lightly and shook his head. "It's a mildly successful family business. My uncles are contractors, my dad was an urban planner by trade. Callaway and Sons was their first baby. My cousins, Tom and Drew, are more operations types, and I have an MBA, so—" He paused, cleared his throat.

"So you're like the heir to the throne?"

"No," he said firmly. I watched a muscle in his jaw twitch and I wondered why that suggestion made him uncomfortable. "Anyway, we mostly do residential projects. Not the commercial stuff you're thinking of. That's where the millionaires play."

"Residential. Like cul-de-sacs?"

"Yeah. I've been trying to convince my dad to get into commercial for years but he's not a big risk-taker, so we stick with subdivisions, flipping multi-units. I own a couple of them myself for some side income."

A waiter came and took our orders and filled the coffee mugs that were upside down at our place settings. Nick gulped his.

"You must be handy then." I sipped my rich, Costa Rican brew, stifling the urge to moan.

He nodded. "My cousins and I have flipped a couple of smaller projects ourselves on the side."

"I'm about to buy a house," I blurted. "It's sort of a, um, fixer-upper."

Nick's eyebrows slashed inward. "You're buying it alone?"

I wasn't sure if that was a smooth way of finding out if I was single or another judgment on my ability, but I decided to give him the benefit of the doubt. "Just me. I'm sort of between homes at the moment."

He looked adorably alarmed.

"I'm staying with my parents."

"So, you're in a rush," he said, his lips twitching into a fraction of that smile he'd given me yesterday.

"Understatement."

We shared a knowing laugh and I felt like maybe he'd confessed something to me too. A bond of recognized misery. Was it wrong that I wanted so badly to know what caused his? I'd known him twelve hours.

I fluffed the hem of my skirt. "Anyway, I really want it."

Nick seemed to consider that, consider me. Finally he smiled, showing me his perfect picket-fence teeth, and the truth one. "I bet you'll have it then."

My chest filled like a balloon. He didn't know me either, but apparently Nick's first impression of me was a girl who said she was going to do something huge and meant it. I liked that girl.

CHAPTER FIVE

Confessional

Brit

"Fuck," Nick whispered. It was the third time he'd cursed on the small set of rollaway stairs we were climbing, boarding what the ticket agent had affectionately called a "puddle jumper." Except the puddle we were jumping today was the Caribbean Sea.

Nick had let me go first, probably not out of chivalry, and he was a few steps behind me, muttering under his breath.

"I'm sure they fly this route all the time," I said like I had any freaking clue how flight paths worked. I was mostly just trying to say something positive to put Nick's mind at ease. "At least we won't be jammed in between two people we don't know. Unless you fly first class. I don't ever fly first class. Come to think of it, I don't ever fly. I mean, a few times, but not enough to say I have flight habits. Except maybe forgetting to pee before I board and being forced to use the plane bathroom. Which sucks, right? This plane probably doesn't have a bathroom."

He didn't respond.

I plopped into the first seat I saw and watched him duck his head to come into the cabin. He tossed his bag on a seat and sat across from it. Then he thought better of it and pulled the bag onto his lap, wrapping his arms around it. I'd already told myself to quit imagining he was smuggling drugs in that thing, but he wasn't making it easy to be a blind believer.

Although, a drug smuggler would probably be better about flying. Like that Tom Cruise movie where he was the pilot doing runs from Central America. They were on planes all the time.

I got up and took the seat his bag had given up. "This is like a bucket list item, right? Propeller plane over the ocean?"

"Sure."

Nick's phone buzzed from the pocket of his shorts and he pulled it out and frowned at the screen before typing out a message with his left thumb. Then he set it screen-down on the seat next to him and rubbed at the back of his head.

The muscles in his neck were like granite. I went to school for massage therapy for a little while. I'd never finished because my father had suddenly insisted I spend that summer at our house on the Cape and the commute was unbearable. I suspected that was his plan.

Sean had always raved about my shoulder massages, though. I'd offer Nick one, earn myself the Travel Companion of the Year award, but that would probably be inappropriate. Maybe the person on the other end of that text would think so too. I looked out at the water, ignoring the curiosity sparking alive in my chest.

The pilot climbed in and gave us a thumbs up. He pressed the button to make the engines come alive and I had to admit there was a *whomp, whomp* sound to it that wasn't entirely comforting.

"Nick," I said. "If we die today, I feel like I should confess something." The propeller offered a clicking sound to the Scary Noise Symphony as it powered on, and Nick's fingers curled around his armrest. "Nick!"

"What am I? A priest?" he snapped.

Geesh. For all his pulling out chairs and complimenting me on my deepest insecurities, he sure had a prickly side. I studied his profile. From this side he did look kind of like a priest—somber, capable like he'd heard it all before but he'd still give a polite amount of gravity to your plight. He even had a small medallion around his neck that looked like the kind that had a saint engraved into it. I was pretty sure priests were only that hot on TV, though.

Whether he was prepared to take my confession or not, the way I saw it, we were either going to become best friends or die together. Might as well just blurt it. "I'm here because I skipped out on my wedding."

That got his attention. Nick's head whipped around, and he seemed to have forgotten the death rattle of the plane's windows.

"You left someone at the altar?" He scanned my outfit again like he was wondering where I'd stashed my veil.

It was worse than that, though. I'd never planned on going through with it in the first place. I'd been playing a long game with everyone I knew and now with this three-fifteen thing, and missing the ship, I was starting to worry I was being punished by a larger force than just my father.

The pilot slipped on a pair of headphones, speaking in Spanish to a man in a flight suit and mirrored aviators. It felt kind of like *Top Gun* but with the reject planes.

Apparently, everything I knew about planes came from Tom Cruise movies.

"I didn't leave him at the altar. I called it off before the actual day." I winced. "A week before."

Nick didn't say anything. I'd known him less than a day, but I was sure he'd never reneged on a deal in his life. His tight jaw and stress-creased forehead said he took his responsibilities seriously—took everything seriously. Maybe that was why I'd hitched myself to his side. I was looking for a judge, an unbiased party who could tell me that I'd done the right thing, even if it took lying to my family, and I was exploiting the fact that he thought we were near death to get his truth. He'd given me a taste of it last night when he'd said he envied my peace, and now I was like an addict sniffing out my next hit.

"Anyway, I thought I should tell you because it's possible I'm being punished right now and you're going to be collateral damage." More silence. I smoothed my skirt over my knees. "I mean, you missed the ship on your own, but this plane, it might be my fault."

I looked up to see him staring at me and my cheeks pinked. "What?"

"Do you really think that's how it works?" The look on his face was haunted, like I'd carelessly brushed a wound.

I swallowed. "I don't know," I whispered truthfully.

The plane lurched and started to taxi. Nick turned forward again, his posture going stick-straight. "Look, Brit," he said, "if this plane goes down, I promise not to hold you accountable, okay?"

I nodded, my throat tight. It wasn't an absolution of my crime, just from the karmic consequences, but I'd take it. He didn't even ask me why I did it. Which was fine because I'd never see him again after this day was over.

But it really would have been nice to tell one person the truth.

CHAPTER SIX

Repent

Nick

"How are you feeling? Sick? Nervous?" Brit smacked a piece of strawberry-scented gum, staring at the side of my face. She had her head resting on her hand, that peacefulness evident in her smile even though we still had hours of travel hassle before we got home.

"I'm fine," I lied. She still thought I was afraid of flying, and I let her believe it. Mostly because I didn't want to tell her I was edgy and sick because there was a high possibility I was going to fail at my brother's dying wish.

I'd be back in New York by tonight, and then what the hell was I going to do? Bring the rest of the ashes back with me? Hand them to my mother in this stupid tin that we used to keep coins in when we were younger? Alex would rest for eternity collecting dust on her mantle instead of tossing around the ocean.

That would be the ultimate hell for him—sitting still. He

told me as much the day he took over as president of the company and moved his stuff into my dad's office. He'd flicked the sign on his door, his usual *don't give a fuck* smile on his face. "Where dreams go to die, right?" he said.

He was partially right, it was just that it was my dream that was dying.

Brit calling me the heir to the throne had pressed on a bruise I'd been nursing for years. My cousin Tom and I had been counting down the days until Callaway and Sons was ours since we were kids, but for some reason when Alex turned thirty, my father gave him the title like it was some sort of participation trophy.

Alex, who had a degree in graphic design and never gave a single fuck about the family business.

I have no idea if he knew how much of a gut punch that was, watching my father hand him everything I'd ever wanted just for him to treat it like a prison sentence, but it tainted everything that came after. Including the last moment I ever had with him. That was why I owed him this. Why I was going to do everything possible to finish this list.

I scrubbed a hand over my face, replaying that day again in my head for the thousandth time. Whatever Brit did to make her think the plane would fall out of the sky, she had no idea that, if anyone, it was me who deserved it.

"Is that your girlfriend?" Brit asked, pointing to the text I'd been typing out to Willow. I promised I'd send her daily updates, though I'd been dreading telling her about this setback before I figured out how to fix it. I still had two items left on the list and I had no idea how I was going to complete them now.

I hit send and put the phone away. "No."

"Wife? You're not wearing a ring."

"Not my wife. Just . . . a friend."

She scrunched her nose. "Hmm. What's that?"

I'd pulled Alex's letter from my bag when we took off and it was clutched in my fist.

"It's a letter," I said. I'd almost worn a hole through the corner of it from pinching it between my fingers, so I folded it in half and shoved it back into my pocket.

Her eyes somehow grew even bigger. "Love letter?" she asked. "Ohhh . . . prison pen pal?"

"No." I tried to serve her a look, but the corner of my mouth tugged upward. She was cute.

"I have a secret document too," she said. She reached into her tank top and produced a piece of paper folded into one of those little triangle footballs I used to make in school. She used her bright pink fingernail to tug at the folds until she got it open, smoothing it out in her lap. "You want to know what it is?"

I did but I wasn't going to play "I'll show you mine if you show me yours."

"Don't worry," she said, reading my mind. "This can be my day for show and tell."

She smoothed the paper out over her lap and read. "*I promise to always listen to what my heart is trying to say even when the words are rough. I promise to put me first and work hard for my dreams. From this day forward, there will never be anything more important in my life than me.*" She smiled. "They're my wedding vows. I changed all the *you*s to *me*s. I wrote them to myself."

I nodded.

Her smile flickered and I realized this was one of those moments when Alex would throw something at me and jokingly tell me to quit talking so much. "I mean, what made you want to address them to yourself?"

"Because you have to love yourself before you can really put someone else first, or else it doesn't mean as much. I could promise to take care of you when you're sick, but if whenever I'm sick, I just ignore my symptoms until I get worse and worse and don't take care of myself, then why would you believe I would do any better for you? Not you, of course. Hypothetical you. Him. Whomever."

"Is that why you left your fiancé? You didn't love yourself enough to marry him?"

"It's complicated," she said.

"Getting home after missing a cruise is complicated. Breaking off an engagement seems pretty cut and dry. Did you want to marry him?"

"No."

Something inside me was relieved at how vehemently she declared that. "There you go. Not complicated."

Her pretty brown eyes sparkled like I'd said exactly the right thing and it crossed my mind that any guy who had the chance to make her face light up like that and didn't take it was an idiot.

"Folks, I'm going to need you to buckle up as we approach our landing." The pilot's thickly accented voice came over the speaker, despite the fact that he was about six feet away.

I hadn't unbuckled since we took off, so I just readjusted in my seat, planted my feet on the floor, and slipped my arm through the strap of my backpack.

The plane banked to the right while Brit was still buckling and I shot her the same look my mother used to give me when I'd take off on my bike while still strapping on my helmet.

"It's fifty-two and raining in Houston," the pilot continued like he'd recently flown Delta and memorized the captain's speech.

Brit shimmied in her seat. "Brrr. We're going to need some more clothes before we fly back to New York. And I'm starving. Do you think they have a gift shop or something at this airport?"

I couldn't help the laugh. I was starting to think this woman had never been anywhere in her entire life.

CHAPTER SEVEN

Leaving on a Jet Plane

Brit

Houston Hobby Airport did, in fact, have a gift shop. Actually, it had an entire shopping center. Nick didn't seem surprised by this, which meant he was just being nice when I'd wondered out loud if I could get a Snickers bar while we went through Customs.

That was an adventure. I'd planted myself behind Nick, fingers curled in the back of his T-shirt while an impatient crowd of people much taller than me jostled suitcases around us. He walked me through the declaration kiosk-thingy, patiently waiting while I figured out how to scan my passport, then to this little mall in the middle of the airport.

"It's too bad we couldn't get on the same flight," I said as I pawed through a rack of Houston-branded hoodies. Nick had booked his flight through some third-party website this morning, while I'd called my father's travel agent and begged him to do it for me and not tell my parents that I'd needed the help.

This little detour was testing my new competent and in-control persona. I hoped Nick was still buying it.

I picked out a navy-blue sweatshirt and slipped it on over my tank top. "You should get a matching one. People will think we're one of *those* couples."

Nick leaned against the drink coolers, sipping a coffee that he'd insisted be our first stop. I tossed him the same sweatshirt in an extra-large and he looked at the tag and tucked it under his arm. "You need a bag," he said, watching me juggle my stuff. He looked at his phone. "And we need to get to our gates."

"You're a guy who learns a lesson once," I said. "I like that."

He pointed to a row of tote bags embroidered with the words *Welcome to Texas, Y'all* on the side. I scrunched my nose. "It's a bit much with the sweatshirt."

A little muscle in his jaw twitched and I bit back a giggle. Twelve hours stranded with someone teaches you a lot about them. Nick was annoyed but too polite to say anything. I had the overwhelming urge to poke the bear.

"Maybe we should go to another concourse," I said. "I think they had a travel store back there."

"I don't think we have time, Brit."

"What's the worst that can happen?" I mused. "We miss our flights and have to stay on vacation forever?" That would actually be catastrophic considering the auction was in three days, but I kept playing with him. I pressed my index finger to my cheek like I was thinking long and hard. "Hmm. I guess I'd rather stay in Costa Rica if I had the choice."

"You don't," Nick mumbled, pushing off of the cooler where he was leaning and marching toward the cashier.

I scurried after him like a little lapdog.

I bought the Y'all bag and it *was* ridiculous. I was like a walking billboard for this state I'd probably never return to.

Nick hadn't put his sweatshirt on yet so I was stuck repping "H-Town" on my own.

He walked me to my gate, slowing to toss his empty coffee cup in the trash, and I looked out the bank of windows to the dreary, gray sky and the tarmac dotted with colorful planes. It was fitting, the gloom. Once I boarded this flight, my vacation from the real world was over. I'd be on my way back to the mess I'd stirred up. My disappointed mother, my father's *what now?*s.

Sean. Even though our relationship was over, I was never getting away from him completely. Our futures were tied up in purse strings. That was the thing about your fiancé—ex-fiancé—being second-in-command at your father's company. I could avoid him, but I would never be completely free. That thought sat about as well as my dinner of gift shop candy and soda.

"I guess this is it," Nick said. He took his hands out of his pockets and I thought maybe he'd hug me, or at least shake my hand, but he just rubbed the back of his neck. He was still holding that letter from the plane. "If I had to endure this travel nightmare," he said, "I'm glad it was with you, Brit."

It was a nice compliment, but disappointment pinged through me. Funny, we'd spent the last seven days on a ship together without knowing it, but now that I did know him, I was sad to see him go. Maybe it was those weird eyes that had me hesitant to walk away. Once I got used to them, they were less of a distraction and more like a rare gem you might find and keep for good luck. If they were, my luck was up.

"Thanks," I said. "You're not so bad a travel buddy yourself."

"Good luck with your house, too," he said. "I hope it all works out for you."

"Your mind's back on business already. At least give yourself the flight to relax."

"Relax?" He looked at me like I was speaking French.

"Sure. You're still on vacation until you walk through your door."

"I'll keep that in mind."

He finally did put his arms out to me—I was so close now, he probably felt like he had to—and I settled against his chest. He was the kind of warm you want to burrow into, and he squeezed me so tightly I felt my insides squish together. I had the fleeting thought that we probably looked like one of those airport farewells you see in movies, and I actually felt a tear threaten to materialize, which was typical of me and mortifying at the same time.

"Bye, Nick," I whispered, suddenly miserable despite having no right to be.

"Bye, Brit." He let me go and turned toward his gate, exiting Stage Left from this little daydream he didn't know he was starring in, and I let out a loud sigh. That was an oddly intense goodbye, but it was definitely a goodbye and I needed to shake it off.

I settled in one of the plastic seats near the window and pulled a granola bar from my new Y'all bag. Nick's plane boarded in fifteen minutes. Maybe I could see it take off from here. Maybe I would tell myself one of the planes I saw was his.

Thanks to Nick's charger, my phone had a full battery, which would be enough to get me to my car in New York, and I pulled it out to distract me from this weird feeling of disappointment in my belly.

I clicked on my bookmarks. The auction house homepage featured a slideshow of properties coming up and mine was number three. I waited for it to appear and took a screenshot so

I could look at it while I was on the plane. Gray, peeling siding, white trim, a stained-glass door—I was in love with every part of it.

Last night before bed, I'd checked my bank account to see my deposit clear. That was surreal. I hadn't had more than four digits in there since I made the final semester payment for cosmetology school.

I clicked over to Pinterest to look for decorating ideas when there was a commotion at the gate next to mine. People lined up at the desk, looking disgruntled and tired. Probably like what Nick and I looked like at the port desk yesterday. The memory of being left behind made me anxious and fidgety. But then again, so did the idea of going home.

The drizzle that we'd landed in had grown thicker, like a cloud of dishwater hanging over the runway. Only one colorful plane tail was visible now, when before I could see a whole row.

The men in reflective safety vests and headphones on the runway had put on bright yellow rain slickers. I pulled my new sweatshirt tighter and shivered despite the muggy reconditioned airport air. Boston would be colder, grayer, more depressing. March wasn't spring in the Northeast. There would be at least a few more weeks of cold. But by then I'd have my house and I'd plant daffodils and decorate my table with fresh flowers. Maybe I'd buy a painting of a Costa Rican beach and hang it over the white-brick fireplace to remind me of this trip. If everything went as planned.

The passengers' gripes in line at the next gate gained volume. I was watching a woman with a blunt bob and thick-rimmed glasses poke at her phone with a scowl, when I saw a familiar navy-blue hoodie squeeze through the line. My heart skipped.

"Nick?" I stood and met him halfway. His hand landed on

my elbow, sending a familiar tingle through my body. "What are you doing?"

"You'll never believe it," he said through gritted teeth.

"What?"

"We're stranded."

Apparently, it was the whole Northeast.

My phone made an alarming beep as Nick told me about the blizzard hurtling toward New York, grounding all flights headed in the vicinity. I pulled it out of my pocket and frowned at the screen just as the monitor behind me changed my flight status to "canceled."

"So now what?"

Nick read from his phone. "New York is supposed to get over a foot of snow today, with more tomorrow."

"You think we'll be here a few *days*?" I knew I was dressed like a bulletin board for Texas tourism, but I didn't actually *want* to stay in Houston. I had places to be.

My mind started to spiral. I needed to call Meri soon. If there was any chance of me not being back by Friday, I had to enact a back-up plan. First I had to come up with one.

"Come on." Nick pressed his hand to my back, steering me away from the line of people forming at the desk.

"Where are we going?"

"We're going to get hotel rooms while everyone else is trying to rearrange their flights. Once they figure out they can't, there'll be a run on the ones on site. I don't want you taking a cab around Houston. It's not safe."

He didn't want me to? Okay, I appreciated his help yesterday with the ship agent, and today navigating the airport, and I knew I'd just been inexplicably wrecked at the idea of saying goodbye to him, but his tone rubbed me the wrong way. I wanted us to be adventure partners. I didn't want him to tag along behind me and keep me alive like a houseplant.

People were forever treating me like I was helpless, using the "it's for your own good" excuse to tell me who to be, how to dress, where to hang out. I found it was rarely *my* good they were worried about. It was my dad's legacy at the private college he'd sent me to, or Sean's absolutely twisted sense of ownership over me even when he didn't want me to begin with. The two of them loved to confer over my life like I was one of their company's investments, and I was *over* it. Time for Nick to get the memo.

"I'm perfectly capable of hailing a cab," I said, keeping my tone firm, not upset. I might not have been one of those polished, put-together women Sean hung out with, but I'd watched them. They took no shit.

"Have you ever done it before?"

I winced. "No. But I've never traveled outside of the country before now either."

He gave me a look as if to remind me how that hadn't exactly turned out well.

"You missed the boat too," I mumbled under my breath.

He crossed his arms over his chest, his jaw working to grind his teeth together. I briefly wondered if a "mildly successful family business" offered dental insurance. "Look, Brit, an hour ago, you were wondering aloud if this place sold food. You had a travel agent book a direct flight for you. We're still hundreds of miles away from home and it just seems like maybe you don't have a lot of experience traveling alone, or I don't know, *living*. I'm just trying to help you."

"Fine, but—"

"But what? Is it more important to you to be stubborn than to be safe?"

"Is it more important to you to be right than to be kind?"

He blinked at me, confused. "I'm trying to be kind."

"Try harder."

"Brit—"

"No, Nick." I stepped into his space, tipping my head back to look at him. "I know I'm a little out of my depth here with this whole *lost on vacation* thing, but you don't know me. I walked out on my whole life to get here. Don't underestimate me, and *don't* treat me like a child."

His steely eyes slid down my face, then over my bare shoulder. I watched his Adam's apple bob. "I certainly don't think you're a child."

I licked my lips, too flustered by whatever that was to reply.

He took a deep breath and his face softened. "Look, I think it would be best to stay here so *we* don't have to deal with getting to and from the airport in an unfamiliar city with no car. That's what I'm going to do. If you agree, we should stop arguing and do it now." He took a dramatic step aside and held his arm out.

I tipped my chin defiantly. I promised Meri I would take Nick up on his Buddy System offer, and I supposed it was still best to stick together. At least until I had a solid plan on how to handle this newest setback.

"Fine, but for the record, I can get to and from the airport by myself. I can do *anything* by myself."

"I'm sure you can," he said, falling in behind me. "But you're safer with me."

CHAPTER EIGHT

Delayed Satisfaction

Brit

After hours of lingering on a stand-by list that we had no chance of making, I was exhausted and starved. Nick pulled his body up from the floor where he'd been resting on his backpack, scrolling weather updates. He always looked like he was lifting concrete limbs when he'd been sitting a while. The man needed to stretch or something.

"Snow's already started in New York," he said. "We're not going to have any luck here. Let's head to the hotel."

To his credit, he'd managed to book two rooms at the hotel directly across the street from the airport, and now that it was getting dark and the rain was turning heavy, I was glad not to have to stand outside and hail a cab.

We hadn't chatted much since our stand-off, and even though he was moodier than a grounded pre-teen, I was starting to regret bickering with my only friend.

"Wanna get dinner first?" I smiled, batting my lashes at him. It was a white flag, and I was really hoping he'd accept it.

But he didn't. "I'm tired. I'm just going to get room service and crash."

"Oh." I tried not to look disappointed. Why I cared so much about having a grumpy, bossy bear for a partner on this adventure was beyond me, but once again, I hated to see him go. "Well, if you change your mind, I'm going to Burger Bar."

He gave me an obligatory nod but I could tell he wasn't considering it. He did wrap his fingers around my elbow before leaving. His hand seemed to always end up there and I could just as easily imagine him tugging me against his chest like a duke on a romance novel cover or locking his arm to keep me at a distance.

"Let's meet back up in the morning. I want to make sure you get out of here okay." He seemed to catch himself, and he softened it with a smile. "Not because I don't think you can. It's just . . . I'll worry."

"Yeah. Okay. Goodnight, Nick." I turned on my heel, feeling a little dejected, though I really had no right to. Hadn't I just equated navigating this huge airport on my own to dismantling patriarchy? I could feed myself just fine without company, and apparently my self-respect depended on it.

Burger Bar was in the other direction, but thankfully not too far. I'd put my espadrille wedges back on this morning, thinking I'd be sitting on a plane right now instead of pounding the tiled floors of the concourse. Now my ankles were starting to swell and the pretty pink ribbon that laced up my calf was cutting into my skin. I didn't dare look in a mirror. I was sure my hair looked equally disastrous. I could really use some dry shampoo and a curling iron right now.

I took a seat at the bar, climbing the stool like a tree before sliding in. Being built like an American Girl doll with curves meant that barstools were not my friend. I ordered a glass of sangria and a basket of fries and started putting together a little movie in my head of all of Nick's facial expressions, assigning them from best to worst.

The top spot had to go to that smile that started out as a cheek twitch, then bloomed on only one side of his mouth. Worst? Definitely the one where his eyebrows slanted inward and his lip curled like a snarling dog. I felt like maybe that one was just for me. His Brit face. I let out a long breath and gulped my drink.

I should have been using this time to work on a blog post or draft some social media content. I planned to create at least three months' worth of posts for my Instagram page so I could mix them in with photos of renovating the studio. Plus, I needed a backlog of video tutorials because I'd be too busy to record them soon.

I tried to brainstorm some catchy travel makeup post ideas, anything that could turn this setback into an opportunity, but this entire day felt like an interrogation lamp shining on the Boss Babe I was trying to be. My cracks were showing. Big time.

A man in a dark suit slid into the stool beside me and waved down the bartender. I counted three other stools he could have taken, and I preemptively rolled my eyes at what I knew was coming.

I was rarely the hottest girl in the room, but I got my share of male attention. I used to think it was because I looked like I gave good conversation, but one night, after a few too many whiskey sodas, Sean explained that my personal brand of self-expression screamed "Daddy Issues." He said men were banking on my bold hair and makeup choices translating into some kinky sexual preferences. Here I thought I was just warm and approachable, so that hurt.

"You stuck here too?" the guy asked. He picked up the menu, but his eyes were on my chest.

I put on a Texas accent just for fun. "Me? Oh, no. I actually come to airport bars all the time. The drinks are weak and expensive, just how I like them."

He blinked at me. *No? Nothing?*

Clearly this guy had no sense of humor. *He should meet Nick.*

"Well, how about I buy you a weak and expensive drink then?"

I turned to face him, debating if I had perky and polite left in me today. Normally small talk was my jam—occupational skill—but this guy had a mean smile, like the male version of Resting Bitch Face. I bet he didn't like kittens or babies or carnivals.

"I'm not sure I'd be good company tonight," I said. *I'm planning to sulk over a cocktail and dissect why my travel buddy doesn't want to be friends.* "Think we can agree to go our separate ways, no hard feelings?"

He turned back to his vodka with a huff. "That attitude explains why you're drinking alone."

My fake smile slid into an open-mouthed gape. *Wow. That one hurt.* Imagine if he knew how many meals I'd had alone over the last couple of years. Or that I wasn't just drinking alone, I was actually on my whole honeymoon alone. Or that Nick would rather eat alone in his room than hang out with me.

Salt burned the corners of my eyes, but I forced down my bruised feelings and spun my stool, getting ready to tell him exactly where he could shove that smarmy—

"Actually, she's drinking with me."

A voice came from over my shoulder, and my head whipped around so fast my ponytail landed in my sangria. "Nick?"

He put his hand on my shoulder and tipped his head, gesturing for the guy to find another place to be.

Just like that, he slinked away.

"Asshole," Nick muttered, dropping into the stool Mean Face had vacated. My heart skipped when he draped his annoyingly sexy arm over the back of my chair, even knowing how pathetic that made me since he'd basically just told me I was helpless, then ditched me for a queen-sized bed and basic cable.

"You okay?" he asked.

"Yes. You didn't need to do that."

"I know."

"What, did you come back because you were afraid I didn't know how to feed myself?" I crossed my arms over my chest and tipped my chin. I was a little lapdog barking louder than my bite and he knew it.

"No, Brit." Nick held a hand up to get the bartender's attention, then ordered a beer. He took a sip, huffed a sigh. "Look, I'm sorry about before."

"Oh." The scowl fell from my face. "I'm sorry" were two words I'd forgotten existed after years with Sean, Sean, Never Wrong—Meri came up with that one. Hearing them was both confusing and like putting on a coat in the rain. "Thank you. I appreciate that."

He ran a hand over his hair. "I came back because I couldn't sleep."

I snorted. "Well, it's only eight o'clock, Nicholas. I can see why."

"Yeah."

"Why are you so averse to having fun? You're like an old

man." I changed my voice to mimic the only old man I could think of—Santa Claus. "Better get to bed." I mimed a yawn. "Early morning ahead."

He looked away without laughing.

I pushed his arm playfully, and when he didn't budge, something sharp poked my already dead and twitching ego. "Is it me? Do you not enjoy my company?"

I doubted he would tell me, he was too polite, but his demeanor was familiar. I was a lot for people to take, so I'd been told. I talked too much, laughed too loud, made some . . . impulsive decisions. Not everyone had a tolerance for it.

Nick swiveled his stool, his eyes rounding the top of my knee and skimming the hem of my skirt before bouncing up to my face. I'd caught him checking me out enough to know he didn't find me repulsive, but that didn't mean he wanted to be friends.

"It's not you, Brit." His eyes turned sad around the corners and he leaned closer, dragging his fingertip down my arm. I shivered. "I'm just . . . this isn't a pleasure trip for me."

Oh. I scanned his tight jaw, the set of his shoulders. That heaviness I'd felt from him last night was back, right here on display. "Do you want to tell me about it?"

He shook his head and gulped his beer. "No. But I do want to have a drink and forget about it for a while."

A flower bloomed inside my chest. "Well, Nicky, you came to the right girl."

CHAPTER NINE

Looking for a Sign

Nick

I had no idea why I'd come down here. I should have been sleeping, preparing for another day from hell trying to get home. But as soon as I'd gotten to my room, I'd realized I was about to be alone for the night with a whole bunch of thoughts I didn't want to be having. Brit had successfully filled my brain-space all day with her constant chatter and those big doe eyes, and I missed it immediately.

We moved to a high table, away from the crowd at the bar that swelled each time another flight got canceled. I pulled her chair out for her and she made a big show of taking her seat, curtseying and bowing before climbing into it.

"You don't find many guys who still do that," she said. "All the highbred men that my ex and my father hang around with, only the ones over fifty do stuff like that."

I shrugged, picking at the label on my beer bottle. "I told you I was old-fashioned."

"How'd you get like this?"

"My dad and my uncle always drilled it into us—open doors, pull out chairs. They said women were the stronger sex, but if you had a chance to lighten their load, you should take it."

She blinked at me, her face flat. "My father thinks women should stay quiet and marry rich."

I laughed in surprise. If that were the case, I couldn't imagine they got along. She'd been telling me where to shove it since the minute we met. It was my favorite thing about her.

Though, she seemed to have lost her spunk earlier. "Hey, you know that guy at the bar was just embarrassed you turned him down, right?"

She turned away and nodded. I reached out and touched her chin, guiding her back to look at me. "Brit. Don't take it personally."

"Of course not." She waved a hand at me with an awkward chuckle before pasting on one of her huge smiles. "I was totally about to tell him to take a hike on the runway."

"Sure," I said, my hand tightening into a fist. When I saw her face crumple like that, I had to stop myself from hauling that guy and his rude mouth outside to kick his ass. I might wear a shirt and tie to work now, but I grew up with two cousins and an older brother. The four of us Callaway boys got into a lot of dirt before we'd cleaned up and become professional colleagues. My cousins still tended to settle disagreements with headlocks and kidney punches, even in the office.

I was feeling guilty about her being pissed at me earlier, but I also felt a weird protectiveness over Brit that I was starting to realize she didn't like much. I didn't want her out of my sight until I knew she was safe on a plane home to Boston. And if not out of my sight meant other guys wouldn't look at her, so be it.

"You never told me what you do for work," I said. "I'm sorry. It was rude of me not to ask this morning."

She shook her head, finishing a sip of her drink. "It wasn't rude. It's not as exciting as buying and selling houses. You probably guessed that."

"I didn't." I hadn't made any assumptions at all. She was unreadable. If she told me she was the Queen of England, I would have believed her just as easily as if she trained circus cats.

"I'm a makeup girl," she said. "You know, like the makeup and perfume counter at the mall." She pretended to spray something at me and for some reason, I flinched. "I call it Dream Training. I get to try out new techniques on customers, learn different makeup lines. The employee discount doesn't hurt since I do events on the side. I'll graduate from cosmetology school in May and then I'll be able to do hair too. I'm going to open my own studio."

"Wow." Okay, I guess I had made a few assumptions and entrepreneur didn't fit with any of them. Maybe it was her miniature size or the fact that she didn't seem to know how airports work, but I hadn't seen that coming. I smiled. She was right about not underestimating her.

"Tell me about it," I said, watching her eyes dance.

"Right now I'm purely mobile, doing weddings and special events on site, plus I run a pretty successful blog, but my business is growing. I need space. That's why I'm buying the house," she said. "I'm going to live upstairs and turn the first floor into a studio. I'll be able to see clients and even sell some of the products I've scored paid partnerships for."

"How old are you?" I asked, impressed.

Brit swirled her drink around, eyeing me like she was waiting for a jab. "I'm twenty-five and three months."

"Just a babe," I said, chuckling to myself. I still remembered that bright-eyed *anything is possible* look. Maybe that was why I couldn't help my fascination with her. I had no idea what she was going to do or say so I was constantly on a hook. It was hell and bliss at the same time.

Of course, the bliss part had everything to do with how pretty she was. In this dim bar, her bare legs crossed in front of me, it was hard to ignore. She leaned closer and the lantern in the center of our table cast a soft light over her cheekbones, making them look even more unreal.

"What about you?" She kicked my foot under the table.

I sipped my beer. "Twenty-nine."

"Hmm. I would have guessed thirty."

"You would have guessed one year older? That's a very precise prediction."

"Thir*ties*, I should say. You're very mature." She said that like it was an insult and a hundred "loosen up" comments I'd heard from past girlfriends echoed in my head. The next sip I took was more of a chug.

"When's your birthday?" she asked.

"It was the day before the cruise." It was my first one without Alex. My mother made a big dinner at her house. She spent the night alternating between locking herself in the bathroom and shoving food at people.

Brit looked at me funny. "Your birthday is March fifteenth?"

"It is."

"Three-fifteen," she said, her voice going soft. She looked a little stunned.

I raised an eyebrow at her.

"It's just . . ." She shook her head. "That was supposed to be my wedding day."

Shit. That's right. This should have been her honeymoon.

For reasons that I didn't want to touch, I didn't like the reminder. I gave her a silent nod, unsure what the fitting response was to that kind of life event.

"Was it a good day for you?" she asked.

"No."

"Me either." She tipped her glass at me. "Happy belated birthday, Nick."

The sincerity in her voice made my neck hot. "Thanks. When's yours?"

"December twenty-fifth."

"You were born on Christmas?"

"Yup." She lit up like she'd chosen the date herself.

"Huh. You're a Capricorn? That makes no sense."

Brit's eyes flew wide and she slammed her drink down, getting a look from the couple beside us. "Shut up," she said. "You know star signs?"

I shrugged, biting back a laugh at her enthusiasm. "My dad is a Capricorn. My sister-in-law is into that stuff. She swears she can guess a person's sign within minutes of meeting them. She's always analyzing us, telling us it's the stars that made us do this or that."

"That's because this 'stuff' is real. And my rising sign is Sagittarius, so, like, there you go." Her forehead wrinkled. "Honestly, you being a Pisces makes no sense either. You don't strike me as a sensitive fish. Unless . . ."

"What?"

She pressed her pink nail to her cheek. "That's why I can't get a read on you."

"A read on me?"

"Yeah, your psychic power is battling my psychic power."

I covered a laugh with a cough. "What are you talking about, Brit?"

She waved a hand at me. "No, this makes sense. Sometimes I can't get a feel for people because there isn't enough in them to pick up on. Not a lot of depth, you could say." She pointed to her temple and made a face that I could only assume would be insulting to those people. "But your energy is almost too deep. You're like the ocean. The more I try to explore you, the darker it gets."

I snorted, but the look on her face told me she wasn't kidding. And as stupid as it was, I was curious. "So what have you been able to pull from the depths?"

She sipped her drink, then pointed it at me. "You're under a lot of stress."

"We're stranded at the airport. You're going to have to do better than that."

"Okay." She crossed her arms, looking determined to blow my mind. "You're very close with your family."

"I already told you I work with them. I hope you don't have a booth somewhere where you scam people out of their money."

She stuck her tongue out at me and I was about to give up on being impressed when she leaned forward on her elbows, pinning me with her big brown eyes for what felt like an eternity. Long enough for moisture to form on my hairline and my pulse to tick up.

"You want to enjoy this," she said, "but you have no idea how to. I don't know why, because I'm not actually psychic, but I can see it in the way you stop yourself from smiling."

My face fell and I blinked at her while I nursed the blow she'd just delivered. I wasn't completely unaware that I did this, but no one had ever said it to me quite like that—so quietly understanding. Usually my shortcomings were thrown in my face after another relationship ended. *You can't ever make time for me, Nick. You don't know how to have fun. You'll never be happy.*

Something about the way Brit said it, though, like she thought I had a choice in the matter, it clawed at me.

She was still leaning into my space, the smell of her shampoo lingering. My eyes dipped to her neck, then lower, and I wondered if she tasted as sweet as she looked.

I'd been watching her since the minute we met, trying to figure out how she seemed to float on air no matter what the world shoveled at us. Even when she was pissed at me for trying to help her, or digging into places in my brain I didn't want her, she was beautiful.

Her bra strap peeked out from her tank top and I imagined pulling it to the side and pressing my face to the dip of her shoulder while she told me more secrets about myself.

Forget it, Nick.

I forced my eyes onto my beer. Brit was nothing I had any business indulging in. I'd asked her to distract me, but I didn't mean it like that. We were temporary friends, and as much as I'd tried when I was younger, I wasn't interested in temporary. I sure as hell wasn't going to have a one-night stand to take my mind off of Alex and his damn list. Not that it was even on the table. *Jesus.* I should cut myself off.

"I'm beat," I said, willing away the hard-on I felt stirring. "Are you finished?"

She tipped the last of her drink. "Yeah."

I helped her down from the stool, keeping my eyes fixed over her head as we left the airport and crossed the street.

"Don't forget to check in with me in the morning," I said when we reached the lobby of the hotel. I took out my phone and handed it to her. "Call yourself so you have my number."

She gave me a simpering look. "You know I'm going to text you all the time now."

I didn't argue.

When she was done, I pocketed my phone and suddenly I didn't know what to do with my hands. I really wanted to hug her goodnight, but I also wasn't into torturing myself. After where I'd just let my mind go, I should probably just walk away before I said something stupid.

She didn't give me a choice, though. She launched herself at me, wrapping her arms around my waist and squeezing with her typical enthusiasm. I had no choice but to hold her, feel her warmth, smell her hair. How did she smell so good after spending all day in an airport?

"Goodnight, Nick," she said into my shirt. "Thanks for keeping me company. You have no idea how much I needed it."

She let me go and I stood there, feet glued to the ground as I watched her board the elevator. She had no idea how much I'd needed it too. I felt lighter than I had in days. For two whole hours, I'd forgotten about all of the pain and pressure of why I was there, and I'd just been a guy talking to a pretty girl in a bar.

CHAPTER TEN

I'll See Your Worst and I'll Raise You One

Nick

"So what exactly are my options?" I was hoping if I kept rephrasing the question, the news would get better, but the older woman behind the desk tapped her nails on the keyboard, unmoved.

"At this point, sir, my best suggestion would be to look at ground transit."

"A car?"

Brit had been quiet thus far, letting me be the sole bane of this woman's existence, but she perked up at that.

"Road trip, Nick!" she said, tugging on the sleeve of my sweatshirt. She'd texted me the moment the sun had come up, asking if I wanted to get a coffee before we started this marathon day of trying to get home. I'd taken her up on it for the same host of reasons I'd spent the night berating myself for, and when she'd shown up with her pink hair pinned up all wild like Medusa, I'd had to laugh at myself at how much I dug it.

She'd also left me hanging on our twin gig when she'd dressed this morning. While I was still claiming allegiance to the Texans, she'd purchased a novelty T-shirt somewhere between the hotel and the airport, and had it tied in a knot above her midriff. The shirt said *Everything is Hotter in Texas.* It was . . . distracting.

I pried my eyes from Brit's stomach and looked back at the woman. "How long does it take to drive to New York from here?" I asked, pulling out my phone to put it in Google before she could answer.

"I was actually going to suggest a combined trip," she said. Her name tag said Darla and she looked old enough to retire before the next customer stepped into line. She was probably questioning her entire career at the moment. "See, darlin', the storm's headed south down the coast. If you drive straight through to New York, you'll likely hit it in D.C. and be stranded again."

Darla's pleasant twang didn't make that news any easier to stomach.

"What's the alternative?" Brit asked. Weirdly, her excitement seemed to build in tandem with my irritation.

"If you drive east, you can pick up the train in Georgia by tomorrow. It's an overnight trip from there to New York, and you'll make better time because you won't have to stop to sleep. I think y'all will be pleased as punch with the sleeper cars." She winked at Brit. "Rail travel is quite romantic."

"Oh, can we, Nicky?"

Brit was practically vibrating now, her huge eyes sparkling.

"You can," I told her. "I'll even drop you at a closer station on the way."

Darla gave me a death glare.

"We're not togeth—" I started to explain but Brit tugged my arm, pulling me away from the desk.

"You know, Nick, driving without me will double your trip time. Think about it. It's—" she grabbed my phone and checked the map I had pulled up "—twenty-four hours of drive time from here to New York. Maybe you luck out and miss the storm, but that's a couple of nights of hotels if you drive by yourself." She swiped the screen. "*Orrr* a half day to Georgia, we split the driving, and sleep the rest of the way home overnight." She cocked her hip. "You kinda need me."

This was the most rational thing that had come out of her mouth since we'd met and still, for some undetermined reason, I had a bad feeling. Maybe it was just the idea of driving east for a whole day when I could just head in a straight line. I'd always been a straight-line kind of guy. Or maybe part of me questioned whether I should commit to being in a confined space with her for that long. I was staring at her stomach right then when I should have been working out a plan.

But she was right. It would take days without someone else to share the driving, and even if I could convince her to just drive straight to New York with me, I'd be damned if I was going to make it all the way to D.C. just to get stranded in the same snowstorm that had stuck us here.

"Okay," I breathed. Brit squealed and clapped her hands. Darla looked "pleased as punch."

Brit hoisted her bag over her shoulder and headed toward the driver's side door of the fucking Range Rover I'd just charged to my credit card. There'd been a run on rental cars too, which I probably should have considered, and by the time we'd finished with Darla and headed to the counter, this was my only option.

I shook my head at Brit and jutted a thumb at the passenger door. She gave me a dramatic pout. This ride was decked-out. I explored some of the features as I slid into the driver's side—heated leather, moonroof, full screen nav. We'd be riding in style, but it was a completely unnecessary expense.

I banked most of my salary since my truck belonged to the company, and I basically lived for free by renting out the other side of the two-story duplex I owned, but if my dad had taught me anything, it was that poor men spent and rich men saved. Making last-minute travel arrangements in competition with hundreds of other people didn't leave much option to save.

We'd need at least one night in a hotel, and the sleeper cars on the train weren't cheap. I cursed Alex as I added it all up.

"So, what's the route?" Brit asked, buckling her seatbelt.

I pulled up the map I'd saved on my phone, forwarding the link to her. "Here. You're the navigator on this leg of the trip." I knew that would make her happy and keep me behind the wheel for as long as I could stay awake. Part of the logic was to share the driving, but after watching her climb in, I wasn't entirely sure she could see over the steering wheel of this thing. "I'm plugging the route into the nav too, but we'll need to make a couple stops if we're going to be traveling for two days. Clothes, food. You're in charge of that, okay?"

She gave me a mock salute.

It was mid-morning by the time we got on the road, and this leg of the trip would be ten hours, give or take, with meals, gas, and a supply run. We'd stop in Mobile for the night, and from there, we'd be five hours to Savannah—an easy drive on a full night's sleep, and plenty of time to spare before the train left. That wasn't something I was willing to cut close.

After I'd given up on trying to get on a stand-by flight last night, I'd resigned myself to breaking the news to my dad. We had two projects up for finance applications, one of which my dad had been planning for over a year, and I had no idea when I'd be back to handle the last-minute paperwork for him.

He relied on me for this stuff in the best of times, but considering how things were with my mom, I needed to be there more than ever. She was a full-time job for both of us now and I couldn't imagine how he'd do it all without me. Which meant that by getting myself stranded, I was simultaneously failing both at completing my brother's list and my job.

I put the car in gear and headed in the direction the robotic voice told me to. The highways looked different down here. Cleaner. My dad told me that most of the roads in the Northeast used to be cattle trails, that was why they meandered and didn't seem to have any logic like the grids in the newer metropolitan areas did. It was a bitch when he had to plan new construction, but I was used to them and they made for an interesting drive. This was just miles of pavement and trees. And Brit.

She was fooling around with the radio, doing this little shoulder shimmy dance move that made her breasts bounce under her new T-shirt. Maybe they'd gotten tired of me trying to keep my eyes off her exposed stomach and wanted to remind me they were still there.

Not that I was ogling her, but my eyes kept catching pieces of her against my will. Her calves peeking out from under her skirt, the huge knot of pinkish-purple hair on the top of her head, that soft stomach, cruise-ship tan. It was going to be a long ride of trying to keep my eyes to myself, but whatever I'd been flirting with last night at the bar, and this morning, had to be stuffed far away if we were going to finish this trip together.

I hadn't been serious about dropping her at the train station alone. Honestly, I was going to do whatever she was going to do from the beginning. I wanted to make sure she got home safe. On the cruise ship, she could stay relatively safe and still complete whatever *conquer the world* mission she seemed to be on, but driving through the night in these rural places by herself? I didn't want to think about how dangerous that was.

And selfishly, I wanted to keep her for a little longer. I remembered how last night she'd asked if my bad mood was because I didn't enjoy her company, and a little screw turned in my chest. I felt like a total dick after that. That was half the reason why I'd stayed at that bar with her as long as I did, my credit card groaning every time I ordered another fifteen-dollar beer. The other half was I just enjoyed listening to her. People always talk about comfortable silences, and I could admit nowadays I preferred it to making conversation, but I'd gotten used to the noise after a day and a half.

I liked how she drowned out the constant loop of worry running through my brain. Was my mom sleeping? Did Willow need me to take care of anything at the house? Brit's peace was contagious. Last night, I'd fallen asleep as soon as my head hit the pillow instead of tossing and turning until the sun came up.

I was glad I could help her even if she didn't need it, and if I were being really honest, I was just glad not to be alone.

And I was glad that it was a whole hour before our first disagreement.

"No way," I said again as I hit the scan button on the radio. I thought Brit's head was going to pop off of her neck and start levitating in a geyser of steam.

"Nick! Is this why you insisted on paying for this car? So you could be in charge of everything?"

"No." I'd done *that* because she'd saved me a couple hundred in gas and hotel rooms by convincing me to take this train, and I figured I owed her. Plus, I just wanted to. I didn't know her financial situation and I was going to have to rent it either way.

She made a high-pitched sound like a grinding gear.

"Brit, be reasonable. It's fifteen hours."

"I am being reasonable, *Nick*, but I can't take any more acoustic emo rock. I'll literally go into a coma." She picked up my phone and started scrolling through my music. "Ugh! It's all like this. How do you function?"

"I gave up listening to happy music with 'Row, Row, Row Your Boat.' This is life, sweetheart. Messy, sad."

"But life is happy sometimes too, Nick. And by the way, 'Row, Row, Row Your Boat' is hella sad."

"What? Why?"

"Did you ever listen to the lyrics? 'Life is but a dream'? How depressing! Life is real and needs to be grabbed by the horns, not pittered away floating downriver. Though, I'm not surprised one bit that your warped young mind thought it was happy."

I squinted at her, feeling a little like my worldview had been shattered. "Okay, well, country music isn't exactly sunshine and rainbows."

"The Chicks are technically cross-over, and we're in Texas. I'm trying to soak up the flavor, and since you wouldn't let us stop at that Tex-Mex stand—"

"Because we already ate and there is no way they had a proper food license for that thing."

"Ugh! Nick, the point is authentic tacos. It's the experience. I'll tell you what, the first person to come up with three famous cowboys gets to pick the music. Go."

I flicked on my blinker and passed a rust-bucket pickup going five under the speed limit. "How about driver's choice?"

"You won't let me drive!"

I bit back a laugh. The slightest provocation sent Brit's drama meter soaring and it was entertaining.

She swiped my screen, brow furrowed. "Even your workout playlist is depressing. I'm going to add some songs."

"No, thanks."

"Too late." She peered at me through her lashes. "Really, though. Why do you listen to this stuff?"

I shrugged. My playlists did tend to be a little melancholy, but they weren't depressing. "I've never really thought about it as sad. It's more that I like to listen to music that's about something real. I guess I just don't like shallow."

She tipped her head, eyeing me. "Okay, I get that. But it's okay to like things just because they're fun. I'm spicing up your music library before this trip is over."

"Fine."

She set my phone in the console and crossed her legs. "Have you ever done this before? Taken a road trip?"

"A couple of times."

"With a woman?"

I laughed. "Does it matter?"

She gave me a sly smile. "You didn't answer, so maybe."

"And if I said yes, what would your follow-up have been?"

"I would have asked if it was as fun as this one."

I shook my head. "It wasn't with a woman, and it was planned, so it had that going for it. My brother and I took a trip to Florida when I was in college to see a Phillies spring training game."

Her eyes went wide. For some reason that excited her. "Did you two party all the way down the east coast?"

"Not exactly."

Alex wasn't even supposed to travel that far away from

home with his condition. But my mother was completely oblivious to the fact that it was spring break, and besides, it was his birthday. Since we all knew every one of those he got was a gift, no one challenged him.

"I turned twenty-one the month before," I told her. "My brother got me so drunk off of rum punch at an ocean-front bar in Myrtle Beach that I was too hung-over to do any of the driving the next day." *Served him right, the fucker.*

I smiled at the memory. I hadn't done that in a while.

"*See*," she said. "Now that's a fun story. You should have led with that."

Brit dug through the tote bag she'd bought at the airport, and I knew as soon as I heard her excited squeal that I wasn't going to like whatever it was she found.

"I forgot I bought this!"

Please don't let it be another belly shirt.

Thankfully it was just a box of what looked like trivia cards. She tore off the plastic wrapping. "Let's play, can we?"

My competitive side nudged me. Alex and I had a fourteen-year-long UNO tournament going against our cousins. It picked back up at every holiday and summer barbeque. None of us could stand to lose, so after each round, we'd up the stakes and start again. Though, I guess it was over now.

"Sure," I said. "We can play." My coffee was wearing off, so at least a game would keep me awake. She set the box on the center console. It was black and red with two question marks positioned like something from the Kama Sutra. "Wait, what is this?"

She wiggled her eyebrows. "It's a game of intimate questions."

I nearly choked on my spit. "Where did you get that?"

"I bought it at the gift shop at the airport," she said. "I'll go first. If you could live anywhere in the world, where would it be?"

That question wasn't particularly intimate. Maybe it wouldn't be that bad. Though, with Brit there didn't seem to be a boundary to be had, so I wasn't convinced. "I'd live where I live now," I said, flipping on my blinker to pass another car.

Brit threw herself against the seat with a groan. "Think outside of the box, Nicky."

I laughed. She was right, but my brain wouldn't entertain another answer when all I could think about was making my way back to Philly. She wasn't having it, though. She hit me with a stare.

"I guess anywhere on the lake," I settled.

"Yeah? You're a water guy?"

"I don't know what a 'water guy' is."

"You know, floats and boats, as opposed to hikes and spikes."

"Spikes?"

"Mountains." She drew a spikey landscape in the air with her finger.

"I . . . guess? My uncle has a camp on the lake. I used to spend a lot of time there." Every good memory I had was set on that lake, the four of us—Alex and me, and our cousins. I hadn't been in months.

"Hmm. I'd move back to Costa Rica, I think."

"Funny thing, that. After the universe tried so hard to keep you there."

She cocked her head at me with a sass I was starting to like. "Was that . . . was that a joke?"

I laughed and she clutched her chest. "My God. A laugh and a joke on the same day? It's almost like you're enjoying yourself just a teensy-tiny bit."

"Don't get it twisted," I said, but I had to force my mouth straight. "My turn."

I picked a card from the box and glanced at it, one eye still on the road. *Oh, for fuck's sake.* I tried to put it back, but Brit caught my wrist.

"No cheating."

I could feel her watching me, a challenge in her eyes. She talked a big game but I had a feeling, when it came down to it, Brit's innocence extended past her lack of travel experience. I wasn't above letting myself ponder the implications of that. "Okay. You asked for it. Name a sexual act you haven't tried, but want to."

Brit's eyes went wide, a pink flush blooming across her cheeks and down her chest. Now I was really pondering it.

"Um. These are a little more intimate than I thought."

"I'm not sure what you expected." I pointed at the box.

She plucked the card from my fingers. "Okay, maybe this was a bad idea. Let's stick to the platonic ones."

Smirking, I picked three more cards, tossing them into the back seat. Finally, I found one that was remotely appropriate. "What's the worst thing that's ever happened to you?"

"Easy," she said. She pulled her knees under her and sat up in her seat, hand over her heart. She looked like she was preparing to recite a Shakespearean tragedy. "When I was a little girl I had this stuffed rabbit, Floppy. He had white fur and his ears were made from some sort of wire. I would bend them in different poses to suit his mood."

She used her index fingers to mimic bunny ears, posing them in different directions while she made faces—two fingers up for happy. One up, one down for confused. She bent both and pouted, looking sad. For some reason, I was mesmerized by this.

"Anyway, I brought him everywhere, dressed him in little outfits. He had an amazing wardrobe. He was my best friend. One day, my nanny—"

"Woah, you had a nanny?" I couldn't help the incredulous noise I made. I might have been passed around a village of aunts and uncles during my mom's worst bouts, but at least they were family.

"She was an au pair, actually. I had a few. Anyway, she took me on a bunch of errands, all over the city. I had Floppy when we left the house, and then I didn't. I was devastated. I still think about it sometimes and my heart hurts imagining him in a ditch somewhere, wondering if I'd come back." She narrowed her eyes. "What?"

Clearly I was doing a piss poor job at hiding my confusion. "Didn't you just break up with your fiancé days before your wedding?"

"Oh, right."

"I guess I just assumed that would be higher on the list than a stuffed animal gone missing."

Her shoulders fell and she pulled her knees into her chest, wrapping them with her arms. "It wasn't just a stuffed animal," she muttered. "And besides, breaking up with Sean wasn't the worst thing to happen to me. It was the best."

Sean. I stored his name in my brain, already hating him more than I should for someone I'd never met. Her whole posture had changed when she said his name, like she'd wanted to curl into herself. It was the opposite of everything she'd shown me so far.

I hadn't picked up that she was trying to confide in me on the plane. I'd just thought she was over-sharing like she did, and my heart sank a little, like I'd missed an opportunity. He'd obviously hurt her and the thought made my hands itch to break something.

Instead I reached across the console and tugged the end of her hair. "Why was it the best thing, Brit?"

She waved a hand at me as she stared out the window at the passing trees. "It's a long story."

"We're stuck together for at least two more days. I have time."

She considered me for a moment, but then she put on a smile I hadn't seen before. It was smaller than her usual ones and it had no light behind it. I knew it was forced. "We do have time," she said. "But I'm not wasting any of it on Sean."

She sniffed and did a little shoulder shimmy like she was shaking off the mood. Then she pinned me with her big brown eyes. "What about you? What's the worst thing that's ever happened to you?"

I turned back to the road. "My brother dying."

Brit went still and I felt like I'd just scratched a record in the middle of a party. The back of my neck heated. I immediately regretted opening my mouth. Why couldn't I just play this stupid game with her? I could have easily lied and said the worst thing to happen to me was the Phillies losing the World Series. But for some reason, I didn't want to lie to Brit.

My brother died two months ago, Brit, and it hurts so much that sometimes I think I'll be sick.

She studied me wordlessly, long enough to make my skin start to tingle, then she launched herself over the center console, wrapping her arm around my middle while I tried not to swerve the car.

My stomach tightened at the unexpected affection.

"This game sucks," she whispered, her head tucked onto my shoulder.

"Yeah, it does. I'm sorry."

"Don't be sorry." She shook her head and her hair tickled my chin. "Not for me."

I cleared my throat, desperate to change the subject away

from Alex. "You're still in charge of finding us a store. How's that coming?"

She squeezed me once more, then went back to her seat. "Take the exit after next. There's a Target close to the ramp. One-stop shopping for clothes, food, and most importantly, fun."

CHAPTER ELEVEN

Target Practice

Brit

"We should pick out each other's clothes." I held up a Hawaiian shirt with enormous pink hibiscus flowers to Nick's chest and pretended to consider it.

He kept walking. "No."

"Do you know any other words, Nicholas?"

"Nope." He reached around me, grabbing two plain black T-shirts and a white Henley off a rack. *Sigh.*

"Come on, it will be fun." I bumped him with my hip. "I can feature you on my Insta. Have you ever modeled before? You could."

He shot me a look that was slightly horrified.

"People are going to think we're married, walking around Target together in the middle of the day. Should we pretend to have a fight in housewares? I can cry on demand."

"Maybe we should get the things we came for and get back on the road. Does that option work for you?"

He grabbed some plaid cotton boxers and a package of socks, then looked through a pile of jeans. I peeked over his shoulder to peep his size, desperate for a little more Nick Knowledge.

He'd put a wall up since our game in the car, or at the very least, a screen door. He hadn't meant to say that to me about his brother and my mind was spinning with questions. I wasn't going to push him on it, but I definitely wasn't going to let him retreat either. We had a long trip ahead, and something told me he had more to say, whether he knew it or not.

I pulled him into the women's clothes section, looking through the pajama options until I found a bright turquoise onesie. "What do you think about this?"

His lip curved with mischief. "I think you'll look like a My Little Pony." He flicked my hair. "With a rainbow tail."

I gaped at him, touching the ends of my top knot. Maybe I shouldn't make fun of his dreary wardrobe. He obviously suffered from color-blindness. "My hair isn't rainbow-colored. It's called strawberry brunette and I did it myself, thank you very much." The video was one of my most popular to date. "What rainbows have you seen made of mauve and dusky rose?"

He shrugged and picked up a pair of flannel sleep shorts with cartoon penguins on them. "This looks like you. And it will probably be hot on the train."

I plucked them from his hand, pretending to be indifferent even though I loved them. "I thought you didn't want to pick out my clothes."

"I didn't want *you* to pick out *my* clothes. Come on, let's get food and go."

I grabbed a floppy sun hat and a pair of sunglasses, then followed him to the snack aisle, watching as he chose between two boxes of protein bars and threw one in the basket. "You don't need any pajamas?" I asked casually.

"I sleep in boxers."

Of course he did. My eyes instinctively fell to the boxers he'd picked out. "Even in the winter?"

"Yep."

"Alone?"

He chuckled. "Smooth."

"I wasn't trying to be . . . ugh, whatever. Never mind. I obviously don't care." Yet I still held my breath for the two beats he waited to answer me.

"Yes. Alone."

"When was the last time you . . . you know?"

"Seriously?"

I gave him a mock look of offense. "What? I was going to say 'went on a date'."

"My reaction stands."

"Don't be a prude, Nick." I tossed him a box of fruit snacks and he caught it. "Don't you think we should get to know each other a little if we're going to be travel partners?"

He turned to me and tapped my nose, smiling patiently. "I'm allergic to penicillin and my blood type is A negative. That should be sufficient for any emergencies."

I blinked at him. "Honestly, Nicholas? Who knows their blood type?"

I hooked my arm through his and gave him a look like he was breaking my heart. He caved with a dramatic sigh. "I broke up with someone in January."

"And?"

"Her name was Janessa. I met her at the gym, and we dated for three months. It didn't work out."

"*Ha*. Work out." I snorted at his unintentional pun.

He tossed a family-sized package of gummy bears in the cart, which was intriguing, but I wasn't deterred.

"Come on. I'm going to need more details than that. What brought down the epic Nickessa?"

"I don't know," he said. "A few things."

"*Like?*"

"Has anyone ever told you you're nosy?"

"Of course they have. Now spill."

He picked up a coffee energy drink and read the nutrition label, avoiding my stare. "She was kind of obsessed with herself—her body, her clothes."

"Oh." Code for she was gorgeous. Something deep inside my chest withered at his My Little Pony comment.

Nick huffed out a breath and kept walking. "We just had different priorities."

"You don't like shallow," I said, repeating his confession.

His eyes snapped to mine and the little nod he gave me made me feel like a lab rat who'd found its way through a maze.

"And her friends thought I was boring." He tacked that on in a sort of embarrassed mumble and I wondered what that meant. I mean, he was a bit of a hard sell in the fun department, but *boring*? I think I could be entertained for years just wading around in those sea-foam eyes, searching for Nick's puzzle pieces to put together. A gorgeous, dependable man with some depth to him—what more could the Janessas of the world ask for?

"I don't think you're boring," I said, looking up at him.

He stopped in the aisle and turned to me. I was still clutching his arm, so now we were practically chest to chest. He looked at my hair, my mouth. Finally he met my eyes. "That's because you're easy to talk to."

My heart suddenly felt too full for my chest. Having a hunch how hard he had to work to make words come out of his mouth, that felt like an enormous compliment.

I let him go to get some more air, and so he wouldn't see how red my cheeks were. There was a toy lightsaber on an end cap, and I picked it up, pressing a series of buttons until it flashed red light. Then I smacked Nick in the stomach with it. I'd be lying if I said the solid thunk it made on his abs didn't shoot electricity straight between my legs.

Nick took it from my hand and touched the tip gently to the side of my neck. I pretended to be mortally wounded.

"Brit. Do you *want* to get home?"

I frowned at him. Of course I did, but that didn't mean we had to ignore all of the fun parts. Since I'd started this trip, the world I lived in felt smaller and smaller. I'd been imagining adventures like this since I was a kid and I hadn't gotten to live any of them until happenstance and maybe a little bit of fate had set me on this course with Nick.

Nick, whose stress was ratcheting up every second I didn't answer him. "Yes, of course I want to get home." But first I wanted to enjoy the ride. I had a hunch Nick could use the adventure as much as I could.

"I only need a couple more things," I promised. I steered us around the grocery section to my favorite part of any store.

"Makeup?" Nick asked, incredulous.

"It's not for you."

"I didn't think it was." His ears turned pink. *Oh, Nick. You are so adorkable.*

I bent to look in one of the sample mirrors. My face was unrecognizable without my favorite winged eyeliner and pink lipstick. I picked out a tube called Two to Tango, then grabbed a liquid liner and mascara.

"Guys like to think women dress up for them, but it's not

always about you. It's about self-expression, what makes us feel pretty and unique and seen. For ourselves." I swiped my lips with the color and popped them in the mirror. "I just like my face better like this."

He laughed quietly and I pushed his arm. "Is that funny?"

"No, it's just, I like your face too."

I swallowed, sliding my gaze sideways. Nick was casually inspecting a bottle of brush cleaner like he hadn't just slayed me twice in the span of five minutes.

I plucked at the front of my shirt, letting cool air fan my chest.

"How did you get into all of this anyway?"

I shrugged. "It's the only thing I've ever been good at."

He gave me a look like *come on.*

"Okay, it's the only thing I've ever been good at that I loved. I'm also unusually good at algebra but *blech*. I did makeup for all the girls in my high school at one point or another."

Most of the time they were making fun of my outfits or ignoring me altogether, but they were all my best friends whenever one of them had a date.

"Eventually, my mom's friends started hiring me to do it for their fancy parties and it became a little business. Thoroughly embarrassing my mother was one of the perks."

Nick shoved his hands in his pockets and followed me down the aisle. "Why would she be embarrassed?"

"Oh, didn't you know, Nicky? Working for my money is beneath my status." I made a gag sound. "My father paid for me to go to college, because he wanted me to be well-read and well-studied so I could be a good partner for my future husband." I snorted. "He actually said that. Everyone I know thinks this is a silly dream." Even Meri sometimes, I thought, though she'd never admit it.

Nick picked up an oversized powder brush, then put it back. "If you love it, it doesn't matter what they think. But opening a studio is a lot different than doing makeup at some rich lady's house, or at the mall where someone else pays for the space and the utilities. There's insurance, advertising, taxes. Have you ever done anything like this before?"

"Why do you keep asking me about the things I've done before, Nick? There's a first time for everything and this is mine."

He shrugged. "I'm just wondering if you've thought out all of your options. Buying a place is a big deal."

"Of course I've thought it out." And I was ninety-two percent sure that my business plan was based on facts not emotion. Of course, there'd always been a little voice in my head that sounded a lot like my father's asking me what the heck I knew about running a *life* let alone a business.

I was well aware that I'd never even lived by myself, let alone been responsible for the upkeep of a whole house, but the night I decided to leave Sean, I looked around my life and realized I had nowhere to run to. Nothing that was just mine. The idea of this house being some sort of refuge had taken root in my brain. And once my parents saw that I could do this, it might even make up for the broken engagement.

Besides, it was a big chunk of change I was getting. Investing it in real estate was a smart move. Wasn't that Nick's whole *job*?

Nick nudged me and I realized I'd been staring at the same eye shadow palette for longer than I should have.

He pressed his thumb to my bottom lip, popping it out from between my teeth. "I'm not trying to tell you what to do," he said softly. "I just meant that I know a little bit about it. If you want any advice, I'm here. We'll keep in touch, okay?"

I smiled. "Okay. Thank you."

He kept walking. "You're young, Brit. You have plenty of time to have it all."

"Okay, old man." I rolled my eyes at his subtle rank-pulling, but I sort of liked the idea of having someone to bounce ideas off of. An ally. Someone who'd done this type of thing.

I'd been growing my blog and socials for over a year now. I was confident in the world of follower counts and web traffic. And I'd gotten a bunch of contacts through my job for makeup gigs. I'd been hired for proms and special events, even some weddings. But running an actual physical space was a whole new world. Something Nick seemed to be somewhat of an expert in.

I opened my wallet and found one of the mock-up business cards I'd made, smiling at the illustrated sketch of a woman's profile, the sprawling font over a smudge of pink meant to look like blush. The aesthetic matched my blog but there was a place at the bottom for a real address, and I had printed the credentials I'd have when I graduated next month after my name.

I slipped it into Nick's hand.

He studied it, then glanced at me, his cheek twitching into a smile. "It's the same color as your hair."

"Be the brand, Nicky." I held my hand out but he put the card in his pocket. "Do you really want to know what made me decide to do this? Like *really* do it."

He nodded, eyes serious.

"When I first got the job at the mall, it was just that—a job. I needed money and I wanted to get away from my life, especially Sean. It was a few months before I noticed it, but there was a woman who would come in at least once a week, sometimes more. One day, she told me she lived at a women's shelter and every time she had a job interview, she'd come there to get her makeup done for free by me because she wanted to look like her old self. Before things went bad for her.

"I started teaching her things when she would come in, different techniques. That's how I realized I was good at that part. I posted some tutorials and recommendations on Instagram, and people liked them, so I started the blog. I even got paid partnerships with a couple of different lines and it helped me pay for school. Hair and makeup at first, then I added electives and made sure my training was well-rounded. It was the first time I realized that it wasn't just rich people and fancy parties who I could help."

Everyone deserved some of the power that came from looking the way you felt inside. Sometimes I wondered if that power was exactly what Sean and my parents hated about me having this business.

Nick looked down at me, a smile lifting one side of his face. It felt a little like respect, that smile, and I slipped it on like a crown.

"You don't think it's silly?" I asked.

"No, Brit. I don't think any of that is silly."

I hooked my arm through his again, beaming.

We rounded the corner to the men's aisle and I bit my tongue as Nick picked out some shampoo/body-wash combination, as if those two things were remotely the same. I picked up a stick of men's deodorant, giving it a sniff. I read the name, smiling. Rock Solid. *That about sums him up.*

I held it up to his nose and he nodded for me to throw it in the basket when my phone vibrated from my bra. I pulled it out.

"Hi, Daddy."

"Bridget. Where are you?"

I balanced the phone on my shoulder and picked up a bottle

of Axe body spray, wiggling my eyebrows. Nick made a face and I giggled. "Um, Louisiana? Maybe."

"Louisiana?" My father's sharp tone wiped the smile from my face. "You were supposed to be home. We have things to discuss, young lady."

Nick slid his arm out from mine and took a few steps ahead to avoid eavesdropping.

"Missing the ship was an honest mistake. And—"

"So you decided to extend the vacation I'm paying for by taking the long way home?"

I shrank at the accusation. "I could hardly help the blizzard."

"You can't run away from this, Bridget. You may have no issue ruining your own reputation, but now you've ruined ours. Not to mention Sean's."

"I think Sean's reputation will be just fine, Daddy. This isn't an episode of *Mad Men*. Sean's relationship status doesn't affect his work. Besides, you're his boss. Aren't you the only one he has to impress?"

"Sean has always impressed me. That's not the issue."

"And me not so much?" I hated the way my voice sounded. I hadn't heard that voice in days. Not since I'd put hundreds of miles between myself and my family.

"I've been paying my own way since I got to Houston," I reminded him.

"Yes, I see. Gift shop trinkets, drinks at the airport bar. Did you forget that I'm a signer on your account?"

How could I? He'd set it up that way when I was sixteen. I wasn't stupid, I had my own account too, but I had to keep my deposits going into this one so he wouldn't know. He'd only stopped going through it with a fine-tooth comb once I moved in with Sean. I guess he was back to it.

"Are you seriously tracking my purchases? Why can't you just trust me for once?" I hissed.

"Because you've proven yourself unfit to make decisions in your own best interest, Bridget."

"Right. Of course you think that." I'd followed Nick to the self-checkout. He was loading the bags into the cart in his lane, but he turned over his shoulder at my raised voice.

"Everything okay?" he mouthed, staying a respectable distance away so he couldn't bear witness to my humiliation.

"It's fine," I snapped.

His mouth clamped closed and the way his eyes turned sympathetic made my saliva form a ball in the back of my throat. I'd almost believed it for a moment there, that I deserved the pride on Nick's face when I told him my plans. But here I was, being scolded like a child by my father.

My new crown tilted, nearly sliding off my head in shame. I lowered my voice to a whisper. "I'll be home soon."

"See that you are."

CHAPTER TWELVE

Sightseeing and Souvenirs

Nick

Back in the car, Brit busied herself beside me, opening and testing all of her new products. I kept one eye on the road and one on her, watching as she gave herself a makeover in the passenger side mirror. I thought she was beautiful bare-faced, but I had to admit whatever she'd done to her eyelids and lips was sexy as hell. Plus now she smelled like some sort of tropical flower, so there was that.

She took a picture of herself after finishing another step, her lips pursed, eyes wide. Her freckles popped in the sun. Damn, she was cute.

Great. Now I'm going to have to get an Instagram account.

I liked watching her work, but I didn't like the new quiet that had settled in. I'd done my best to avoid listening to her phone conversation in the store but our proximity for the foreseeable future didn't allow much privacy. I could tell it wasn't pleasant.

"Why'd you choose that name for your business?" I asked.

Brit peeked at me over a makeup brush the size of her forehead.

I dug the card out of my pocket and read it. "*Álainn*. Does it mean something?"

"It's pronounced *aw-len*. It means 'beautiful' in Gaelic. My father used to call me that when I was little."

I glanced sidelong at her, thinking about the parts of that phone conversation that I could hear, her face when she'd hung up. "He doesn't call you that anymore?"

"Can't remember the last time."

"*Álainn*." I said it again, pronouncing it right, and she pressed her hand to her heart and smiled.

Listening to Brit talk about her business had me swimming in a whole bunch of memories—nights on the lake when Tom and I would lay out on the dock at my uncle's camp and talk about being the next generation of Callaway and Sons. The things we'd do when the company was ours, how when we grew up we'd have our own sons to pass it down to. We were going to run the world.

But first we would make Drew our permanent coffee bitch because he had the misfortune of being born two years later than us.

I hadn't let myself think about those plans since my father chose Alex to be president of the company. He made it clear what my place was that day—to be there when he needed me, to carry his torch instead of trying to light my own. But Brit had that hunger that I used to have. Seeing it was kind of like looking at a photograph from the past.

Brit tossed the brush in her bag and picked up her phone. "Oh! Up here, a mile off of the next exit is a place we should check out. It's a state park that has a haunted bridge. There's a waterfall!"

I flicked a look in her direction. We were already behind schedule. The trip to Target had eaten all of my allotted bathroom/meal/shopping time combined. "Sightseeing isn't on the itinerary."

She giggled like I'd told a hilarious joke. "*Itinerary*. Nicky, you've scheduled almost two days for a fifteen-hour trip. We have time to see some sights."

"If we make it to Mobile before we stop for the night, we'll have time to sightsee in Savannah tomorrow." I had a schedule, and I didn't care if Brit thought I was being uptight for wanting to get there early. The last thing we needed was to miss another ride. I couldn't take another day to dwell on how many ways this trip had gone wrong.

Alex's unfinished list felt like a fifty-pound weight in my back pocket. Though, I was starting to care less and less about whether or not I completed these tasks. I did my best; now I needed to get home.

Even as I thought it, I knew "I did my best" wasn't how my family handled things.

Brit huffed, seeming to give up, but a few minutes later, she crossed her legs and started doing some squirming, shaking dance in her seat. She turned to look at me, pulling her newly pink lip between her teeth.

"What?"

"I have to pee."

Christ. "That's convenient."

She pushed her lip into a pout. "It's rather *in*convenient, actually, given that I'm stuck in this moving vehicle."

I pointed to the grassy shoulder. "I'll pull over up there."

Her jaw dropped. "Nick! I am *not* going to pee on the side of the highway."

Of all the ridiculous things, this was what she took

exception to? I blew out a breath and tried to ignore her puppy-dog eyes. "Let me guess, this park has public restrooms?"

She nodded, that lip between her teeth again, and the puppy-dog eyes won.

I put on my blinker. "Ten minutes."

I grabbed Brit's arm, steering her around a puddle at least ankle deep. It turned out the puppy-dog eyes weren't the only tool she had at her disposal. After she'd used the bathroom in the visitor center, she'd turned that pouty lip on me and I was like a robot programmed to do whatever she said. That was how we ended up going to see the waterfall.

We were a quarter mile into the woods, far enough that I couldn't see the car anymore, and I looked down at her flip-flops. "Did you put any thought into your footwear when you decided we should do this?"

She shrugged. "I'm not going to let my wardrobe constraints keep me from seeing a bridge haunted by the ghost of a dead blacksmith."

I watched mud splatter up the back of her calf when her shoe slapped her heel, then looked back at her perfect hair and makeup. I shook my head, seriously torn between annoyed and turned on.

"You don't really believe in this ghost stuff, right?" I asked.

"You mean this particular story or the afterlife in general?"

"In general, I guess." I chewed my lip, wondering why I'd even broached this subject. I had my own thoughts on the matter, and lately I was intolerant of anyone who talked about Alex living on in some other realm like that was supposed to make him not being in this one any better. Brit was talking about campfire tales and kids' stories. It wasn't the same, but I had to know if she really bought into it.

She looked over her shoulder at me and I knew I hadn't gotten away with anything. She knew why I was asking. "What do you think?"

"I'm not the one looking for a dead blacksmith haunting a bridge."

"Well, we all know I'm the fun one." She gathered her skirt up, giving me a glimpse of thigh, and jumped over a rock in the trail, landing in more mud. "I don't know, Nick. I don't think any of us do. But I think sometimes people just need something to believe in and we should let them have it."

I nodded at the top of her head, thinking about my mother and Willow and the way they thought it mattered where these ashes in my pocket ended up, how they believed it was a piece of Alex and not just a pile of dust. I didn't believe any of that, yet every time that tin got lighter, I felt more alone. Until I met this beautiful woman stomping around in the mud.

A few more brush-covered feet, and the sound of water rushing overpowered the sound of the mosquitos.

"Here," she said, pushing ahead of me. I followed, ducking under a low branch, and found myself at the edge of a wooden bridge that didn't look like people should be enticed to visit it. Now I was wondering if the blacksmith died trying to cross this rickety thing.

Below us were rapids that I was hoping we could avoid exploring, but across the river, draped over the jagged edges of a slate wall was a waterfall that glowed green from the moss growing behind it. The canopy opened directly above it and the sun poked through in fingers, like it was plucking at the water. The air around us was fresh with mist.

We'd just spent a week hopping from one gorgeous destination to another by boat, but something about this spot in the forest in the middle of nowhere took my breath away.

"Well, water guy?" Brit said, looking up at what was probably a dopey look on my face. "Isn't it gorgeous?"

"It is."

"Are you glad you came up here with me?" She climbed onto the railing in her damn flip-flops and I fisted the back of her dress, holding her safe.

"I am very glad I came here with you."

She pulled her phone out of her bra and held it out to try to take a selfie. Her arm was too short to get us both, so I took it and wrapped my arm around her waist. She was nearly my height while standing on the railing, and I pressed my cheek to her temple. She turned her face so her strawberry breath brushed my skin. "Say cheese."

"No," I said, just to mess with her, but I still smiled, big and ridiculous. It was becoming a habit with her.

Brit made a face, and I snapped the picture. She took the phone back and grinned. "I'm going to keep it forever."

"Hey," I said, pulling her closer and telling myself it was for her safety. "If I wasn't here, would you have done this by yourself?"

"If you weren't here, I'd still be on a dock in Costa Rica, waiting for a ship."

I grinned at the back of her head. "So, you admit it. You need me."

She turned in my grip, leaning back on the railing to look at me. "Look at that smile on your face, Nicky. You need me too."

Back at the car, Brit used a T-shirt and what was left of my Dasani to clean the mud off of her bare feet. She tossed her flip-flops in the back and laced those sandals from yesterday up her calves. I was saved from having to pretend I wasn't watching by my phone buzzing in my pocket.

I pulled it out to see my cousin Tom's name on the screen and I could almost hear myself deflate, wondering what warranted a middle of the day call. Tom and I were born three months apart, him first, he loved to remind me. He was more like Alex than me—laid back, always smiling—and we looked nothing alike other than our pale eyes, but when we were together people always assumed we were brothers because apparently we just looked close.

I hated that now seeing his name on my screen made me anxious.

"Hey, Tom. Hold on." I covered the receiver. "Brit?" She smiled up at me and I tossed her the keys. "I have to take this. Will you please stay in the car?"

She twirled the key ring around her finger. "Does this mean I get to drive?"

"It means you get to pick the music." She pumped a fist, and I jogged a few steps, calling over my shoulder, "Please stay here."

She saluted me, eyes on the radio.

"What's up?" I asked Tom.

"Who were you talking to?"

"No one."

He chuckled. "Sounded like a female no one."

I knew it wasn't an accusation, but I still felt guilty considering what we both knew I was here to do. "You need your ears checked," I said.

"Yeah, all right. Where are you?"

"Somewhere in Louisiana."

"Have you talked to your dad?"

My pulse tripped. I'd sent him to voicemail twice when Brit and I were at Target. "Tell me it's not my mom."

"She's fine. It's the Clayborne job. He's got it in his head you're going to be back to run the final budget numbers before we submit them. I told him it was unlikely."

The Clayborne job was a planned neighborhood of ten houses that overlooked a man-made lake the town had just finished. It was our biggest job to date and we'd just won a hard-fought bid to get it. Now we had to go to the bank with our budget for the development to secure funding and we had a pretty razor-thin margin.

We used to have a CFO, in addition to my dad and uncle, but when I got my MBA, I inherited responsibility for the financials—and the business development, and the acquisitions—while Tom and Drew handled the contracting side of things. "I'll be back in two days," I said. Another brick fell onto my shoulders. As if not finishing Alex's task wasn't enough, now I had a deadline.

"He can handle it, Nick. I know it's bad timing, but you just have to tell him you can't do it all."

"Yeah, because he listens to me."

"A lot of shit would be different if he did," Tom said. "We both know that."

I dug the toe of my sneaker into the dirt, tension building in my shoulders at his implication. The day my dad put Alex in charge, Tom and I went out to drink too many beers and lick our wounds. He told me it should have been me and then we never spoke of it again. It was there, though, in comments like that. "I'll give him a call," I said, ready to change the subject. "I need to check in on my mom anyway. Any news for me there?"

"She's the same. Listen, Nick, you got a forced vacation here, one we both know you won't get again for a long while. Make up an excuse with your dad. Hell, slash your own tire if you need to, but take your time. Drew and I will cover for you. Like always," he added, jokingly, since I spent my teenage years covering for those assholes.

I laughed at the jab, but I wasn't going to take his advice. Even if they could swing it without me at work, I needed to be back for my mom.

Sometimes it felt like there wasn't a single person who didn't need something from me.

"I'll be back in two days," I told Tom, my chest squeezing even tighter.

CHAPTER THIRTEEN

Hunger Pain

Brit

Nick was right. I was too small for this car.

He finally let me drive after a big back and forth about whether or not I could see over the steering wheel. He insisted that I demonstrate that I could back out of the parking spot at the waterfall while he stood in the lot, arms crossed over his chest like a driver's ed instructor.

Because he was outside, he couldn't see how I'd had to come to a full stand to reach the brake and see over my shoulder. I wouldn't have been able to do it without the backup camera. But so what? That was its whole purpose!

The whole thing was kind of hot, if I'm honest. The way he watched me from behind his sunglasses, smiling that half-smile when I managed it. I'd never tell him the truth.

Ever since he'd told me he liked my face—a weird, and yet entirely *him* compliment—my mind had been a torturous place to be. I wondered what it would be like to have Nick as a friend.

I wondered what he did with his free time, who he hung out with. I couldn't imagine that many people passed the guard he had up. But he was also weirdly charming when he wanted to be. Like a secret weapon he let gleam from his hip.

What I wouldn't give to take my chances on a full dose of that charm. Now he was sitting in the passenger seat, elbow propped on the window in a way that made his bicep pop while he frowned at his phone. The man was entirely too pretty to be in small spaces with.

And *that* was why I was staring out the windshield, hands ten and two, my eyes laser-focused on the road to keep from looking at him. Was that his plan?

It had been two hours since we left the state park, and my stomach started to grumble. We'd crossed most of Louisiana, but Nick had it in his head that we would drive to the route I-10 split before stopping for dinner. That way he could check the current traffic conditions while we ate, and choose one of two routes to Savannah. It was all very organized, but that was—I pinched the nav screen and zoomed out—three hours away.

"Can we stop?" I asked. "I'm getting hungry."

He jerked like he'd been in one of those highway trances, then he made a face. "It's only four o'clock."

"Yeah, but we didn't really get lunch." At least *I* didn't count the snack selection from Target with a side of drive-thru coffee as a real meal. And I'd only had a double chocolate muffin for breakfast at the airport.

Nick had a protein bar and juice, which might be why he had those abs.

He gave me a long-suffering look and glanced at the dash. "It's almost like you forget the way you got left in Costa Rica because of your poor time management skills."

"I got left behind because of my poor listening skills. You knew exactly when to be there and you still missed it."

He mumbled something about donkeys and bananas, then poked at his phone. "I'll search what's at the next exit."

"Okay, maybe something with outdoor seating. It's so nice out. No tapas or anything, though. I'm so hungry I could eat a horse right now. Oh! Try and find a taco place since we missed out on the food truck."

"Horse tacos. Got it."

The whole googling thing was a lie, though, because when a red and green pizzeria sign greeted us first thing off the exit, Nick insisted we just eat there.

The parking lot was jammed, cars circling brake lights like vultures. Nick tapped his foot and huffed the entire time I searched for a spot big enough for this behemoth vehicle. Finally, I found an empty space around the side of the building. I made a big show of maneuvering it—*thank you, luxury vehicle equipped with park assist*—and backed it into the spot.

He grabbed his backpack and pushed out the door before he could congratulate me, but I'm sure it was on the tip of his tongue.

Nick ordered a mushroom and pepper pizza the size of the table and we sat across from each other in a squeaky wood and pleather booth. I watched him devour a folded slice in two bites.

"You were hungry," I said.

He finished chewing and took another slice. "Like you said, we didn't eat lunch."

I studied him. "Your color looks better. I didn't even notice how pale you were. Nick!"

His head popped up, eyes wide. "What?"

"Is this a habit for you? Not taking care of yourself?"

"I didn't realize I was hungry until we got food. I'm fine."

"It's not fine. You can't go into hypoglycemic shock and crash the Rover. I need to get home and buy a house." I reached across the table and pinched the skin on his hand to check the elasticity.

"Ow. What the hell?"

"You're dehydrated too." I pulled up the fitness app that I'd downloaded last summer then promptly ignored. "I'm going to start tracking your water intake."

He plucked my phone from my hand and put it face down on the table, then served another slice of pizza onto my plate. "Tell me more about your house," he said.

I knew a subject change when I saw one, but this one was too enticing.

"It's a dump." I blew a raspberry and frowned. "I mean, right now it is. But I'm going to fix it up."

Nick folded another slice in half and took a tidy but huge bite while I sawed off the end of my slice with a plastic knife.

"And it has room for your studio?"

The excitement I'd felt when I first saw it bubbled back up at Nick's attentive eyes. I was a popped champagne bottle, spilling over. "It was built as a single-family home, but the first floor was converted to a dentist office in the nineties. The waiting room needs to be redone and I need to knock down a few walls. Obviously I have to redecorate the whole thing, but it has this really cute wooden signpost out front. I can't wait to hang my sign there. That's how I'll know I made it. A sign hanging from a post."

He chuckled and shook his head.

It would be one step at a time. I needed to replenish my savings account, which was a barren desert after paying for cosmetology school. Then I could quit the job at the mall. I'd set up an office to run the blog and my socials and edit videos. Then I'd pick at the renovations until I could get it in good enough shape to see clients there.

I had visions of bridal parties sipping champagne near the fireplace while I made them feel good about themselves. Mothers bringing their daughters in for prom. They'd leave feeling special and happy all because of me. It was a five-year plan at best, but it didn't matter because the first step would be done. I'd have some solid ground to build on.

"It's going to auction on Friday," I told him. "And my realtor said there hasn't been much interest. I have a good chance."

"Wow. Auction." He raised an eyebrow. "Not many buyers can pull off a cash sale."

"I have a trust," I admitted. "It kicked in when I turned twenty-five." I chanced a look at Nick, trying to read him. I hated telling people about that. It made it a lot harder to claim my emancipation from my parents' world when I was using family money to do it.

Part of me wanted to explain all of the things I'd had to give up for this inheritance—agency, self-respect, love—but I knew to a hard-working guy like Nick, I'd just seem ungrateful. "I know you probably think that sounds privileged, and I know that it is, but I'm using it to build something. I worked my butt off to make it this far. I paid for every dollar of cosmetology school myself."

Nick tipped his head to look at me. "Hey. I'm not judging you, Brit. I had a whole business handed down to me. I know it still takes a lot of work."

My face softened at his quiet understanding. I'd set out to do this completely on my own, to prove that I could, but if I let myself, I could get used to having someone like Nick in my corner.

Not *like* him. Him, specifically.

I grabbed my phone and pulled up the real estate listing. "Wanna see?"

He wiped his hands on a napkin and took it from me. "This is it?"

"Yes." I took a bite of pizza, trying not to fidget while Nick examined my hopes and dreams.

"You were right about it being a fixer-upper," he said, but his lip curled up in a smile and I knew he approved. It meant the world.

"It's a long way from Liberty Ave."

He raised an eyebrow.

"My parents' house in Chestnut Hill. Currently the posh digs of a homeless runaway bride."

"Don't be so hard on yourself. Everyone needs help sometimes."

I stifled the urge to reply with a bashful "some more than others." That crown had reappeared and I liked the way it felt.

I took the phone back, scrolling to the interior photos. Those were even worse. When I showed Nick, he laughed, but it was in commiseration.

He leaned back in his seat, eyeing me. "Why do you want it so bad? What is it about this place?"

I smiled, remembering the way my heart had knocked on my ribs when I'd seen the listing for the first time. "I just had a feeling this house was going to change my life somehow," I said. And that I'd finally found something that needed me as much as I needed it. "Do you think that's crazy?"

"Not even a little."

I blinked, pushing away all the bad that had led to this point and focusing on the future. "Anyway, I think me and this house understand each other. We're both a little bit of a mess."

Nick licked his lips and stared at me. "A mess isn't so bad." He lifted his drink to his lips. "Sometimes it's good to get your hands dirty."

He winked and I completely missed my mouth. A big, saucy bite of pizza dribbled down my chest into my lap, leaving a trail of red on my T-shirt that made me look like the victim of a heinous crime.

Nick snort-laughed, nearly spraying his sip of soda all over our lunch.

"Really?" The first time he gave me that full laugh and it was at my expense. Whatever, I was so intoxicated by it that I didn't care. But I did toss a balled-up napkin at his head. "Laugh it up, Nicky. That was your fault."

"I'm sorry."

He wasn't, and his grin grew as I blotted the front of my shirt. "*What?*"

"You just . . ." He pulled a napkin from the table dispenser. "Here."

He pressed his big palm to the side of my face, tipping my chin, and touched the napkin to my cheek. His lips turned up into one of those rare-gem smiles. There was a reason he kept those smiles at half-wattage most of the time. They were like a bullet straight to the heart—all rounded cheeks and crinkly-eyes.

A picture of that smile pressed somewhere on my body assaulted my brain and made me sigh audibly.

Oh my God. What was I thinking? I'd never survive a kiss from a man like Nick. All that brooding sexual intensity would incinerate me on the spot and I'd be left a pile of bones and mascara in a cute T-shirt. A cute, sauce-smeared T-shirt.

"I'm going to the car to change my shirt," I blurted, nearly knocking over my drink as I stood. I looked at my dress-turned-skirt and saw the trickle of red had gone further than I thought. "Actually, my whole outfit."

Nick's smile dropped and he reached for his backpack under the table. "I'll go with you."

"You want to come watch me change?" My voice was all *flirt like I hadn't just imagined committing suicide by lip lock.* What the hell was wrong with me?

He cocked his head in response, and I wasn't sure if it was meant to flirt back or chastise me for such a ridiculous thought. "The car is behind the building," he said. "We don't know this neighborhood."

Right. Not flirting then. I needed some air.

"It's still light out, Nick. Besides—" I pointed to the winding line "—we'll lose our table to these vultures. I'll be right back." I shoved out of the booth and half-jogged to the exit before he could stop me.

I blotted frantically at my shirt as I pushed out the door. It was my Hotter in Texas one and I wasn't sure if it was salvageable. Losing it would be a major bummer. That was definitely why I'd run out of there like the place was on fire. Not because I was afraid if I stayed there any longer, I'd say something stupid like: "Hey, Nick, what do you think our children would look like?"

I could not be trusted.

Was I imagining that he and I kept having these weird moments? Sometimes I was sure he was going to leave me on the side of the road, and sometimes he looked at me like all of his secrets were behind a locked door and he really wanted me to find the key.

Boring. Pshh. Janessa, you fool.

I reached into my bag and clicked the unlock button on the key fob, listening for the beep as I crossed the wavy, heat-soaked parking lot. Nothing. I clicked it again and my pulse skipped. I must have forgotten to lock it. Good thing I didn't let Nick come with me. Depending on which one of those moods he was in, I might never hear the end of it for putting our snacks and extra underwear in such profound danger.

But as I rounded the corner, my feet skidded to a dead stop, my wedge espadrilles nearly twisting my ankle. It took a minute for my eyes to accept it, another for the little gatekeeper of bad news in my brain to let it pass, but sure as this ridiculous crush I had on Nick, the Rover was not where I'd parked it.

Instead, a rectangular white sign with blue letters that I'd somehow not managed to catch in the back-up camera glared back at me.

No Parking Anytime. Violators will be—

Ohhh no.

CHAPTER FOURTEEN

Losses and Gains

Nick

"I'm not mad." I shoved a hand in my hair and tugged while I paced the parking lot.

Brit sat on the hot asphalt in front of the restaurant, her eyeliner melting in the evening sun and her clothes still covered in pizza. She looked at me with Sad Eyes. "It's just that your face looks kind of mad."

Okay, I was fucking furious, but not at her. I know I'd given her a hard time earlier about missing rides, but I didn't see the sign either. I wasn't going to put this on her. Though, she seemed to expect that I would, which made me feel a whole lot of other things besides anger. Like guilt and more of that protectiveness she didn't like.

I sat down beside her and squeezed her shoulder. *I have the little green tin*, I told myself. Everything else could sit at the tow lot for a little while. At least, I hoped it would only be a little while.

I left a message for the tow company thirty minutes ago. If

we didn't get this squared away quickly, we'd be driving well into the night to make it to Mobile. *Fucking hell.*

"I really am sorry," she said quietly.

"Brit, I'm not mad at you. I promise. Come on, let's find somewhere cooler to wait." I stood and tugged her hand until she was standing beside me. Her forehead was damp, her cheeks a little too rosy. I could at least use this time to find her some air conditioning and a more comfortable place to sit.

According to the GPS on my phone, the closest shelter seemed to be a strip mall a block away. I was hoping maybe we'd find a coffee shop or somewhere we could rest and charge my phone, but Brit saw something else.

She pumped her fists in the air. "Yes! It's saved!"

"What's saved?" I followed her through the door, relieved that the air conditioning seemed to be on full blast. Inside, a beige tile floor was dotted with colorful plastic chairs and the walls were lined with stackable laundry machines. The sign said *Wash and Fold* and advertised free Wi-Fi and cable TV.

"My outfit," she said. "I can get the stain out."

"How's this going to work?" She was only wearing one layer, and I would not put it past her to strip down right here. Public decency laws aside, I could definitely not handle that.

She pressed a hand on my chest and I allowed myself to be pushed into a seat, then she reached for my backpack.

"What are you doing?" In hindsight, I probably should have been more concerned when she pulled the extra pairs of boxer shorts out of my bag, but I was too worried about her finding the tin.

I didn't want to have that conversation. My dad had always made a big deal about keeping family business close—God knows he had his reasons with my mother—and this felt like family business.

More than that, I didn't want her to know because she seemed to see things about me I didn't mean to let show. I didn't want her doing her psychic energy schtick and seeing how I really felt about this task my brother had given me.

I shoved my hand in the bag, scooping up the tin at the same time as she whipped out the black T-shirt I'd worn on the zip line. Then slept in. Then wore all day in the airport.

I stuffed the tin in my pocket. "That's dirty," I said, grabbing for the shirt.

She jumped out of my reach, a mischievous look on her face as she held it to her nose. "Mmm. Man musk."

"You're so weird."

"Got any clean ones?"

I gave her a look. "Yeah, in the car. With yours."

She waved off my tone. "And the boxers? Clean?"

Part of me wondered what she would do if I said they weren't, but I really didn't want to know. "Yes. They're clean." They'd been in there since the zip line too—my last pair. I'd forgotten I had them since I'd bought new stuff at Target.

"Good." She tucked them under her arm. "I'll be right back."

"Hurry," I called after her. "The tow company could call any minute." And if they did, we weren't waiting for a wash/dry cycle. *Sorry, Brit's T-shirt.*

I rubbed at my temples as she marched off to the hallway with a restroom sign. I needed to regroup, come up with a plan now that my first one had been blown to hell. I had to admit, I was annoyed that we'd be off schedule *again*, but I didn't feel the dread in my stomach like I did when my flight had been canceled. What was it about being around Brit that made my pulse race and lowered my blood pressure at the same time?

My phone rang in my hand as I was plugging it in behind a chair.

"Hello?"

"Is this Nick Callaway?" a voice filled with tobacco and motor oil asked.

Finally. "Yes, this is him."

"Got your call. We have your vehicle here."

"Great. Thanks. How can I get it back?"

I heard him swallow something, then he said, "Hundred and seventy-five bucks."

I groaned. "Fine. Where?"

He rattled off an address and I typed it in a text to Brit as he spoke since I didn't have a pen.

The chirp of her phone startled me, and I spun around to see her standing behind me in my red boxer shorts and dirty T-shirt, the sleeves rolled up and the bottom tied in her signature crop-top knot just above her navel.

All the blood drained from my brain. I thought she was beautiful the moment I saw her, but she had a sweetness in her eyes that had helped my mind steer clear of the gutter. This look though? This was sexy as fuck.

She still had her heels on—*Christ, how does a woman so tiny have such long legs?*—and I forced my eyes away from her thighs onto her face. It didn't help. She'd pulled her hair up in a ponytail on the side of her head and her mascara had melted into a thick line of charcoal beneath her eyes. She looked like a stripper dressed as Punky Brewster for Halloween and my dick sent a whole host of images to my brain without my permission— Brit sitting open-legged on top of one of these washing machines while I pulled that T-shirt over her head. My mouth on her stomach, her pink nails digging into my shoulders.

So much for my pep-talk when we'd left the airport.

"Well? Can you be here then?" The tow-truck guy barked in my ear.

"Uh. Sorry. I didn't hear you."

"I said I'll be back at the lot at eight-thirty. Be there then or I'll see you in the morning."

"Wait. Eight-thirty? We have to be in—" I heard the call disconnect "—Mobile . . . Fuck!"

What kind of back-woods, one-man show was this guy running where he had to hold my car hostage all evening before taking my money?

Brit fell into the chair beside me, looking up at me with her charcoal-stained eyes. "Bad news?"

"We're not getting the car back tonight." Eight-thirty was too late. By that time, we'd only have a few hours before we'd need to stop again, and I'd rather sleep now and be rested for the marathon we'd have to do tomorrow.

"I'm sorry, Nick."

"It's not your fault," I said, forcing my voice steady. "It's just—we should have had hours more driving time before we had to stop for the night."

"So, we'll just find a place to sleep here." She crossed her legs, forcing my boxers to ride up her bare thigh. I wished I had a blanket to cover her up with. Seeing her in my underwear was too much. I was going to have to start reciting baseball statistics in my head to keep from walking around with a permanent tent in my pants.

She scooted closer to me and dropped her head on my shoulder. *Not helping.*

"You're already tired," she said. "I can see it in your eyes. We'll rest and reset and make up for it tomorrow."

I looked down at her and immediately felt the fatigue hit my muscles. She was right. I was exhausted but I'd just promised Tom I'd be back on time. "Anything goes wrong and we'll miss the train."

"We'll make it," she said, patting my thigh. She smiled up at me with those pretty pink lips and I stared at them, thinking dirty things. This time I didn't fight it. If nothing else went right for me today, I was at least going to enjoy looking at her while we were stuck here.

I sprawled out over a row of chairs, resting my head on my backpack, and got to work answering emails while Brit took her clothes to the washing machine. I was in the middle of combing through a quote from a contractor for a renovation I was overseeing when one of those metal rolling carts crashed into my knee.

I looked up to see Brit sitting on one of the folding tables across the room, swinging her legs.

"What are you doing?" she asked.

"Work." I turned the cart around and kicked it, sending it rolling back to her. She caught it with her feet, then climbed into the basket, sitting cross-legged.

"You're always on that thing," she said, gesturing to my phone.

"Yeah, well, I'm not playing Candy Crush."

"What exactly do you do?"

What didn't I do? I set my phone aside and sat up. "When my dad finds a property he likes, a foreclosure or maybe some land he thinks we could develop, he sends it to me and I make sure it's a good investment. I research it, run the numbers on what we need to make for a profit. If we need financing, I secure it. If it's a bid project, I write up the scope of work. Then there's the inventory we keep to rent out. I basically manage the whole portfolio."

Her eyebrows shot to her hairline. "When do you sleep?"

For the last couple months, rarely. But that wasn't because of my job. My dad had always leaned hard on me to the detriment of anything else in my life. He had to when we were younger, on account of Alex being sick. I knew I was lucky to be healthy and I couldn't complain. Still, as an adult, I looked back sometimes and wondered if it was too much. It was more important to shelter Alex from the tough shit, though. We had to keep his stress down.

"It's a lot," I told Brit, "but it's my family's legacy. I like the work for the most part. I like finding value in things that other people overlook. It's the responsibility of it all that's stressful. Between contractors and tenants. You know, there's a lot of money at stake."

"So like all the stress of buying my house but times a thousand and every day."

"Yeah. Sort of."

"Do you ever get to pick the properties you invest in? I think that would be fun."

I pressed my finger to my phone, spinning it on the plastic chair. A few weeks ago, I'd gone to my dad with a commercial project I wanted to invest in. Something Tom and I had found. The two of us had done all of the research, but it was still sitting on my dad's desk weeks later even though the clock was always ticking in this business.

"If I see something I like, I bring it to my dad. We don't always agree, and he has the final say."

She chewed her lip, studying me. I shifted uncomfortably, hoping she couldn't see that sore spot the way she saw everything else.

A buzzer echoed off of the linoleum and metal but Brit didn't move. "That sound means your wash is done."

"Oh!" She pushed off of the table and sent herself sailing toward the machine, not quite making it. She gave me a pitiful look and I got up and pushed her the rest of the way.

She moved her dress from the washer to the dryer, making it much harder than it needed to be by not getting out of the cart, but she seemed to be amusing herself.

"Seems kind of expensive for hot air," she said, feeding quarters into the machine.

"Says the girl with the trust fund." She stuck her tongue out at me and I hit the start button since she couldn't reach it from the cart. "You've never had to pay for laundry before?" I asked. "Did you live in a dorm?"

"I lived there but I didn't usually stay on campus on the weekends."

"Bet you missed a lot of fun."

"Not really. Did you go to a lot of parties in college?"

"Enough." Truth was, I wasn't one to talk about missing out on fun. I did the party thing, the drinking, the football games, but I didn't enjoy any of it like I should have. In the back of my head, I was always worried that something would happen to Alex or my mom while I was gone. I couldn't shake the feeling that every good time I had was like the montage scenes in movies, right before it all goes bad.

Brit leaned back in the cart, letting her legs hang over the side, and I took a longer look than I should have. "Why didn't you want to stay on campus?"

"My dad knew someone in the admissions department so my freshman year, he made sure I was assigned to room with the daughter of one of his business associates. It would have been nice to make that decision for myself, but that's life with my father."

It was interesting, I thought, the way she seemed to be begging the world to give her more responsibility when I'd spent my whole life wishing I had less.

She tugged at my boxers, sticking her fingers in the waistband

and rolling them once. "Anyway, I guess you could say we weren't a good fit. Or I wasn't."

"That's kind of hard to believe," I said.

"What is?"

I pushed the cart with my foot, making it spin, and she giggled. "Someone not liking you."

I couldn't imagine a world that Brit wasn't the queen of. If I had to guess what her life was like, I'd imagine her as the centerpiece of every table. She was sweet, witty, fun—I had a feeling if I'd met Brit when I was twenty-two, she would have broken my heart a million ways to Sunday. She still might if I had any intention of touching that.

"Growing up, I didn't get to pick my own friends," she said. "And the ones my parents picked didn't really get me." She swept a hand over her body, gesturing to her hair and her outfit.

I followed the path she'd just taken, admiring all of those things they "didn't get" and shook my head. "Their loss, Brit."

She dipped her head in a sort of demure move I hadn't seen her make yet. "You're sweet."

I huffed a laugh. I'd never had a woman call me sweet before. Uptight, withdrawn, difficult—I was used to that, but not sweet. I scratched the back of my head, turning to watch the dryer spin. "I think we both know I'm not."

"You're sweet to me."

Yeah. I'd started to notice that too.

CHAPTER FIFTEEN

Room Service and Lip Service

Brit

It was after dark by the time my clothes had finished washing, and Nick called an Uber to just drop us at the nearest hotel. We were in the middle of nowhere, he reasoned, so we had to take what we could get.

The air in Louisiana was like hot soup even in March and when the cold breeze from the lobby brushed my cheeks as we pushed inside, I nearly moaned in relief. I wasn't made for this heat unless there was a pool and a frozen drink involved. Boston would be forty-degrees and snow-covered right now, and I certainly wouldn't be chafing on my inner thighs.

"Good evening," the man behind the counter greeted. "Do you have a reservation?"

"We'd like to make one," Nick said. He glanced at me side-long and let his hand fall from where it had been resting on my lower back. "Two, actually."

"Oh." The man's smile tightened, and I knew immediately

that we weren't sleeping here. Based on Nick's lack of a scowl, he hadn't figured it out yet. "I'm sure you've heard there's a blizzard crippling the Northeast at the moment."

"Yeah," Nick said, rather snarkily. "That's why we're in Louisiana looking for a couple of rooms."

"Well, I'm afraid there's a conference in town. Between that and the overflow from the airports due to the storm, we're fully booked."

That would explain the rush on that crappy pizza place. I watched Nick's cheek twitch.

"You don't have anything?"

"I'm sorry."

Nick dragged a hand down his face, looking like he needed a break from travel negotiations. Marco had been indifferent, but Darla really hadn't liked him. I stepped in front of him and stood on my toes to lean on the desk, trying to look weary. "Are you able to check any nearby places for us? We've been driving for hours and we're sort of stranded."

The man—Greg, according to his nametag—smiled and started punching keys on his computer. "Of course. We have two other properties nearby."

Nick wandered over to an upholstered bench and flopped down, pulling out his phone.

"It looks like there's one room left at The Cypress, and three available at Serene Stay Motel, but that's not in the greatest neighborhood."

"How much is the room at The Cypress?"

"It's a river view suite. The normal rate is five hundred a night." He must have seen my face fall. "You could probably shave a few dollars off booking this late in the evening."

A suite sounded amazing after hanging out in a laundromat for hours, and I didn't like that Nick had paid for the car himself. It was my turn. I slipped out my credit card and slid it over. "Will you book it for me?"

"Of course," he said. "It's a fifteen-minute drive. I'll call ahead and let them know you're coming."

"Perfect." I turned to Nick. "Honey! Hope you like to cuddle."

Nick was still grumbling about me paying for the room as he slid the keycard into the reader and let us in. This place was . . . *whew*. Stunning. The carpet was a rich maroon with gold detail, the headboard was upholstered and real, as in not bolted to the wall. One whole wall was covered in velvet drapes that I was sure would reveal a view to rival the cruise ship when we pulled them open.

I pushed past Nick and launched myself face first onto the mattress, letting out what I realized too late was a very sexual-sounding moan.

He gave me an uncomfortable look and let the door close behind him. "This room is ridiculous."

"Come on, Nicky. Live a little."

There was a stiff-looking couch, one of those modern, boxy things, across from the foot of the bed and he started unpacking a few of his toiletries there, preparing his den. "If you were going to overpay for something, you could have bought yourself a real meal instead of all this pizza and candy."

"You bought the candy, and did it ever occur to you that you shouldn't comment on a woman's diet? You know, given your enviable body-fat percentage."

He raked his eyes over me and scoffed. "It's hardly done you any harm, all the chips and chocolate."

I didn't have time to react to his confusingly cranky

compliment. His phone buzzed from his pocket, and I watched the color drain from his face when he looked at the screen. He marched to the bathroom to answer it, closing the door with a solid thunk behind him.

"Weirdo," I whispered.

I couldn't tell if it was the utter extravagance Nick was uncomfortable with, or the fact that he was sharing it with me. This place was way out of my league, and I imagined his. Sure, my parents had money, and Sean did extremely well for his relatively young age (not entirely because he was engaged to the boss's daughter) but he always made an excuse for me not to come with him when he traveled. I'd be bored, he'd tell me. Or he needed to use his room to work. *Lies.*

A lump tried to work its way into my throat, the memory of a receipt from a hotel just like this on our kitchen counter when I got home from wedding dress shopping. My mother had taken me to New York for the weekend in a completely out-of-character gesture of maternal interest.

I'd been putting off wedding activities for months, making carefully planned excuses for why I couldn't attend to whatever item was next on her checklist. But when she'd suggested the trip, the idea that she might genuinely want to spend time with me had been too big of a pull to sabotage with a fake mall makeup-counter emergency.

Sure, she made the usual comments about my taste. *The ruffles are a bit much. I believe floor-length is the tradition for civilized people. Bows are for little girls, darling.* But it didn't matter because I knew I was never going to wear whatever dress I let her pick. It was the laughter and afternoon champagne that I did it for. Like I was living someone else's life.

It must have been the magic of that life that tricked me into believing Sean when he told me he was going golfing with his brother for the weekend. We got home the same morning, and as I pulled into the driveway, he was getting out of his car in slacks and a rumpled dress shirt, his tie in his hand. His face had registered the tiniest surprise, then he'd kissed me on the cheek and helped me with my garment bag, making zero excuses for his blown cover.

He carried my wedding dress into our house smelling like perfume from another woman, and he didn't give a damn. When he'd emptied his pockets, he'd left the receipt face up on the kitchen island, and I'd always thought maybe it was his way of saying "Hey, at least I didn't bring her here."

Small kindness, I suppose.

Nick's muffled voice kicked up a notch and I flipped onto my belly, craning my neck closer. I couldn't hear much behind the heavy bathroom door, but it didn't sound like a pleasant conversation. Nick's default setting seemed to be Stress-Case regardless of our current set of travel woes. At least it wasn't just me that made him that way.

When he finally came out, his face was stone.

"Everything okay?"

"Yep."

I deflated at his one-word answer and the way he avoided my eyes. Between Nick's expression and the sinking feeling in my chest from the memories I'd just been dredging up, we'd both already tainted the energy in this room. And we still had all night to sit in it.

"We should go out," I blurted, the idea coming to me in a flash of excitement.

Nick moved to the fridge, uncapping an eight-dollar bottle of water. "That sounds like a terrible idea."

"Why? It's early. Let's make a drink from the minibar and go check out the nightlife. When will you be back here again?

That's what travel buddies are for. So you can explore without looking like an anti-social loner."

"Or in your case, without getting trafficked and sold into sex-slavery."

"That's not funny." Though, he'd just unwittingly reminded me of his kryptonite—his complete and utter lack of faith in me as a human who could maintain Status: Alive without his assistance. He'd never let me go alone.

I reached into his backpack and pulled out the bag of gummy bears from Target, then ran a finger along the bottles of booze on the bar. "I suppose you can stay here if you want," I said, uncapping a bottle of white rum and sniffing it. I emptied the bag of gummy bears into the ice bucket.

"What are you doing?"

"Pre-gaming." I may not have spent much time on campus in my undergrad days, but I picked things up here and there.

I tipped the bottle, watching as it chugged out into the bucket, covering the candy.

Nick looked like I'd punched him in the stomach. "That was a seventy-five-dollar bottle of rum."

I ignored him. "I'll send you some pictures of the club I pick, so you can list them under 'last seen at' on my missing posters."

"*That's* not funny. And you aren't going to a club by yourself, Brit."

I popped a Rummy Bear into my mouth, coughing at the burn. They probably needed to sit a while. "So, you'll come?"

His eyes ran the length of me, bouncing like one of those little red balls that help kids learn to read—eyes, neck, chest, legs. Away. "Sorry. Not happening."

My shoulders sank, tears rushing the corner of my eyes. I didn't know why this was suddenly so important to me, to get out of this room, but I did know I'd been distracted by one mishap or another since I got left on that dock, and I couldn't bear the thought of slowing down, sitting in a quiet hotel room and letting my thoughts go all free-range. It was too early to sleep, so I wanted to keep going. And I really wanted him to come with me.

Sometimes when Nick and I looked at each other, the forces that seemed to be keeping us together buzzed between us undeniably, and sometimes I felt like he was merely putting up with me. Would he really rather sit here alone? What was it about me that was so damn unlikeable?

I'd worked myself into a huff about it by the time he was finished lining his toiletries on the dresser like toy soldiers. I was tired and hungry again and, *God*, every single reason that I was here was painful and miserable and I was trying to make it fun. Couldn't we at least make a few memories?

Nick turned around and did a double take at my face, which I was sure was splotchy and red. This was why no one took me seriously. I had all of these brilliant points lining up in my head: Feminism! Carpe Diem! But instead, my teeth were clenched shut and a solitary tear had squeezed its way free from my left eye doing a tell-all tour down my cheek.

"Brit . . ." His face softened and my heart flickered with hope.

"Please, Nick?"

We stared off for a few heavy breaths and I started to doubt my effectiveness. But then his eyes rolled closed and he did that nose-bridge pinch thing. The heaviness of his sigh told me he couldn't refuse me. "Can I take a shower first?"

A smile bloomed across my face and I felt wings sprout. "Yes!" I turned to the bed where my bag was splayed open, then looked back over my shoulder. "Thanks, Nicky."

He shook his head, but he was smiling. "You're welcome."

CHAPTER SIXTEEN

Angels and Devils

Nick

It was the tears that got me. Those two little circles of red on her cheeks as she tried to hold it in. I had an aversion to it these days, crying, but Brit crying had nearly gutted me. Twice now seeing her upset had flipped some sort of rational thought switch in my brain. Whether it was considering kicking some guy's ass at the airport or calling an Uber to take us to a bar in rural Louisiana when I should be sleeping, I wanted to do whatever I could to fix it.

After I'd done a quick wash-off of the grime and sweat of the road, I threw on the jeans and black T-shirt I'd bought at Target and was now stuck with until we got the car back. Brit had used the same amount of time to transform herself from road trip tourist to belle of the ball—or, I guess, belle of this outdoor country bar.

She'd ditched her T-shirt and turned her skirt back into a dress with some girl magic. Her face was already done up, but she'd pulled half of her hair up into a knot, the rest hanging in big curls over her shoulders. She was gorgeous. I knew she would be, which was half of my hesitation at the two of us going out together. Too much low light and booze—memories of her in my boxers. The other half was I didn't really want to share her. I wouldn't have minded hanging out with her tonight, just the two of us, but saying no to her was something I was finding increasingly harder to do.

At least the bar she'd picked didn't suck. I worried she would drag me to some dance club with artificial smoke and bad mash-ups, but here people danced on packed dirt and threw darts at boards nailed to tree trunks. It was easy to imagine you were just hanging out in a friend's backyard.

My cousins had a backyard like this—a fire pit and yard games. Like me, they'd invested in a duplex from the company inventory, and they lived on either side. If either of them knew I was here when I'd turned down a hundred offers to go out for a beer after work, they'd be pissed. Then again, if they'd seen Brit crying, they'd probably understand.

So here I was, at a bar in a Louisiana swamp with my temporary friend who looked like an angel in that white dress. To my own surprise, or maybe not, I wasn't hating it.

"Ha!" Brit pumped a fist when her beanbag thunked into the hole she'd been aiming for. "Beat that."

She'd challenged me to a game of cornhole on the boards the bar had set up in a stray patch of dirt. It didn't take a lot of convincing.

I stepped to the line on the ground and lined up my shot, weighing the bag in my palm. I was killing her, so I decided not to put too much effort into my throw.

I made it anyway.

"Beat *that*," I said, nudging her arm.

"Ugh. Do you have to be good at everything?"

I chuckled, feeling myself settle into the warmth of an oncoming buzz. Those damn Rummy Bears were potent, and she'd already made me shoot tequila with our first round of drinks. My head was in that perfect place where the edges of the world started to blur but I could still function enough for games that required hand–eye coordination. At least I could.

I winked at her. "Sorry. Perfectionism isn't something I can help."

I watched her size up her next toss. She didn't have an efficient bone in her body and she spent a ridiculous amount of time stretching and covering one eye for better aim, only to have made two shots the entire night.

"I can teach you how to throw better," I said, sipping from my bottle of IPA.

"And I could teach *you* how to be less patronizing," she shot back. "But I'm in the middle of my turn."

I laughed, unwounded. I liked her comebacks. They reminded me of the Shakespeare quote: "Though she be but little, she is fierce." It eased my mind a little when it drifted to all the ways she could have gotten into trouble without me here.

"Come on," I said as she made a show of stretching her hamstrings. "I've been playing this since I was a kid, that's why I'm beating you." I put on a cocky smile I'd forgotten I owned and bumped her with my elbow. "I'll show you how to be a stud like me."

Her eyes narrowed but they flashed with just the tiniest bit of something else. Nerves maybe. Whatever it was, I liked it.

"Okay, then," she said. "Show me."

I stepped behind her and took hold of her elbow. She settled against my chest, head just below my chin, and my eyes inadvertently dropped to her cleavage. Thankfully, she didn't notice.

"Just toss nice and easy," I said, showing her how to weigh the beanbag. "Don't chuck it."

She nodded and I guided her hand back and forth a few times, letting her weigh it, feel the right motion.

"You got it?"

"I got it." Her tongue peeked out to wet her bottom lip and she stared at the target. I forced myself to step back as she lined it up just like I showed her, bending her knees to toss it.

And she completely missed the board.

I groaned. "You're killin' me, Smalls."

Her mouth hung open as if the possibility of failure hadn't even occurred to her and it was so adorable, I wrapped my arms around her shoulders, laughing. Brit giggled with me, a little snort punctuating the rise and fall of it, and I was fucking smitten.

"I need another drink," she decided.

"That's not likely to help," I whispered in her ear.

She tipped her head, smiling. "Rude."

I let her go and followed her through the crowd, waiting a step behind while she put more drinks on the tab I'd started. The bartender liked her better and I didn't want to wait all night.

She'd just ordered when the guy beside her slid down the bar until his arm touched hers. It didn't matter where you were in the world, some things were always the same: As soon as a pretty girl leans against a bar, Some Fucking Guy is in her space. This guy had a backwards camo hat and his hand brushed her lower back while he whispered something in her ear.

My fingers curled into a fist, but I forced myself to stay put, let her handle it. She'd made it clear she didn't like me looking out for her. And I wasn't entirely sure looking out for her was where my reaction was coming from anyway.

She came back with a beer for me and a cocktail for herself. Plus two more tequila shots balanced in her palm. I took them from her and downed mine. "What'd that guy want?" I blurted.

She raised an eyebrow, and I knew how it sounded, but I still wanted to know.

Flipping her hair over her shoulder, she said, "That's Dean. He was just being friendly."

I made a neanderthal grunt sound in the back of my throat, and took my beer.

"What?"

"This is why I didn't want you to come here alone." *Good job, Nick. You made it thirty seconds.*

Brit smiled like a patient babysitter. "Why? Because a guy might hit on me?"

"I don't like the look in his eye." Caveman shit aside, he was still staring at her and it wasn't just impolite—it made the hair on the back of my neck stand up. I stepped closer and rested my hand on her hip, letting him see me claim my spot as her friend or personal protection or whatever the hell I was there to be.

I whispered in her ear, letting him see that too. "Be careful, please."

She held my eyes, a challenge on her lips, but a group of rowdy women wearing plastic tiaras and hot-pink sashes pushed up to the bar around us, forcing us apart. I let go of Brit and she gave the women the same open, friendly smile she'd given that guy. She really had no sense of danger whatsoever. To her, everyone was a new adventure.

"Cool bracelets," a short redhead said.

"Thanks." Brit shook her wrist and a seashell charm caught the light. "They're from Nicaragua. Handmade."

"No shit." They all came closer to get a better look.

"Is this your boyfriend?" one of them asked, pointing at me like I was part of the decor.

"Mm-hmm," Brit said at the same time as I assured them I was not. Brit's eyes snapped to mine, her lips parted, and I felt like I'd said the wrong thing, though I had no idea why.

"Oh," Brit whispered. "Was that a *wingman me* look? I thought it was a *help me* look. My bad."

What the hell was she talking about? I hadn't given her any look and I certainly didn't want Brit to *wingman* me. Of all the—

"I got you," she said, giving me an exaggerated wink. She turned to the group of women. "Just kidding! This is my friend Nick." She shoved me, and because I wasn't expecting it, I actually stumbled forward. "He's like a bazillionaire. Owns a ton of property in the Northeast."

The women oohed and Brit joined them. *Jesus Christ.*

"I'm not a—"

She put her hand to her mouth and made a poor attempt at a whisper. "He drives a Range Rover."

I shot her a look that said knock it off.

She ignored me. "Anyway, he's kind of shy."

"Bridget," I ground out, but she was fully invested in this now.

"We're from out of town, and well, he's sort of terrible at making friends, talking to people, smiling." She pouted. "Think you ladies can show him a good time?"

A tall blonde, whose sash said *Maid of Honor*, stepped toward me. She had on a tiny denim skirt and cowboy boots, and her tank top stopped high enough to show off a strip of hard, tan stomach. I preferred the view of Brit's midriff. It was softer, like you could sink your teeth into it.

That thought burst in before I could stop it and I huffed out an exasperated sigh at myself, at her, at the fact that I was there at all. How did this night turn around so quickly?

The other women sucked Brit into their boisterous circle, but the blonde had cornered me with the beer I'd been enjoying not five minutes before.

"Are you really a bazillionaire?" she asked. She was all flirt, her red fingernail pressing into my chest just hard enough to pinch, and I felt my neck get warm.

I had no problem talking to women, at least in the beginning when there was nothing of substance to say. I could flirt when I wanted to, be charming when there was nothing on the line. But I didn't want to. I'd only agreed to come here for Brit, and I was irritated that she'd shoved me off on this woman instead. *And where the hell did she go?*

She was just beside me a minute ago, but now I couldn't find her.

I looked over the blonde's head. "I'm not," I said, nervous when I didn't see any white dresses.

"That's fine," she said with a smile that was pure sex. She flattened her palm on my chest, leaning close enough that I could taste her perfume. "I'm not looking for a sugar daddy. I own my own business and—"

"That's great. Look, I have to find my friend. She's really unpredictable. She should probably be medicated. Brit!" I called for her but the music drowned me out. Were all of these people here before? How hard could it be to find a little bouncing ball of light? "Brit?"

A loud cheer erupted from the other end of the bar and I turned to see the rest of the women from the party, and Brit, all lined up. They laughed with their heads tipped back like baby birds while the bartender came by and squirted some sort of pink liquor into their mouths. A pack of college-age guys cheered them on.

I pushed past the blonde, making my way toward Brit, but before I got there, one of the women in a tiara and a faux-leather dress hauled herself up on a bar stool, then stepped up onto the bar itself.

For fuck's sake. As soon as I realized what was about to happen, I knew Brit was next. She couldn't help herself; she was like a magnet when it came to reckless behavior. With a little push from one of the frat boys, she climbed up, raising her drink over her head while she twirled and laughed with the other women.

The guy in the camo baseball cap had found her too. I still didn't like the way he was looking at her, his tongue lapping at the corner of his mouth like a dog eyeing a steak. When his hand fell to his belt buckle, I elbowed my way in front of him. "Eyes off, asshole."

He shoved back, spitting a couple of profanities my way, but I had pounds and inches on him and he must have decided I wasn't worth it. "Brit! What are you—"

She tossed me a smile and the admonishment died on my tongue. The hue from the stage lights made her skin glow and her hair look like autumn leaves on fire. I stared up at her—rosy cheeks, that dress tied around her pretty neck, mile-long legs. She lifted the hem of her dress as she danced, teasing me with a glimpse of her thigh. When my boxers had ridden up on her giving me the same view, I'd felt it in my cock. But now the pressure was in my chest, thudding against my ribs. Every once in a while, she'd turn over her shoulder to look at me, make sure I was still there standing guard, then she'd twirl again. I could have watched her forever, spinning in that white dress.

Then her shoe slipped, and her drink sloshed, and it was like someone dumped cold water on my head.

Be responsible, Nick.

"Brit, please get down," I called over the music. I'd learned my lesson about telling her what to do, but she really needed to get on solid ground before she broke her neck, so I asked nicely. "You're in heels on a bar covered in beer."

She gave me a dramatic eye-roll but there was laughter in it. "Please?"

She stepped to the edge of the bar and I reached a hand out to help her step down onto a stool, but instead of taking it, she handed her drink to one of the other girls. Then she jumped, arms wide, eyes closed.

Jesus. Fuck. I caught her in a bear hug, stumbling backward. Despite her miniature size, the impact knocked the air out of my chest, and when I pulled it back in, I choked on a sound I wasn't sure I remembered. It tumbled out of me, unchecked— my own laughter.

Did she really just do that? Jump off of a bar on a fucking wing and a prayer? It was ridiculous and holy shit, I couldn't stop laughing.

"What is this?" she asked, clutching her chest with one hand. She clung to me, shaking with giggles. "Is this Nick Callaway . . . *laughing?*"

I shook my head. "You're out of your mind. How did you know I would catch you?"

"Oh, Nick. I don't think you've ever let anyone down in your whole life." She leaned in and pressed her cheek to mine, her laughter petering out to a sigh.

I squeezed her tighter, turning my head just enough that I could feel the dampness of her breath on the corner of my mouth. "I need to keep a better eye on you."

"I like it when your eyes are on me."

Fuck. What were we doing? Hadn't I already told myself no to this? My eyes slipped closed, my heart pummeling my chest. She had to have felt it.

"I'm not being a very good wingman," she whispered.

I laughed at the ridiculous idea of giving any other woman at this bar my attention. "I didn't want you to."

"I know."

I moved a hand to the back of her head, threading my fingers through her hair. She was so warm and open, and *God damn it*, just like last night at the airport, I wanted to kiss her. Just an inch to the left and I would be.

I looked down at my other hand on her thigh, dangerously close to the hem of her skirt, at her soft curves pressed to my front. We were sharing a hotel room, a car. The last thing I wanted to do was be inappropriate and make her uncomfortable, or scared, or . . . I don't know. But she didn't look any of those things. She looked as affected as I was.

I hadn't been able to tell up until now if her casual flirting and sweet smiles were just part of her personality, something everyone got, or if they were really for me. I hadn't let myself contemplate it too hard because if they were, it was going to be a lot harder to tell myself to ignore it. Brit had me whipped from the first conversation we shared and now her lips were parted, brushing my cheek, and my whole body went rigid at the thought of that room waiting for us. The one with only one bed and none of our luggage. Whatever she was going to sleep in tonight, I already wanted to take it off.

I let her go and she slid down my front, landing on her tiptoes, arms still circling my neck. We were locked in a sort of half-slow dance, half-hug when the band slowed to a soft, twangy ballad. *The fucking timing.* Was the whole world conspiring to load these moments until they burst? Either way, I was done sharing her for the night.

"We should go," I said.

Brit didn't hear me. She spun on her toes and the light from the bar caught in her eyes. Still so fucking beautiful. "Dance with me," she said.

I shook my head, my throat suddenly tight. "I can't."

She laughed. "You can't dance? That's not surprising."

"Not right now."

She grabbed my hand, holding it above her head, and turned beneath my arm like a ballerina in a music box. "Look," she said, spinning. "You're learning."

The humidity stirred up the tropical scent of her shampoo, holding it in my nostrils, and I pulled a deep breath of it into my lungs. "We should go," I said again. "It's late."

She looked up at me through her lashes, seeming to get what I was suggesting. I watched her throat work on a swallow, and she nodded.

I settled my tab, which took way too long, and we pushed out into the parking lot. My arm was around Brit's waist. We were both buzzed, laughing together about absolutely nothing, and when she leaned into my side, every place that our bodies touched felt like foreplay.

There was a bench at one end of the building, and I sat, pulling out my phone to get an Uber. The closest one was twenty minutes away. I wasn't sure I was going to make it.

I was watching Brit sing along to the music, wondering what was going to happen when we got back to our room, when something caught my eye across the street. A river ran parallel to us, and light from the homes on the other side made the water look like flickering diamonds behind a tall, shadowy mass I couldn't quite make out.

I let my vision blur until the lights became a streak of white and the shadow came into focus. It was a tree, large enough to block half of the view, with vines that hung almost to the ground. I recognized it—the type of tree. *Holy shit.*

An idea cut through the fog of lust and booze in my brain, and I shoved my hand in my pocket, running my thumb over the metal tin. I hadn't dared to leave it in the hotel room. I'd had enough bad luck on this trip and I wasn't leaving anything to chance, but now it felt like I was supposed to have it with me.

"I'll be right back," I said, already on my feet. I turned back to look at Brit under the glowing beer sign. "Please, Brit, stay on this bench and don't go anywhere."

CHAPTER SEVENTEEN

New Friends and Old Enemies

Brit

I stood there blinking after Nick as he took off across the dirt parking lot like he was on some sort of mission. Where the hell was he going? Had I completely misjudged the reason he'd dragged me out of the bar?

No, I definitely hadn't. He'd been laughing with me, the kind of laugh where you couldn't catch your breath. And then he'd pressed that smile so close to mine that most people would have called it a kiss. A fraction of his mouth had been on a sliver of mine and he'd held me so tightly, I could feel his heart beating beneath his shirt even over the bass from the band. Even if it wasn't a kiss, at the very least, he'd wanted to.

And then he'd left me standing here in this parking lot.

I kicked an empty beer can laying in the dirt. *Gawd*, leave it to Nick to be just confusing enough to make me analyze and wonder and *obsess*. I'd thought when he suggested we leave that maybe he was suggesting . . . well, I don't know what I thought, but it was obviously stupid of me.

Now I was really obsessing over what he might be doing over there in the dark. Only because I knew enough about Nick to feel how unspontaneous his heart was. Darting away into the night was about as un-Nick-like as not knowing where you were going to eat next or wearing a color other than blue.

I stood on my tiptoes, my flattened hand to my brow, and squinted. I was trying to spot Nick's silhouette, study his posture for any signs of how he might be feeling, but he was beneath a willow tree large enough to block my view with its tendrils.

Hidden from me again, Nick. How tragically metaphorical.

I walked to the corner of the building so I could hear the music while I waited. I was contemplating going back in, when I felt a hand on my hip and the heat of another body behind me. I let myself soak in that little touch before I turned around and gave him hell.

"Took you long enough. What the heck were you—" *Oh.*

Instead of Rock Solid, I got a nose full of some spicy, too-strong cologne. This wasn't Nick's hand. It was Dean. My stomach sank with disappointment.

"Your boyfriend leave you out here all alone?" He smiled and I saw a flicker of what Nick was talking about. Just a tiny hint of nefariousness in the way his eyes raked over me. My heart gave a little warning blip.

"He's not my boyfriend," I said. I probably should have kept up that charade, just to be on the safe side, but for some reason playing pretend about me and Nick made my chest hurt.

Besides, we were in a well-lit parking lot. There was a big

guy in a Security T-shirt just inside that door. *See, Nick?* I could be safe on my own. I didn't need Nick to keep me alive. And I certainly didn't need him to keep me company when other people were more than happy to actually talk.

Dean grunted an acknowledgment and his fingers, still on my hip, curled tighter, shifting my weight until I stumbled forward and fell into him. My body instantly rejected the contact. That blip in my heart rate turned into a thump.

I braced my hands on his chest and pushed, but his other hand came up like a viper and caught my wrist. Now a whole symphony of alarm bells clattered in my brain. I tried to look over his shoulder, search again for Nick, but Dean was too tall.

"You looked awful pretty up there on that bar. Dancing like that." His breath smelled like cheap beer and chewing tobacco, and I stifled a gag. "How about you come back to my place and dance just for me?"

Fear licked at the back of my neck but my gut told me to keep from pissing this guy off until Nick came back. And he would come back. He wouldn't leave me for too long. He was too responsible and had zero faith in me. *Nick! Where the hell are you?*

"No, thank you," I said. I forced a smile and tried to pull out of his grip but he was too strong.

"Come on," Dean said. "You know you want to. I saw you in there, smiling at me."

I managed to jerk my body free and took two steps backward, but he caught my forearm, his meaty fingers pressing hard enough that I could feel a bruise forming. It was pure instinct, what happened next. I spun in his direction, my eyes scrunched shut, and jabbed out and up until I connected with something solid.

"What the fuck?" Dean brought a hand to his bloody lip and tears flooded my eyes.

"Ow. Ow. Ow." I cradled my hand. *Shit, that hurt.* Damn it. I hadn't thought about how hard a jaw and teeth might be when colliding with my fist. I saw stars, but my adrenaline was still surging, telling me to go. Now.

CHAPTER EIGHTEEN

Weeping Willows

Nick

I skidded to a stop on the muddy embankment across the street from the bar and looked up at the enormous, ancient weeping willow tree. It was the kind that you picture when you think of the Bayou, long vines reaching to the ground, sturdy arms.

I shook my head. It was number nine on the list—the top of a tree. When I'd read it, I'd imagined leaving some of the ashes on a palm tree on the beach at one of the tropical places Alex was sending me. When we'd boarded that plane to Houston, I was sure I'd lost my chance, but this—a *willow*—standing alone on a small strip of grass overlooking a river was a sign I couldn't ignore.

I stepped cautiously toward the lowest branch, wrapping my mind around how I knew this was the tree I was supposed to be at and how I'd stumbled upon it in the most random way—how I was never supposed to be in rural Louisiana of all places. It was eerie.

The branch seemed to hold my weight when I hung from it, so I put a foot on the trunk to get some leverage. When I'd parkoured my way high enough, I swung my leg over the droopy branch. It groaned but it held.

I tipped my head back against the trunk and closed my eyes, pulling hot muggy air into my lungs. This wasn't getting any easier. Each time I performed a task from this treasure hunt from beyond, a bitter taste crept into the back of my throat, and my fingers shook.

As much as I hated that he'd sent me to do this, I knew that once I was done, this tangible connection to Alex would be lost. There'd been a little bit of relief mixed with the stress when I thought I wasn't going to get to finish it. I didn't want to do it and I didn't want it to end and I wasn't sure how to reconcile those two places in my brain. I couldn't reconcile any of it.

It was impossible to believe Alex was anything but alive. I could still feel him here. In the first few moments of every day before I remembered. In the weight of the tin, still in my pocket. In the way my heart seemed to beat double every time I poured his ashes somewhere new--one for me, one for him.

In the way my whole body had ached to kiss Brit just then, and my first instinct was to ask my big brother what the hell I should do about it.

Whenever life got heavy, I would drive to Alex's house and sit out on his back deck, mostly silent. He'd talk and Willow would pop her head out to nod in agreement. He always knew exactly what I needed to hear.

Tonight, for the first time in my life, just acknowledging something was irresponsible wasn't good enough to strike it from my brain, and I didn't know what to do with that new feeling. I was still getting used to the fact that when I talked to Alex now, he didn't talk back.

I perched my back against the tree and flicked open the tin with my thumb.

"You can see the water from here," I said, hating the way I could barely get the words out, the way my eyes burned. "It's a willow tree." Now another laugh snuck up on me like it had at the bar, this one coming out as a choking sound. "How the hell did I . . .? Anyway, Alex, I'm trying my hardest to make this up to you. I hope you know that. I hope this is what you wanted. Rest easy, bro."

I tipped the tin until ashes spilled out onto the branch, forming a little mound of gray dust that trickled over the side.

It was a good spot. Peaceful, other than the bar across the street. The sun would hit this place in the daytime. The wind would take the ashes, I knew, but some would stay maybe. They'd get trapped in the cracks in the bark and stay here forever in the warm Louisiana sun.

I pulled out my phone and tried to take a picture through the branches, to get the view of the diamond water. I nearly fell out of the tree twice stretching to get the right angle, then I sent it to Willow.

Nine down. Almost done.

That was all I could think of to say in the moment and I started to wonder if Willow was disappointed in what probably seemed like a lackluster effort toward my brother's dying wish.

Alex never had a problem finding words. Even the instructions he left for me read like fucking poetry. And I checked them off and wrote out terse text messages to his widow.

I ran a hand down my face, wallowing in one of those rare moments where I felt more than just the numbness and muted melancholy. I felt the balmy breeze in my hair, and the uncomfortable scrape of the bark of the tree through my T-shirt. The river gurgled and rushed in the near distance. I closed my eyes and let the setting seep into my bones so I could remember this place where I'd never be again and my brother was going to stay.

A quiet yelp broke the quiet, and I whipped my eyes back to the parking lot where I'd left Brit. I saw a brief flash of her white dress, then my view was blocked by a male figure. The guy in the camo baseball cap, and he was standing too close to her, maybe touching her.

I couldn't see her face, but that sound wasn't a *happy to see you* noise.

I jumped down from the tree, landing hard and clumsy, and took off running.

I barely remembered crossing the street, but my hand was on the guy's collar before I even knew it. Rage and adrenaline pumped through my blood and I hauled him up by his shirt against the front of the building, rattling a neon Bud Light sign in the window. I drew my fist, ready to bury it in his face, but blood already poured from his swollen lower lip.

The sight of it jarred me and he broke one arm free, shoving me back from his space. Brit was to my right, shaking her hand out, crying. My brain tried to put two and two together, but I wasn't sure I believed what I was seeing.

I got the upper hand back, my forearm slamming across his chest. "Did you put your hands on her?"

"Fuck you," he spit through his swollen mouth, pushing against my arm.

"Wrong answer." I pushed back with my chest, pinning him, then a heavy hand hauled me back by my shirt and my shoulder slammed into the wall.

The bouncer. Where the hell was he two minutes ago?

I didn't give a shit if this guy worked here, I shoved him off and took a step toward the guy in the camo hat just as he threw a sloppy punch in my direction. His reflexes were dulled by booze, and it was a glancing blow, but it was enough to split my lip. And enough to snap what little control I had over myself.

I lunged for him, but Brit's arms wrapped around my waist from behind, squeezing. I felt her face press into my back, felt tears soaking through my T-shirt. "Nick, stop!"

The guy took advantage of the hold she had on me, booking it across the parking lot and disappearing into the treeline.

The bouncer was still looming. He stalked toward me but before he could throw me out or punch me, however they handled these things at this middle-of-nowhere bar, the Uber I'd ordered pulled into the dusty parking lot.

Brit ran toward it, pulling me by the wrist, and I stumbled behind her, holding the back of my hand to my mouth. She shoved me in, then climbed in beside me and slammed the door, rattling off the address of the hotel to the driver.

The car took off, and I spun in my seat to face her. "Do you see what can happen, Brit?" My muscles were still vibrating, and I drove my fist into the back of the passenger seat with the satisfying crack it had been looking for.

"Dude!" The driver took his foot off the gas, but Brit held up her hands.

"It's okay," she said. "He's okay. Nick!" She hissed at me, fingers curled into my T-shirt. I barely registered the contact.

I needed to get a hold of myself before I got us kicked out of this car, but my pulse was pounding in my ears and I couldn't catch my breath. He'd just walked right up to her. What would he have done if I hadn't shown up? I shouldn't have left her alone.

Brit reached for my hand still pressed to my mouth. I yanked it away and looked at my fingers. They were dry—the bleeding was done, but I wasn't. "What if you had been alone? You need to be more aware of your surroundings!"

"Nicky. Let me look at your lip."

Fuck that. I wasn't going to let her take care of me right now. "Not everyone is your friend, Brit. I told you that guy was trouble." The adrenaline still surging in my veins made my voice come out angry, and her lip trembled.

She nodded her head, her eyes wide and unblinking and—

Fuck, she was shaking. All the fight drained from my body and I slumped against the door. "I'm sorry. I'm sorry. Come here."

I tugged her wrist until she slid across the seat, falling against my chest. I wrapped her in my arms, breathing through her hair. She hadn't even seen the way that guy looked at her at the bar. She hadn't even sensed the danger. He must have followed her out there. I didn't think I'd ever get that look out of my head. I shouldn't have fucking left her.

"Are you okay?" I whispered.

"Yes."

Her voice shook, and I felt something pierce my sternum. "Brit."

"I'm sorry," she said. She wiped at her eyes with her palms. "Whew. That was just . . . scary."

"Don't be sorry." I took her hand and inspected it. She had a bruise on her knuckles already, but it wasn't swollen. "You hit that guy?"

She nodded again.

"How did you learn how to do that?"

"I took boxing lessons for a while. Well, three classes."

I laughed unintentionally. "Jesus."

"I know." A tiny hint of a smile brushed her lips.

I shook my head, fighting my own smile. In the middle of all the emotion coursing through me, I was fucking proud of her. "You busted that guy's face."

"I got lucky. He wasn't expecting it. Thank you. For, you know . . . coming back."

I rubbed my thumbs under her eyes. They came back black from her eye makeup and she laughed through her sniffles. "Are you sure you're okay?"

"Yes. I'm just emotional because I'm tired."

"All right." I pressed a kiss to her forehead, letting her have that excuse. "Let's go home."

Back in our room, I MacGyvered an ice pack out of the shower cap in our bathroom and held it against Brit's knuckles. "You can move it okay?"

She flexed her fingers to show me she could. It didn't look like we were dealing with a sprain or anything worse. I said a little *thank you* and flopped backward onto the bed. Shit, I was exhausted. I didn't know how I was going to manage ten hours behind the wheel tomorrow.

Brit was unusually quiet, and I could see the events of the night running through her head. Her eyes were glassy, her body still. I wanted to put her in bed and hold her until she fell asleep. Which wasn't at all what I'd imagined we'd be doing when we got back to this room.

I grabbed the toothbrushes we'd asked for at the front desk, and she followed me into the bathroom. We brushed together and I tried not to wince as the mint burned my split lip. It was going to be ugly tomorrow, I could already tell.

"Put some ice on it," Brit said, watching me in the mirror. "My hand is fine. Use the pack for yourself."

I spit and shook my head. Apparently I was going to be a macho idiot about the whole thing.

Brit rinsed her mouth, then stormed into the bedroom, grabbing the ice pack. She pressed it to my face, not entirely gently.

I met her eyes in the mirror. "Can I rinse, please?" I asked, my voice muffled by the toothbrush and the ice.

She huffed but let me. "I'm sorry."

I wiped my mouth. "Don't apologize, Brit. You make me feel like a real asshole when you do that."

"You're not an asshole. If I'd listened to you, your mouth wouldn't be bleeding."

"No. If I hadn't left you alone, or if I hadn't swung on that guy even after you were out of danger, then my mouth wouldn't be bleeding." I took the pack and put it on my face, going back to the main room. "It was my fault."

Brit was at my heels. "Why'd you do it?" she asked. "Go after him like that, I mean. Your face was scary."

"I was angry." I turned, nearly bumping into her. She looked up at me with pleading eyes, and I was too tired to lie to her. "And scared."

"For me?"

"Yes."

"Why?"

I closed my eyes, thinking of the moment my flight was canceled. How I'd told myself to walk straight to the hotel, that we'd already said goodbye and she was surrounded by people whose job it was to help her get home. And how even as I thought it, my feet were already carrying me to where I'd left her. Brit could get home without me. Like she said, she could do anything without me. Half the time, I think she was just humoring me and my need to have control over everything. Until tonight.

I lowered the ice and looked down at her. "Because I wasn't with you."

Her head tipped nearly all the way back to look at me with those pretty eyes. I wanted to hold her that way, crush my mouth over hers. But I also wanted to get out of the room and away from her for a few so I could process everything that had just happened—the fact that I'd just lost another few ounces of my brother, and the way I'd admitted to myself how badly I wanted her. How the enormity of those two things happening in the span of an hour was too much. I'd never been more conflicted in my life.

She took a step back and unhooked the halter of her dress. "Turn around."

I spun toward the wall, grateful for the break in eye contact. I reached for my backpack, finding the boxers she'd borrowed, and tossed them over my shoulder to her.

"Thank you." I heard the smile on her face.

I stripped down to my underwear, tossed my clothes on the chair, and went to switch off the light.

"Sit with me?" She'd climbed under the duvet, her head sinking into the overstuffed pillow. "Please?"

Ignoring every intelligent thought in my brain, I crossed the room and climbed in beside her, pulling the blankets over us. "Hey."

"Hi." Her voice was tiny and shaky, and my heart fractured another splinter.

I tucked her hair behind her ear. "Are you scared?"

She shook her head. "Not anymore."

I reached for her hip, sliding her closer. There I was touching her again, but I got the feeling she wanted me to, and she was lying beside me with all of that bare skin on display. I only had so much willpower.

She brushed the pad of her middle finger over my mouth. "Does it hurt?"

"Not really." I swallowed, watching her every move. Her eyes were wide, and I could hear her breath coming in an uneven rhythm. It felt like the world was evaporating around me, leaving just her tiny noises and the heat of her body.

She pulled her fingers back and pressed them to her own lips, kissing them, then she touched me again, feather light. I wasn't sure if she was afraid to hurt me, or afraid of what I'd do. I held her wrist, pressing her closer, kissing her fingertips. It stung like hell, but I didn't care.

"Where'd you go?" she asked. "Earlier, when you left."

"I had something to do."

"Duh." It was a whisper. A soft nudge.

I couldn't explain myself to her right now, though. My thoughts raced, my body fighting me. I still felt every bit of the desire I'd had holding her on the dance floor, and now we were inches apart with the entirety of this night—of this trip—in bed with us.

I ran my hand down her arm, making up my mind about where to stop as I went. I landed on her waist and squeezed. "It wasn't important."

"You're lying. But you'll tell me someday." Her fingers tangled in the chain around my neck. "The clasp is in the front."

"So?"

I watched her chest rise and fall as she looked up at me with hooded eyes. "You're supposed to kiss it and make a wish."

I smiled. That was so ardently her. "Says who?"

"Um, like everyone? Were you ever a kid?"

I just shrugged. If I was, I couldn't remember.

I held my breath as she leaned in and pressed her lips to where the clasp lay on my collarbone. "There," she said. "Make your wish."

I didn't make a wish. Instead, I cupped the back of her head, holding her cheek against my chest. She melted into me, her body loose and pliant, and I wanted to touch more of her, forget myself in the feel of her skin. I nuzzled my face into her hair, brushed my lips over the curve of her shoulder. She made a tiny noise of surprise in her throat and I groaned. Christ, she tasted good, and that bit of vulnerability was too much to take.

Every boundary I'd set started to crumble again. If I thought I wanted to kiss her at that bar, I had no idea what it was going to be like in this bed, listening to the shudder of nerves in her breathing. I'd spent a lot of time alone since Alex died. I didn't want to talk about it and I didn't want to lie, so I kept to myself. But Brit wouldn't let me do that no matter how hard I tried. She was in my face, bright, loud, making me do stuff like search for waterfalls and eat Rummy Bears.

My hand slipped over her hip, to the curve of her ass, and I wanted to push it further. I wanted to wrap her thigh around my waist and press myself into the space between her legs, watch the reaction on her face when she felt me hard for her. I'd been thinking about it every minute of this trip, how good it would feel to give in to this attraction to her, this fascination.

Her hands were in my hair, our chests pressed together and it felt good to touch another person, to hold *her*. So fucking good.

And I couldn't do it.

I let her go and flopped onto my back, my heart pounding. *Fuck*. What was I thinking? This was one of those moments Brit had called me out on, I realized as I felt the headiness leave my body, making room for a piercing sense of guilt. Guilt for touching her like this when she was vulnerable. Guilt for wanting yet another thing for myself when I hadn't done what I'd come here to do. Alex's ashes were in my backpack across the room while I lay in this bed feeling Brit up.

I'd forgotten for a moment, the reason why I was here with her. What I owed him. It was happening more and more since I met her. The weight would lift just enough for me to take a deep breath and then it would double once I remembered. If it was any other moment in time, I'd have her in a second. I'd take anything she was willing to give me and be thankful to get it, but this whole trip was a funeral march for Alex, for fuck's sake. Here I'd been doing shots, laughing, thinking about taking her clothes off—I wouldn't even know her if Alex was still here.

That thought felt like a punch to the gut and my skin instantly went cold.

"Nick?" Brit reached across the space I'd put between us, and I caught her wrist. I pressed my lips to her palm, shaking my head.

"I should go to the couch."

"Please don't." Her face crumpled into disappointment, and I had to close my eyes because the sight of it was unbearable.

"You can stay," she whispered.

"I'm sorry. I can't." My voice was rust and thorns and dirt, and not for the first time since she'd come into my life, I hated the sound of it. "You just broke off an engagement and—"

"You don't know anything about that, Nick. Stop making decisions for me."

"It's not just that." I rolled over, swinging my legs off the side of the bed. The cold air rushed my skin like another slap of reality. "I told you this isn't a pleasure trip for me. This isn't what I'm here for."

"You can't just sleep here?"

"No. I can't." I reached behind me and squeezed her arm before standing. "I'm sorry."

CHAPTER NINETEEN

Rest Stop

Brit

When I was a kid, I wanted to be a mermaid. I dressed up as one for Halloween four years in a row, until finally my nanny said the tattered costume had finished its run and I'd have to choose something else.

I dreamed about being different, but not like the way I was different in my real life where people weren't sure how to handle me. I wanted to be the kind of different that people treasured. Rare different. Special different. People would long to touch my colorful hair. They'd watch me swim, my tail shimmering in the sun. And if I felt those painful human emotions sneaking up on me? Well, I'd dive into the ocean and swim away.

Today I wasn't a mermaid and there was nowhere to swim to. I was stuck in this car with Nick and I couldn't decide if I was furious with him or heartbroken.

We were finally on our way to Savannah and the sky was a

dreary gray. Nick had his hat on, his eyes shielded by the brim. Not that he was looking at me anyway.

I had no idea what had happened last night when he'd had his hands on me, then suddenly bolted. I didn't understand a thing he did. After almost three days with him, I had more questions than answers about Nick. All I knew was there was this connection between us when we touched, like the click of a lock latching into place. But just like all of his smiles, he kept cutting it off.

From the moment his eyes had opened on that stupid hard couch, he'd barely looked at me, giving me one-word replies. He insisted we skip the gourmet breakfast that came with our ridiculously expensive suite in favor of drive-thru because it was quicker, but I think he just didn't want to sit across from me at a table. We had plenty of time. It was barely seven a.m. by the time we got the car out of impound.

That had gone swimmingly. Burke, the guy who ran the lot, had decided that despite the quote he'd given Nick over the phone, he'd forgotten to mention that leaving it overnight would double the price. I thought Nick was going to have an aneurysm when he'd realized his own miscalculation. I'd offered to pay since I was still feeling awful about missing the sign, but that had started another argument about how this was absolutely not my fault, and could I please drop it and also stop doing that thing with my face.

I could only assume he meant smiling. I was happy to oblige.

I sipped my coffee, happy at least to be back in the Range Rover where there was a whole console between us with no chance of him touching me and then acting like he hated himself for it.

Last night, I'd wanted him to stay so badly it hurt.

The whole thing hurt. Like the fact that he chose to sleep on that hard couch rather than share a bed with me. We were two adults, mostly clothed, on a king-sized bed, and I knew from experience how easily you could avoid touching someone in that scenario if that was what he wanted.

I should have learned this lesson by now—that some people can only handle me in small doses. Sean told me as much, even as he asked me to move in with him, then proposed. And I'd stayed despite that, hoping I might grow on him. There were a lot of similarities between that and this crush I'd let myself develop on Nick. Things I didn't want to see. I'd made Nick go to that bar. I'd made him lay in bed with me. Hell, I'd made him take me on this trip. And I'd confused those moments with a connection because sometimes, when his eyes wandered over my body and then shifted away, I caught a longing there. Something hidden that I could feel bursting through his seams. But once again, Nick's cooler head prevailed, and this time *I* was the thing he was talking himself out of. Me and him, touching like that.

"How's your lip?" I asked begrudgingly when I noticed a slight wince from him as he sipped his energy drink. Damn it. Hating him was hard when I remembered he'd literally bled for me last night.

"It's okay. How's your hand?"

I opened and closed my fist. "Also fine."

He nodded his approval. "Do you know where you want to stop for lunch?"

"Nope." He was trying to make conversation, but I'd learned some things from all of the humiliation Sean put me through over the years. I knew how to build myself a wall, somewhere safe to hide. I pushed the button to recline my seat and put my bare feet on the dash because I knew it would piss him off. It was a passive-aggressive wall.

"It'll save us time if we have a plan," he pushed.

I wasn't really into Nick's plans at the moment. Nick's plans could go screw themselves. "I'll figure it out. You put me in charge of stops. Don't forget it."

He grumbled something, then switched on the radio. I swatted his hand away. He'd put me in charge of that too and I was scrambling for purchase in the control department.

I was scrolling through the satellite stations when Nick's phone rang from where he had it stuck to the dashboard. The name "Mom" scrolled over the screen.

It rang again and I turned to see his knuckles white on the steering wheel. He tossed a sideways glance at me but continued to ignore it.

"Nicholas, your mother is calling you."

"I can see that."

"Are you going to answer it?"

His soft cheeks sucked in as he chewed the inside of his lip. Why did he not want to answer it in front of me? Fine, he didn't want to touch me, but was I really such a stranger? *Still?*

I reached over and hit the answer button and he snarled, swiping the phone from its cradle and switching it off of the Bluetooth.

"Hi, Mom." A beat passed and he lowered his voice. "Where are you right now? Is Dad home?"

Silence.

"Can you go back inside, please?"

Okay, clearly I wasn't meant to hear this. I picked up Nick's energy drink and pretended to read the nutrition label.

Nick pulled the phone from his ear and rubbed at his eye with the back of his hand. I heard a woman's voice, a whimper, and my throat thickened.

"Please don't cry, Mom." Now he was nearly whispering.

"Yes, I know, but it was late by the time I got to the hotel and I didn't want to wake you." He shifted in his seat, leaning further into the door as if he could keep me from hearing. "Okay . . . Yes . . . Everything is going to be okay, Mom. I'm sorry. I promise I'll see you soon."

He ended the call and tossed his phone in the center console, running a hand over his mouth. My heart tripped. The air in the car grew tense and I knew I'd just been privy to a private conversation. One that hadn't gone well, based on his expression.

He stared out the windshield for the next few miles, silent.

"Nick?" I said quietly. He rubbed at the back of his neck like he was trying to massage a stone. "Are you okay?"

He flipped on his blinker and switched lanes. "I'm fine."

He wasn't though, and I felt like I witnessed something I shouldn't have. But maybe something I needed to.

Puzzle pieces were falling into place before my eyes. I wasn't sure how I'd missed it. Maybe I'd been too busy trying to decide whether he was looking at me with pity or affection, and I'd stopped paying attention. Nick and his tense shoulders. Nick and the way he cut all of his smiles short, except for those brief moments where he forgot himself. He'd told me this wasn't a pleasure trip for him, and me being me had thought, *Well, that's silly. Fun is all a state of mind.* But maybe Nick's mind didn't have that setting.

All morning, I'd been taking my broken feelings and stabbing them back at him without any consideration for whether any of this was hard for him.

I studied the side of his face, the thrum of his pulse in his neck. "I think we should talk."

"Fuck, Brit. Not now, okay? Please?"

The way he said "please" made my breath catch. There was

pain in it, a plea not to press it. But how could I just let him sit there in all that hurt? He'd been there for me over and over again since this trip started. Last night I'd brought myself to tears over a trip down memory lane and he'd saved my whole night by going with me to that bar. No matter how it ended up. We were the only friends we had right now, and I was going to be a good one.

I leaned forward scanning the side of the road for a mile marker or something to tell me where we were. Finally, I spotted an exit sign. "Get off here."

"What? Where?"

"The next exit. I want to eat there."

He huffed out a sigh, but he did what I asked. He always did.

CHAPTER TWENTY

Lay Your Head on my Shoulder

Nick

I figured Brit had some other reason for wanting to get off of the highway, since there wasn't a restaurant around here for miles. The whole time we drove around looking for food, I braced myself for what I knew was coming. She was quiet, painfully so. I knew she was mad at me for leaving her in that bed last night. I just wished she knew how mad I was at myself.

Eventually, we found a convenience store that sold sandwiches. There weren't any tables but I assumed this wasn't a conversation for a public place, anyway.

We drove to a rest stop set in a park and I didn't complain when she suggested we get out of the car and sit under a tree, picnic style, even though we really didn't have the time. I'd do whatever she asked if she'd just stop looking at me the way she was, with all that hurt on her face.

The sun was high in the sky now, and the constant humidity

in the air made the ground feel wet. Brit laid her sweatshirt down and sat cross-legged on top of it.

She unwrapped my sandwich and handed it to me. Then took a bite of her own. "I'm mad at you," she said when she'd finished chewing.

I'd seen it coming but I still flinched. "I could tell."

"I'm mad, but I think I've been wrong about some things and I want to apologize."

My throat worked on a swallow, my muscles relaxing a fraction. I was waiting for a blow, but it didn't look like one was coming. "Wrong about what?"

She blew out a sigh. "I don't know. Maybe everything up until now. I don't need you to take care of me, Nick. I don't want to be some problem you deal with because you're a nice guy. That defeats the whole purpose of why I'm here."

Guilt warmed my neck. That was the absolute last thing I thought about her. "I don't think you're a problem, Brit. I didn't mean to—"

She held a hand up and I clamped my mouth shut. "This is my apology. I'll take yours later when you don't look so sad and worn down."

I blinked at her. "Okay."

"You're being bossy and over-protective, and I'm so tired of being bossed and protected. But last night, with that guy, you were right, and I appreciate that more than the way I've been acting. I also think I see now that it's something you can't help." Her smile softened. "I'm trying really hard to accomplish something right now," she said. "And I was supposed to be doing it on my own. Sailing off on that cruise, buying the house—I'm proving something to myself. But I think maybe meeting you has helped me be even more brave because I know you won't let me fall."

"Because I don't let people down." She'd said it at the bar, but I couldn't tell if it was a compliment. It had never been one before.

She slipped her hand into mine and sweat pricked the back of my neck, both because I had no idea what she was going to say, and because after last night, I had to be careful with the way I wanted her.

"Do you want to tell me about that phone call?" she asked.

I stared at her, wondering how much I wanted to say out loud. It seemed like she was giving me a pass here, but I couldn't tell. Remembering her face last night, though, I couldn't let her think anything but the truth. She wasn't a problem. She was the only good thing about this. And I owed her at least half of an explanation.

"My mother drinks," I said tentatively. Not everyone was gracious about it. Though I should have known there would be no judgment on Brit's face. Just those curious eyes. "She has since I was a kid, but it was never a danger to me. It wasn't like that."

"What was it like?"

I blew out a breath. "Exhausting. My brother was born sick—heart defect. His was complicated. There were times when it looked like he was going to be okay, and times when we didn't know if he'd make it another year. She couldn't handle it, you know? The ups and downs. The constant hospitalizations."

She squeezed my hand.

"I don't know why I'm telling you this."

She shrugged. "Because you need to. Keep talking."

I hesitated but even just not having to lie about that phone call already made the air in my lungs feel lighter. I'd lied about so many of them—to friends, girlfriends, colleagues. "She's a lot of work when she gets like this," I said.

"Work for you?"

"Mostly. Sometimes she starts out her day fine, and then realizes halfway through that she can't handle it. She has a few drinks, then calls me like that, crying, needing to be talked down. Other days I won't hear from her all day until I call to check in. She'll still be in bed, and I'll have to leave work or somewhere else and force her to get up and shower and eat. It's almost every day now since—" I paused, wiped a hand over my mouth. "Alex died two months ago. He was thirty-two."

A swift pain caught me in the chest and I realized I hadn't had to talk about it yet. My best friends were my cousins, so everyone was going through it just like me. There was no need to speak it out loud, to hear what it sounded like in my own voice.

He died two months ago. Eight weeks, that was all.

I looked up at Brit and her eyes were red-rimmed. "Oh, Nick," she whispered. "That's so recent."

I nodded, her sympathy making me uncomfortable. "I know I've been killing all of your fun," I said.

She shook her head. "No."

"This whole trip was a terrible idea. She's losing her mind over it. She needs to lay eyes on me every few days, you know? Make sure I'm breathing."

But Alex didn't think of that when he sent me on this trip, how everyone would be right now. How I would be. "Brit, last night, I . . ."

"You don't have to apologize."

"I want to, though. It's just . . . I'm under a lot of pressure." Even though I'd somehow found a way to check another item off of Alex's list, the whole thing sat like a boulder on my chest. I was trying to finish this for him, but to do it, I knew I was leaving my parents to struggle at home.

Brit tilted her head, studying me, then she let go of my hand and stood. She made a rolling motion with her hand. "Lay on your stomach."

I stared at her. "What? Why?"

"Just do it."

In my head I told her no way, but I was already rolling over. She kicked off her flip-flops and I tensed when she stepped up onto my lower back. She wasn't heavy but it was awkward, having a woman stand on me. "What are you doing?"

"Shh. Trust me." She balanced on the balls of her feet, one on either side of my spine and fuck it felt amazing. When she took a step, I nearly moaned.

"People are looking at us," I slurred. I sounded half drunk.

I felt her body lift in what I assumed was a shrug. "Who cares?"

"Please don't break my back."

"I took ballet until I was in high school. My teacher taught us how to do this. You'll be fine. Keep talking to me."

"My dad," I said on a rush of breath. "He needs me. He's too old for this. Having a sick kid aged him. Both of them. But it's too much sometimes."

I don't know why I said it. Maybe she was using some sort of magic on me, or maybe it was just that with her standing where I couldn't see her, my face buried in the bend of my elbow, it was easier to admit all of these things.

"When I was a kid, I would get jealous of Alex. How he never had any responsibilities. He could just do what he wanted, no one expected anything from him. No one needed his help. Fuck, that sounds awful."

"It doesn't."

"I've never told anyone that. I can't believe I just said that out loud."

She moved to stand between my shoulder blades, rocking from her heel to her toe. "Have you ever told them how you feel?"

I froze and she stopped rocking. I could feel her eyes on me. "I did. Once," I said. "But I shouldn't have."

Brit's weight lifted off of me, then I felt the heat of her wrapped around my lower back as she straddled me. It was a silent cue to keep talking, but I didn't take it. Not at first.

But when she leaned forward and pressed her cheek to my back, I couldn't find a single excuse I wanted to use. "The day Alex died, he asked me to go snowboarding with him. We'd had a storm the night before and he was in my office being a pain in the ass about it, talking about how great the powder was and giving me his *seize the moment* crap, but I wasn't in the mood for it. Janessa had just broken up with me for bailing on plans with her for the hundredth time, we had sales closing that *he* was supposed to handle. I was so damn tired of it and I . . ."

"You what, Nicky?"

Part of me wished I'd never started this conversation with her. Another part of me wanted to go further back, to tell her how angry I'd been when my father gave him that job in the first place. He never wanted to run the company. Alex. He never took it seriously. I was the one who worked every summer building houses with my uncles. I double-majored in business and construction management. I put myself through grad school so I could do things with this company that my dad and uncles never had the drive to. It was my life. And my dad gave it to Alex and he treated it like a hobby he could pick up and put down whenever he wanted.

"I said some things." I blew out a breath and closed my eyes. "I told him it should have been me who Dad put in charge of the company. I told him he didn't deserve it. He smiled at me in that infuriating way he had, like he had the world figured out and he was just waiting for you to catch up. He smiled like that and he said, 'We both know it'll be yours soon enough, Nick.'

"And then he went snowboarding by himself and I stayed in my office and sulked. His heart finally gave out on the mountain and that was the last time I ever saw him."

"Nick." Brit's fingers curled into my T-shirt.

"I should have gone with him."

"It couldn't have changed anything."

"No. But I could have made sure the last thing I said to him wasn't *that*."

She was silent for a while and even though I could practically hear her combing through everything I'd just confessed, it didn't feel like the judgment I was expecting.

"Why are you here, Nick?" she finally asked. "On this trip?"

I rolled over and she laid down beside me in the grass. And then for some reason, even after everything I'd just confessed, I lied about this. I didn't tell her about the ashes and Alex's letter. Maybe because if I told her, she would have been a part of it. I liked that I had this little flicker of bright light in her, completely separate from the task I was failing and the pressure to get home. Like at the airport bar when she'd made me feel normal for a few hours over beers. I wanted to keep that.

"I just needed to get away," I said.

And I've been sailing around the world and it didn't feel like getting away at all until I met you.

I knew she didn't believe me, but she let it go anyway. My limbs felt heavy and my eyes burned. I rubbed my fists into them. This conversation was taking all of my energy, and after what little sleep either of us had had, I didn't have much to spare. I felt drained and hollow and like I might even let Brit drive the Rover when we were done here because my head was a mess.

"Nicky." She scooted over until her body was pressed next to mine and even through the exhaustion, my skin reacted to her, heating. "How about I promise to tone it down a little, not jump off of any more bars or spike any more candy, and you promise to try to let go of some of this stress? Just for a little while, Nick. There is nothing you can do for anyone right now. Let yourself off the hook."

Silence lingered, the sound of kids laughing weaving in and out of the air between us while I imagined what that might be like—just accepting my circumstance, letting it go. I rolled toward her and laid my head on her shoulder, pressing my cheek against her warm, bare skin. I probably shouldn't have. I was probably too heavy, but she held me and I let her. I fucking let her because she was right, what she said at the bar. I did want to enjoy this. Not this painful confession she'd pulled from me, but everything else. I wanted to enjoy *her* but I didn't know how. "Brit?"

"Yeah?"

"Please don't tone yourself down."

I felt her shiver beneath my cheek and she squeezed me. "That's the nicest thing anyone has ever said to me."

CHAPTER TWENTY-ONE

Song of Savannah

Brit

It was pouring with rain when we pulled into the train station in Savannah, big blooming thunderheads darkening the sky, but inside my heart was clear and glowing.

After our conversation in the park, Nick had fallen asleep for almost forty-five minutes, his head on my shoulder, our backs in the grass. I laid there, listening to his quiet puffs of breath, thinking how the things he'd just shared with me were more intimate than anything we could have done last night in that bed. When I'd finally nudged him awake so we wouldn't miss the train, he'd sat up and rubbed roughly at his eyes, wincing in what I assumed was more guilt for taking those few moments for himself, but it felt like a gift being trusted with those confessions, and his sleep. I treasured it.

Nick returned the Rover at the Enterprise desk in the train terminal. I'd been oddly sentimental about it, which amused him. He'd gifted me another one of his crinkly-eyed smiles and

we raced up the sidewalk to the tracks, laughing about the terrible job we were doing of staying dry.

He was right about not having time to sightsee. When I'd
admitted as much as we boarded, he smiled, brushed a rain-
drop from my cheek and said, "Sorry, sweetheart." Then he'd
taken my bag and my hand, squeezing so hard my fingers were
numb.

I looked around the sleeper car, feeling jittery like I'd just
downed a few packets of sugar. My hands were shaking, but
there were too many things to blame it on that I couldn't decide
how to make it stop.

For starters, the space was tiny, and Nick and I were sharing it.

This wasn't like sharing the hotel room, which was practically a small apartment. Here, there was nowhere for him to go
where I wouldn't be able to feel his body heat or smell the rain
on his T-shirt. Not that I was trying to avoid that. In fact, I was
back to soaking up every bit of him I could. *Before all of this
ends.*

Secondly, and even more jarring, the cabin number above
the door read *315*. My arms broke out in goosebumps when I
saw it and the cold from my wet clothes kept them there.

There were two seats by a window that would fold down
into a bed, and a bunk that pulled down from the wall above it.
I assumed that was where I'd be sleeping because Nick wasn't
fitting up there. I hung my bag on a hook and turned around,
bumping into his chest.

"Sorry," he said, smiling as he pressed his hands to my
shoulders and shuffled around me. He hung his backpack, then
put his hands on his hips, looking like he was coming to the
same conclusion about whose bed was whose and how close we
would be for the remainder of this trip.

"I, um . . ." I tugged at the hem of my wet T-shirt. "I think I'd like to change."

"Oh. Right, yeah." His eyes fell to my chest then flew away. "I'll go take a walk so you can settle in," he said, jutting a thumb over his shoulder toward the door.

"Okay."

He didn't move and his teeth sawed over his lip. He was nervous now, after last night. I got it now. I'd let him have this.

"I won't leave the room," I promised. "Give me ten?"

"Of course. Sure." He took a step backward then stopped, reaching a hand out to cup my cheek. "I'll be close."

I bobbed my head in reply, suddenly mute.

Nick closed the door behind him and I stripped my T-shirt over my head like it was on fire, my chest heaving from holding my breath.

What had started out as a harmless—and let's face it, typical for me—crush on Nick had recently turned into a thing where we held hands and he touched my face and said things like "I'll be close." A simple crush I could deal with, but I didn't know what to do with that.

I decided to call Meri. The ticket agent had warned us we may not have cell service for large chunks of this trip. Since we were leaving in twenty minutes, I should probably check in.

After I pulled on some shorts and a tank top from my Target haul, I climbed onto one of the plush seats and propped my feet on the windowsill. It was dark out now, and there were only a handful of people on the platform who hadn't boarded yet.

The phone only rang once before Meri picked up. "Brit. What state are you in?"

"Georgia. I'm on the train."

"Oh, thank God." She sighed in relief. "Has your itinerary changed?"

I laughed softly at the spectacular implosion of Nick's itinerary. We still made the train, though, even if a sliver of my heart was disappointed by that. "We're on schedule," I said. "We go to sleep tonight and wake up almost in New York."

"*We* go to sleep," Meri repeated.

I'd said it that way on purpose, nudging open a door. She'd dutifully taken the bait. "Me and Nick."

"Mm-hmm."

I heard water sloshing and I knew she was in the bath reading. Probably a textbook or an autobiography or something super-smart. The bubble bath was Meri's most cherished ritual, and it was a rare night that she didn't fit it in. Justin would catch up on sports news for the day and she'd spend an hour reading in a cloud of bubbles. She swore that hour apart was what kept them together. Maybe she was right because I had a tendency to stick like glue to guys and look where it got me. Except Nick didn't seem to mind. He was stuck to me too.

I'll be close.

I shivered, my eyes darting around the bunk like someone might hear me reciting Nick's words in my brain.

"So, how *are* things going with your hot travel partner?" she asked.

My jaw dropped. "Um, when did I say he was hot?"

"I can hear it in the way you say his name. 'Me and *Nick.*'" She changed her voice to that of a seventh-grade girl—fluttery, a little out of breath. She was right. I'd absolutely said it like that.

There was no sense in denying it. Not to Meri. "He's so hot, Mer," I groaned. "You should see his jaw line, it's not even fair. But more than that, I don't know, he's just . . . good."

That was what got me the most. I guess I'd kind of always wondered if that existed. People in my world were mean, calculating. But Nick? He drove me mad with his hovering and worrying, but it seemed that every intention he had was solid gold.

I hadn't just attached myself to Nick's side because he knew how to get home. I liked him from the minute we met. I liked how his deep-set eyes and full lips made him look dangerous and sweet at the same time. I liked his sarcastic comments that were always softened by that sparkle in his eye. I liked how steady he was, how he didn't sway with the wind. That had always been my biggest flaw, getting tugged by everything that caught my eye and forgetting my destination. Nick let me hang out of the window and feel the breeze, while making sure I never fell.

Though, it certainly felt like I was falling now.

"Define *good*, Brit. A nice jaw does not make a good man."

Fair point, and my track record gave her a full two legs to stand on with her skepticism. I'd once fallen hard for my mailman because I saw him pet the neighbor's dog. He was ten years my senior and turned out he did hard time before joining the postal service, but in my head I'd woven an epic story of the rehabilitative power of love.

This was different, though. Unlike the mailman, Nick and I were sharing a tiny little room and he was *looking* at me.

And he'd also become my friend. One who trusted me with precious things, which was rare. And one who I trusted back in a way I couldn't explain.

I wasn't dumb enough to tell Meri about Dean to make my point. Not over the phone. She couldn't do anything but worry, and Meri didn't know Nick. If I told her I was fine because I was with him, she would have no reason to believe me. But I could tell her one thing.

"He hasn't tried to lay a hand on me once. Shared hotel

rooms, cramped cars." *When we were wrapped around each other in that bed.* "You know. He could have."

Maybe I wanted her to confirm that it really was Nick's goodness that kept him from taking things any further last night, as opposed to a billboard-sized sign that he didn't have any interest in tangoing with the weird girl who'd hitched a ride in his Range Rover.

"I know what you're thinking," Meri said when I blew out a sorry-sounding sigh into the phone. "Where does this Nick live?"

"Philadelphia."

She groaned. "Brit, you're about to buy a house *here*. How do you see this developing?"

"I haven't really thought about the logistics."

"And do you think getting involved with someone right after you end an engagement is a good idea?"

Was that what we were doing? Getting involved? It seemed so much more cosmic than a decision about distance or the appropriateness of the timing. It felt out of my hands. Fateful.

I'm so ridiculous.

There was a long silence, then more splashing. "Okay, listen. I don't know your Nick, but maybe your whole psychic thing is rubbing off on me because I feel good that you're with him."

"I'm not psychic," I muttered. "If I were, I'd never have to wonder how anyone felt. I'd just read their mind." I winced, imagining myself peering into Nick's brain and finding him looking at me the way Sean did—confused and a little disgusted with himself. "Or maybe I wouldn't. I'm too fragile."

Meri barked a laugh. "Fragile like a bomb, babe."

I laughed too and salt water rushed my eyeballs. "Thanks, Meri."

"Stay safe with your Nick and call me when you get to New

York. Justin and I are making ourselves available for any crises. Not that you'll need it," she rushed, careful not to insinuate that my reputation preceded me. "But we'll go to dinner after the auction, to celebrate, okay?"

I smiled, letting myself roll around in the feeling of excitement I got when I pictured that house. "I wouldn't miss it for the world. I'll see you soon and we can drink wine and make Pinterest boards for every room."

"Oh, you know I am down for that. Night, Brit."

I ended the call and pulled up the real estate auction site, running my thumb over the picture of the gray clapboard siding. I just needed to make it mine.

Though, a tiny voice whispered in my ear, reminding me that getting back also meant the end of nights sleeping in the same room as Nick. Of spending long days trying to make him smile for me. Melting when he did. Everything was changing but not even close to the way I'd attempted to force it to.

The thing about having a ticking clock hanging over your time with another person is you have to gorge yourself on every piece of them before they disappear from your life. You've got to dig into their soul and suck up every little detail, so you can remember it when you're alone and missing them.

Luckily, some cosmic shift had occurred and Nick was letting me do just that.

"Oh! This is a good one," I said, plucking another card.

He tossed a Rummy Bear in his mouth. "Do you have any idea what's going on in this scene?"

I'd convinced him to pull out the bottom bed—his bed—for the full slumber party experience, and now we were watching *A League of Their Own* on my phone. Well, he was. I was sitting

with my legs slung over his lap, torturing him with the rest of
the intimate question cards.

"I've seen this movie before," I said, waving the card in his
face. "What is your best physical attribute?"

He groaned and I giggled. He was so humble for a guy who
looked like him. I wondered if he knew.

"Jesus. I have no idea."

"Come on. You told me you go to the gym. You're not above
a little vanity." *Also, I saw your abs. Those were on purpose.*

"I go to the gym because I like to eat." He glanced down at
his body, then shrugged. "My arms?"

"No. It's definitely your eyes," I blurted.

His lips tipped into a cocky grin, and I realized what I'd just
let slip—that I'd thought about this enough to have an answer
on the ready. I guess I was just going full confessional now. *I've
been drooling over your face since we met, Nick. I'll probably
never forget it.*

"Yours is your hair," he said.

I scoffed. "You called it rainbow hair."

"Why would you think that was an insult?"

"Because you said I looked like a cartoon horse!"

"Pony." He grinned wider. "And maybe My Little Pony is
my favorite childhood toy. You don't know."

I smiled back, appreciating that he chose the most adorable
way he could think of to apologize for that. "I'll be saving that
tidbit," I said. I made a little scribble gesture on the air.

He reached over to take the card out of my hand, brushing
his fingers over mine. "Watch the movie with me."

I turned around to put the game away, and when I looked
back, he'd opened his arm for me to settle beside him. I hesitated, my heart beating wings in my chest. It was one thing
flirting from a safe distance, but I didn't really know how to

touch him after what had almost happened last night. Every brush of our skin felt like touching a live wire, but then, when he laid his head on my shoulder at the park, it felt comfortable and right. It confused me, the way he could make me feel both of those things.

That little sliver of space he'd left me was calling to me though, and I lowered myself against his side, wrapping my arm over his stomach. He made a sleepy, content sound and my eyes turned to little hearts.

Lying next to Nick was pure bliss. The heat he radiated could warm a small home and he smelled like something spicy that I wanted to lick. I peeked up at his face, watching his eyes move along with the action on the screen. His lip was still slightly swollen, but it looked better than it had last night. I wished I could run my fingers over it again.

His phone was face down on his stomach, and it buzzed, startling me out of my creepy inspection of his face. It hadn't stopped since we left Houston, always vibrating and beeping, and I was beginning to think Nick might be the president of a small nation, or like a really popular celebrity, with all of those notifications. People sure were anxious to get a hold of him, but unlike every day so far, tonight he didn't seem to care.

"I haven't seen this since I was a kid," he said, ignoring the call without looking at the screen.

I turned back to the movie. "I've seen it a hundred times."

He tipped his chin to look at me. "What do you like about it?"

I tried to think of a clever answer, but his eyes were bearing down on me, making me squirm. Truth was the only possibility. "The outfits."

He laughed, his chest shaking beneath my cheek, and I couldn't keep in the sigh that rushed from my mouth.

"You're a very comfortable pillow. I wouldn't have thought it with all that muscle, but it's like you just absorb my weight."

He snickered and reached for more candy. "You weigh about as much as an extra layer of clothing."

"What do you weigh?" *Oh my God.* I was so desperate for more, I'd resorted to compiling stats.

This time he gave me a full laugh. "You don't need those cards to be nosy, I see." Blood rushed my face, but he tightened his arm around me. "No more questions. Just sit with me."

"We're not sitting. We're cuddling." I half expected him to jolt at the realization, but he didn't even flinch.

"Cuddle with me then."

That was an invitation I couldn't refuse. I burrowed closer into his side, my legs squeezing together when his fingers tangled in my hair, stroking. I dared to let my palm slide over his ribs, my pinky skimming bare skin where his shirt had ridden up. God, this was pure blissful torture.

After a while the battery light on my phone turned red and I looked up at him from under my lashes. "Do you want to use yours?"

As if it were balking at the idea of being used for entertainment, his screen lit up with three new notifications. He reached across himself, and touched my cheek. "We should go to bed."

"Okay," I said, disappointment squeezing my stomach. I peeled myself out from his embrace, and he laughed at me while I did an awkward log roll/crab walk over him to get out of his bunk.

"Thanks for the help. What happened to all of your chivalry?"

He shrugged. "It was more fun to watch."

I shook my head, amused that he could still surprise me. What was I going to do with all of these pieces of Nick I'd collected when I had to leave him tomorrow?

I straightened my clothes and glanced at my bunk. "Am I ever going to see you again, Nick? After all of this?"

He looked up at me, eyes serious. "Yes."

"How?"

"I don't know. But you will."

I climbed the ladder to my bed, smiling. That was good enough for now. I switched off the light. "I'll see you in New York, Nicky," I whispered.

CHAPTER TWENTY-TWO

A Dream is a Wish

Nick

"Nick!"

I startled awake at the sound of someone whisper-yelling my name. I couldn't have been asleep more than a few hours based on the way my limbs were frozen and my brain fought to clear away the fog. I'd been having a hell of a dream. I was sitting at a huge, polished wood desk, across from a man in a suit, but I was wearing these boxers and no shirt. Brit was on my lap wearing the get-up from the laundromat. Her hands were in my hair, silently stroking the back of my head while I searched my backpack for something I apparently owed this guy and hadn't brought.

"Let me just make a call," I'd said, but instead of pulling out my phone, I'd turned and pressed my mouth to the side of Brit's neck. She moaned my name and then—

"Nick! Psst. Nicky Mouse."

"Nope," I mumbled. My voice was hoarse, and I dragged myself up to sitting. "That's not gonna be a thing."

She laughed and I realized the remnants of my dream were lingering. I reached down to adjust my shorts. That was going to take a minute. Good thing it was pitch-dark. "What's the matter?"

"The train isn't moving."

I covered a yawn with the back of my hand. "Maybe they stopped to change the tracks. What time is it?"

"Three in the morning."

I pulled the curtain aside and squinted out my window. What little light shone from the train reflected off of white as far as I could see. Snow. Even though it was plenty warm on the train, I shivered at the sight of it. We were definitely a whole lot north of where we started, but I had no idea where. And we were clearly in the middle of a forest.

I hauled myself out of the bunk. The room was the size of a Dixie cup and when I straightened, Brit and I were almost nose to nose. She was on her side, her head propped in her hand, smiling, and I had a reflexive urge to tuck her hair behind her ear and finish what I'd started in my dream.

I stumbled backward, bumping into the sink. "Uh, let me put some pants on and I'll go find out what's going on."

"Should I turn around?" she asked, mischief in her voice.

My eyes involuntarily slid over the curve of her hip, down her bare thigh. She wiggled her toes to show me she'd noticed. I just shrugged, leaving it up to her.

Then I turned away from her to change because I didn't want to know what she decided.

I put on jeans and sneakers and made my way down the narrow hall. A few other passengers had stuck their heads out of their rooms and we exchanged *what the fuck?* looks. I wandered all the way to the dining car before I found someone in a uniform. Three someones, actually, all in a huddle discussing something that had their brows furrowed.

"Excuse me."

They jumped apart and one of them looked at his watch. "Yes, sir. How can we help you?"

"I was hoping to find out where we are." I looked out the window of this car. Still nothing but white. "And why we're stopped."

"I imagine they'll be making an announcement any minute," the man said. He took a step toward me, as if to usher me back to my room, but before I could tell him I was going to need a better answer than that, another man wearing a gray conductor's hat came into the car.

"Welp," he said, his eyes on a tablet. "The shit and the storm have officially mated. Baby shit storms everywhere."

One of the uniforms cleared his throat and the conductor looked up, meeting my eyes. Then he picked up a walkie-talkie from his belt and pressed the button. "Time to break the news."

It wasn't Darla's fault. She was right about hitting the storm if we'd driven straight through from Houston. With our route, we missed the worst of it. But what Darla couldn't have foreseen was that the damage from the storm would still be screwing with travel plans even after the last snowflake had fallen. In this case, the freezing cold temperatures had turned the thirteen inches of new snow into ice. The weight of it had taken down an enormous pine over the tracks somewhere in Northern Virginia and the engine had plowed right into it. No one had been hurt, but the impact was probably what had stirred Brit awake.

Long story short, we weren't going anywhere until they

could clear it. We were less than eight hours from New York City by car, but we were stuck in the middle of a forest on a broken-down train.

Brit had climbed down from her bunk and was sitting on my bed now, her thumbnail between her teeth. She'd put a sweatshirt on, but her feet were still bare and dangling from the side of the mattress. She was taking this a lot harder than when we'd been left in a foreign country with just the clothes on our backs.

"What does this mean?" she asked.

I scrubbed a hand over my emerging beard. "It means for the third time in three days, we're fucked."

"Did they say how long it would take to move the tree?"

"They said to settle in. To me, that didn't sound like a quick job."

She rolled onto her back and covered her face with her elbow.

"Hey." I sat on the edge of the bed and picked up her foot, setting it in my lap. "It's going to be okay."

She gave me a look like I had two heads. Okay, so stressing was kind of my job, and I could feel the anxiety needling me. I knew I already had voicemails from my dad and uncle about this project—probably the source of the "bank in my underwear" dream—but for some reason, my first thought hadn't been what my dad would do without me, or how tonight would probably be a bad night for my mom once I told her I wouldn't be home on time. Or that I still hadn't completed the last item on Alex's list, and I had no idea how I would.

Instead, when the conductor broke the news, the whole of my thoughts were focused on the fact that if this train hadn't plowed into a tree, I'd be saying goodbye to Brit in a couple of hours.

My first reaction was relief.

CHAPTER TWENTY-THREE

Stranger Things Have Happened

Brit

The train was creepy when it wasn't moving. The lights were still dimmed since some of the passengers had attempted to go back to sleep. It being the middle of the night and all, it made sense, but I couldn't sleep. I had too many signs to decipher.

I walked down the hall to a tiny staircase that led to the second level, wondering if I'd see anyone else at this hour. I'd left Nick in the room, claiming I was going to explore. He'd given me his usual litany of warnings with a side of stern look, but I needed a few minutes to sort this out, to figure out what all of these feelings were that vied for my attention.

Today was the auction. I was supposed to use every cent I owned to buy the beginning of my new life. I'd been planning this for months. My heart started to pick up speed in my chest. What if I didn't make it? What if I should have been taking these delays more seriously instead of relishing the adventure and the distance from my parents? I'd just assumed it would all work out, but I was inching closer to crisis territory.

More disturbingly? Even knowing that this latest setback could be catastrophic, the auction wasn't where my thoughts went first. When Nick told me what had happened, and I realized that I'd just been granted a precious few more hours with him, a whole bunch of tension I didn't know I'd been holding was released. Like a bus had been hurtling in my direction and I'd dodged it at the last second.

How could I ignore the way fate seemed intent on keeping us together, scribbling messages on the wall at every turn? But on the other hand, *what the hell was I talking about?* It was just a storm. *Right?* I tossed between committing my life to this sign and starting a YouTube channel dedicated to debunking my own ridiculous conspiracy theories.

Nick and I had been doing this weird dance between friendship and longing stares since Houston. But I knew myself. I had a habit of throwing myself on top of a spark with the hope that it would catch fire and consume me. More often than not, I just ended up smothering it or getting severely burned.

We had one moment in the hotel. One concrete thing that had almost happened. The rest—the way he'd let me in at the park, the way he touched me now—it could be friendship. God knows I didn't have a ton of experience with friends. Or it could be my mind wanting something and making it so. It was the thought of never finding out that made me fidgety and scared.

I checked the time. If the train got back on track in the next three hours, I'd make it home in time. There was still a chance, but it was narrowing every minute this pile of metal stayed stationary.

Maybe I should tell my parents about the house and ask them to send someone to the auction to bid for me. My dad was a signer on my account but there was no guarantee they'd agree. They had never approved of a single dream of mine before, and they were very, very angry with me.

Meri and Justin had said they'd be available for crises and being stuck on a train certainly seemed like one, but I honestly didn't know how it worked. Could she bid for me? How would I get her the money from here? I felt so naive all of a sudden. So unprepared.

A woman appeared in the doorway, dressed in pajama pants and a cardigan, and she startled when she saw me sitting there in the dark. "Oh. Sorry, I didn't think anyone else would be up here."

"I don't think we're supposed to be." I shrugged. "But what are they going to do, kick us off the train?"

She laughed and sat down two seats away. "I'm Annie."

"Brit."

"So this sucks, huh? Are you heading home or away?"

Ha! Good question, Annie. There wasn't an answer that fit completely either way. I was headed back to where I came from, but home didn't feel entirely accurate since the place I lived was, at best, a temporary shelter. When my father had called me and demanded to know when I'd be home, my first inclination was to tell him I had no idea where that was these days.

As far as my chance to get away from all of that? It was hanging by a thread.

"I'm headed to another stop on the way," I answered.

"My husband and I are on our way home to New York. I'm trying to decide if I'm annoyed or thankful for the holdup."

"I definitely get that."

"Chocolate?" She offered me some M&Ms from a sandwich bag she was carrying. *Girl after my own heart.*

"Thanks." I liked her, I decided. We were both in pajamas

eating candy, like some weird destination slumber party and I started to get the urge to spill my guts. I twirled the end of my ponytail around my thumb, staring out at the white, and decided to go full Brit Donovan.

"Do you believe in fate, Annie?"

Her eyebrows jumped, then she laughed lightly. "That's a deep question, but I suppose if there was ever a time to contemplate that, it would be when you're stuck on a broken train staring into the snowy abyss."

"You read my mind."

She pulled her knees underneath her and turned to me. "I like to think it's real. But I also think it can be a crutch."

"How do you mean?"

"Most things worth their salt are hard, right? So if you tell yourself it wasn't meant to be when the road starts getting tough, you'll miss out on what you could have had if you had just worked a little harder."

"Right." I couldn't help but think of my parents. How they'd always accused me of giving up on things, things they'd chosen for me. "It's just hard to know when the tough is trying to tell you something."

"I think you just have to listen to your heart. It has a way of speaking louder than your brain." She smiled. "Not every detour is a disaster. Sometimes they keep you from running into a tree."

I laughed but she was right. All I could do was listen to my heart, and at least in the immediate moment, my heart was telling me that whatever force had me stuck on this train, I shouldn't waste the time I had left with Nick.

CHAPTER TWENTY-FOUR

Unstable Connection

Nick

I paced the three steps that made up our room, stressed and missing Brit. When she left me here to go exploring, I lost the soothing distraction of her company, and the excuse not to look at my phone.

The conductor told us we might lose service here and there, but if we had, I wouldn't have noticed. I hadn't touched it since we boarded, too busy playing cards and eating candy. Cuddling with her.

I checked my email first, the bile in my stomach churning. Note after note popped up on deals I knew my father was stuck dealing with because I wasn't there. I went through each one, answering as many as I could without access to my computer. Tom was right, he could handle it, but it was my job. I forwarded only what I couldn't answer, giving him as much instruction as I could. Then I moved on to the voicemail.

The first one was from Willow and my spine straightened

like I'd been caught doing something I shouldn't. It wasn't far from the truth. I'd been avoiding her since last night, and she was catching on.

"Hey, Nick. I haven't heard from you in a bit. I know you're working your way home and I'm sorry this has been such a mess for you." She blew out a breath like she was feeling guilty and I made a mental note to try to sugarcoat my travel updates. I didn't need to put anything else on her plate.

"Please check in. Your mom's worried. I'm a little worried too. Listen, I put something together with the pictures you've been sending. Check your email. I think you'll like it. Thank you for doing this, Nick. I know the weather and all of these disruptions weren't part of the plan, but what you're doing means more than you know. Look at what I sent you. I'll see you soon."

I sat on the bed and clicked open my personal email account, scrolling through a bunch of subscriptions and spam until I saw one from her. I didn't bother reading the text, I just clicked the attachment and waited while it loaded on the bogged-down network.

And my heart dropped into my stomach. A picture came into focus. The living room at Willow and Alex's house. She'd moved the couch aside and there were ten frames stacked against the wall, different sizes overlapping but spread out enough so I could see some of each one.

I recognized the view from the willow tree first. I was propped against the cold metal wall of the train, but I could feel the mugginess of last night on my skin, the way the hair on my neck had stood up at the coincidence of finding that tree.

The other frames were filled with shots from different stops on the trip. All of the places where I'd left Alex's ashes— the top of the volcano in Nicaragua, the zip line in Costa

Rica. The one in the front was empty. It was rectangular, hori-
zontal. It was meant for a panoramic photo. The last one. My
brain filled it in with a snapshot of what it would have looked
like. A white ship railing in the foreground, bluish-green
water, pink and orange sunset. That was the plan. But now
what?

I hadn't called Willow because I didn't want to lie to her.
There was no way I was going to complete Alex's list, and I'd
been actively ignoring that fact since I started enjoying little
parts of this trip, or at least one part of it.

I was getting tired of this mission, the constant stress.
Worrying about Alex had gotten me stranded in a foreign
country, stuck in an airport, stuck on a train. It was why I left
Brit in that bed last night when all I really wanted was to dive
as deep into her as I could. I really didn't give a fuck if I finished
this list anymore.

At least that was how I felt sixty percent of the time. The
other forty was a mixture of guilt and failure. I owed him this.
Was I really going to let him down? Let all of them down? Alex
wasn't the only one counting on me. Willow, my mother—they
needed this the most. It didn't matter what I wanted and I knew
I should stop pretending it did.

I dropped my head in my hands, squeezing my temples. I
had a headache that wouldn't let up and now my throat was
stuck shut with something viscous and bitter. My outward
breath choked on it, and I felt my chest tighten around an emotion I didn't want.

But that was the other thing I'd learned from my father—
how to cut that shit off at the knees.

I launched myself off of the mattress and gripped the back
of my neck.

"Shake it off, Nick. You'll figure it out." Maybe I would, but

I was still pissed at Alex for setting me up like this in the first place.

I was always covering for him. When we were kids it was lying to Mom, telling her we'd been at the park when he'd actually made me hop a fence with him to jump on the Shaw's trampoline. Or patching up my own scrapes and bruises after falling off the home-made skateboard ramp at his friend Randy's house so she wouldn't see them. It was my job to make sure she didn't find out he'd been out doing something that could have killed him. He dragged me along with him as his cover and his accomplice. And now, I was going to have to apologize to Mom and Willow for one last adventure gone wrong.

I ripped my backpack off the hook and dug out the tin, setting it on the bed.

"God damn it, Alex." The echo of my anger off of the metal walls egged me on. It was like someone had twisted a pressure release valve in my chest. I couldn't stop. "I'm tired of carrying your load, man."

I took a step back and bumped into the sink, knocking Brit's hair products into the bowl. "At work, at home. All of this 'live like you're dying' bullshit when we were kids. You could live like that because you always were dying! And we're not kids anymore. I have enough pressure because of you—the business, Mom and Dad. You're dead and you're still—"

The door creaked open and I spun around to see Brit standing there, wide-eyed.

I froze.

"Who are you talking to, Nicky?"

I shook my head, my jaw clenched shut. She'd just caught me talking to a metal box and now I couldn't make my words come out to defend myself. But what was I going to say? *I was yelling at my dead brother, Brit. No need to be alarmed.*

"It's nothing." I shoved the tin back in the bag and stepped toward her, so glad she was back. I just needed her in my space again, to pretend I had everything under control.

But when I reached for her, she didn't come to me. "It didn't seem like nothing," she said.

I forced a casual smile. "Don't worry about it, Brit."

Her face fell into a frown. "Of course I'm going to worry about it," she said. "If you start hiding from me again, I'm going to worry and I'm going to wonder. I came back here because I missed you, Nicky, but you're gone again." She tapped her temple. "In your head."

I ground my teeth, irritated. Maybe because I'd heard this all before—*You're so difficult, Nick. I have no idea what's going on in your head*—or maybe because it wasn't true this time. "I've told you more than I've ever told anyone."

"And yet . . ." She pointed to the letter in my hand. I'd forgotten I was still clutching it.

"It's complicated," I said, stealing her line from the plane.

She shrugged. "We've got all night."

"Why are you pushing this?" I turned to put the letter away but she caught my wrist.

"Because I'm tired of having no idea what version of you I'm going to get. The one who lets me in or keeps me out. My friend or a stranger who I happen to be stuck on a train with."

I swallowed, silent despite how much it hurt that she thought that. I just wanted to keep her out of this one part. Just this one. And not because I didn't want to lay a little bit of it down. God it had felt good to do that in the park, to speak those decades-long grudges out loud, but I was ashamed that I needed to. I hated this feeling.

"Nick. Please just talk to me."

I gave her a pleading look to drop it, but I knew she wouldn't.

It was the best and worst thing about us, the way I couldn't say no to her. "I'm failing, okay? Are you happy?"

The words burst out more angry than I'd meant them but wasn't that what everyone wanted from me? *Say it, Nick. Speak, Nick.* And I did that one time with Alex, I said exactly what I was feeling, and I'd regret it forever. Maybe I'd regret this conversation too because even though she was staring at me, eyes wide and mouth hanging open, I couldn't stop. It was all crashing down on me, the incredible helplessness of it all. I couldn't stand having my hands tied. Couldn't stand sitting still when there was so much I had to do. Even if sitting still with Brit had been the best time I could remember.

And it was, and I wanted to keep doing it, but I couldn't have both.

"I have real responsibilities, Brit. People counting on me. Everything's not going to magically be okay because you gave me a back massage in the park and told me to take deep breaths. This is just an extension of your vacation," I reminded her. "Well, it's not for me. Do you know how badly I wish I could just have fun with you?"

The empathy on her face slid into something harder. "I don't know, Nick. Because you're being very confusing. One minute you *are* here laughing with me, having fun, *touching* me, and the next you're just . . . gone. I have no idea what you're thinking about, what you want!"

What I was *thinking* about? I was thinking about her! Her smile, her hair, her pretty legs always stretched out in front of me. The purple polish on her toes. Her fucking adorable little snort-laugh. That freckle just east of her belly button. Hell, I was thinking about her in my sleep before this happened.

I was thinking about her when I should have been thinking about Alex.

That was the crux of it. The sharpest part of my guilt. I unclenched my fist and held up Alex's list.

"Here," I said, unfolding it. "This is why I'm here, hundreds of miles away from home, stuck on a train in the middle of nowhere." I picked up the tin. "These are Alex's ashes. He sent me on some goddamn scavenger hunt from the grave, a list of places I was supposed to leave him. After the funeral, my sister-in-law gave me this." I held the letter up to her face. "I've completed them all, everything he wanted me to do— except one."

I read Alex's blue chicken scratch out loud to her, my voice shaking.

"*Way to go, Nicky. End of the line. You did good. I can say that, even though I won't be there to see the end result, but damn if I don't know my little brother, right? Now, I need you to save the last drop for the ride home. Whatever the hell you do, don't give me to Mom or Willow. The last thing they need is a little bit of dust sitting around collecting, well, dust. So I want you to dump the rest in the ocean. Maybe I'll wind up on that same beach in Jersey where we went when I was nine and you were six and we jumped waves and got sunburns with Dad, and Mom was pissed but she bought us ice cream anyway.*"

I felt my eyes burn and I wiped at the corner, the paper crinkling in my fingers.

"*Maybe a seagull will eat me and shit me out on someone's picnic blanket. That's the best part. I'll never know. And neither will you.*"

I looked back at Brit. "I promised his wife I'd do it on the way home, the last one. Over the side of the ship. Somewhere near here, actually. And I'm going to let him down. And Willow down. And a lot of good I get for failing, because I'm still not going to be home in time to help my dad out and *that's* going to let everyone else down. Do you have any idea how that feels? The pressure?"

She set her hands on her hips. "Yes, actually. I do."

"Why don't you tell me how, Brit, because from where I sit, I see a privileged little girl taking a vacation from her perfect life and calling it running away."

I clamped my mouth shut, flinching at the hurt in her eyes. I wanted to take it back as soon as I said it. I knew better than that. I knew what she was running from just as well as I knew I envied her for being able to do it. Why was I fighting with Brit when it was Alex I was angry with? None of this was her fault. It was my fault for being so distracted, so hooked on her. For wanting her so damn bad.

But Brit didn't crumble.

She came at me, pushing a finger into my chest. "Fine, Nick. Maybe you're right. But do you want to know what I see? I see a self-made martyr with control issues."

Well, fuck. That arrow hit its bullseye. Even I knew she was spot on. It didn't mean I knew how to be any better. I opened my mouth to, I didn't know what, muddle together a defense, but she wasn't done.

"Now it's my turn to play 'did you know?' Did you know I called my wedding off because Sean cheated on me like it was a sport? He didn't even try to hide it. Did you know I stayed for a long time because I had nowhere to go besides home to my parents? And you know what? No one would have cared, least of all them. They would have wanted me to work it out because business is the most important thing and Sean is *oh*, so good for my dad's business."

I stared at her, regret sinking onto my shoulders. I wished she had just popped me in the mouth like she did to that guy at the bar.

"He's their top guy, you know? That's what they said when I told them I was leaving him. My mom said, 'Bridget, how will this look?' But my dad?" She gave a humorless laugh. "The first thing he asked was if Sean was quitting. I'm their daughter, but they were pissed. At *me*. So, yeah, I know a little bit about disappointing people, Nick. About expectations.

"And maybe I did have a perfect life to some people, but it wasn't *my* perfect life. So much of it has been awful, and I'm doing everything I can to get away from it. I wanted to come on this trip and prove to myself I could do it alone and *you* wouldn't even let me have that!"

She pulled her finger from my chest and we stared at each other, her lip trembling, her eyes wet, me wallowing in my guilt. I didn't have a clue what to say to any of that.

Then she pressed her palms to my cheeks and whispered, "No one should have to be unhappy just because someone else has it worse, Nick. Someone else will *always* have it worse. You only get one life. Stop wasting the one you have because you feel guilty that not everyone got the same. That Alex didn't get the same."

His name on her lips hit me like a wave I hadn't seen coming. The pain I'd been keeping at bay with all of this manufactured anger tore through my chest, sharp and stinging. Pain for Alex, for me, for the things I did and didn't say.

For the thought of Brit crying over some asshole who dared to treat her like anything less than a gift. That was what she'd been for me. So beautiful and funny, and even after what I'd said, she was still holding me up.

I stepped closer until she had to tip her head to keep her tough stare aimed at me, and then my hands were in her hair. "I'm sorry." It was all I could choke out. "I'm sorry I said that."

"That was mean."

"I know, I—"

She pressed her finger to my lips and *shh*ed me. "Stop. I've already forgiven you."

She took the letter from my hand. "Do you still want to do this, Nicky?"

"Do what?"

"The last thing on the list." She put her hand on my chest. "Look, I didn't know your brother, but I can't imagine he intended for this trip to be a second funeral. Look at the things on this list. Mountain tops and beaches and zip lines. It looks to me like this was written by someone trying to get you to live a little. This was for you, Nick."

My stomach dropped like I'd just crested a hill on a roller coaster. Was that true? Was this all some fucking dare like the rope swing or the racecar driving? Brit didn't even know Alex, but shit, that was the most Alex thing I'd ever heard. And she'd figured it out before I had.

I stared at her, slack-jawed and she poked me in the ribs, cracking a smile. "Were you always this dense, Nicky? Or is it the grief?"

"I . . ." Was she teasing me now? I could barely keep up.

"I understand if it is," she said. "But I'm here to tell you, cut the crap and do what your brother so clearly wanted for you."

I shook my head, so in awe of this woman, my voice would barely work. "How?"

"The snow!" she said, laughing. "It's a frozen ocean and we're stuck in the middle of it." She pointed over my shoulder and I turned to look out the foggy, rectangular window in our cabin. "And you know where all this snow is going to end up when it melts? It's going to trickle down the side of these ravines, and land in a brook. Then it's going to slide over rocks and plants and dirt, and it's going to end up in that very same ocean we were supposed to be sailing in."

Holy shit. My eyes snapped back to hers. I was going to get whiplash. But . . .

"They'll never let us off the train."

She dropped the letter on the bed and reached for her jeans. "We'll just explain it to them."

I caught her hand. "No way. I'm not playing the dead brother card."

Brit shook her head and giggled. "Okay, Nicky. Just remember, you're the one who wanted to lie."

CHAPTER TWENTY-FIVE

Melting Hearts

Nick

"You can't be serious." My elbow banged off of the wall as Brit tugged me down the narrow hallway to the next car. She sucked in air, faking these huge gasps, and she'd somehow made real tears spring from her eyes on command.

"Go with it or it won't work." She flagged down a man in a conductor coat and hat. "Sir!"

"Yes? Is everything all right?" His wide eyes bounced from a now-hysterical Brit to me. I summoned everything I had to turn my face into a mask of grave concern.

"I'm . . . I'm . . ." She tossed me a look over her shoulder that said, *Your line, idiot.*

"She's feeling claustrophobic," I supplied on cue.

Brit winked at me then went back to gasping. "I cannot spend another minute on this train, sir!"

She pressed her hand to her forehead and swayed, her voice

turning vaguely Southern. Sort of Scarlett O'Hara-ish. This performance was confusing. Maybe that was her angle.

"I need some fresh air. Please. Can we get off for just a few minutes?" She fell back onto my chest dramatically and I barely caught her.

The guy was shaking his head before she even finished. "I'm sorry, miss. I can't let you off of the train. It's dark and we're surrounded by forest. I can page a nurse?"

"She just needs a few minutes," I said. His eyes swung to me in commiseration while Brit ramped up her tears. "I'll go with her. We'll be right there where the lights from the window are. We won't go anywhere else."

I clutched the tin in my pocket and Brit started rocking back and forth on her heels, still breathing weird. She pretended to sob.

She had him. He looked over his shoulder to make sure we were alone. "Fine," he said. "Make it quick. I could get in serious trouble for this."

He opened the exit door and Brit darted for it. I chased her down the stairs, cursing when I jumped from the last step into the crunchy snow. It rushed past my sneakers, freezing my ankles and shins like tiny shards of glass. The air was painfully cold, burning my windpipe with every breath.

Brit was hopping like a rabbit, the snow up to her knees. It was pitch black, except for the lights from the train, and the line of pine trees beyond us creaked and groaned under the weight of the ice and snow.

"Jesus. Come here. It's freezing." I jogged to catch up to her, wrapping her up in my arms.

"Are you ready?" she asked. Her breath came out in white clouds, the tip of her nose already bright pink.

"Where should I do it?"

She looked around the sea of white, then pulled me to the crest of a soft slope. She kneeled in the snow and started digging, shaping the crusty top layer into a bowl. "Here. We'll cover them over so nothing disturbs it."

I dropped to my knees and pulled out the tin, looking down at Brit like some sort of lifeline. My chest was pounding.

"Do you want me to wait over there?" she asked, pointing behind us.

"No. Please stay." She nodded and I pulled her into my side, flipping the tin open with one hand. The other dragged down my face.

This is it. I'd been carrying this around for so long, dwelling on the inconvenience of this mission because anger was a softer landing than grief, but now it felt like the last tether I had to Alex was snapping in front of me. I was finally free of this task right when I'd figured out what it had all been about.

My hand shook as I tipped the tin, letting the first gray ashes pour out and pool on the white snow. I hadn't really let myself think of this dust as my brother. Alex had dark hair like me, but his skin was lighter. He was skinny because building houses with Tom and Drew and I wasn't an option, but he always felt bigger than me, like his presence just took up more space. Now I was looking down at this ant hill and realizing this was his last physical presence on this earth. It stole my breath how much that hurt.

I closed my eyes and bit back the ball of emotion in my throat. I knew I should say something. I wasn't sure I could put anything I felt into words, but I couldn't let this moment pass with my usual silence—I'd regret it for the rest of my life.

I sucked in a cold breath and tried twice before forcing out the words.

"Alex, I, um. I'm sorry. I've been kind of shit at this whole eulogy thing so far. I guess you probably knew I would be." My voice tried to crack and I pressed my palm into my eyes, breathing through a swelling sensation in my chest.

Brit wrapped her arms around my stomach, and I threaded my fingers through her hair, holding her to me. "You always knew what to say, you know? How to handle everything with Mom. Now she's falling apart and Dad is acting like it's normal. Fuck, I guess it is normal, but everything is worse now and the one person who gets it is gone."

I felt a tear roll over my cheek and I wiped it away, sniffing up at the sky. "I don't really know who we are now without you. Who I am. It feels like a crack opened up in the middle of my world and there are parts of me I can't get to anymore.

"I was so mad at you for making me do this, Alex. I've been cursing you out for weeks. But I see now that this was your way of leaving the best part of you here, with me. I still don't know if I passed your little test, but I get it and I'm trying. I will try. I love you."

The tin was empty and I tucked it back in my pocket. I stayed there for what felt like forever, mute, while Brit scooped snow up with her bare hands to cover the ashes. I thought about that rope swing at my uncle's camp, remembering a day I went there with Willow and Alex when she'd first gotten her license. He and I took turns doing these crazy jumps into the lake while she called out our scores.

Alex's ashes might be in a forest covered in snow, but I hoped that was where he was.

Finally, the snow had soaked through my pants, biting at my knees and shins. I stood, pulling Brit up with me, and wrapped her in my arms. I could feel her breath through my T-shirt, and I felt oddly peaceful.

"Thank you," I whispered.

"Are you okay?"

I took a deep pull of cold air, scented by the tropical flowers in her shampoo and blew it out into the sky. "Yeah. I am, actually."

Because of her. She'd changed everything. *Everything*.

Every day of my life had been clouded—Alex's illness, my parents' needs, all the pressure—and what I was holding right now, this was the sun. Bright and beautiful and foreign. And I couldn't imagine going back to the dark.

She moved to pull away, but I squeezed her tighter. "Brit . . ."

"Nick."

Neither of us blinked and the lack of white mist between us told me we were both holding our breaths, waiting to see what this moment was going to do to us. I felt something in my chest coiling tighter and tighter with every touch. I was afraid any minute I would wake up and she'd be a memory, because nothing in my life had ever felt this good. And I'd just promised not to waste that feeling.

I cupped her cheeks, tipping her face toward mine, and she stared at me through her long lashes. "What are you thinking about?" she whispered.

I leaned closer until my mouth hovered just over hers. "I'm thinking about kissing you."

She swallowed, eyes wide. "Are you talking yourself out of it?"

"No. I'm just trying to do it right." I ducked that last inch to press my mouth to hers, and she wrapped her arms around my neck, sighing like I'd just taken something heavy from her. She kissed me back, our tongues sliding, mouths pressing. She tasted like candy and tears, and holy shit, I saw stars.

I ran my hands down to her ass, lifting her off the ground,

and she wrapped her legs around my waist, parting her lips for me. It was sloppy and desperate and I told myself to slow down, kiss her right, but I couldn't seem to calm this deluge of raw need.

At the hotel, the tension between us had felt frantic and directionless, like a top spinning out of control. The thought of trying to catch it in my hands, command it, had felt impossible. Now it felt like a rope pulling me in. Holding on and following was the only thing that made sense. It was like someone dropped her on that dock in front of me so I could finally feel what it was like to breathe.

"I should have done this days ago," I said into her mouth.

"You wasted a lot of time."

"I'm going to make up for it."

She was so warm and giving, and I wanted everything. I wanted to lay her down and love every part of her until she felt everything I couldn't say. *Thank you. You're the most amazing woman I've ever met. You feel like everything good in the world, rolled into a tiny package.*

"Hey!"

I jumped at the sound of someone yelling and turned to see the conductor waving a flashlight at us. Brit fell into a fit of giggles and I stumbled, tumbling us both backwards until my ass was in the snow. She buried her face in my neck, laughing so hard her whole body shook.

"If your girlfriend is all better, please get back on the train."

I swallowed down my own laughter and gave him a salute, then I turned back to Brit. "Time's up."

"No," she said, her voice low. "We have all night."

I was going to use every minute of it.

CHAPTER TWENTY-SIX

I've Been Here the Whole Time

Brit

I've heard people use the phrase "Now I can die happy" but until that moment—standing under the icy moon and flickering stars, Nick's mouth and hands moving over me—I'd never understood what it meant. And now, his back plastered to the door of our room, looking at me like he wanted to devour me, I wasn't entirely sure I hadn't already passed on.

"Nothing has to happen if you don't want it to," he said. His voice was doing that growly thing again and I could tell the thought of me stopping this here was killing him. Hell, it was killing me and I had no intention of it.

"Are you turning me down?" I breathed.

"No, sweetheart."

My legs squeezed together involuntarily. The first time he'd called me that it had been condescending, exasperated. Now it was so affectionate, I wanted to get it tattooed across my chest.

"I'm just making sure this is okay," he said. He stepped closer. The corner of his mouth lifted, probably in reference to the swoony look on my face, and a shiver wracked my body. He pressed his fingers to my cheek. Just as quickly as I'd gotten the smile, it fell. "You're freezing."

I was, but I wasn't sure that was why I was shaking. This thing that was about to happen had my body in a state of pulsing anticipation. But it was also a little terrifying. I was twenty-one when I slept with someone for the first time, and it was Sean. I couldn't say it wasn't good sometimes, but there was always this undercurrent of hierarchy. He was the experienced one. He was the one who chose me. I should feel lucky.

Nick rubbed his hands over my arms, something entirely different than that in his eyes. Something . . . reverent.

"You're taking care of me again," I whispered even as I dissolved against his chest.

He responded with a grunt of acknowledgment but he didn't stop. He smoothed my hair away from my neck and pressed his warm palms to my skin, giving me his body heat. I thought of the way I'd demanded he stop looking out for me at the airport. Now all I wanted was to be wrapped in his arms and coddled.

Walk me through this, Nick. I'm out of my depth.

I pressed my face into the cotton of his long-sleeved T-shirt, breathing in the scent of frost and skin. "Your shirt is wet from the snow," I whispered. I wasn't just being obvious, I wanted him to take it off.

It worked. He let me go to tug it over his head, and my throat made a little "eek" sound. *All that skin. Right there.*

I reached a tentative hand out, exploring his broad chest, the six distinct ridges over the flat plane of his belly. I dragged my flattened hands over his shoulders, down his biceps, touching all of the pieces of him that I'd shamelessly gawked at from the passenger seat of the Rover.

Nick watched, lips parted and eyes hazy as I studied every dip and curve of muscle like I was going to be tested later. When I ran my finger along the dark trail of hair leading into black boxers that peeked from his jeans, his stomach muscles bunched.

"The eyes still have it," I said shakily, reminding him of our card game. "But there are some serious contenders for second-best physical attribute."

His smile was playful exasperation and it felt like a fluttering in my chest. "Are you done?"

I definitely wasn't. At the edge of his Adonis belt, a little white line puckered his skin. I pressed my thumb over it. "Appendix?"

"Yes." He tugged me closer, kissing a spot beneath my ear that made my head flop over like a ragdoll. His hands mapped me now, down my hips, around to squeeze my butt, soft then greedy while he murmured against my skin.

"I was in fifth grade." He moved to my neck. "Alex was in the hospital at the same time getting his first pacemaker. We thought it was cool, but my mom definitely didn't." He pressed his teeth against my pounding pulse. "As soon as I got back to school, I checked out all of these books on nutrition from the library. Thought maybe I could keep all of my other organs from stressing her out."

I blinked up at him, wondering how many of these little stories he kept tucked away. "I want you to tell me every thought you've ever had, Nick."

He laughed, scooping me off the ground. "Later."

I held his cheeks and kissed him for the two steps it took for him to set me on his bed. The sheets were bunched up against the wall, his pillow folded in half from earlier when he was asleep here. His scent was everywhere and it felt like I was climbing inside of him.

Nick dropped to his knees and pulled off the faux-shearling boots that I'd bought at Target and just ruined in the snow. Stripping off my socks, he held my freezing bare feet against his belly to warm them. I wiggled my toes making him laugh. The sound was like sunshine.

"Better?" he asked.

"Yes."

His hands ran up my ankles and over my thighs, warming me through my jeans. When I reached down and unbuttoned them, his eyes went dark.

"Need some help?" A whisper of a smile crossed his lips.

My God. This is really happening. My heart was a fireworks display. I lifted my butt, and Nick peeled the pants off of my damp skin, down my legs, letting them drop with a wet thunk onto the floor.

We stared at each other, him naked from the waist up, me in just my underwear from the waist down. My stomach was a swirling ball of nerves and affection and pure lust. I wanted this man so bad it hurt, and I knew by the drunk look on his face that he wanted me too.

I'd been sleeping next to a man for years, but I'd never been looked at like this—with such hunger. I'd given up on ever having a moment like this.

Nick climbed up to sit beside me and this close to him, I could hardly believe the color of his eyes. They were otherworldly and they were staring right into my soul.

"Why are you looking at me like that, weirdo?" I forced a playful smile even though I was more than a little intimidated.

"Because you're beautiful and you're not wearing any pants."

I burst into a laugh. That was exactly what I needed to calm the butterflies in my stomach—Nick being blunt, joking, being my friend. This was the same man who said he liked my face and made it sound like a sonnet. Who took a punch for me in a dark parking lot and slept on my shoulder. Who let me sit with him during what was probably one of the hardest moments of his life.

Suddenly all of my nerves evaporated like a candle being blown out and I pulled to my knees, throwing one leg over his lap to straddle him.

Nick tugged my hips until we were chest to chest, pushing at the hem of my oversized hoodie. "Can I take this off?"

I nodded and he stripped it over my head, quick and clumsy. My hair got caught and he made a little growl of frustration as he worked to untangle it.

"Look at you," he breathed when he finally tossed the shirt on the floor. I was perched on his lap in just a tank top and purple cotton boy shorts. He leaned back and dragged his eyes over my body—my small chest, my slightly-too-big-for-my-frame butt, my non-existent abs. His pupils were black, his breath shallow, and I felt that crown reappear. Nick was checking me out and he liked what he saw.

"I've thought about this," he said, his voice low and rough. "Have you thought about this, Brit?"

"Yes," I admitted. "Last night at the hotel, I wanted you to stay."

"You have no idea how much I wanted to."

He kissed me again, that tenderness from before giving way to a hunger that we'd both just admitted to. Nick tugged my lip with his teeth, hands pushing beneath my tank top to wrap around my rib cage. I spread my knees, dipping to brush against the hardness in his jeans.

His eyes rolled back. "Fuck."

"Are you going to take your pants off too? Please? Take your pants off, Nick."

He chuckled against my ear, easily lifting me off his lap. I watched as he unbuckled his belt and slid down his zipper. I'd already felt what he had hiding in there, but to see it was a whole other thing. Sean wasn't small, or so I thought. I didn't have much to compare it to. But Nick was much bigger.

He saw my eyes bulge and he gave me a wicked smirk. *Oh my God, this man.* He may not know his face should have poems written about it, but he knew what he was packing.

"Should I be scared?" I asked, only half joking.

His burst of surprised laughter briefly cut through the heady tension we'd built, but then he cupped my chin, bringing my eyes to his. I had to force myself not to blink away from the intensity. "I'll be so careful," he whispered. "I thought about that too, how careful I'd be at first."

My belly swooped. "At first?"

He licked his lips and his eyes dropped to my chest. "Until you ask me not to be."

I shivered, affection and want making me sway.

Nick shoved his jeans off, and I was back on his lap with just two thin layers of cotton between us. I could feel him pressed between my legs, hot and solid, and I rolled my hips, chasing friction while we kissed. His hands were everywhere, beneath my ass squeezing, pushing up under my tank top, thumbs stroking my stomach. I could have been kissed by him for hours but I was drenched and buzzing from the anticipation. "Touch me. Please?"

He groaned with what I assumed was restraint. "I'm definitely going to do that."

"Nick. Now."

Something on his face broke and he wrapped an arm around me, flipping us so I was on my back. He barely had enough room to pull to his knees above me. Even with my bunk tucked away, he had to hunch his shoulders. He propped his fist on the mattress beside my head, his other hand darting to the waistband of my underwear.

"That T-shirt you had on the other day," he said. "The one you knotted, showing off your stomach. It's been haunting my dreams."

"I like that," I said. "Being in your dreams."

He dipped lower and the chain he wore pooled on my collar bone, cool metal on hot skin. "I'm going to touch every inch of you," he said. His teeth dragged across the swell of my breast and my hips jerked.

He shifted his weight to his knees and pushed my tank top up my belly, bending to nuzzle his face against my navel as he slid my underwear down my thighs.

When he brushed his fingers over me, I cried out loud enough to echo in the tiny tin can of a room.

"Shhh." He covered my mouth with his, grinning. "We have to be quiet. We're already in trouble."

I pressed my teeth into my lip and nodded, but I was sure I was leaving nail marks on his back.

"Can you be good?" he asked, circling me with his thumb.

I don't know who he thought I was, but calm and composed while Nick was saying those things and touching me like that was not something I could commit to. "I don't know."

He curled his fingers and when I gasped a little too loud, he shot me a look that was half warning, half pride. He quieted me again with his mouth, his hips rocking against my thigh in a way that made me feel wanted and powerful.

"You're going to have to because if someone knocks on that door before I get inside you, I'm going to explode."

I nodded, deciding I could give him what he asked but only because I wanted him inside me too. I wanted him everywhere.

"I'll be good," I slurred. "Please don't stop. Please."

He stretched one arm above my head, his other hand working a pattern, patient and determined, turning me into a moaning, blubbering, *begging* mess. "Don't stop," I repeated.

"I won't."

"Please, Nick."

He laughed into my neck. "I'm not going to—"

The fire that had been building in my belly exploded, pulsing downward until I was clenched around his fingers, my legs shaking in a way I couldn't control.

Nick smiled against my open mouth. "Shhh," he reminded me, but what I'd thought was building into a scream came out as a whimper. Every nerve in my body was dancing and the pleasure of it all stole my breath. I couldn't make any noise if I wanted to.

Nick shifted so his whole body covered mine, the heavy length of him pressed into my thigh, and he kissed me with so much affection. His mouth was sweet and slow, his fingers careful, but relentless. He held me as I twitched and shuddered from the shock of it, smoothing my hair and kissing my jaw instead of rushing me.

"Good?" he asked, nuzzling my hair.

I sighed out some unintelligible reply, but the answer was a resounding *holy fuck*.

He sucked at my neck. "I need to be inside you."

"Yes, please. Be inside me, please."

His laugh was a burst of hot air on my ear, then his tongue was there, flicking the lobe. "I have a condom in my wallet."

"I have an IUD," I said, holding on to his arm so he couldn't leave me. "And I've been tested . . . because, Sean . . ."

Nick's jaw ticced and I turned away. I was feeling open and emotional and if I saw that protective look in his eyes one more time, I might make a fool of myself with orgasm tears.

He pressed his thumb to my bottom lip. "I have too. Are you sure you're okay with it?"

"Yes." I reached down, clawing at his boxers while he smiled and pulled them the rest of the way off. He kissed the top of my thigh, my hip, then stretched out over me, our stomachs sealing together in the humidity we'd built up. The walls must have been sweating.

"You're beautiful," he said.

"And I'm not wearing any pants."

"Still wearing this, though," he said, pushing my bra strap off of my shoulder.

"Take it off."

He did, unhooking it and lifting it over my head with my tank, much more gracefully than he had my sweatshirt. And that was it. Nothing left between us but his heavy breaths and my slight tremble.

Our eyes locked as he pushed my legs apart with his knee, settling between them.

"Tell me if I hurt you," he whispered.

"You won't."

He held my hip with one hand, his cock with the other, watching as he lined us up, then his eyes lifted to mine and with one slow and careful thrust, we were a whole lot more than travel buddies.

Nick sucked in a ragged breath and I whimpered as he hit that same spot that had just sent me crashing. "You okay?"

I shifted, rolling my hips to adjust to the stretch of him. "Yes. More."

He fisted my hair, a look of pure relief on his face as he started to move. His normally shrewd eyes glazed over, the grumpy little frown he usually wore turning into a growl of pleasure against my breastbone when he found a rhythm.

I pushed my fingers into his hair, relishing the way he let me hold him while his hips pumped. He found my mouth and we laughed into sloppy kisses.

For days I'd been catching glimpses of this charming, playful man just underneath all of Nick's brooding. He'd forget himself for a moment and smile, and the impossible softness of it would shake my world like a child with a snow globe. Now he was giving it to me without measure and I wanted to scoop up every happy noise he made and keep them in my pocket.

"I want you to come again," he whispered. His voice was strangled and hoarse despite the smiles.

I shook my head. "I can't."

But then he reached for my thigh, wrapping it around his waist, and suddenly he was hitting a new spot that made white flash behind my eyelids. He tilted my hips and slipped a hand between us. My eyes rolled back. "Just like that, sweetheart," he said. "You drive me fucking crazy, Brit . . . so pretty . . . so sweet."

The praise made pleasure rush from my belly to my toes and suddenly I was squeezing around him again.

"Oh fuck." He held my hips, driving faster than before. His eyes were clouded with lust, near wild, but he kept his promise, being so careful while taking everything he needed.

Finally his weight collapsed onto me, and he groaned into my neck much louder than he'd just shushed me for being.

A giggle bubbled out of my still-dazed, sort of squished body. I absolutely loved that I'd made him do that.

Nick's shoulders shook with silent laughter. His fingers blindly fumbled around my chin and cheeks before pressing lightly against my lips to close them.

"You okay?" he asked, panting against my skin.

"Yes."

"I was too rough there, at the end."

I smiled. "No. Shh. I liked it."

All of his weight was on me now, his breath heaving into my neck. "I fucking loved it."

He rolled to his side and laced our fingers. "You sure you're okay?" he breathed, his lips on my forehead.

"Better than okay."

"Me too." He tucked my hair behind my ear, grinning down at me. "We should have been doing this for days. I might have been better company."

I knew there was a sliver of self-consciousness in that, and I held his cheeks, nipping up at his chin. "You've always been good company, Nicky."

He smiled, kissing me. "Are you cold?"

As if on cue, a shiver snaked through my shoulders and I wiggled in his grip. "A little."

He kissed my cheek and rolled off of the bed, leaving me even colder.

He came back with a towel and gently wiped the inside of my thighs while I lay there, boneless.

He pulled his boxers back on and dug in his bag for a clean T-shirt, tossing it to me, and I slipped it over my head, tugging the collar to my nose and sniffing with zero shame. When he'd climbed back in, he hovered over me, forearms bracketing my face as he touched small kisses to my cheek and jaw and forehead.

"Still okay?" he asked, grinning at me. His eyes were

dancing, and I wondered what it was about my face that made him keep asking. Did I look on the outside like I felt on the inside—shaken down to my soul?

"I'm okay," I whispered. I wanted to lay my head down in the perfect notch of his shoulder and cuddle him all night. I wanted to sneak outside and detach our car from the rest of the train so we'd be left behind here together forever. I wanted to do it again.

All of those rapid-fire thoughts made me realize I actually had no idea what to do next.

I shifted over, squishing myself against the wall so he could lie beside me. It was a tight fit but quite possibly the best place I'd ever been.

Still, I knew I shouldn't assume. "Do you want . . . um. I can't pull my bunk down by myself."

There was a latch I couldn't reach and, *oh, please, Nick, don't make me leave.*

His forehead crinkled. "You're sleeping in your bunk?"

"Oh. I wasn't sure . . ."

He laughed and then I *really* wasn't sure. He tightened his arm around my waist and rolled so his weight trapped me. "Sorry, Brit. I'm not pulling your bunk down. If you want to leave me, you'll have to grow a few inches."

His lips turned up into a sweet smile and I giggled into his arm. Happiness bubbled over in my chest. Nick wasn't leaving me, and he wasn't making me leave and, oh my God, I was going to touch him all night long. And for as long as I could after that.

CHAPTER TWENTY-SEVEN

Changing the Script

Nick

I wasn't usually into morning sex. Most days, I woke up with a to-do list written on the backs of my eyelids, and as soon as daylight hit, I wasn't able to relax long enough to enjoy it. There were too many pulls on my attention, too many places I needed to be that I couldn't let myself accept the indulgence. But this morning, my list consisted of waiting for this train to start moving again and watching Brit sleep, and all I could think about was getting back inside of her.

She was beautiful, all sleep-teased and warm. After all the time I'd spent stealing glimpses of her in the passenger seat, I couldn't believe I had her like this, cheek on my chest and bare leg thrown over mine, her perfect little ass in my hand. I stroked my fingers up and down her back, impatiently waiting for her to wake up so I could touch her again, put my mouth on every part of her. But I also wanted to show her how much she meant to me.

I'd been lying there, grinning at the top of her head like a fool. My face was sore from it, which was a pretty potent reminder that I hadn't used these particular muscles in a while. I had no idea how I got to this place.

Most of my relationships fizzled early when women realized I was spread too thin to give them what they needed. Only a few had drifted into real feelings territory, enough so that I'd been disappointed when they ended. But this? It had been a matter of days and I knew I wasn't coming back from this.

Brit shivered when I skimmed my fingers over her hip, and I watched her eyelids blink open. "Hey."

"Hi." She dragged a hand over her mouth and lifted her chin, looking all shy and cute.

I, on the other hand, already had a hard-on that was bordering on uncomfortable. She definitely noticed, and for a few moments we just lay there, smiling at each other, adjusting to everything that had changed.

"Nick," she said, her hand walking down my stomach, making me swallow.

"Yeah?"

"Pass me some of the gummy bears."

I cracked up. "The sun's barely up and you're eating candy."

"Either that or I get out of this bed to brush my teeth."

I weighed the options. There was only a little rum in them. And I really didn't want her to leave. *Sold*.

I reached to the little cubby above my head and pulled down the bag. Brit sprawled out over my chest and grabbed a handful, stuffing her mouth. I did too. I was still chewing them when she crushed her lips to mine.

"You're adorable," I mumbled around the candy.

"And you're the sexiest man I've ever seen."

I laughed and shook my head, running my hands down her

back to palm her ass. She was still naked from the waist down and I let my fingers creep lower until her eyes rolled closed and her lips parted on a pant.

Every time she reacted to me, my chest felt full, like my heart was beating more vigorously than it ever had, pumping blood to all the parts of my brain that remembered how to enjoy things. I was enjoying the hell out of Brit squirming against me, so eager and wanting, and a little surprised at herself.

I'd been right about her not having much experience, but it made me incredibly angry to think she'd been planning to marry someone who hadn't even bothered to fuck her properly. If she'd give me the chance, I'd change that. I'd stay on this broken-down train as long as it took to show her exactly how good I could make her feel.

"I missed you while I was sleeping," she whispered.

"Let's make up for it."

She kissed my jaw and I closed my eyes, letting the unfamiliar sensation of relaxation, that peace she gave me, warm my blood and loosen my muscles.

I'd already decided what to do about Willow's picture. When I got to New York, I'd head to the harbor and take a picture of the horizon over the Atlantic. Alex wasn't there yet, he had a long journey ahead of him without me, but that was where he'd end up. With that settled in my brain, all I had left to do was enjoy being away from the rest of the world. Just me and Brit.

And when we got off this train, I wasn't letting her go. Last night while she was curled under my arm, sighing in her sleep, I'd given a long, hard thought to what she'd said about only having one life. If I didn't take that to heart now, I'd have nothing to show for all of the shit Alex had put me through on this trip.

It was going to be hard. She lived five hours and sixteen minutes away—yeah, I'd mapped it out right after she'd told me her parents' address—but this wasn't something I was going to walk away from. This felt . . . *she* felt like finding a piece of myself I hadn't even known was missing. She was all of the smiles she'd accused me of holding back, all of the good things I'd been afraid to feel wrapped in this beautiful, pink-haired, amber-eyed package.

I was already thinking about driving to see Brit whenever I could, flying her out to see me. I had about ten years' worth of vacation time I suddenly wanted to use to explore every inch of her body. I felt like a kid planning to run away from home, but I found myself drunk off the idea of it—me and her and miles.

"What's that smile for?" she asked, grinning back at me.

"You."

She inched backward, crawling down my body and I nearly pinched myself. Was this another dream?

Brit picked her head up and smiled at me, that mischief that usually made me nervous dancing on her face. I swallowed hard, my stomach muscles clenching as she gathered her hair on top of her head and slipped an elastic band from her wrist to tie it up.

Then there was the screech of metal on metal and the train jolted, sending her tumbling forward.

Her face bounced off of my stomach.

"Shit. Are you all right?" I tucked her hair behind her ear and swallowed a laugh.

"Ow. Yes. Your abs are ridiculous." She rubbed her cheek. "Hey, we're moving!"

I sat up and took stock of my equilibrium. We were definitely in motion. I knew I was supposed to be happy about that, but I couldn't help the way my chest deflated like a day-old balloon.

Brit stretched over me and pulled the curtain aside, her face twisting in confusion.

"What's wrong?" I pushed up to my elbows and watched the pine trees start to blur as we picked up speed.

"We're going the wrong way."

As soon as she said it, a commotion started outside of the door. It was loud enough that my face burned at the thought of what all of our neighbors must have heard from our room last night.

"Oh no, oh no, oh no." Brit was already on her feet, pulling on her underwear. I reached for her wrist.

"Hey, wait up." I glanced down at my lap. "I'll go. I just need a minute."

But her face drained of color. "Nick, if I don't get home today, I won't make the auction."

CHAPTER TWENTY-EIGHT

Switching Tracks

Brit

I frantically hit redial on Meri's number. It was barely sun-up. When it finally woke her, she was going to kill me.

The conductor told us it would take a crew the day to demolish the tree that we'd run into, and it turned out twenty-five miles up the track, a snow drift had covered the tracks overnight. Big enough that it needed to be plowed. Another engine had been sent while we were sleeping and it was hauling us back the way we came to a tiny town two hours south.

The absolute worst case scenario had come true. Right after the absolute best.

I looked at Nick as the phone rang endlessly, my bottom lip raw from worrying my teeth over it. "They're going to help us make arrangements to stay the night," I told him. "In the morning, we'll get back on the train to New York." By then it would be too late.

My brain was reeling. What if Meri didn't answer in time? What if she couldn't help me?

"We'll get a car," Nick said. "Drive straight through to Boston."

"We don't even know if there's a place to rent a car in this town." I added up the time it would have taken us to drive even without the detour. "We'll never make it."

He pulled me into his side, pressing his lips to my hair. "We're going to figure it out, Brit."

I nodded, trying hard to mainline some of his confidence, but when Meri picked up on the next ring, the tears sprang to my eyes. "It wasn't my fault," I blurted.

"What happened?"

I didn't miss the fact that she sounded less than surprised. I wiped my eyes with the back of my hand and sniffed. "The train hit a tree. Last night."

"*What?*" she screeched. "Are you okay?"

I waved a hand at the air. "Yes! Yes. I'm okay. But I'm stuck . . . somewhere in the woods." My voice cracked and Nick squeezed my shoulder. "Mer, the auction."

"Oh. *Oh.*" There was a shuffling on the other line, then she sounded much more alert. "What do you need?"

"It's a lot to ask."

"I told you we'd be available for crises," she said.

I blew out a breath. "I was really hoping I could do this without one of my messes."

"Brit, this is beyond your control. And that's what friends are for, okay? What do you need me to do?"

Thankfully, Nick had experience buying properties for his father at auction. I put Meri on speaker and listened as he explained how the bidding worked, who to pay, and what would happen when we won. I'd already paid the money to be allowed to bid, and with my trust clearing, I had enough in my account to cover the total cost in cash. I had to order a bank check made out to the auction house and she could pick it up on the way.

Nick said Meri just needed to hold up the paddle with my number on it. Simple.

Meri wrote it all down and promised she would bring Justin to read over the contracts.

I was still going to make this happen.

I thanked her profusely then hung up, turning to Nick, eyes wide. He took my face in his hands and his smile dried the last of my panic tears. He kissed my forehead. "You did it, sweetheart."

I pressed my fingers to my pulse. "It feels a little bit like I barely made it out alive."

"No way. You just had your first crisis as a business owner and you handled it." He lifted his palm. "You're badass, Brit."

I high-fived him with a giggle, my heart pulsing with affection and the unfamiliar warmth of being the object of someone else's praise. For as long as I could remember I'd had a script of reassurances that I played for myself in my head. *You can do this. You're stronger than you think you are. They're all wrong about you.*

But hearing it from someone else hit differently. Hearing it from Nick felt like being hoisted on someone's shoulders and ferried through an adoring crowd.

I beamed at him, watched those round cheeks pull upward with the sweetest smile, and a drop in my belly reminded me of something I'd been ignoring. By handling this, I'd solidified my plan to leave him.

I swallowed, the unfairness of it tasting bitter in my throat. It would be fine, I told myself. The drive from Boston to Philly would be nothing after this marathon road trip. It was less than half a day. I could take the train, they were kind of our thing now, and use the travel time to update my blog or edit videos.

Of course I could. I was a badass.

Besides, we had one more night before we had to figure all that out and I was going to make the most of it. I pushed Nick's bare chest until he fell backward on the bed and I straddled his waist. "Nicky? When we get to town, we're getting one room again, right?"

His sea-foam green eyes turned stormy. "Absolutely."

I fell onto his chest and squeezed him. I was going to get my house and an extra night with Nick and I was giddy about both. I'd figure the rest out later.

CHAPTER TWENTY-NINE

Lessons and Plans

Brit

The train ferried us backward toward a tiny, one-stoplight town where we'd be spending the night. They could only scrounge up a couple of buses to take us from the tracks, so we had to go in shifts. It was after noon by the time Nick and I checked into a little roadside motel.

The exterior left something to be desired, with its gaudy orange doors and the bulbs burned out of the O in "Motel" but the rooms were clean and modern.

Nick opened the door, and I kicked off my shoes, dancing my way to the bed. "Look how big," I said, climbing up to bounce in the center of the mattress.

He dropped our bags on a chair and caught me around the waist. "We're back in Brit-worthy accommodation," he said, his mouth already working down my neck.

I fell backward and he crawled over me, arranging us both

so our heads were on the pillows. His eyes rolled closed and he breathed warmth into my neck. "This is nice."

"Should we take a nap? We were up half the night." I was teasing, of course. I might never sleep again as long as he was in the same bed.

He wrapped a big hand around my waist, flipping us so I was underneath him. "Better idea," he mumbled against my mouth.

"Oh yeah? What's that?"

"I was thinking I might see what it was like to fuck you on a real bed."

My belly did a somersault. The way he talked to me sent a thrill through my body. It was rougher than Sean, lacking in charm and finesse, but it was so real. Everything about him was that way, from the scratch of his unshaven face to the natural scent of his skin. The sheer size and weight of him on top of me.

I smiled into his kiss, wrapping my leg around him to press that weight where I wanted it. He groaned, grinding slow and deliberate, until my breath was short and my chest damp with sweat. Our clothes came off piece by piece—a T-shirt over my head, him standing to let his jeans pool at his feet while I watched. Then he was back on top of me, pressing me into the mattress, trailing slow, open-mouthed kisses down my stomach before moving down to suck at the skin on my hip.

He traced the line of my panties with his tongue, then pulled them off, eyeing me with his face still between my legs.

My pulse thrummed a chord in my neck. "What are you doing?"

"You know." He smiled, gliding a finger over me as he kissed my inner thigh. My knees knocked together of their own accord, nearly catching his chin. *Smooth.*

"You don't like it?" he asked.

"I . . . don't know."

He thought I was being coy. His smile turned cocky and I knew instantly he was good at this. "Tell me what turns that into a yes."

"No, I mean . . ." Ugh, this was suddenly so embarrassing. I felt foolish in my inexperience while he was looking at me with such confidence. Heat swept over my cheeks, down my neck, and I squirmed in his grip. "I don't know because no one has ever done it."

"What?" He seemed genuinely confused, which I thought was the sweetest thing I'd seen from him yet. He propped himself on his elbows. "This morning you—I mean, you knew what you were doing."

With the auction details taken care of, we'd spent the rest of the train ride trying to be quiet while fooling around in our cabin. I thought Nick was going to pass out when I'd finished what I started.

"*I've* done it," I said. And Sean loved to give me pointers, so I'd gotten pretty good. "I've just never . . . received."

Confusion, then something darker flashed in his eyes. "You're kidding me. Your fiancé never even offered?"

I shook my head, my lip between my teeth. Then his angry expression slid into that little half-smile that turned my insides into a knot. "Can I be the first?"

"Would that make you happy?"

"Yes."

How could I say no to that? I blew out a nervous breath and unlocked my knees. Nick kept my gaze as he nudged my thighs farther apart with his elbows, settling between them. He dipped his head and my heart slammed against my chest bone, making my body jerk.

"You okay?"

All I could see was the top of his head, the cowlick in his hair that had been freed when he took off his sweatshirt earlier. Was I okay? If I wasn't, I didn't really want to be.

I nodded. "I'm good."

He nodded back, a little agreement between us that he would take it from there. Good thing because one slow stroke of his tongue and I was convulsing. "Oh my God."

He smiled and I *felt* it. "I think you're going to like it."

Understatement. If he stopped right then, I would have marked that down as one of my favorite things to have ever happened. I settled into the mattress, focusing on the warmth of his arms wrapped under my knees, the slow slide of his tongue. The quiet groan he made like he was taking pleasure. Was he? Did he like doing this?

My brain shuffled through a million questions and curiosities until one slipped out. "What do I taste like?"

He pulled away and licked his lips, his pupils dark. "Rummy Bears."

"Nick!" I kicked my feet against the mattress, and he caught my ankle, laughing.

"I'm kidding." He crawled up my body locking eyes before catching my mouth in a deep, tongue-sliding kiss. "That's what you taste like."

My God.

He pulled up to his knees and grabbed the back of his shirt, hauling it over his head. I thought maybe he'd changed his mind and just wanted to get to it, but then he lifted my hips, dragging me down the mattress until my body curled into a C. My back and bottom were flush to his chest, my shoulders pressed into the bed.

He spread my thighs open just below his chin and licked his

lips. I was boneless and in some sort of state where lust mixed with shock. I just stared at him.

Nick smiled with the patience of a saint and the expression of a man who was about to ruin me. "Put your legs on my shoulders," he instructed.

Right. I wasn't sure why I didn't think of that instead of letting them hang awkwardly in the air like I was doing Pilates.

I hooked my ankles behind his head and Nick lowered his mouth, his eyes on mine until the last possible second. "Good?" he asked, one cheek hitched into a devastating smile.

I gurgled some sort of unintelligible sound. My mouth was stuck in an O, eyes wide like I'd just witnessed an angel from heaven appearing to tell me this was all a reward for some kindness I'd committed in another life.

I tried to tilt my body so I could reach him, touch him back, but he let go of one thigh to push my hand away. "In a minute," he whispered, leaning over me to lace our fingers on the mattress. His other hand wrapped around my stomach, holding me to him. "Focus." He blew the word out, warm breath over sensitive skin and I choked on a half-cry.

Determination flashed across his face, as if he'd given up trying to impress me with torturously precise technique and let himself get overwhelmed by the rush of it. And overwhelmed was a good word because all of my senses were locked into the scratch of his stubble against my thigh, the greediness of his tongue, the *sound* of it. I thought maybe I owed Sean a debt of gratitude that he hadn't ruined this for me yet.

"I don't want to finish like this," I said when I felt my thighs start to shake. I needed him closer.

"Tell me what you want."

"I just want you."

"Be more specific," he said, his voice like sandpaper.

"I want you to stop being careful."

The corner of his mouth hitched up and in an instant I was on my stomach, Nick on his knees behind me. His fingers tangled in my hair, guiding my head back for a bruising kiss that made my heart slam in my chest. It was pure excitement, though. I knew even when he wasn't being soft, that Nick would always be sweet.

"Lift up," he said, tapping my butt. I did as he said, scooching to my knees, my cheek still flat on the pillow. He traced my jaw with his thumb. "Goddamn, this is a nice view."

I giggled, then gasped when I felt the tip of him nudge me, then his big hand splay over my hip, squeezing tight and rough. He reached around my stomach, between my legs, lining us up to bring us together in a thrust that was anything but soft.

I bit down on my lip to keep from crying out. The last thing I wanted was for him to stop. I wanted that hard edge, that slip of his control. He was holding me to him so tightly, he couldn't pull all the way out, fucking me with just a rough rock of his hips. He mumbled into my shoulder, telling me how perfect I looked beneath him, asking me to come for him, telling me how much he liked to watch it. It was like a layer peeling away, revealing this needy possessiveness in him. It was so unexpected and intimate and raw, and where I'd just been feeling playful and excited, now the intensity made me shiver.

A whispered "*Come on, sweetheart*" sliced through my tiny fear of letting it happen like this, in such a vulnerable position, because I wasn't wrong about Nick or the way he would catch me. He slipped his hand behind my neck, tilting my face toward him, and fell with me, eyes wide open and smiling.

We slept for hours, naked and tangled, finally stirring when the room was cast in shadows from the setting sun. I lay draped over Nick's hips, my face half-buried in a pillow. Nick's hand was on my butt, not moving, not squeezing, just resting. I thought maybe he was still asleep, until he pulled in a deep breath and turned to face me. "Can I ask you something?"

"Mmm."

"How'd you pick a guy like Sean, one who treated you so poorly? I'm not implying it was your fault at all, I just meant, what attracted you to him?"

"Oh. Um . . ." I stuttered. This was an unexpected turn. "He picked me, actually. Plucked me right out of the crowd at this company event. A harbor cruise for my dad's firm because they'd hit some benchmark for the year—string band, sunset, all that. My father insisted I go. Sean had just started there a few months before so I hadn't met him yet. He walked up to me and said, 'You're the prettiest girl on this whole boat. Want to dance?' It wasn't a big boat."

A flicker of irritation flashed in Nick's eyes. He didn't like my self-deprecating humor.

"How'd you get all the way to engaged, though?"

I shifted, pulling my bent arm beneath my cheek. "I told you, he works for my dad. It was good for everyone involved."

"You were going to marry him to make your dad happy?"

"It's not what you think," I said, wondering how to explain it without sounding like the pushover I'd been. Dating Sean was my decision. He was handsome, successful, oh so charming. In the beginning we had fun. He seemed to like my quirks. It crossed my mind that being with me was some sort of rebellion of his own, that maybe there was something in him that was more like me than he realized and he just wasn't brave enough to embrace it.

I had reasons, but I couldn't say the approval that our relationship got from my parents wasn't a carrot on a stick. That was what convinced me to ignore my own gut, and that was where my shame lived.

"I didn't go into it with that intention," I told him. "It was more that I had finally done something to earn my parents' acceptance after twenty-plus years. Once I got a taste of that, it was hard to go back to The Looks."

Plus, I had no idea how bad it would be, how cruel. I just thought maybe I'd accept that, though Sean and I weren't in that fairy-tale kind of love I'd always dreamed of, we'd be happy *enough* and then I'd earn my place.

I took a deep breath and snuggled deeper into the pillow. "The first time I caught him, we'd been engaged all of six months. I thought, no way. He'd never put his career in jeopardy by cheating on the boss's daughter, not that carelessly. I assumed it was a mistake, a misunderstanding even though I had the evidence right there in black and white." A filthy email exchange that had made my cheeks red and my throat burn bitterly. "But then I realized something. He didn't care because he knew as well as I did who they'd back. They wanted it so badly, me and Sean."

I still couldn't be sure he hadn't known that from the beginning, planned it that way.

Nick wrapped an arm around me, his fingers curling in my hair.

"The second time was even more blatant and that's when I decided I was done. I thought I could get my trust and buy the house before I had to marry him, except they moved the wedding up—him and my father. It wasn't supposed to be until June. I mean, who gets married in March in New England? But my father wanted Sean to become a partner and they thought him being 'family' would help his cause."

In the end, it became my biggest failure to date in their eyes.

A broken engagement and a move back to their house. Plus, ruining their plan for Sean. It was just another check-mark on the list of ways I'd humiliated them.

"You never told them the truth? Even after you left?"

"I was embarrassed," I said, feeling a little prickle of defense on the heel of that memory. "It's no different than what you're keeping from your family. We all have reasons for the things we choose not to say."

Nick's jaw ticced. That didn't seem to sit well and I felt a stab of guilt in my belly. I hated to have any tension between us when the skin between my legs was still wet from him.

I expected him to keep arguing, but when I didn't get a comeback, I looked up to find him staring at me, looking . . . contrite. "I didn't mean to make you upset."

I shrugged. Talking about Sean didn't upset me. I just didn't like Nick thinking of me that way. Helpless. Stupid.

"I'm not upset."

He reached for my wrist, tugging until I unfolded onto his chest. His lips found my neck, soft, tender comfort that I relished. "For what it's worth, I think you're the prettiest girl on any boat."

I giggled and his kisses turned to bites as he flipped us over and pulled to his knees. "I'm going to take a shower. Want to come with me?"

I shook my head. "No. I'm going to be lazy a little while longer."

"Okay." He rolled away, then back for one more kiss. "See you in a few."

"See you in a few."

Nick grabbed his toothbrush from his backpack and closed the door to the bathroom. I peeked at the ancient alarm clock beside the bed. Meri would be on her way to the auction now.

I'd ordered a cashier's check that she was supposed to pick up in an hour and from there, she'd take it to the auction and she and Justin would place my bid. I knew there was still the chance of getting outbid, but I never discounted my gut feelings. Like I'd told Nick, from the moment I saw that house, I knew it would change my life. How could I not win?

I rolled over and closed my eyes, intending to nap while Nick showered, but my phone buzzing from somewhere on the bed startled me. Unlike Nick's, mine had been fairly quiet this trip. Besides Meri, there was no one to miss me back home.

I found it under one of the pillows, a picture of my father and I outside of our house on the Cape lighting up the screen, and I grimaced at the prospect of explaining my latest travel detour.

I pulled the sheet up over my chest and answered. "Hi, Daddy. So I've hit a tiny snag—"

"Did you think I wouldn't find out?"

The cool anger in his voice made me flinch. "What?"

"A cashier's check for hundreds of thousands of dollars and you didn't think the bank would notify me?"

The bank? Why would they call my father? My brain scrambled to catch up. My throat closed, my skin going clammy. "It's my account," I whispered.

"That I opened for you," he growled. "I'm the primary signer and you have a spending limit. It was a stipulation I set up when you were sixteen. Then, it was to keep you from doing anything foolish, but I see that protection is still needed."

"It's not foolish. It's an investment." Panic eased into indignation. How dare he? He had no idea the planning I'd put into this. He just assumed because it was my idea, it was foolish. "I've been waiting years for that money," I said. "You can't take it away." I might have misunderstood some things but I knew that much.

"No, but I can make sure you don't waste it before we discuss what you're using it for. I canceled the check request and froze your access to the account." His voice was calm and smug compared to my rising one. "You can use my credit card for any travel-related expenses, but you're to come straight home and not spend a dime over what's required to get here."

I knew he could see my transactions, but I didn't know he could stop them. "No. I—you *can't* do this."

"This is unbelievable, Bridget. Truly. Come home. Now."

He hung up and the tiny click of the line disconnecting felt like a bomb exploding in my chest. My mouth hung open, desperately gaping at the phone like it might start laughing and let me in on the joke.

This wasn't happening. I handled it. A freaking tree had tried to stop me but I handled it. Ducks were put in neat little rows and lists were checked and rechecked and I *handled* it.

And with a flick of his powerful wrist, my father had swiped it all away.

I forced my jaw closed and swallowed against what I assumed was a swelling sob but nothing came. My muscles were slack with defeat. My eyes dry.

All of the time I'd spent dreaming about this house, I was never going to get it. None of the setbacks even mattered because my father had made sure that every single thing I did had to have his approval. He was like the final boss on a video game, the one I was never good enough to beat. And I'd been naive enough about the way the world works that I hadn't even known the extent of his power. He'd kept me sheltered on purpose.

I'd failed. Game, set, match. He won.

I fumbled with the phone in my hand, pulling up the screen to text Meri. My fingers were barely strong enough to push the keys.

She was already on her way to the bank. I told her to turn around, that I didn't need her after all. She had a million questions but I couldn't face them. I thanked her for wasting her night and told her I'd call her soon, then I shut my phone off and sat in the middle of the bed, my arms wrapped around my knees, tired and beaten and numb.

Until I heard the shower turn off and the curtain slide against the rod.

Nick.

Sudden humiliation burned hot across my face. His words flicked through my brain. "*You're badass, Brit.*" The way he'd said, "*You did it, sweetheart*" with such pride in his eyes.

Then, "*How'd you end up with a guy like that?*"

He'd been quick to say it wasn't my fault, but wasn't it? Kind of? Wasn't all of it?

I couldn't tell Nick about this. He couldn't know that I was the mess he thought I was when we first met. I couldn't stand it.

Just as quickly, my heart tugged in the opposite direction. I wanted to curl into him and break down, tell him how all of my dreams had been shattered and let him hold me and tell me it would be okay. He would. He'd make it better. But then he'd know.

I jumped off the bed and ran to my bag, started pulling out clothes.

The door clicked open and Nick came out, a towel wrapped around his waist while I was pulling on denim shorts over a pair of colorful tights.

"Going somewhere?"

"Can we explore a little?" I asked with a bat of my lashes. I needed to get out of that room. It would be much easier to sell him on my *everything is fine* smile if we were out with other people instead of here, alone.

I pulled my hair out of the bun it had been in and combed through pink curls with my fingers. The color suddenly felt childish and ridiculous and I scooped it back up and re-tied it.

"You okay?" he asked, eyebrow raised.

"Of course."

Nick set his towel down on the armchair in the corner and wrapped his arms around my waist, bending to kiss my neck. "Where do you want to go?"

I reached up to stroke his wet hair, lowering my voice to a sexy whisper while sweat formed on my brow. "I want food."

Nick laughed. "Okay, sweetheart. Let's go see what this town has to eat."

CHAPTER THIRTY

All I See is You

Nick

I threw on some jeans and a Henley and Brit and I walked out onto the snow-covered sidewalk. Neither of us had a jacket, so I wrapped my arm around her shoulders and pulled her into my side. I had a feeling she was going to want to escape for fresh air before the night was over. She was always restless, it seemed. It made me want to capture her and show her how good I could make her feel if she'd just sit still for me. But it also made me want to follow her just for the moment she got tired and fell into my arms. Christ, I had it bad for this woman.

The sun was a fiery ball in the sky, streaking orange over the tops of the snow banks. I hadn't even looked at the time when we left, only realizing it must be dinnertime because my stomach had growled as soon as she mentioned food. We were existing in some weird dimension where I had nowhere to be and nothing but Brit.

Another part of that weird timeless existence was that I

could pretend she wasn't about to invest everything she had into a place that was hours away from me. I pushed down the unease in my belly. It didn't matter where she was. I was going to make it work.

"Have you talked to Meri?" I asked. It had to be time for the auction to start.

"Yup," she said. "Spoke to her right before you got out of the shower." She pulled her lip between her teeth.

"Everything's good?"

"She knows what to do. I like it here," she said, changing the subject. Maybe she didn't want to think about the end of this trip either. I took a small amount of heart in that.

I looked down at her. "Yeah?"

She gestured to the eclectic mix of storefronts, strung together by cobblestones. "It looks like the sort of place where people love to come to work."

I nodded. "There's a neighborhood just like this near my office—old charm, newer businesses. There's more foot traffic to sustain those businesses but the vibe is the same."

"Yeah?" Her eyes lit up. I loved when they did that so I kept talking.

"It's sort of up and coming. A lot of opportunity. When I approached my dad about getting into commercial business, I suggested we buy some of the more run-down storefronts, turn them into something, but I couldn't convince him. It's been our biggest disagreement."

Her voice turned soft and she twisted her fingers in mine. "It sounds nice," she said. "I'd like to see it. I bet I'd like Philly."

I smiled despite the wheel of regret turning in my head. God, I wished I'd met her before she'd found a place she loved. I could have bought her one. Or built her one somewhere closer.

Maybe I'd move to Boston. Would she even want me to?

Yeah, right, Nick. You can't even take a vacation to fulfill Alex's last wishes without giving yourself an ulcer over Mom and Dad.

That was the old Nick, I told myself, but still I squeezed her hand harder like someone was going to come and snatch her away. It was probably crazy to even think about stuff like that, but I knew the time we had like this was running short and it made my chest feel tight.

I pulled her closer. "Hey. I like this, you and me. I know it's only been one night of, you know, but I've liked it since we met on that dock. I like being with you."

"I like it too." A shy smile crept onto her face. The kind that undid me.

"Let's stay here another night."

Her lips twisted as if to say "Sure, Nick." Her skepticism made me double down. "Let's just stay. It will take a few days before you need to be there for the auction paperwork and I—" *don't give a shit anymore* "—I can take another day. We'll skip the bus, spend tomorrow doing whatever you want. Then we'll rent our own car. Finish this trip by ourselves."

"Really?"

"Absolutely."

One of her huge smiles bloomed across her face and she hugged me so hard my breath rushed out in a grunt. "I like that idea."

"Me too." I squeezed her back, lifting her off the ground. "And I'm going to like sharing a real bed with you tonight. Are you?"

"Depends," she said, tipping her chin at me.

I leaned down until our noses touched. "Oh really? On what?"

"If you're going to snore all night again."

I barked out a laugh, setting her back on her toes. "You try sleeping with a hundred-pound weight on your chest, missy." It was the best night's sleep of my life.

"I offered to go to my bunk."

"That wasn't an option."

"Oh yeah?"

"What, and miss you moaning my name in your sleep?"

Her eyes bugged out and I laughed, kissing the top of her head. God, she was cute.

"You're going to be cocky now, huh? I see how it is."

When she smiled at me like that, it was hard to be humble. And hard to keep my hands to myself. I steered her up against a brick building, cupping her face, and kissed her slowly, the way I'd been too impatient to up until now. She melted like an icicle in my arms, blowing a soft, strawberry-flavored sigh into my mouth. My tongue slipped between her lips, sliding in the heat of her mouth and I felt myself thicken in my jeans. She made me feel heady and impulsive, and the experience was so new that I couldn't help but gorge myself on it.

"Going in?" A man's voice snapped up my attention and I pulled away from Brit, realizing we were standing in front of a tavern. I glanced at the sign on the door. It said *Madge's* and featured a mermaid holding a pint of beer while a sailor eyed her assets.

"Brit?" A woman with a beanie on her head stepped ahead and waved.

"Annie! Hi." Brit looked up at me. "Annie and I met on the train."

"I didn't know you were traveling with someone," Annie said. She gestured to the man who had just interrupted us. "This is my husband Jonathan."

We introduced ourselves and Annie looked between the

two of us. Brit's lipstick was smudged in the corner of her mouth and I quickly wiped my lips, feeling like the cat who ate the canary.

"Are you two on your honeymoon or something?" Annie asked, a smirk on her lips.

Brit threw her arms around my neck. "It's our anniversary, actually."

I laughed, shaking my head. Nothing she said surprised me anymore. Besides, we'd never see these people again. If she wanted to play pretend, I wasn't going to argue. Though I did wonder how she got so good at acting all these different parts.

"The motel told us this was the only place in town to get food," Annie said. "We figured we'd see a few familiar faces. Want to join us?"

Brit looked up at me, hopeful.

"Sure," I said, holding the door. "Lead the way."

CHAPTER THIRTY-ONE

Mirrors

Brit

Jonathan and Annie were here to party and it was exactly the distraction that I needed. When they'd invited us to hang out with them, I could tell Nick would have preferred more alone time. Trust me, I would have too, but it was easier to pretend that my world was intact in a group of strangers. Even after a few days, Nick knew me too well.

After I had a burger and most of the ice-cream sundae I made Nick share, the four of us claimed a spot in the corner by the jukebox. He pressed up against me, his chest to my back, his chin resting on my head. I imagined him like a blanket wrapped around me—cozy, safe—and I let myself accept some of that safety this time. My heart could use all of the protection it could get.

He fed a five-dollar bill into the machine and pretended to argue with me about the songs we were awarded while discreetly running his fingers under the hem of my T-shirt. He was shameless with the touching, and the fact that he hadn't toned it down for our new company had me more buzzed than the tequila Annie kept trying to give me.

"Rules of the road still apply, Nicky." I tipped my chin to look at him. "You said I was in charge of the music."

"That rule expired when you got the car towed."

I pushed an elbow into his ribs and he pretended it hurt. "For that, I get two Taylor Swift songs."

He groaned. "I knew you were too pretty to be kind."

That comment dripped over me like honey. I made my selections, then leaned into his chest while he chose the one song I allowed him. It was "Thunder Road" by Bruce Springsteen. Classic and crowd-pleasing, but the kind of lyrics you were too busy belting at the top of your lungs to realize how devastating they are. That was who Nick was. Perfectly hidden devastation.

I sighed inwardly at my secret. Maybe that was who we both were now.

"You two are adorable," Annie said, tipping her drink at us, her words starting to slur. "Aren't they adorable, Jonathan?"

Jonathan smiled at his wife. Annie's pale cheeks were bright red, her shoulder-length brown hair pulled hastily back with a clip she'd found in her purse. "Absolutely."

"You must be thrilled to have your vacation extended," Annie said. "Even if it's in the middle of nowhere."

I winced, looking at Nick and remembering his face in the airport when he'd said, "This isn't a pleasure trip for me." But he was looking at me like he hadn't heard a word Annie said.

"You want another drink?" he asked in my ear.

"Please." I wanted more tequila. More of Nick's touching. More distracting.

But I really had to pee. "I'm going to the ladies' room."

"I'll come with you." Annie stood, her foot getting tangled in the chair before Jonathan steadied her.

Nick curled his fingers into my waistband, covering my mouth with his. He tasted like whiskey and the sex we'd been having all day, and for a moment I actually felt like I'd won a round despite coming out of this day in the negative. "I'll be at the bar," he said.

I gave him a thumbs up and followed Annie to the bathroom, my heart on a see-saw.

Annie and I each used the bathroom and I let her wash her hands first in the one sink that worked. She swayed, humming along to the music from outside.

"You think this place is always this busy?" I asked.

"I doubt it. I bet that little train wreck of ours is paying the bills tonight."

I snorted. "I don't think it should be referred to as my train wreck. I can only handle one at a time."

She looked me up and down, taking in my tights under jean cutoffs, the gift-store T-shirt that said "Fueled by Coffee and Glitter."

"What's wrong, Brit? You've had a gorgeous man hanging off of you all evening but you look like your dog got run over."

I guess I wasn't doing as well as I thought. I blew out a heavy sigh. Keeping this from both Nick and Meri had me itching for a friendly face to spill my guts to.

"Almost everything," I said. *Everything except that gorgeous man.* "I've made a mess of something, as usual."

She leaned against the wall while I washed. "Of what?"

"I'm supposed to be at an auction right now, buying a house. But the tree, and some other things happened, and now I've lost everything I've had my heart set on."

Her face fell. "I'm sorry."

"Thanks. It's just . . . sort of expected of me, these types of disasters. I thought this time was different. But my life continues to be a comedy of errors."

Annie crossed her arms and gave me a once-over. "Don't apologize for your circus, Brit. Besides, looks to me like that boyfriend of yours is the ringmaster."

"Oh. He's not really my boyfriend," I confessed, hoping she would forgive my fib. "We just met a few days ago."

She snorted, then fell into a fit of giggles.

"What's funny?"

"Cutie-pie, do me a favor and don't tell him he's not your boyfriend until you leave here. We're all having a good time and I couldn't bear to watch you ruin that man."

I watched the soap rinse from my fingers, trying to mask my goofy smile. "I think you're exaggerating, Annie."

She pulled a paper towel and handed it to me. "I'm serious. Look, all I'm saying is last night you were asking about fate, but I don't think it's all or nothing. One path or the other. It seems like maybe you found something to smile about in spite of it all. Enjoy that. Life is about finding the chewy center inside all the hard."

I would have chalked that up to drunken bathroom wisdom, but Annie had already given me some solid advice on the train. I couldn't ignore it.

"It's going to be okay," she said, squeezing my hand. "And as far as that man goes, I haven't seen lovestruck like that in a long time. If you're going to break his heart, don't do it tonight." She held out her pinky and her smile softened with sincerity.

I laughed, letting myself smile at the ideas she was putting in my head. I hooked her finger with mine. "I promise."

"Good. I'm going to find Jonathan and try to match your

cute. Maybe get myself some tonight." She waved to me over her shoulder as she turned to leave.

I faced the mirror and fluffed my hair. My makeup was just a suggestion of what had once been and I wiped beneath my eyelid with the tip of my pinky, catching a smudge. I looked like a feral cat but my eyes were bright with Annie's comment. Maybe there were some parts of this smile I didn't have to fake.

When I came out, I spotted Nick talking to two guys at the bar, both dressed in Sean's after-work uniform—dress shirts with loosened collars, rolled-up sleeves, flat-front chinos.

He saw me and his face turned up in a smile that made my chest tight and fluttery. I made my way through the crowd and tucked myself into his side.

Nick introduced me.

"Hey, Brit. I'm Brad," the first guy said. He pointed to his friend who was chatting with two women. One was blonde and sharp-eyed, the other had jet-black hair and killer lipstick. "This is Todd and Whitney and Stacey."

Brad swayed a little as he wrapped an arm around the blonde. I waited to see if Todd would claim Whitney, but he didn't and she flicked her dark eyes up and down Nick's chest before glancing at his hand on my rib cage with blatant confusion.

Yeah, I know, Whitney. I can't believe it either. That was what my snarky brain said, but my brief good mood shriveled. Where was Annie? I liked it better when Nick and I were "adorable" instead of confusing.

I looked around for her, but she'd started a game of pool with Jonathan.

Whitney fixed her face and smiled as she sipped elegantly from a stemmed glass of red wine. I knew these women. I'd had to make conversation with plenty of them from my dad's firm at various events. They were who my parents always dreamed I would be, and for a long time that hurt.

When I was younger, I'd try to mimic them in social settings, these elegant, put-together women. But it didn't work. They always saw through me.

Looking at Whitney's silk blouse and sky-high heels, then down at my maroon tights and furry boots, I felt that same heat of embarrassment creeping in.

The bartender handed me and Nick our drinks and Brad clinked our glasses in turn. "Are you two from that train that pulled into town?" he asked.

Nick chuckled. "We're already local news, huh?"

"Is that where you two met?" Whitney asked, fishing.

Nick looked down at me, uttering a single "No" and I felt a pinprick of irritation at his lack of elaboration. Of all the times to go back to his one-word replies.

Tell her how we met on a dock in Costa Rica, Nick. Tell her how you held my hand in the park and kissed me on the train. Tell her how we woke up naked and tangled up in each other's arms this morning and again before we came here.

Nick twirled my ponytail around his fingers, which would normally make me swoon properly, but now it just made me wonder if Whitney thought my hair looked like a My Little Pony.

The look on her face said yes.

"What do you do, Nick?" Todd asked, just like Sean would have. It was such a douchey thing to ask, I'd always thought. Why did people always lead with that? Why didn't they just exchange cards and be done with it if they really don't care about who the person is?

Nick ran his father's business, but that wasn't the most interesting thing about him. But Nick didn't seem to mind the shallow question. "I'm a real estate developer."

"No shit," Todd said. "I'm a broker. Commercial."

Nick seemed interested in that, probably because of what he'd just told me about his dad and the plans he had. The two of them tossed the conversation back and forth—interest rates, zoning laws, a whole bunch of stuff I didn't understand—and I felt my ability to participate in the conversation evaporate. It was all so *professional* and here I was, a busted dream in a weird outfit. The odd man out. Again.

I didn't like this new feeling. Five minutes ago I'd been thinking about all of the places Nick was going to touch me tonight, and now I felt like the girl in those teen movies who gets asked to prom by the quarterback as a joke.

I couldn't help but think of my parents, and the way they molded me and changed everything they could about me before trotting me out at one of their parties or fundraisers. I'd always been a misfit toy without an island. You'd think understanding the root of an insecurity would help you get over it, but not me.

Whitney turned to me, tipping her head to look down her long, elegant nose. "What do you do, Brit?"

She was being kind, maybe. Trying to involve me. Or she was expecting the exact answer I would give and amusing herself. Either way, my face burned. Was I really going to stand here and tell this woman in two-hundred-dollar heels that I worked at the mall like a teenager on summer break? Or try to impress her with the follower count on my blog?

I would have a few hours ago. I would have told her my business plan, shown her a picture of my studio-to-be. I would have stood tall with Nick's hand on my waist and told her all about it.

Now, on the heels of yet another Brit Mess, all I could think of was that little smirk Sean would get when someone asked me what I was doing these days. As if it were a private joke that he'd set up. God, I hated this.

I took too long to answer, and Nick tipped his head to question me with a look. He raised one eyebrow just for me, as if to say, "Where'd you go?"

I ignored him and looked Whitney straight in the eye. "Cruise ship captain," I said, sipping my drink.

Whitney screwed up her face like she didn't believe that for a second and Todd ignored it altogether. I felt Nick's hand on my side go still. He kissed the top of my head and played along with my lie, but the air thickened.

A familiar song started on the jukebox, and it was like the sea parting, giving me a way out of this conversation. "This is the one I picked," I said, tugging on Nick's shirt.

He laughed. "I think most of them are yours, sweetheart."

"You owe me a dance," I said, hopeful. *Please don't turn me down in front of these people, Nick.*

He smiled, slow and sweet. "I do?"

"Yes. From the bar in Louisiana. I seem to remember a guy who looked an awful lot like you refusing me."

His pretty eyes sparked with affection. "That guy sounds like an idiot."

I tipped my chin at him and he leaned down until our noses touched. I felt the tension ooze out of my muscles. Just like that, we were in our own little universe again, breathing the same air, electricity sparking between us.

Not bothering to say goodbye to our new friends, I tugged Nick to the wooden floor where no one else was dancing. Annie made a *whoop* noise from the back of the room, then whistled at us. Nick wrapped me in his arms so tight, it was hard to turn.

See this, Whitney? I thought, but being bitchy didn't make me feel any better.

"Why did you do that back there?" Nick asked just loud enough to hear over the music.

"Do what?"

"Lie about your job." He tucked a piece of my hair behind my ear. "You're always changing depending on who's in the room. It's like you can't decide if you want to stand out or blend in."

I tried not to shrink at his critique. When did he become the nosy one?

"Brit," he said when I didn't answer. "Why not just be you?"

"Not everyone likes *me*." It came out bitter and insecure. God, I sounded so far from the woman I'd set out to be when I'd left that port in New York. The woman I'd been a few hours ago in bed with Nick.

I felt his fingers brush my chin and I opened my eyes even though I knew they were wet. "Not everyone has to like you. *I* like you."

You like the me you thought I was. Now I'm back to being nothing. A failure. The thought I'd been trying to fend off came bursting into my brain. I liked being liked by Nick, I more than liked it, but all it took was one interaction to reframe our entire time together.

Just because Stuck-on-Vacation Nick liked me, didn't mean that Dress-Shirt-and-Tie Nick would. His friends, his family—his *people*. What if they were like Sean's people? What if he realized, like Whitney had, that I'm a mess? Nick had enough mess in his life. He didn't need more screwed-up people searching for safety in him.

"I'm a lot sometimes," I said, repeating back a phrase I'd first heard from Sean. After that, I realized the same sentiment lingered in the exasperated looks my parents had been giving me my whole life.

"What does that mean?" Nick asked, his voice low.

"You know, like, my personality is a lot. I'm weird or whatever. People get tired of me."

Nick looked like I'd just stabbed him in the heart. "Why do you think that, Brit?"

"I don't want to talk about this anymore," I said.

"Why not?"

"Because we're having fun. Can we just drop it?" I could feel the tears rushing my eyes. Again. God, I wish I could stop doing that. It would be a lot easier to blow off conversations like this, play them off as no big deal, but I was cursed with these weak tear ducts and this heart that was so soft, it bruised like a peach.

I bit down on my lip and begged him with my eyes to let it go.

"Hey." Nick ran his thumbs over my cheekbones, wiping at the tears that hadn't fallen yet. "I'm sorry, okay? We can just dance."

But I didn't want to anymore. I wanted to get the heck out of this weird place that was trying to shine a flashlight through my Nick bubble. I wanted to be alone with him, to let him remind me that right now, he still enjoyed my company.

I pushed up on my toes to place a kiss at the hollow of his throat. Then I let my hands travel down to the back of his jeans, hooking my thumbs inside. He leaned down, his lips grazing mine until we were kissing with a slightly inappropriate amount of tongue.

"You wanna go back?" he asked in a strangled voice that filled my chest with an explosion of butterflies.

Yes, please. I wanted to go back to the hotel, I wanted to go back to just us.

CHAPTER THIRTY-TWO

Somebody I Used to Know

Nick

By the time Brit and I got back to our room, we were all over each other. It started on the walk back—her giving me bedroom eyes, and me completely unable to control the way my hands traveled over her body, despite being on a public sidewalk.

I'd barely closed the door when she unbuckled my belt. "Off," she said.

Jesus. That little command. I stepped out of my jeans, then tore my shirt over my head. Brit did the same, pulling down her shorts, then slowly rolling off the tights. She stood in front of me in her bra and panties, watching me take her in. Her breath was short, making her chest heave while we stared at each other. "You're worked up," I whispered.

"I just want you." She wrapped her fingers around me over my boxers and my hips bucked against her grip. I groaned a long "*Fuuuuck,*" fighting to keep myself from jumping her. I sure as hell wasn't complaining about her enthusiasm, but she seemed desperate all of a sudden. Something nagged at me from behind it that made me uneasy. Something left over from our conversation at the bar.

"I want you too," I said, using every ounce of self-control I had to pull her hand away. I backed her up against the door and pressed a soft kiss to her neck. "Easy. Let's slow down."

Her body went loose, her shoulders sagging. Something was off. She was so vulnerable all of a sudden. "Hey." I grinned, whispering against her mouth. "I just want to take my time with you. Do it right."

"Do what right, Nick?"

If I started naming all of the things I wanted to do to her, we'd be here all night. But screw it; all night was exactly what we had. "I thought we could start where we left off," I said, moving a hand to her breast. "You on the tip of my tongue."

I felt her stiffen in my arms and I pulled back. "What's wrong?"

"Nothing's wrong." She touched me again, working me with her palm until I'd swelled to fill her fist. "Do you like this?" she asked, her voice small.

This wasn't flirting––she was actually worried. I know I'd only been inside of her a handful of times and all of them had happened in the span of twenty-four hours, but I was fairly certain something had changed from this morning when she'd murdered me with a sexy smile while she took me in her mouth. "Brit, sweetheart, why are you so nervous right now?"

"I'm not." She cast her eyes to the corner of the room. "It's just that, I don't know what you like yet. We don't really *know* each other."

I leaned back, giving her an incredulous look that I hoped would put her at ease. "I know *you*."

Her lips twisted and I brought my hands to a more innocent place on her hips. "I know you're happy and sweet." I kissed her forehead, then her cheek. "And it's half because you eat a lot of candy and listen to pop music." She rolled her eyes, but there was a hint of laughter in it. I kissed her nose. "But the other half is just you. Beautiful Brit." I dragged a finger between her breasts. "Do you want to do this with me?"

"I don't really know what we're doing," she whispered.

That took me by surprise. But I guess it shouldn't have. This—me and her together—it hadn't even been a conscious thought. It was just like someone had snapped their fingers and we just *were*. But I hadn't exactly stopped touching her long enough to tell her that.

She looked up at me, cheeks flushed, eyes huge, and I was reminded just how young she was. How, as far as I could tell, the only other time she'd been involved with someone had been painful and full of little cuts to her confidence.

I kissed her again, slow and sweet, telling her with my mouth how I felt about her. How it hadn't ever been like this for me. "I hope we're doing everything, Brit. I want this. You and me."

I couldn't remember ever wanting anything like I wanted her.

She laid her head on my chest, her arms wrapping my waist. "I want that too."

I ran my thumb over the bow of her lip, something heavy pressing against my ribs. She was so warm and soft and *pretty*. And I was so hard it hurt.

She stood on her toes and pressed a kiss to my jaw. "Don't stop."

I studied her face for any signs I should stop, but her lips were parted, pupils huge. I felt that base need flare. I needed to be inside her again, show her how she was already mine.

I turned her around against the door, tracing her shoulders

with my palms. With her standing like that, feet apart, chest and cheek pressed against the door, I took a long, lingering look at her body. I ran my fingers down her spine, then cupped her ass, squeezing. She pulled in a sharp breath as I nudged her feet farther apart and pressed myself between her cheeks. She had on a light blue thong that I definitely hadn't seen her buy. If I had, I would have been thinking about it every second of this trip.

"I like this," I said, pulling it to the side, then letting it go with a little snap.

Her head fell forward on a pant. "I bought it for you. On the off chance you'd see it."

That confession made my blood pump harder. "Do you think it was an off chance?" I asked. "I'm starting to think it was always going to end up like this." I wrapped an arm around her belly, pulling her ass against me. "Feel that? You've been doing this to me for days."

She reached back and took my hand, bringing it to the wetness between her legs. "Me too."

Fuck, I had to have her right there.

I spun her around and wrapped a hand around her thigh, trying to hike it up around my waist. She pushed all the way on her tiptoes, but she was too short. She whined and we shared an exasperated laugh, her giggling into my neck. "Maybe we should go to the bed."

"No way." I hefted her into my arms, pinning her against the door with my chest and she wrapped her legs around me, eyes wide. "This okay?"

She nodded, and I slid one hand behind her head, the other between us, hooking her panties to the side.

One hard thrust and I was panting against her neck. "God, Brit. You feel so good. I want to do this forever."

She moved against me, whispering my name. I got a hold of myself, thrusting again, and she cried out so loud it bounced around the dark room.

She slapped a hand over her mouth, and I laughed, pulling her fingers away and pressing them to my lips. I was glad we weren't in that train car anymore because I wanted her to keep doing that all night long. "Make all the noise you want, baby."

There was no one around to hear us. It was just Brit and me.

We finished the last of the Rummy Bears and half-watched a movie before going again in a much slower, quieter session. After that, Brit passed out, her face plastered to my chest, and that was where she stayed.

I slept like a rock after her back-walk in the park, but tonight I was wired. I surfed the shitty cable package until I found a rebroadcast of a Nats game from a year ago, lowering the volume so I wouldn't wake her. I played with a lock of her hair while I let my mind drift to the last twenty-four hours— they'd maybe been the best of my life. Screw the cruise and all of the beautiful places Alex's list had taken me to. This, being holed up with Brit, laughing and eating candy, her naked body draped over me while she slept off her orgasm, this was paradise.

And she was the one snoring, for the record. It was so adorable, I wasn't even going to tease her for it.

Around the second inning, my eyes started to go blurry with exhaustion. I reached over to turn off the lamp, and a blinking light from my phone caught my eye. A voicemail. This time I couldn't even blame missing it on no service. I'd willfully ignored the thing all day.

Even though it was the last thing I wanted to do, I lifted Brit's cheek and slid out from under her. I found my boxers on the floor and stepped into them as I walked to the bathroom. I knew who would call me this late. I knew exactly what it was, and I didn't want Brit to wake up and hear this conversation.

The voicemail was time-stamped one in the morning. I pressed play and my mother's familiar slurred greeting played back. I could tell she'd been crying.

I'd expected this, a relapse after Alex died. You usually had to quit something in order to call it a relapse, but there'd been a few years after Alex and Willow got married that she'd seemed like she'd turned a corner. Now she'd been like this since the funeral, always differing degrees of self-medication.

I closed the bathroom door and dialed her number. I'd only missed it by twenty minutes. Maybe I could talk to her now and she'd go back to bed.

But my dad's rough and worn voice answered instead. "Hey, Nicky."

"Dad." My brain shifted roles on a dime. "Why are you up so late?"

He laughed, trying to play it off, but all of his laughs were sad now. "I should ask you the same."

I had a beautiful naked woman in my bed. But I wasn't going to tell him that. My father didn't know much about my personal life, what little there was of it, but I think we both liked it that way. The company was what we had in common. "I woke up and saw Mom's call."

His heavy exhale crackled over the line. "Your mother's having a rough night."

"Is she in bed?"

"Yes."

"Good. You know you shouldn't let her have it in the house—"

"Nick, we need to talk about work."

My pulse tripped at the way he switched gears without warning. I'd hoped maybe I could enjoy a full twenty-four hours of being done with Alex's list but I could already feel that tightness in my chest returning, reminding me that the commitments never ended. "I'm sorry I haven't been in touch," I said. "I'll be home soon—"

"I have to tell you something." I heard him release a shaky breath. It was the most emotion I'd ever gotten from him. Even at Alex's funeral, with my mother breaking down between us, he sat stoic. This made me feel off-balance and unprepared and I wanted to make up an excuse to hang up, crawl back into bed with Brit and forget about this for a little while longer, but that wasn't happening. "The job in Clayborne."

His voice trailed off and my hair stood up. "What about it?"

"I screwed up, Nick. The bank didn't approve the loan because I didn't have the right permits."

Dread settled onto my shoulders. That was my responsibility, checking the packages before they went to the bank. He was covering for me. "All right," I said, my mind racing. "So just get the right one and schedule another meeting, Dad. I can take it when I get home."

"Our subs were supposed to be paid upfront. They're bailing. Without them, we won't meet our schedule for the development and the city wants to re-bid it."

Christ. Anger flickered behind the guilt. I knew I wasn't there but this wasn't his first rodeo. This was low-level admin shit for *his* project. "How could you pull the wrong permits?"

"I was rushing."

I squeezed the back of my neck. A year's worth of work and it was all going to fall through because he'd forgotten a basic step. I'd been walking him through the package remotely for days. And where the hell was everyone else? For all of the assurances that things wouldn't fall apart while I was gone on this trip, it sure seemed like they had. How could he—

Oh. I sank down onto the sink. "You had something come up?" I asked. That was how he liked to refer to it when my mom got balls-out drunk and one of us needed to drop what we were doing and deal with it. Leaving Little League games early when I was a kid, work meetings when we were older, our aunt Janey coming over when Dad was working late, feeding Alex and me while Mom went upstairs to lie down. It was a secret code known only to the Callaways.

"Wednesday," he said. "Emily called me." Emily had been my dad's assistant since before we were born. She knew the drill. "Your mom came down to the office. I brought her home and I guess my mind just wasn't right."

Wednesday. Two days ago. I'd been at a bar doing shots with Brit.

"Why didn't you call me?"

"What could you have done, Nicky?"

Fuck, I don't know. Something? I could have talked to her on the phone, maybe. Called Tom or Drew. Remembered for him. I'd been doing it my whole life. I'd been doing everything for everyone my whole damn life.

I leaned against the mirror and rubbed my chest as a memory from when I was a kid reached up from beyond and clawed at me. Alex was home recovering from a stint in the hospital, and Willow was over. The two of them started dating when they were thirteen, so she was already family.

I had plans to go to the movies with friends and I was primping in the mirror. Alex was pale and skinny from the last surgery, and Willow was in a pair of *Little Mermaid* pajamas, but the two of them still heckled me while they held hands on the couch. I popped a baseball cap on my head and gave Alex the finger, then we heard glass breaking from the kitchen and my father's muffled voice.

I rounded the corner in time to see my mother on her hands and knees, cleaning up a broken wine glass. I'd gotten used to this scene, but I was getting old enough to have an attitude about it. It's funny how much anger can build in that time between blindly wanting to please your parents, and finally understanding them as fallible human beings who didn't have a clue what they were doing.

I tried to bolt out the door, make it to my car before my dad saw me and peel out of the driveway like a getaway driver, but he grabbed my elbow and yanked me into the room.

"Take your mother outside, Nicky. I don't want Alex to see her like this."

I'd been working construction all summer with my uncles. I had fifty dollars and the keys to my first car in my pocket. All of my friends were going to be there.

And why the hell didn't it matter if *I* saw her like that?

"I'm supposed to be at Ben's house in ten minutes," I'd said, my voice as firm as adolescence allowed.

It was no match for a man trying to keep his family together, but I didn't know that until later. He looked at me like I was trying to serve him a spoiled piece of meat. "Tell them something came up!"

And that was how we got in this situation, me as my mom's therapist, my dad's cleanup crew no matter what I had to give up to do it. Now, I was the only one who had anything left to give.

I nudged the door open with my elbow and looked at Brit lying asleep on the bed, a hint of a smile on her face from whatever she was dreaming. My heart squeezed around a thousand knives.

I was going to have to break out of this little fantasy world and go home and fix things, but I didn't want to. I'd given enough, goddamn it. That was what Alex was trying to teach me, but because he wasn't here anymore, I had to come up with the how of it by myself and I was at a loss.

"I'll handle it, Dad." I didn't have a clue how, but I would take it off of his plate at the very least. Let him think I had it under control. "Send me everyone's contacts tonight and . . ." The words caught in my throat, holding on for dear life, but I forced them out. "I'll be home tomorrow."

I heard him cough to cover up a sniffle and I nearly lost it. I had to press the heel of my hand to my eyes.

"You're a good man, Nick. I've always been so proud of you."

"Thanks, Dad."

If only being a good man ever got me what I wanted instead of what I deserved.

CHAPTER THIRTY-THREE

Heart on a Wire

Brit

I woke to a slice of bright winter sun across my face, feeling groggy and disoriented. I'd slept in so many beds over the last week, that it took me a moment to remember where this one was. The scent of Nick on my skin reminded me, and I smiled, rolling over to reach for him, but instead, I found a cold, empty spot on the mattress where he was supposed to be. I frowned, stretching to see the clock. It was barely seven.

The last thing I remembered from last night was being so thoroughly destroyed by my last orgasm that I'd lost the ability to form complete sentences. I'd mumbled something about seeing Nick in the morning, then passed out like a freshman at a keg party. But here I was *not* seeing him in the morning and a prickle on the back of my neck told me that something was wrong.

I sat up and found him at the desk by the window, hunched over his phone. He was in just his boxers and the snow-covered scenery behind him made me want to wrap him in a blanket. Those hands that had been everywhere on my body last night were typing furiously, and stress was etched all over his beautiful face.

"What's the matter?"

His eyes snapped to mine like I'd startled him, like he'd forgotten I was there, but then the corners crinkled affectionately. "Morning."

I climbed out of bed and pulled on his discarded T-shirt. "Morning. Have you slept?"

"Of course," he said. "I'm just catching up. It's not important."

That felt like a lie, but he pulled me onto his lap and kissed the side of my neck so I let myself believe it. "I didn't realize you were behind on work."

"I've been a little distracted," he said, patting my butt. His expression turned playful but there was a worry line on his forehead. "I had some stuff come in last night that I can't ignore."

"I didn't mean to keep you from your work." I'd learned from my father, and then from Sean, what a cardinal sin it was to interfere with business.

"You didn't," he said. "I mean, it was my choice."

I studied his face. I supposed I understood ignoring the real world. Wasn't that exactly what I was doing? Yesterday, I dropped a bomb on Meri, then left her on "read" and shut my phone off. I hadn't seen Nick pick his up once since we got off the train. He didn't even bring it with him to the bar last night.

We'd been gone for days. He was bound to have to work.

I stood and walked to the coffee maker on stiff legs, feeling the memory of last night in my muscles, the most delicious soreness. I didn't think I'd ever had that much sex in one night.

Nick noticed, giving one of his cocky smiles. "You're walking funny, Brit."

"You're incorrigible." I tossed him a flirty grin. "But you've earned it. Should I go downstairs and book another night?"

His face fell, his lips parting in surprise, then he ran his hand over his eyes. "Shit."

"What?"

"I'm sorry." He winced and my heart crawled up into my throat. "I actually need to get home."

"Oh."

"Something came up that I have to deal with. With work. My dad—"

I glanced at his phone clutched in his fingers. "Just now?"

"Last night."

My first inclination was to assume it was an excuse, but this was Nick. Sturdy, honest Nick. I didn't truly believe he'd lie to me.

Still. He'd said . . .

He reached an arm out and I went to him, letting him pull me between his legs. He wrapped his arms around my waist and kissed my stomach. "Brit, I really am sorry."

Something twisted inside my chest. A sinking feeling mixed with a little panic as I searched his apologetic eyes for something more. Other women weren't like this, I knew. But other women didn't have experience lodged in their ribs like shrapnel. The memory of broken promises that eventually turned into crying over your dinner alone with your fiancé sleeping somewhere else and not bothering to call.

But that wasn't what this was. I was being paranoid. Codependent. Nick didn't look disinterested. He truly looked sorry.

Just because I'd lost any reason to go home, didn't mean Nick could hide out here too.

"It's fine," I said, forcing my face to smile. "At least I'm saved from your terrible music, right?"

He frowned. "Right."

He let me go and went back to his phone while I pulled on some clothes and packed my things. I thought about Meri's bubble-bath hour, and how since Nick and I started sleeping together we'd barely been out of each other's personal space, but shouldn't there have been a lead up to the bubble-bath hour? Shouldn't it have taken longer to need a break?

I definitely didn't need a break yet, but if *he* did, I could give him that. "Nick?"

He popped his head up from his screen and the light in his eyes made me swoon.

"I think I'll go down to the front desk and check on the status of the buses."

His forehead creased. That wasn't exactly a Brit thing to do and he knew it, but I felt like I needed some distance to clear my head of all of these thoughts.

"I'll go with you," he said. He looked down at his phone again, then back at me, his face conflicted. "Just gimme ten."

"It's okay, Nick." I grabbed my Y'all bag and left before he could say anything else.

My stomach was a rock when the train pulled into Penn Station. We gathered our bags and deboarded, struggling to stay side by side in the crush of people. Nick had been staring at his phone the whole trip, his hand clenched around mine, but his eyes on that damn screen. I wanted to ask him about his work, what had him so worried, but I kept chickening out. Afraid I'd see the excuse.

Oh, for God's sake. *This is why this happens, Brit. You're acting needy after a day of being together.* Or whatever we were. I was doing the same thing I'd done last night, making up a story in my head.

I knew there was another piece to the wall I felt between us and it was my fault. I had to tell him about losing the auction. Last night I'd let every one of my insecurities show and he'd told me it was fine with his hands and his mouth and the way he'd held me while I slept. He'd told me he didn't mind that I'd gotten weird on him.

I could tell him. I was stupid not to. We needed to figure out where to go from here, me and him, and I had to be honest if we were going to be together. "Nick—"

"How long is your drive?"

I swallowed. "Over three hours. You?"

"Half that." He rubbed the back of his head, avoiding my eyes.

We reached the desk for the shuttle to the parking garage and he turned to me. His eyes were full of remorse and I started to sweat. He cupped my cheek. "Brit, I—"

"Don't go home, Nick." My fingers curled into the front of his shirt. "Come to Boston with me. Get in my car and we'll just go."

His brows slashed inward. "You know I can't do that."

"Then let's go somewhere else. Anywhere."

"I told you I have to get home, Brit." His voice was soft, placating. "You have to be home too. You just bought a house."

I shook my head, suddenly feeling manic, like I was trying to hold a gallon of water in the cup of my hands. "I didn't, actually."

"What?"

"The auction. I didn't get the house, Nick. There's no reason for me to go home."

His jaw fell open. "You lost the house? When?"

"My father, he . . . There was a hiccup with the funds. It doesn't matter. The house isn't mine. I have no reason to go back to Boston. I could come to Philly. With you."

He huffed a laugh and I felt something crack inside my chest. "I don't even want to go to Philly." He sighed, running a hand through his hair. "Brit, it's not a good time."

"Okay, well, maybe in a couple of weeks," I said. "I could fly out."

He swallowed, his eyes darting between the ground and somewhere over my shoulder. "I just need a little time to try to get my head above water," he said. "At work."

"How long?"

"I don't know if I can answer that yet. We'll figure this out, though. I'll call you as soon as I get home, and I'll see you as soon as I can."

"You'll see me as soon as you can," I repeated, my voice robotic. "Okay. Yeah, I guess I'll see you around, Nick."

I tried to turn away but he caught my wrist. "Come on. It's not a line, Brit." He pulled me closer, pushing his hands into my hair and my body went warm for him, betraying me. "Some things have come up that I need to take care of. That's all."

His voice was desperate but so was I. I'd already lost my house and the one thing I still had out of this whole experience was Nick. The chewy center in all the hard, like Annie had said.

Except apparently he didn't want me too close.

I couldn't wrap my hopes around one more thing that would turn to dust. I didn't have it in me. I pushed off of his chest. "It's fine . . ."

"Brit—"

"Take the out, Nicky!"

"What?" His hands dropped to his side. "Brit, please. That's not what this is."

"Prove it. Come with me."

"You're being irrational."

Irrational. Silly. Ridiculous. So that was what he thought of me despite everything he'd said. Hurt and confusion wove together in a noose to choke me. "You said you wanted to do this forever."

"I meant it."

"Just not now."

"It's not like that. It's . . ." He squeezed the back of his neck. "Don't do this, Brit. I don't have a choice here."

"I'm sorry you think that, Nick, because everyone has a choice. I don't know who told you that you were the exception to that, but they were wrong."

"Like you had a choice with Sean?"

I froze. "What about it?"

"What was it you called me? A self-made martyr. Hell, you were going to marry a guy just to make your dad happy. If that isn't martyrdom, I don't know what is." We were chest to chest now, his height forcing him to look straight down. "You understand this better than you're pretending."

I glared at him. "I didn't tell you that so you could throw it back in my face, but while we're at it, were you just pretending to understand what your brother was trying to teach you? I mean, for fuck's sake, Nick. It took what? Two days for you to go right back to being Mr. Play It Safe."

He laughed unpleasantly. "God, you're just like him, you know? Do whatever feels good at the time. It doesn't work like that in the real world."

"In the *real* world? I'm standing right here, in the real world, giving you the option to take what you say you want. But you can't do it. At least I fought for what I wanted. I might have lost it all but at least I didn't just give up."

"Jesus, I'm not giving up on anything. I'm just asking for more time, Brit. Why can't you just give me that?"

"Will it even make a difference?" I crossed my arms over my chest, chin trembling but tipped. "What are you going to do, Nicky? Blow up your whole life for a girl you've known a week? We both know you're not that guy."

He blinked at me in stunned silence but he didn't make any move to correct me, to tell me he *was* that guy. To promise me the things he'd promised last night. He just stood there.

How could I have been so stupid? I'd let myself believe that Nick and I had this cosmic connection, some unflappable bond, because what? We'd spent a week together stuck in various confined spaces and then we'd ended up sleeping together?

But that was just it. Six days wasn't a long time in the *real world*, but when you were sharing space and secrets the way we were, it felt like an eternity. We'd been trying to get home for almost a week—a week to get from Houston to New York! The snowstorm, the car getting towed, the train running into a *tree*! How could I not believe the universe was trying to tell us something?

God. That thought was so *me*, it was sickening.

Nick needed comfort and distraction. He'd been at the top of a roller coaster of emotion when I met him. Now he was safe at the bottom and he didn't need me anymore.

"Don't leave me, Brit," he whispered.

I shook my head. "No, Nick. Don't spin it. You're leaving me. You're the one with no choices."

"Brit . . ." I watched every emotion cross his face—sorrow,

anger, exhaustion. He started to say something then stopped. A tiny ray of hope dawned in my chest, then he ran a hand over his face. When he looked at me again, his expression was flat, like a switch had been flipped. "Maybe you're right."

I turned on my heel and started running.

CHAPTER THIRTY-FOUR

Deluge

Nick

When Alex died, I got a lot of cards in the mail. Family members, friends I went to school with, even business contacts—everyone wanted to tell me how sorry they were through canned messages they'd bought at the grocery store. I skimmed them and tossed them in the recycling, but there was one that stuck with me. It was from my high school English teacher, and the outside had a picture of a full moon hanging low over the ocean. Inside it said: *Grief is a wave, ebbing and flowing, and all you can do to survive it is to learn how to swim.*

If that were true, I was drowning.

The front door to my apartment stuck from the constant frost heaves and I gave it a cathartic shove with my shoulder, dropping my bags on the hardwood floor. The thunk echoed through the stark, clinically tidy rooms. It might as well be another hotel room, it seemed so empty and sterile. A realtor could show this place today and no one would believe anyone was living here. It made sense in a twisted, metaphorical insult kind of way. Could I call anything I'd done before I met Brit living?

I'd gone through the motions of getting the picture for Willow, making my way down to the crowded pier where everyone I encountered looked happier than they had a right to be. I'd turned my phone sideways and snapped a photo of the harbor without bothering to look at the final result. I made it all the way to the end of the pier before guilt pushed me back to the spot I'd just been. I tried again, getting closer to the edge, setting up the shot. I took my time with the frame, centering the ball of sun hovering over a horizon of blue.

After I got a postcard-worthy shot, I cast one more look at the water just as an old, rotted sneaker floated by. In that moment I thought my brother might be the stupidest asshole I'd ever met, but I had to pull my cap down low and haul ass back to my truck to keep from breaking down.

My phone had been buzzing non-stop for the whole trip and I pulled it out of my pocket, scrolling while I went to the kitchen to scrounge up something to eat. I found a package of Saltine crackers, shoved a few in my mouth and flopped down on the couch.

I'd been gone two weeks now. I should have probably ordered some food, put away my clothes from the trip, but my father had sent me a list of sub-contractors I was going to have to beg to and it was a mile long. I had tonight and tomorrow morning to get it done before I had to take my mom to Sunday Mass and to visit Alex's headstone. Plus I needed to comb through the entire bid package to make sure my father hadn't missed anything else. Sunday night would be for catching up on my own projects.

So much for a weekend.

I flipped on the television while I worked. Usually the background noise distracted me, kept me from my own thoughts, but tonight it didn't sound right. The voices were wrong and no one had anything clever to say.

My phone buzzed again and I chucked it onto the carpet, squeezing my temples. I missed Brit. Her chattering beside me as we drove. Her breathing in the bunk above me that first night on the train. The vague hint of tropical flowers that had been in my nostrils since Louisiana. I couldn't stop imagining what Brit's laughter would sound like in this space. How she'd look sprawled out on my bed in those penguin shorts. What her makeup and hundreds of bottles of hair products would look like all over my bathroom counter.

How she said she would move here and I laughed.

I missed her so much it felt like my chest was splitting in two, making a hole for my heart to climb out and go running back to her. But she was five hours away in a completely different world than the one I knew her in.

When she'd said she would come to Philly, I wanted to scoop her up and run to my truck before she changed her mind. But I knew if I took Brit home from this vacation and brought her into the chaos of my real life, she would see firsthand just how much of my time wasn't mine to give. It had always been too much for any relationship I'd tried to maintain. She'd decide she didn't sign up for this, and then I would've uprooted her whole life because I was selfish and wanted her here.

God, I wanted her here, but if she couldn't understand this, how was she ever going to put up with the late nights at work, the calls at two a.m.? Brit wanted something big, something I wanted to give her, but promising that wasn't enough. Just like Alex, she didn't understand there was a time and a place for these blow-up-your-life gestures. And just like Alex, she'd tested me. And I failed.

We both know you're not that guy.

That accusation felt like glass shattering. I'd *been* that guy for the last two days. I liked that guy. Brit was the one who convinced me that I could have more out of life—she and Alex—and yesterday, I was ready to uproot my whole life and do something crazy. But last night reality had yanked my leash back. I wasn't the guy Alex wanted me to be, the guy Brit needed me to be. This was my life. All I could offer her was disappointment.

My stomach tightened like a fist and I rolled over to my side on the couch. It physically hurt to not check in to make sure she got home okay, but I didn't know if she'd answer. I could never predict what she was going to do, and, instead of feeling invigorated, I was back to feeling helpless to keep up.

I fetched my phone from the floor and opened up the last text Brit sent me last night from the bathroom at the bar. **I think Annie's going to puke.**

I brushed my thumb over the screen like I might be able to feel her soft lips. I made Siri read it to me, but it didn't sound like Brit.

I just needed to know she wasn't a figment of my imagination, something I'd conjured up in my dreams. That she was a real, live person who lived on this earth, even if I couldn't have her. I typed out a text with my thumb. I knew it was a juvenile, cowardly thing to do, but if I called her, what would I say? I had no more answers than I had when she'd left me a few hours ago. And if she didn't answer, I'd never know why. Was she telling me to fuck off, or was she just in the shower? So I typed out the only thing I could say: **I miss you.**

CHAPTER THIRTY-FIVE

The Trouble with Wanting

Brit

When I pulled up to the steep, pillar-lined driveway at my parents' house, my face was puffy and red from hours of highway crying. Just the sight of this place made my stomach hollow—the perfectly pruned pine trees, the pretentious address sign on the gate. God, what I wouldn't give to be back in a dirty roadside motel with Nick.

Nick, who I'd left speechless in a train station. I'd replayed the conversation in my head a million times on the ride home, waffling between indignant anger and panic that I'd done the wrong thing. I'd settled on a sinking, aching depression.

I parked my car in front of the three-bay garage where my dad kept his vintage cars that were worth more than the college education I'd wasted, and for the first time, I had a good look at my outfit—cheap yoga pants and my Texas sweatshirt. My face was smeared in black mascara Halloween-style, and my hair was living off of dry shampoo and the scrunchie that had been on my gear shifter for going on a year. I looked like a caricature of the mess everyone thought I was.

Everyone except Nick. He looked at me like I was the Picasso of messes—something beautiful hidden under the chaos. I felt my throat close around another sob.

Steve, the guy who'd been tending my parents' lawn since I was a kid, waved a gloved hand to me from behind a snow blower on one of the brick paths. I stepped out of the car, arms loaded, and nearly slipped and fell on my butt. Somehow the snow and ice here weren't nearly as magical as the woods beside a stopped train, or a middle-of-nowhere town with Nick.

Steve turned off the snow blower and rushed to my aid. He hefted my bag out of the snow and brushed it off, handing it back. "How was the cruise?"

The question seemed to be from another lifetime and it took me a minute to find an answer. It was jarring to look at Steve's face and realize that nothing that had happened to me in the last week had a single witness. No one to corroborate my whole life changing. Since I'd last been here, I'd failed pretty much as hard as you could at a solo vacation, I had my heart broken worse than I'd ever experienced, and I lost my dream house, so really . . .

"The cruise was great!" I said with a cheerfulness I should have won an award for. It wasn't a lie. When I'd been on that ship, I'd only been recovering from a broken engagement to a serial philanderer. What an easy task compared to letting Nick go to come back here.

Maybe my father did know what was best for me. Maybe me being at the helm of the USS *Brit* had me destined for an iceberg.

I thanked Steve and treaded carefully up the stone steps to the house. The heavy oak door swung into the foyer and I kicked off my boots. I should probably have just tossed them in the garbage at this point, ruined as they were, but I didn't have the heart. Everything I had on my person was a souvenir from my time with Nick.

I heard my mother's heels clicking on marble tile and I prepared myself, running a thumb under my eyes one more time. Yup. Still caked in what used to be a perfect cat-eye.

"Bridget, my God." My mother was wearing a tailored pants suit and she looked at me like I was a dead mouse a cat had dropped at her feet.

"Hi, Mom." I set my bags on the floor and instinctively straightened for her appraisal. I'd been gone for two weeks, half of that time I'd been lost and making my way home in precarious fits and starts, but she didn't make a move to hug me. I pretended that didn't sting and tugged at the hem of my sweatshirt.

"What on earth happened to you? Where did you get those clothes?"

I snorted. Only my mother would ignore my red-rimmed eyes and mascara streaks to comment on my off-brand outfit. "Target and a variety of gift shops throughout the southern states, Mother."

Her ageless face twisted in a sort of bored confusion. "Well, thank God you're home safe, darling. Why don't you go run a bath, hmm? You can take care of your things later."

It was actually quite the concession from her, so I took it. I padded in my socks to the winding oak staircase that led to my wing, but not before my father appeared in the archway from his study. "Bridget."

My puffy eyes turned to slits. "Dad."

"After you've gotten yourself together, we should have a chat."

"About what? How you've ruined my life?"

His laugh was a papercut on top of a gaping wound. "You can't honestly think I would let you go through with this."

"Yes, I honestly thought I had a say in my own life."

"I did it for your own good, Bridget. First Sean, now this? I won't let you continue to be careless with your future. And I certainly won't let you use your inheritance to do it." He fiddled with the cuff of his dress shirt, not even having the decency to look ashamed. "It's my one job as your parent to steer you around these pitfalls."

"Funny, I thought your one job as a parent was to love me." His nostrils flared and I turned for the stairs, my heart trailing behind me in a puddle.

CHAPTER THIRTY-SIX

Not All Willows Weep

Nick

Willow told me not to bring anything, but I knew my mother would disown me if I showed up to someone's house empty-handed. Even if that someone was family. I balanced a bottle of wine and a box of Alex's favorite pie and knocked on the cheery peach-colored front door that still had a balsam wreath left over from Christmas, the needles burnt orange on the tips.

Willow appeared on the stairs, barefoot in a flowy, hippy-style dress, her blondish hair in a loose braid over her shoulder. I watched her face break into a smile through the side-light and I breathed a little easier. She opened the door and pulled me into a hug.

"Nick." She pushed my shoulders out, inspecting me like I was a child who'd grown a few inches since we last saw each other. "It's so good to see you."

It was good to see her too. Though I'd come here beating

myself up for the way I'd made her chase me down for updates the last few days, her expression told me she hadn't given it another thought.

"Come in." She took the pie from me and I followed her up the short steps to the main floor. Alex and Willow had bought this split-level the same way I'd bought my duplex and Tom and Drew had bought theirs. He'd used the Callaway and Sons buying power, flipped it, and sold it to himself for cost.

When Alex picked this place out, the walls had been covered in seventies-style pine paneling. The dining room had an orange shag carpet. I'd been impressed when, in the first year, Willow had completely transformed it. Now the walls were a quiet stone color with tasteful abstract art hung around the room in between family photos. The gray suede couch in front of the fireplace had been Alex's since college. Willow had covered it in a hundred fluffy pillows.

I hadn't been in this house since Alex died, shitty brother-in-law that I was, and every beer-fueled heart to heart he and I had ever shared on that couch came rushing at me. I knew if I sat there it would be like sitting next to his ghost, so I put the wine on the kitchen island and pulled out a stool.

Willow searched a drawer, coming up with a corkscrew, and sat down across from me. "How are you?" she asked, turning the cork and popping it. "You look thin."

I couldn't imagine that was true after almost a week on the road living off of takeout and airport food. Rummy Bears and strawberry gum. But then, I couldn't actually remember having eaten a real meal since I got back.

"I'm . . ." I couldn't bring myself to say "Fine". *Devastated, losing my mind about work, wishing for a wall to drive my fist into.* "The same."

"I was afraid of that." She pushed a glass of chardonnay my

way and I put my fingers around the stem like I intended to enjoy it.

This might have been a bad idea. The last thing Willow needed was me bringing my sulking here, especially if the hole in my chest where my heart used to be was going to be so glaringly obvious.

"I have your picture," I said, changing the subject.

Willow's face split into a slow smile. "It feels weird, right? Being done?" She sipped her wine. "I wonder if he considered that, that it would be another goodbye."

I wondered if he considered any of it. Alex wasn't known for his well thought-out plans. But I'd made my peace with that. He and I had it out one last time on that train and then I let it go. Or rather, a tiny woman with rainbow hair had pried it out of my clenched fist. And changed my whole life by doing it.

"Anyway, I'll send it to your email so you can print it in whatever size you need. Thanks, by the way. My mother will love it . . ." My voice wanted to crack so I trailed off.

Willow smiled knowingly. "Your family will always be my family, Nick. *You'll* always be my family."

I nodded, not knowing what to say. How was she so much better at this than me? I should be here taking care of her, but instead I was barely holding it together and she knew it. I wasn't sleeping, I wasn't eating. The truth was I was stumbling without Brit. I'd let myself draw too much strength from her, have a little taste of leaning on someone else, and now she was gone.

This was worse than right after Alex died. I'd been the same tired, cranky shell of myself then too, but at least I'd known there was nothing I could do but bear it. Death was final. You could wish and pray and scream about how unfair it was until you were blue in the face, but when it came down to it, there was a freedom in knowing you had no power to change it. You had to move on because you had no choice.

I kept going over and over my choices with Brit. Had she really been the one to leave me? Or had I taken the out just like she said? She'd struck first at what we had, and it had fucking hurt like nothing else, but I'd hardly put up a fight to keep it. I'd sulked off and nursed my wounds. And I'd felt so damn sorry for myself.

But then I'd reached out and she ignored me.

Willow was still staring at me. "Talk to me, Nick."

For once my jaw felt loose, like maybe I could get some of this out. Alex loved Willow, and as fucked up as it was, she was the strongest one of us all right now. Maybe talking to her would be a little bit like talking to him.

"I met someone," I said. "On the trip." I ran my hands over my face like I could erase the weakness I knew was there. "I met someone and then I lost someone and I just . . . I guess I'm not dealing with it well."

And I've never met anyone like Brit before, and I'm afraid she was some cosmic gift to me from Alex and I lost her.

I knew that wasn't true. I knew Brit was her own person who'd found herself sitting across from me on that dock through her own actions, and everything that happened afterward was because the two of us chose it. I also knew that no one could make Brit do anything, cosmically or otherwise. But Christ, if there was anything in this world that even remotely resembled destiny, I couldn't help but believe she was it.

If Willow was shocked by my story, she tempered it well. She reached across the table and squeezed my wrist. "You know, Alex used to tell me that out of everyone, he was most worried about you." She laughed. "I thought, *Nick?* He's a rock. He's the glue holding everyone else together—but that's the thing, I think. Everyone else—your parents, Alex—they already knew they were broken, so when the pieces started to come apart, they were expecting it. You haven't had a single moment to let yourself fall apart, to grieve. I know it's scary, that part of it. Like you're drowning, looking for something solid to grab on to. And in your case, everyone else is grabbing on to you."

I looked away. What she was saying was the truest description of my life right now, but God, did it make me feel like an asshole. Everyone else was grabbing on to me because they needed me and I'd made a promise to be there. When I was born healthy, that was the deal. We all knew it. It was unspoken like most everything, but we all knew it.

My mom once told me how hard it was for them to decide to have another child after Alex's diagnosis, how scared she'd been, and that I was a miracle. I always felt like she was telling me they had me as some sort of backup. A promise that they wouldn't be left childless. And now they were adrift and they were calling on that promise. How could I admit that every cell in my body wanted to push them all off of me and swim as far away from this as I could?

"This girl," Willow said. "Where is she now?"

"Boston."

"Mmm."

I almost smiled. "What? What's 'mmm'?"

She sipped her wine. "It's not the other end of the world."

"It is when you have this many fucking commitments, Will."

I knew how this went. I'd been here before. And this wasn't Janessa getting pissed when I had to bail on brunch because my mom was having a day. Or Katy, the girl I'd dated freshman year in college, deciding she wanted to be with someone who laughed more and didn't take life so seriously. Brit was the best thing I'd ever found and I couldn't even keep her happy for a week.

Willow held a hand up at my tone. "I get it, Nick. But the thing with commitments is you can only use the information you have around you to make them. When those circumstances change, the people who love you will understand."

"There's a lot of people to ask to understand."

"Who?"

I looked up at her and her eyes flew wide. "Me? You feel like you need to be here for *me*? Well, cross that off your list, buddy. I won't be the reason you're unhappy. Alex would haunt me. So give me another."

"Fine. My mom."

She leaned back in her chair, eyeing me. "That's valid. Your mom is sick in a different way than Alex, but it's still a sickness and I don't think anyone would wonder why you felt like you needed to be there for her. But let's just say that didn't entail a twenty-four-seven vigil. Let's just say you had someone who would be willing to share that load with you."

Was she offering herself? I guess I'd always just assumed when Alex died, Willow would take the first exit off of that hellish highway. Sure, she'd visit and still be a friend, but to take responsibility? "You don't need to take that on."

"Your mother has been part mine for twenty years, Nick. She gave me Alex. I love your family and I'm not going anywhere. So give me another reason."

I blew out a heavy breath. "The company," I said. "You know, while I was gone, I actually thought what if I just don't go back?"

Willow's head tilted. "But you love the family business, Nick. Your mom showed me pictures of you as a kid drawing the company logo on your toy trucks with a Sharpie. You've been wearing Callaway and Sons T-shirts since you could dress yourself."

She gestured to my chest to prove her point and I absently touched the navy blue logo. "It just feels different ever since . . ."

I ran a hand through my hair, hesitating to admit this to another person. Telling Brit had been hard enough. "The day Alex died, we fought about it."

She nodded like she knew this even though there was no way she could. She was working when we got the call from the hospital. He'd gone alone to the mountain after I'd turned him down.

"It's been my dream for as long as I can remember but it's all twisted and wrecked now. For the first time in my life, I don't even know if I want it. Not if I can't have her."

And still here I was, letting her slip through my fingers because of it.

"The company has been your life since you were a kid, Nick. But you can't believe it's all you were ever expected to want."

I shook my head. I didn't believe it mattered one way or another what I wanted. That was half the problem.

"Look, I'm not going to give you some speech about how you should follow your heart, and everyone else be damned. That's a nice platitude, but it's not real life. I get that. I do. But what I will say is there has to be a balance. You've lived your whole life like you owed everyone something, Nick—your parents, Alex. You've had all of this responsibility since you were probably too young to handle it. But you also have a responsibility to yourself. Something tells me this is the moment you're finally realizing that. Because of whoever this woman is."

I couldn't even count the things I was just now realizing because of Brit. That I'd wasted a lot of time feeling sorry for my brother for being sick, when he was never looking for my sympathy. That I'd been stuck in the anger stage of grief so long, I didn't know any other way to live without him. That girls with rainbow hair understood the world better than everyone else.

Brit understood me better than *everyone* else. She'd taken one look at me and figured out all of my pain. She'd looked at me in that airport bar and read me like a book, and I'd been instantly defensive, but then a familiar comfort had seeped into my bones. The comfort of not having to explain myself, of being with someone who saw the things I struggled with the most and let me have them. Only two people had ever been able to see through me like that. And now they were both gone.

"I think I'm in love with her." I laughed nervously and scratched at the back of my neck. "That's crazy, right?"

"Why would it be?" Willow sounded genuinely confused and my heart sang a little in my chest.

"We just met," I said. "Two weeks ago, I didn't even know her."

"I was twelve when I fell in love with Alex. People told me I was crazy too, but what's falling in love besides letting someone burrow through all of the blood and bone and scar tissue until they get to our beating hearts? I was lucky enough to meet my person before I'd built all of that up. Maybe you were lucky enough to meet yours when your heart was hanging on the outside."

"I want Brit to be my person."

"Then make the room. No one is going to love you any less for setting some boundaries, Nick. In fact, maybe we'll all love you even more once we finally get a chance to meet you. The real you." Her expression turned teasing. "The you who fell in love with a woman after only a few days."

I groaned and she patted my arm. "Sorry. Big-sister teasing is worse than big-brother teasing. Deal with it."

I smiled. "I got it, you know."

She gave me a sly smile. "Got what?"

"The point he was trying to make with the list. Or, I should say, Brit got it. She showed me." I rubbed at my chin, laughing. "And then she said something about grief making me dense."

Willow barked out a genuinely delighted laugh. "It sounds like Alex would have liked this girl."

"I think so too."

She held her arms out and I stepped into her hug. "He always knew what you were carrying, Nick," she said. "This was his way of apologizing to you."

I nodded, knowing that without Brit, I would have missed it altogether.

CHAPTER THIRTY-SEVEN

The Prodigal Daughter

Brit

"I won't do it." I crossed my arms and glared at my father from across his desk. I'd slept fitfully, waking every few hours and missing Nick's warmth and scent. His arms around me as I slept. I'd stumbled downstairs when the sun came up, and I'd barely forced down a muffin and fruit before my father called me into his study.

I'd expected a campaign from him to get me to speak to Sean, from both of them actually, though my mother seemed to have sat this one out. But this was too much.

"You're going, Bridget. You knew that because Sean works for me he'd be part of your life no matter what happened between you two. This was what your mother and I wanted you to consider when you couldn't work things out."

Oh, I'd considered it. I'd just been naive enough to believe my own parents wouldn't make me spend the evening with my ex-fiancé when the refunds from the wedding had barely cleared.

"So this is how it is now?" I asked. "I make nice with Sean or I can't have the money I rightfully inherited? I seriously doubt extortion was what was intended when you were made the trustee."

"Watch your accusations, little girl." I flinched at his tone. "The money is still yours. I've simply put a pause on your access to it. It's within my rights as a signer on your account."

"For how long?"

"Until I'm satisfied that you know what you're doing with your life."

"You mean satisfied that I'm doing what *you* want me to. You knew the money would be deposited in that account and you made sure you would control it. You've planned this since I was sixteen."

"Yes, Bridget, I've made stipulations that allow me to protect you from yourself since you were a child, and clearly you still need them." He steepled his fingers, looking down at me. "Now let's discuss what I need from you."

"Your work has nothing to do with me. I don't see why I have to go to some silly gala."

"My work paid for everything you have. It's important that my family attend these things, and that we all look well and happy together. All I've asked of you is to show up to parties, Bridget. It's not a tough life you lead. And you owe Sean an apology. It was humiliating the way you left. This is the least you can do."

Humiliating? For him? My brain raged around inside my skull, but I kept my face neutral. I was so tired and broken that I nearly spit out all the disgusting details. The texts Sean would get late at night, his assistant who I had to make conversation with at last year's Christmas party when I had intimate knowledge of her lingerie collection thanks to those texts he didn't bother to delete. The cliché as fuck lipstick on Sean's collar. The way he'd told me it was a one-time thing, at least six or seven times, then stopped bothering at all. These parties and events weren't the cake walk my father thought they were.

But I hadn't told him or my mother that because *I* was the one who was humiliated. And I couldn't stand to find out if I was right—that it wouldn't change a damn thing.

"Bridget, Sean's family and I sit on the same boards. We handle important business together and you've made it awkward for us all to be in the same room. Now you're living here for free, fresh off of a cruise that I paid for. I won't even mention the money you lost me when you canceled your wedding. You'll do this for me. Be pleasant to Sean, to his family. Make it right and maybe we'll talk about what you'd like to do with your money."

Make it right. What exactly would Sean need from me to make it right? I wondered. Looking at my father's face, I realized it didn't matter to him one bit.

After being dismissed from my father's study, I drove to Meri's. She'd been calling since last night and I owed her an explanation after disappearing on her. I was huddled on the couch in her living room, drinking tea because Meri was an elderly woman dressed as a millennial.

"Oh, Brit." Meri rubbed my back as I hiccupped through another round of tears. "I'm so sorry. We'll start looking for other places."

I'd spoken to my realtor as soon as I got home, hoping for a miracle. Occasionally these things fell through—checks didn't clear, or there were issues with deeds—and a property could end up back on the market. But the house sold to a developer from Watertown, one with a solid reputation and someone who would no doubt have the money to complete whatever plan they had for it. Maybe they'd even tear it down. That felt symbolic in the worst way.

"My father has basically revoked my trust. I can't afford to buy a place on my salary, and all of my revenue from my business goes back into it. That's how it works in the beginning." My paid partnerships floated the cost of running the blog and my socials, with a little cushion to buy equipment and supplies. Which I now had nowhere to house.

I was proud of my success but it was hardly real estate investor money. I needed to keep my job at the mall to afford a place to live, which meant most of my weekends would be unavailable for makeup jobs. No one would ever take me seriously working out of my car, or my parents' house anyway. I needed square footage, a sign on a post. That was the plan.

"I've made a hundred decisions leading up to this, Mer," I said. "All based on the promise of that money coming to me. Now I've got a half-baked dream and no heat to cook with."

Meri chewed her lip. Even she couldn't find a way to spin this into the positive. "Maybe you could rent a space. You'll be able to save a ton of money while staying with your parents."

I groaned at what that meant for me, how I'd been home for one day and they'd already reminded me how my place with them was conditional. The thought of going back to that version of myself after all that had happened felt like a failure of epic proportions.

"Maybe everyone was right, Mer. Maybe I'm not cut out for this."

"That's bullcrap and you know it. I'm not going to let you even think about giving up."

I sighed. "I'm not. I'm just . . . re-evaluating. Everything."

Meri took a slow sip from her teacup, studying me. "This isn't about the house."

Dual waves of heartache and comfort swamped me. She knew me so well. "You're right. It's about how everything I try to grab onto slips through my fingers."

"Brit—"

"There's something I need to tell you," I said. A beat of silence passed with Meri's gaze hardening and my lip between my teeth. Then I blurted it. "I slept with Nick."

Her blue eyes popped open and she choked on her tea. "What!?"

"On the train, and like, a lot of times after that." My chest squeezed with memories—Nick above me, his full grin pressed to my mouth. Nick's arms wrapped around me while we slept. "I'm sorry I didn't tell you. Once it happened, we were kind of all up in each other's personal space until . . . we weren't. I couldn't exactly call you."

"You slept with your hot travel buddy?"

I sniffed a laugh at how trite that description was. It had maybe never been the case between us, but at least the last two days we were so much more than that. We were happy and together, and he said he wanted to do it forever. Yet, here we were.

Meri gave me a once-over—curled into the fetal position, makeup smeared and dangerously close to staining one of her throw pillows—and her eyes narrowed. "Tell me what he did."

I knew what she was thinking and, of all things, protectiveness for Nick was my first reaction. I wanted to scream: *He told me he wanted me, then changed his mind.* But that wasn't the whole truth, was it? I knew I'd forced his hand, but I also knew it was coming and I'd saved both of us the painful path to get there. And besides, he'd agreed, hadn't he?

Maybe you're right.

"He didn't do anything," I said, wondering where the truth was in all of these one-sided conversations I kept having in my head. But that was the thing. I'd given him the chance and he didn't do *anything*.

All I'd wanted Nick to do was choose me, but to convince him, I'd laid out all the reasons I didn't think he would. I'd loaded him with ammunition then acted surprised when he shot it back at me. Now I was in an eternal state of tumbling backward from the impact, unable to get my feet beneath me.

I knew it was crazy after only a week, but I felt like I could handle everything else if I just had Nick with me. Grounding me. Asking me pointed questions about my plans and my experience. Questions that made me defensive, then made me think. He was a straight and sturdy axis that I could spin around, free but tethered. It was the first time being tethered had felt safe instead of suffocating.

"I just don't know if it was ever what I thought it was," I whispered.

Meri leaned forward and pushed my hair off of my face, her voice soft and coaxing. "What did you think it was?"

Love. I wanted to shake myself at the absurdity, but it was my best guess as to what that felt like. Nick was good-hearted, supportive, deep. He was so sweet in a way most people might miss at first glance. And he was funny and charming for the people he decided to let in. And he had let me in. I wanted to wrap myself in him like a blanket and stay warm forever.

"I thought we had something, I don't know, *epic*, but I asked him to come here with me and you would have thought I'd asked him to lop off a finger. He didn't even consider it."

Remembering his look of utter disbelief made my stomach turn.

"And then what?"

"I told him I'd go there, to Philly. He said it wasn't a good time." I winced with embarrassment. "And then I ran away. Literally."

Meri's eyes narrowed. "Have you heard from him since?"

I pulled out my phone and showed her the text he'd sent me last night. **I miss you.**

I'd broken into an ugly, gulping sob when I read it. Now I ran my finger over the screen, my chest aching. "I didn't answer him."

Meri threw herself backward on the couch with a theatrical groan. I'd always said the two of us would have made an amazing acting duo. Like Rosemary Clooney and Vera-Ellen in *White Christmas*. She'd be Rosemary, obviously. She had the judgy eyes down pat.

"So, let me get this straight," she said. "You asked him to move to Boston, where by the way you don't even have a place to live, after you'd known each other for a week, and he said no, and so you think this means he doesn't care about you?"

Yes, Mer. It was a test. Shame on me, maybe, but he failed. "He said he didn't want me there either."

She pointed to my phone. "Did he? Or did he say it wasn't a good time?"

To be fair, I was already in a spiral when he said it, so I couldn't answer that truthfully. The end result was the same, though. He was there and I was here. One text and a selfie from the waterfall to remember it all by.

I buried my head further into her couch. "I do this, Mer. I fall in love with people, things, ideas. But they never fall in love with me back." I wiped at my cheeks and looked at her. We both whispered, "The mailman."

"It's not always that harmless, though. I did this with Sean too, and I almost bound us together for life."

She gave me that look she saved specifically for when I spoke Sean's name. It was kind of like she'd just smelled a rotten egg. "Those two things are *not* the same, Brit."

It felt the same. Me writing fairy tales in my head about someone else's intentions.

"My dad wants me to go to the Saint Mary's gala," I told her. "Sean will be there, at our table. He said it would be best if things looked the way they had in years past."

That finally cracked Meri's diplomat act. "Oh, fuck that," she said.

The surprise of hearing an F-bomb flying out of my perfectly poised friend's mouth startled me and I actually stopped sobbing.

"I don't have a choice."

She gave me a look. "You do."

God, this conversation sounded familiar and it was making me squirm.

"He insinuated I might be able to have the money back if I did it."

"It's not worth it!" She set her teacup down and threw her hands in the air. "Sean is an egotistical asshole who purposely tore you down bit by bit for years, and you've been carrying around this picture of yourself that he drew ever since. As if it's the only one. As if it's even remotely accurate. Sean told you who he wanted you to be because it was the most convenient version of you for him, Brit. He told you that you weren't good enough and then he used you. He doesn't deserve to ever see your face again."

"He's not the only person who thinks that."

"Well, screw your mom and dad too! Brit, you're a gorgeous, vibrant soul who brightens every room she walks into, but you've been kept in a jar your whole life. There's a whole big world out there that your parents and Sean don't dictate. And look what happened, the minute you stepped out into it, someone fell head over heels for you."

I sighed. Was that what she got from this story? Because it sure didn't feel like the ending I remembered. "More like I fell head over heels for him and he weighed the options. I came out at the bottom."

"I don't buy it. What man personally chauffeurs a woman from Costa Rica to New York unless he cares an awful lot about her? And you *do* do this, Brit. You fall in love easily, but that's one of the best things about you. You're kind and happy even when the world isn't. You treat everyone as if they're going to be your next best friend. A lot of times they don't deserve it, but that doesn't mean you're not going to be right one day. Broken clocks, and all."

I sniffle-laughed. I felt like a broken clock, no sense of place or time. I used to think my life would be forever divided into acts—Before Sean and After Sean. But this devastating phase I was in right now felt like it should be labeled "After Nick."

God, I missed him. I missed the person I was when I was with him, me but . . . stronger. I felt like I was tugging against the stars by not being near Nick, not sharing his space. The universe had thrown us together in a series of ridiculous circumstances, and the intimacy between us hadn't grown at a natural rate. It had exploded in fits. One minute, we were splitting supplies at Target, the next we were sharing everything from our deepest fears to our bodies.

But at least I was prone to epicness in my own fantasies.

Nick may or may not have even had a fully functioning pulse when his brother sent him on that trip. What did I really expect of him?

"He's lost something big," I said. "The whole reason he was on the trip, everything between us—it was rooted in grief."

I hadn't told Meri Nick's secret. His letter, his brother, the pain that had been part of his aura since we met. She considered this new information, then she covered my hand with hers. "Don't forget where you were when you two met, Brit. Your world was in pieces too. How can you say you were clearheaded about it, but he was blinded by circumstance?"

I sniffled, remembering how I'd lied to him about the auction even as I dragged uncomfortable truth after painful confession from his broken heart. "I guess I'm afraid neither of us was clear-headed."

"You should at least answer him. How do you know he's not curled up on his best friend's couch thinking the very same thing?"

I knew he wasn't. Even hundreds of miles away, I knew Nick. He was back to buttoning himself up. Nose to the grindstone to keep himself from feeling things he didn't want to. I couldn't handle imagining he was curled up anywhere thinking about me, and I knew he wasn't on his best friend's couch because his best friend was dead.

I left Meri's around eight, managing to avoid my mother while sneaking back into the house. I hadn't spoken to her since my meeting with my father and I still wasn't sure what her absence meant. She'd been behind the French doors of her study, phone to her pearl-decorated ear, and I'd slipped by to hide out in my room.

I brushed my teeth in my en suite and put on the penguin

shorts that Nick had picked out for me at Target. I settled into the eyelet comforter on my childhood bed and booted up my laptop. My browser was still open to the listing for my house, frozen in time before I'd set out on my honeymoon alone. I took a deep breath and hit refresh, watching the "for sale" status turn to "pending." I imagined the same red letters appearing over my head as I fell backward into the pillows. Brit's Life: status—pending.

After I'd managed to calm my Nick Tears enough to have a solid conversation, Meri and I had gotten to work on plan C. Or was it D at this point? I couldn't remember.

I needed to regroup. Losing the house was a huge setback, but I still had my business. Summer was coming and I could book more weddings and events, bank more cash until I saved enough for my own down payment. If I had to cut back my hours at the mall to make time for those events, I'd save money somewhere else.

Blowing a kiss goodbye to the screen, I closed the real estate site and pulled up my website. The first picture I'd taken on the cruise ship scrolled by, flipping to a link for the manicure color poll I'd posted on Instagram. The limited content I'd uploaded while I was sailing had been super popular. People loved my video on how to pack light for a trip with five makeup basics.

I scrolled through some of the comments, the first smile I'd had in a day and a half tugging at my lips.

Love how you incorporated the sunset colors in your palette.
   You're so creative!
—Meg62581

So glad I found this account. Your face always brightens my day.
—Blondeandbeachy

Going to Hawaii for my honeymoon next month. Thank you for
   these tips!!
—KeriK

I clicked over to the short blog post I'd managed to write, scrolling through the pictures I'd taken after Target. The step-by-step tutorial I'd done in the Rover, ending with the selfie I'd taken with Nick at the waterfall. His voice flowed through this new current picking up in my thoughts. *"You just had your first crisis as a business owner, Brit, and you handled it."*

I could handle this one too. I pulled a notebook out of my bedside table drawer, popping the cap off of a pen with my teeth. *I'm creative, dammit. I'm badass.*

I'd get to work on increasing my follower count. Then I could charge more for paid partnerships. The three I already had had sought me out, but I could be more proactive there if I was going to stay mobile for the time being. I could shift more of my own funds into the online side of Álainn, flip my timeline.

I could still have this. It would just be different.

And it would also be alone. I could do this by myself. I could do anything by myself, but now doing it by myself felt less like an accomplishment and more like a punishment. Nick was my personal hype-man for the last few days and I missed his encouragement, his gentle steering. Especially while hiding upstairs from my parents like I was planning a bank heist instead of a business.

When I finally did save enough for a deposit on a studio, it couldn't be here. At Meri's, it had occurred to me that everything I'd built to this point wasn't tied to any particular location. My career was completely mobile and if I'd learned one thing on this trip, it was that a little distance from this place was freeing in a way I didn't know was possible.

I remembered what Annie told me. Not every detour is a disaster. A detour is meant to keep you from avoiding a hole in the road, some danger. Maybe that hole was trying to do this under my parents' watchful eye. My dad had already proved he would ruin whatever was in his reach just to get me to comply.

Meri was right too. I'd been kept in a jar, and sure, I'd wanted that studio, but more than that, I'd wanted to show them I could make this happen. Sean and my father were always against me. Nick was the first person to tell me that I should—that I *could*—go for it.

If I couldn't have him, at least I'd have that.

CHAPTER THIRTY-EIGHT

The Heir to the Throne

Nick

Monday morning, I prepared myself to go back to the office. I went through the motions of ironing my clothes and picking out a tie. It was navy blue, the shirt was pale blue, the slacks were a charcoal gray. I looked like a storm cloud with no rainbow in sight.

When I'd woken up on the couch that morning, I'd thought for the briefest of seconds that Brit was in a bunk above me, that I could hear her breathing. Then I saw the plain white drywall of my ceiling and I remembered.

Now when I entered my office Tom was in my chair, his boots on my desk. With his dark beard and flannel shirt, he looked like he'd gotten lost on the way to the local brewery.

"Get the fuck up," I said.

He laughed and bumped his fist against mine, taking that as the "It's good to see you" that it was meant to be.

He made a show of looking at his watch as he exited my spot. "Still on Caribbean time?"

"I've been in the States for five days trying to get home."

"Sounds like the trip from hell."

I pictured Brit's bare feet on the dashboard of the Rover, legs crossed, head tipped in the sun. Then the back of her head as she ran away from me. "Some of it."

"So what's the plan?" he asked, getting straight to the point. Thankfully. I wasn't in the mood to chat. "Your dad is losing his shit."

I pulled out my computer and made room for it on my desk. "It was my fault."

Tom gave me a hard look. "We both know it wasn't."

"I usually take these meetings."

"You weren't in the state, Nick. This is his business, and he's been running it since before we were born. You're here now to clean it up, so don't take the blame for this."

His voice was sharp and the admonishment caught me by surprise. Tom and I had been close since we were kids, but lately it was in more of a *let's grab a beer and talk Fantasy Football* way. Now he sounded like Alex.

"Either way, it's my problem now, right?" Even I could hear the bitterness in my words. I waved a hand over my laptop as it booted up.

Sorry you didn't get the girl, but here's a lifelong albatross around your neck instead.

Tom sat back down, this time on the edge of my desk. "I was hoping maybe you'd stay away a little longer."

"Thanks, asshole." I tried for a joke but then I realized I was the only one kidding. Tom's jaw was set and I felt the air in the room shift away from business. My skin started crawling with the urge to leave. The last thing I wanted was to have a heart to heart while I was trying to keep it together. Not if it wasn't from my brother.

"I'm serious, Nick," he said. "You've always pushed yourself too hard, but since Alex . . . It's not sustainable."

That was rich considering no one else had picked up my slack while I was gone. I pushed my hand into my hair and squeezed. "If you wanted me to stay away, why didn't you handle this shit for me while I was gone?"

It was unfair and we both knew it. My dad wanted me on the projects he thought were important. He didn't trust anyone else.

Tom eyed me, his expression neutral. "Go ahead," he said, holding out his hand. "Go off."

"What?"

"You wanna be pissed off, go ahead. God knows you deserve it."

I blinked at him. My brain was in a fog and I couldn't tell if he was fucking with me.

I thought about telling him about it. Brit, my mom, the way I felt buried by all of it. How the thing I'd always wanted had turned into a consolation prize, but even worse, now I wanted something else and those two things weren't in the same place. And one of them wasn't speaking to me.

I thought about flipping this desk over and storming out but I barely had the energy to sit there and scowl at him. "It doesn't matter," I mumbled.

A familiar knuckle rap on my door made me jump. "Nick. You're back."

I didn't look up at the sound of my father's voice. I hadn't spoken to him since the phone call that had cost me Brit and I didn't know what he'd see if I met his eye. Something I couldn't take back.

"I told you I would be." I looked at the clock. "Where's Mom?"

"She's with your aunt Janey."

Tom and Drew's mom. Good. At least she was taken care of for a few hours and I could get this done.

My father cleared his throat and took a seat across the room. "So, the Clayborne job . . ."

"I'm handling it." I clicked the file on my desktop. "I've been in contact with the subs and I'm pulling up the bid package now."

"Good." He nodded once, tossing another folder on my desk. "I found something else I need you to take a look at."

I looked at the folder, then back at my dad, grinding my teeth.

He tapped the folder. "I think this is the next thing we should put our time into."

"You mean my time."

His gray eyebrows jumped and I realized I'd said it out loud. "What's that mean?"

I don't know what came over me. Maybe it was Tom pissing me off right before my father came in here, or the fact that I hadn't slept in three days, but I felt like a stick about to snap. "I don't want to put my time into whatever that is."

He looked at me like I'd grown wings. "What's going on here, Nick?"

"I think I need some time off." I pushed away from my desk and stood. My breath had started to strangle me, a fine sheen of sweat forming on the back of my neck, and I tugged at my tie. I was nauseous and too hot.

"You just came back."

"I know, I . . ." I shook my head. "No. You called me back. I only came back because you said you needed me to."

"I did need you and you were on your way home."

"I wasn't. I wasn't on my way home. I'd just finished Alex's list and I was dealing with that, processing it or whatever, and I was with someone and I was happy to be there. With her."

I swallowed, glancing to the side to see Tom staring at me, eyes watchful.

My father took a breath through his nose, his jaw tight. He was measuring his reply. "Nicky. I rely on you because I know I can always count on you. I can't do this without you."

"Is that why you gave the company to Alex?" I tensed. That had slipped out, but fuck it, we were doing this.

He blinked at me, confused. "Is that what this is about?"

"I don't know, maybe. It's about a lot of things but that's the one I want to talk about. I have been here every time you've called," I said. I pictured Brit sleeping in that bed while I promised him I'd leave her and come home and my temper flared. "I've put out fire after fire in this family starting back when I was just a kid. Even Alex knew it. Christ, he sent me on a goddamn apology tour. But you? You gave away the one thing that was mine." I pushed a hand into my hair. "And that one decision ruined everything."

My father's face hardened with familiar sternness. "He was my first born . . . Alex was . . . He was the oldest."

"Fuck. Glad to know you had a solid reason, Dad."

"Nicky—"

"No!" I slammed my palm on my desk. "He was the oldest but I was the one who carried everyone. You put too much on me. This was too much."

The dull ache in my chest that I'd woken up with grew sharper. I rubbed at it through my shirt. Sweat formed at my collar and I loosened the knot on my tie further to get more air. Then I ripped it over my head.

Tom got to his feet beside me. "You all right, man?"

I couldn't answer him. I was afraid if I spoke, I'd lose it. Suddenly my office felt way too small for all of these people I didn't want. It was like there was a finite amount of oxygen and I wasn't getting my share.

"I need some air." I pushed past Tom, heading for the back door. I was going to throw up or pass out. I wasn't sure which, but I needed to get out of that room. I threw open the heavy metal door and landed in the parking lot, sucking at the cold air.

Fuck, it was thirty degrees out, but I ripped open the top three buttons of my shirt anyway. Willow was right. I'd been holding myself together by a thread, not letting myself fall apart, and I felt it all rushing at me at once. Alex was gone. Brit was gone. There was too much pain without them, and I couldn't hack it.

I leaned against the brick building, sliding down to sit on the cold pavement. Adrenaline made my head pound and I dropped my face into my hands, trying to catch my breath.

The door creaked open and Tom came out, rubbing at his arms in the cold. He slid down the wall beside me and laced his fingers around his knees. "You all right?"

I glanced at him sidelong, my hands shaking.

He nodded, then after a few moments, "Who's the girl?"

A half-laugh broke through my heavy breaths. "Wouldn't you like to know."

Tom leaned his head against the wall and sat there silent while I wiped the back of my hand under my eyes. "I miss him," I said, my throat thick.

He gave a single nod. "Me too. I know it's not the same for me—"

I sniffed. "We all grew up as brothers, Tom. It's the same."

"Maybe. But Drew and I had the luxury of living in a different house all those years. We got all of the good parts of Alex, the wild times and the bad fucking ideas, but you were the one making up for it on the other end. What you said in there was true, and whatever it took for you to finally say it, that's what you need more of."

"Nicky." My father stepped through the door Tom had left open, his Carhartt jacket pulled up to his chin.

Tom and I jumped to our feet like kids called out. "Dad, I—"

"No. You asked me a question and I want to answer it." He ran a hand over his tan and weathered face, breathing deep. "The job. I knew you wanted it and that me giving it to Alex hurt you. I'm sorry for that, Nicky. But I thought maybe if I gave Alex this responsibility, it would . . . I don't know, ground him here somehow. Like maybe if I made him indispensable then I couldn't lose him. At the very least he'd be beside me while he was here, instead of off running." His voice turned wistful. "He was always running."

I dipped my head, a wave of memory sweeping over me, burning my throat.

"But when you left on that trip he sent you on, I realized something. I'd done wrong by both of you, because that was what he wanted. To be free for as long as he was here." His voice cracked. "I should have let him."

My shoulders sank with realization. I always thought of Alex as the defiant one. It burned at me the way he constantly found a way to duck around responsibility and everyone seemed to let him off the hook. But I knew Alex never wanted to work for my dad. Him taking that job was just as much of a concession to our father as me watching it happen.

Knowing Alex and the way he always seemed to understand things better than I did, it was unlikely he hadn't seen exactly why my father was doing it. Taking that job to make my father happy was a choice. One I never gave him credit for.

"You did your best," I said. "Alex made his own choices."

My dad grabbed the back of his neck, squeezing in a way I recognized too well. "I'm trying to do right by your mother," he said. "That's why I need you here, Nicky."

The pain in his voice caught me in the chest and I had to close my eyes to breathe through it. "I know that, Dad, but that's not something you and I can handle. Not anymore. Cut the *keep family business close* crap and get her some real help. You can't do it all."

Those words seemed to hang in the air between us. Maybe I was still talking to myself or maybe I was doing what I always did, trying to take care of him. Either way, there was enough guilt and grief between us and someone had to let some of it go.

My father shoved his hands in his coat pockets, casting his eyes to the brick wall. "I'm sorry I let you think you didn't deserve to run this company, Nick. I think it's time I fixed that." He cleared his throat. "Alex's job . . ."

"I don't want Alex's job." I knew now that was never the issue.

He blinked and I stood up straighter, hearing Brit's voice in my ear.

At least I fought for what I wanted.

"Alex's job was just a title," I said. "Maybe that was on purpose, I don't know. But what I want is a seat at the table. If you want me to run this company, let me run it. I promise I won't let you down."

His mouth twitched at the corner, his eyes slightly amused. "No, I can't imagine you will."

He gave my shoulder a squeeze and turned to walk away but

something stopped him. "Nick. Just one more thing. I want you to remember that it's always been your name on that sign. Nothing will change that." He slapped my back, calling over his shoulder as he walked away. "And I'm giving you the title too. It's your time."

It was my time. And I might not have been that guy when Brit needed me to be, but I could be that guy now. The guy who took what he wanted.

I left the office late and went for a drive to clear my head from everything that had just gone down. I wouldn't have guessed it, after days of hassle, but it felt good to be back on the road. Like reliving a fond memory. Except my pickup wasn't a luxury SUV, and there was no beautiful chatterbox in the passenger seat making fun of my music.

I wished I could call her, tell her that I'd taken her advice and that I felt the world open up just a little because of it. Instead, I let myself imagine what it would be like to have her here now, sitting in the passenger side of my truck, maybe going home together. We'd still argue about the music and she'd still make me play stupid deep question games, but I'd put my hand on her thigh as we drove, and she'd cover it with hers and smile.

My chest tightened with a feeling of incompleteness.

Make room, Willow had said. I was working out in my head what that looked like, but even once I figured it out, how could I convince Brit? I still didn't know if she'd run away from me or she'd convinced me to run away from her.

The Bluetooth announced a text message and I slowed to a stop on the side of the road to read it.

Drew: Offer is in. Outlook good.

I grinned, pumping my fist alone in the cab of my truck.

The first thing I'd done when my father left was count the Clayborne job a loss. That was his project and he'd let it die. It wasn't that I didn't want to help him, but the fact was, he'd said it was my time and losing that job freed up some cash. A lot of it. I knew exactly where I wanted to invest it.

Tom and Drew and I sat around the conference table and made the plans. The three of us working together felt like old times. Like when we were kids, coming up with some scheme to pull over on our parents. Of course this scheme had a big financial risk attached to it, but still. I'd missed that since I'd been pretending that anyone who wasn't Alex didn't matter.

I sent Drew a meme of Jerry Maguire saying "show me the money."

He replied with a gif of a man's naked ass as he dove into a pool of hundred-dollar bills. I deleted it.

I pulled back onto the road, a new destination in mind, and ten minutes later, I was edging into a parallel spot and putting my truck in park.

I climbed out and zipped my fleece to my chin. My boots crunched in the snow as I wandered the block, taking a look at my first commercial investment. It was a row of brick on cobblestone, mixed-use space that included a market, some offices. I'd had my eye on it for months. It needed a ton of work but Tom had agreed on the potential. That was his expertise. I ran numbers and reports and he got ideas. We were both damn good at our jobs.

I waited for a car to pass and hustled across the street to get a feel for who our neighbors would be. What kind of customer base was already present that we could tap into when trying to find tenants once the space was renovated. I'd been down here a few times, dreaming, and Drew had gotten us an official list of nearby businesses when we'd decided to do this, but I wanted to look at it again in person now that it would be ours.

I passed a bank, a coffee shop closing up for the evening. A tavern that was just coming to life. It reminded me of Madge's with its glass front and antique wood door, and my chest squeezed as the thought occurred to me. This looked like the type of place where people liked to go to work.

I walked another block or so until I found myself in front of a vintage-looking two-story with gray peeling paint nestled between two newer buildings. My feet came to a stop on their own, something telling me to take a closer look.

The street level had been an office, now it was empty space behind a bay window where a business name had been poorly scraped off. The top floor looked like loft space. It probably had vaulted ceilings based on the roofline. There was stained glass in the attic window and . . .

Holy shit.

I jogged up four stone steps and saw a handwritten *for rent* sign taped to the door.

My heart sped up as an absolutely ridiculous idea started to form in my brain. Maybe I was still high from the wins of the day, or I missed Brit so much I was out of my mind, but I quickly snapped a picture of the address and texted it to Drew. He knew everyone in this business. Inspectors, developers, realtors.

Can you find out who owns this property?
Drew: You looking to move? Because that might be a downgrade.

I laughed. I might have to move here if this didn't work.

It's not for me. Can you do it quickly?
Drew: On it.

If he got me the info, I could do this. The ink wasn't dry on the deal yet, but my dad made it clear that I was the one making decisions now. I wouldn't unless Tom and Drew gave me the okay, but I could almost bank on that. I could do it the same way I bought my house and they bought theirs and Alex bought his—as a Callaway and Sons investment.

Of course, I didn't know if I could convince her, if she'd even take my call, but I'd figure that out later. Right now I was going to channel a little bit of Brit and take a huge leap of faith.

"You're sure this is a good idea?" Tom drummed his fingers on the edge of his desk, eyeing me.

I'd filled him in on what I wanted to do last night after Drew had got me the name of the guy who owned the house and I'd given him a call. Turned out he'd recently moved out of state and had little interest in keeping it rented. When I'd made him an offer for it, empty and as is, he'd jumped on it.

"It's a solid investment," I said. "No matter what happens."

Tom rolled back and forth in his chair, considering me. "You don't need my permission, Nicky. That's what being in charge means."

"I know that, but this is how I want things to be. Us making the calls."

He laughed. "That why you're in my office looking like a kid asking for an extra helping of dessert?"

I sat down on the edge of his desk, scratching at my brow. "You think it'll work?"

Tom dropped the professional tone and smirked at me. "You're asking me for advice on a woman?"

A reflexive longing for one of Alex's talks jabbed at my chest, but it was already duller. "I guess I am."

He made a low whistle and crossed his arms over his chest, thinking. "Welp, I'll say this. If buying a girl a house doesn't work, I think you can safely say you're doing something else wrong."

He winked at me, and I shook my head. "Fuck you."

He laughed. "Love you too, Nick."

CHAPTER THIRTY-NINE

Dancing with the Devil

Brit

I had sacrificed my self-respect for the Donovan family name many times, but agreeing to play nice with Sean after everything that had happened was a sharp, rocky bottom.

My hands shook so hard I could barely hold my champagne flute as I followed my parents around the ballroom. Sean would be here any minute and the thought of seeing him and his snooty parents made my stomach feel like I'd eaten butterfly soup. I thought about my new plan, the things I had in the works for my own life, and gave myself a mental hype speech. *You can do this, Brit. You're not just the makeup-counter manager anymore. You're a badass business owner.*

Who currently looked like a zombie in this silk, flamingo-colored dress with the dramatic slit up the side. My eyes were red-rimmed and bagged, my hair had been professionally done—my mother insisted I ditch the strawberry part of the brunette for this—but I'd flattened the back of it in the town car, leaning dramatically against the window. My feet were killing me in these heels, so even my gait was half-dead. I missed my fake-shearling boots. I missed my Texas sweatshirt. I missed Nick's hand on my lower back, guiding me through a crowd.

I still hadn't returned his text. He hadn't tried again. I was trying to convince myself that Meri was right, that he just needed the time he'd asked for, but no matter what happened, I knew this was the last night I was going to spend doing things like this. I felt like a houseplant that someone had left in a dark room, a tropical flower in the winter. I'd been withering since I got back here and getting out was a top priority.

Unfortunately, I had to dance with these demons before I could slay them.

I gulped my drink and set the empty glass on a waiter's tray. My father worked the room with his easy smile and politician-style handshakes. Everyone here had something he wanted and he was a pro. I, on the other hand, had always been captain of the amateur team.

"Bridget, please try to look like you care to be here." My mother placed a hand on the inside of my arm and smiled wide so that from afar, her critique would look like we were engaging in some mother–daughter bonding. *Goodness, yes, Mother. Gardenias in the centerpieces were a wonderful touch.* Gag.

"I do not care to be here," I said in my most regal voice. "So I have no idea how to look like it."

Her smile wavered. "Are you afraid to see Sean?"

I flicked a look at her. That almost sounded like a sincere question, but I knew better. "I'm not afraid. I just don't want to."

What I wanted to do was take this dress off and go over to Meri's for a movie and pizza. Maybe cry into my pillow for another night in a row, then fall asleep and dream of being a boat on an ocean of sea-foam green.

If my father thought he could break me with this torture, he had no idea what I had the capacity to do to myself.

"Well, I think you look lovely now that your hair is a normal color," Mom said. "So Sean can just eat crow." She squeezed my arm, and I stood there a little dumbfounded. Besides the dig at my hair, that almost felt supportive.

"Ah, you're here, son." My father's voice was joyous and I whipped my gaze over my shoulder to see him embracing Sean despite the fact that Sean was, in no way, his son.

"Wouldn't miss it, sir."

They both turned to me and a wave of nausea threatened to bring the champagne back up. Sean looked the same as the last time I'd seen him—tall, golf-course tan, well-pressed suit. His longish hair was slicked into place, showing off that wave my mother liked to point out would be wonderful for our babies to inherit. Not a cowlick in sight.

He took my hand and pasted on a perfect smile as if he expected a camera to capture this moment. That would be a priceless headline. **Girl's millionaire father ruins her life in the name of business. Because you never can have too much money.**

I hated *business*. Business suits, business calls, business dinners. Business transactions that involved my heart.

"Bridget, it's nice to see you again," Sean said.

"I'm sure the pleasure is all yours."

Sean's winning grin almost faltered. My father made a snarling noise.

My mother clapped her hands. "Well, now," she said. "Let's take our seats, shall we?"

Sean tucked himself into the chair beside me, lowering his

voice. "I'm surprised to see you here tonight, Bridget. I know how much you hate these things. What did you call them? *Adults playing dress-up*?"

"I didn't have a choice. I'm sure you know that. Your image has always been the one to protect." I folded my napkin on my lap, watching my parents carry on with Sean's. None of them seemed overly awkward being in a room together like my father had claimed.

"Speaking of image, that's an interesting outfit," Sean said under his breath. "I can't say I'm surprised you decided to show up to a black-tie event looking like the talent at a bachelor party. I guess I should be thankful I never saw the wedding gown."

I glared at him. "It's called personality, Sean. You should Google it. Maybe you can have Jennifer order you one." Jennifer was his assistant, though she was Jenny in the late-night texts.

He laughed meanly. "Ah, yes. Personality. Well, Jennifer wouldn't be caught dead in an outfit like that. Besides, I've always preferred her with her clothes off."

I froze with my glass at my lips. The conversation around us had stilled at that precise moment, and his little confession landed like a bomb in the middle of the table. My mother smoothed her napkin in her lap. My father's gaze darted between me and Sean, his mouth an unreadable line.

I pressed the back of my hand to my lips, wishing I could crawl under the table and die.

CHAPTER FORTY

Recalculating

Nick

I pulled up to the gated entrance where my GPS told me Brit's parents lived, and rubbed at my eyes. Jesus, this place was a palace. Especially compared to the run-down house she'd been trying to buy. The dichotomy didn't surprise me, though. Nothing that I knew about Brit fit with this lifestyle she'd painted for me. To be honest, I'd wondered if the whole rich-kid thing was one of her acts. But here I was in front of a seven-foot wrought-iron gate that told me it wasn't.

I patted the pocket of my shirt for the purchase and sale agreement I'd folded and stuffed there.

The windows that I could see were lit, but there were no cars in the driveway. Though, I assumed a place like this offered garage parking. I pressed the intercom button and no one answered. My heart sank. I supposed I could drive around the city a bit, come back in a little while and try again. As I was deciding what to do to kill time, the lights from a pickup truck appeared on the other side of the gate. Then it swung open.

The driver pulled up beside me and we both rolled down our windows. "Can I help you?" He had a work coat on over a Henley. There were a few shovels and buckets of sand in the bed of his truck. He obviously worked here.

"I'm looking for Bridget Donovan."

"The Donovans are at the hospital gala. Bridget went with them."

"Hospital gala?" I snorted a little laugh at the idea of Brit at an event like that, but it didn't matter where she was, I was going there.

I considered asking for an address, but I was probably lucky to get that much info out of this guy. Google could give me the rest.

I thanked him and he nodded, waiting for the gate to close behind him before he took off. I turned my truck around and searched the internet for every charity function happening in Boston tonight. It only took a few minutes to hit the jackpot. A dinner benefit for Saint Mary's with Donovan Financial listed as the top sponsor.

I flicked on my blinker, turning into the driveway for The Plaza, and stopped to let a couple men in tuxedos pass in front of me. This plan was getting crazier by the minute. What if I couldn't get into whatever this thing was? What if she told me to piss off before I got the chance to tell her about the house? At least if it was black tie she'd probably be in high heels. She'd be easy to catch if she ran away again and this time I wasn't going to stand there like a mute statue.

Brit told me she didn't believe I'd ever let anyone down, but she was wrong. Every time I'd dropped everything for my family, there was someone else who I'd disappointed—friends, girlfriends, myself. This time it was her, the one person who hadn't asked anything from me, and it was the last time.

I pulled my truck up next to a black Jag and straightened the collar on my wrinkled dress shirt. The T-shirt underneath was stuck to my back with sweat from my heated seats and nerves. I did a brief scan of the cab for a stray tie I might have ditched on a drive home one night, but no such luck.

It didn't matter. I wasn't here to impress anyone. I just needed a few minutes alone with Brit. To say what I needed to say. She'd found a way to remind me who I was before bitterness took over. I wanted to be that guy again. I wanted to feel that way again. And I wanted to be the person who understood her best too. For all of her confidence and quirks, there was so much vulnerability to her. I wanted to be the one who told her every single day how perfect she was. Because she was perfect. And if I had to do it here, so be it.

I pushed through the revolving door to the swanky, gilded lobby, looking for a sign that would point me in the right direction. Well-dressed people hovered with glasses of champagne and tiny plates of appetizer art. I could hear a band playing through a set of wooden doors. A man at a table stood as I walked toward them. He looked like he worked there.

"Is this the Saint Mary's benefit?" I asked.

He eyed my outfit, an unpleasant look passing over his face. "Yes, but the dress code is black tie, sir."

"I'll only be a minute." I pushed past him, trying to imagine Brit at a scene like this but all I could see was her standing in my boxers and sweaty shirt, her makeup smudged and her hair a tornado on top of her head. What I wouldn't give to have her like that again.

I stepped onto the maroon carpet in the ballroom, briefly

sorry for the way I was probably tracking mud from my boots. Shit, there were a lot of people here. Nerves started to swell as I scanned tables of tuxes and formalwear. The staff wasn't going to let me stay here much longer, searching.

But then a flash of color caught my eye and I saw her. In a sea of black and jewel-toned gowns, she was dressed in hot pink. I laughed to myself, despite my heart pounding in my ears. *Always the brightest light in the room, Brit.*

I pulled in a deep breath, the full weight of how much I missed her settling in my chest as I started across the room. Brit and I were back in the same space and I knew more than ever that I needed to keep it that way.

CHAPTER FORTY-ONE

The Beginning in the End

Brit

The table was silent. Maybe they were stunned at the cruelty they didn't know Sean possessed, or maybe they were holding their collective breath, hoping I wouldn't make a scene.

I pressed my fingers under my eyelids, breathing in—*one salamander, two salamander, three salamander*. I'd told myself I was done crying over Sean, but I'd forgotten just how good he was at sniffing out my wounds and digging his claws into them.

My voice croaked as I fumbled my way through excusing myself from the table. I just needed to hold back the tears until I could get somewhere private and let myself have this sob, but my dress caught on the heel of my shoe and I nearly tripped. Beside me, Sean shook his head. That was the last straw. I couldn't control it anymore. The tears flowed faster than I could swipe them away and I clapped my hand over my mouth, frantically searching for an exit.

And that was when I saw them—those good-luck charm,

sea-foam green, alien eyes staring back at me from the entrance to the ballroom.

I clutched my chest. I was dreaming. That was the only way to explain it. All of the stories I'd made up in my head had finally turned into hallucinations. Nick couldn't possibly be here right now.

But he lifted a hand and started toward me. My chair tumbled backward as I pushed away from the table and he was there, catching me by the elbows as I crashed against him.

"Nick?" Despite the shock, I threw my arms around him, burying my face in his shirt.

Sean pushed his chair out with a loud scratch. "What is going on, Bridget?" His tone was part censure, part mortification. It was nauseatingly familiar.

Nick turned to Sean and his face twisted in disgust like the goodness in him innately sensed Sean's douchery. "Who's this?"

He hadn't even told me why he was here and now he was looking at Sean with Murder Eyes. "This is Sean," I said. "He's here for my dad."

Nick looked between us, his eyes narrowing. "Why are you crying?"

Sean hissed a whisper. "Honestly, you're making a scene."

My father stood. "Bridget, do you know this man?"

Nick ignored my father's puffed out chest. "Actually, Sean, I'm the one making a scene because for some reason Brit doesn't think people like her scenes. I'm thinking you're part of that reason?" He turned to my father. "And maybe you?"

My eyes bugged out of my skull. Being spoken to like that was the equivalent of a WWE Smackdown for my father. I wanted to pump my fist and cheer. I also wanted to hide because I knew what was coming.

"Excuse me, young man?" He turned to Sean. "Get security."

Sean trotted off like the lackey he was. If only he knew he was a grown man with free will. And why the heck was Nick here?

It was so good to see him. His hair was a mess like he'd been dragging his hands through it. He'd shaved his face back to stubble and he still had that Costa Rica tan. His eyes were as bold as ever, but the whites were tinged with pink. Worry clouds gathered in my head. Was he sleeping? Drinking enough water? Exhaustion was all over his face.

"Brit." He ignored the fact that my father had just sent his henchmen to alert the rent-a-cop on duty and slid his hand down my arm, lacing our fingers. "God, I missed you. You look so pretty."

"What are you doing here, Nick?"

"I went to your house. One of your employees told me you were here. I needed to see you. You didn't answer my text."

Ha! His one text. I almost threw that back at him until I saw the pain on his face, how much that had cost him. Suddenly that one text was a golden rose. I'd left him speechless in a train station and he'd still sent me one text. Which was more than I'd given him back.

"I'm sorry. I . . ." A million excuses lined up on my tongue. Lies, mostly. But looking at him now, I didn't know if I had the same conviction to keep myself sheltered at all costs. "I was scared."

That seemed to catch him off guard. "Of what?"

"That you were figuring it out." I ran a hand under my nose. "Now that we're not on vacation anymore, you'll get tired of trying to fit my square peg into your round life."

"Why do you think that?" He shoved his hands in his hair.

"You didn't exactly jump at the chance to keep going, Nick."

My voice was high-pitched and breaking. I was only vaguely aware that we were doing this in front of an audience until the ambient scraping of silverware stopped.

Nick didn't seem to care. "You're right. I fucked up, but I was never on vacation, remember? And I'm not going to get tired of you. I miss you so much. I haven't slept since you left me." He swallowed like he hadn't meant to admit that. "I bought you a house."

Wait. "What?"

He pulled his phone from his pocket, handing it to me. I didn't dare look. There was no way I'd heard him correctly. *He bought me a what?*

"Bridget, who is this man?" my father boomed. "He bought you a house?"

"It's not exactly like the one you wanted," Nick said. "But it's the same color and it has a fireplace. It's got a window in front for a sign, but I can hang one on a post for you instead."

My heart. I could barely speak. "You remembered that part."

"Of course I did."

I blinked a few times then focused on the screen. He was right, it wasn't exactly like the one I lost, but oh my God, how I loved it. The siding was similar, an old weathered gray, and it was two stories with white dollhouse trim in the eves.

I swiped to the interior pictures. The upstairs had lofted ceilings and stained glass, and the downstairs was open with pale wood floors and exposed beams. I could picture it, my studio, just like I imagined.

"It needs some work," he said, "but I thought maybe you'd like that."

The back of my throat burned with emotion for how much I liked that. I kept scrolling, glancing up at him when I got to the last picture. "It's in Philly?"

He swallowed. "You said you'd come. I took a chance."

"But you said no."

Sean came back then, a man in a uniform by his side. "Here," he said, pointing at Nick.

"Sir, you'll need to leave." The guard took a tentative step toward us.

I held my hand up and glared at him. "Let us finish."

Nick stepped toward me, ignoring the pitchforks. "I was an idiot, Brit. I should have taken you home when you said you'd come, but I guess it was easier to tell myself you were the one walking away, than to try to make you happy and fail."

I shook my head. "You did make me happy."

"I took your advice. I told my dad how I felt and he put me in charge of the company."

My heart swelled. I was so proud of him, I could cry.

"It's a lot of responsibility and I still have a lot of people who need me, but giving you up is where I draw the line, Brit. I'm going to make the room. So the house is part of our inventory. If you still want to come with me, it's yours." He seemed to get hit with a rush of nerves. "If not, I'll flip it or whatever."

My heart was already getting attached but a terrible thought crept into my head, even as I clutched his phone and the pictures to my chest. "You just want to save me because that's what you do, Nick. You can't help yourself—when you see a mess, you clean it."

My lip trembled. A tsunami of tears was building behind my fake confidence, and Nick could tell. Just like that night at Madge's, he could always tell.

He pressed his thumb to my lip, dragging it downward. "I don't want to save you, Brit. You're not a mess, you're perfect. You think I'll bail when it's not fun anymore? I didn't even know how to have fun until I met you. And you running away from me wasn't fun, but here I am. This isn't a phase or a fling or whatever else you think. I'm in love with you."

That was it. I was a ghost hovering over my body.

Somewhere in the ether, Sean made a scoff in the back of his throat. The security guard walked away.

My mom was silent, jaw unhinged. She might have died of embarrassment, but I was floating. "You're in love with me?"

"I think I fell in love with you when I saw you on that dock, looking like an angel in the middle of one of the worst moments of my life. And then again at that bar when you punched that guy in the face." He laughed. "And then a hundred times after that, Brit. You had this way of making me happy when I was determined not to be. Life's too short to let that pass me by. You showed me that. Please take the house. It's a tiny gesture after all the ways you've changed my life."

I didn't know what to say. It felt like all of my dreams were lining up in front of me and—"Oh, no."

"What's wrong?"

"I . . . can't."

His face fell. "Brit, please, I—"

"No. It's not what you think. You can't buy me a house, Nick, and I can't buy it because I don't have the money. It wasn't just a hiccup with the funds. My father cut off my trust. Without it, I'm broke."

"Your father is going to release your trust." It was my mother's voice and my head whipped around to see her staring at my father, chin tipped defiantly. She shot him a scathing look and for the first time in his life, he looked chastened. "If you want the house, buy it yourself. Don't let him do it. Sorry." She turned to Nick, and he held his hands up to say he took no offense. "That money is yours. It was willed to you."

"But Daddy was very clear I wouldn't see that money without marrying Sean."

My mother inspected her manicure like this was all very gauche, discussing finances. "He doesn't actually have any say in it, legally. Besides, if he hadn't made you go to school for something you didn't want to, you'd have done it on your own by now. He was trying to help you, but he was wrong. We both were. Your father took the opportunities afforded to him and built the world he wanted. You deserve the same. Take it and run, darling."

I wanted to believe this, I did, but my brain was giving me all sorts of warning signals born of years of these kinds of deals—*Learn ballet and we'll buy you a car. Major in what we say and we'll pay for college. Marry Sean and we'll love you.*

"You give it to me now and there will be some string," I said, gesturing to Sean who seemed oblivious to the fact that he was the string. "Something you'll ask of me later."

My mother's face turned up into a warm smile. One I'd never witnessed before. "No strings, Bridget." She stepped closer and took my hand. Had my mother *ever* held my hand?

She waved dismissively at Sean. "This isn't what I want for you. Frankly, I'm relieved to my core that you found a way out of it." Then she turned to Nick, a hint of the mother I recognized peeking out in her shrewd inspection. "Whoever this man is, I hope he's a lot better than Sean."

Sean's mother pressed a palm to her chest, but Marcia Donovan couldn't have cared less. "Oh, Savannah, you know it's true. Your son is a snake and I hope he gets a venereal disease."

Holy, what? Now *I* was pearl-clutching. This was absolutely wild.

Sean cleared his throat, Hulk-Smashing his way into our

moment. I'd forgotten he was there. "Well, this just tops all of your schemes, Bridg. You're going to take off to Philadelphia now? Is this still part of your big-girl independence bullshit?"

Nick's jaw twitched. "Can I hit him?"

"No, I've got this. You can just shut up, Sean," I said, tipping my chin. "So I'm impulsive. So I make heart decisions instead of head ones sometimes. I like that about me." I *liked* seeing where the wind took me. I'd gladly spend my days dizzy from following the whims my heart led me on rather than locked into another thing I would grow to resent. Like him.

"My heart told me to run as far away from you as I could and I should have listened." I turned to my father who was still standing there like a wide-eyed statue. "And you! I'm tired of being the good Donovan daughter."

"Bridget—"

"No. I want more than what you want for me. I'm in charge of my life from now on. Accept it or not. I don't care about your approval anymore."

My father was silent for what may have been the first time in his life. Damn, that felt good. I took a deep breath, my hands shaking with adrenaline. I looked around the room at a hundred eyes trained on us and this ridiculous scene. But there was only one pair I cared about. I turned to Nick. "I'll go with you," I said. "I want to go."

Nick's breath rushed out, his hand coming up to fist his hair. "Really? You'll come?"

I smiled. "What, like it's a hardship to look at this face every day?" I reached up and cradled his cheeks, putting us back in that bubble that seemed to surround us whenever our eyes met. "Do you remember I told you that when I saw that old, run-down house, I knew it was going to change my life?"

Nick nodded.

I shrugged. "Well, it did. In this crazy, roundabout, fateful way it brought me you. I miss you, Nicky. I lost the house a week ago and I'm not sitting around crying about it. Okay, I did at first, but then I realized that my dreams aren't tied to four walls. What that house meant to me was some solid ground to launch from. You've supported me more than anyone else in this room ever has. You're my solid ground."

"You're my everything."

I felt like I had champagne bubbling in my veins and I threw my arms around his neck and jumped. Nick caught me in a tight hug. My heels fell off and clattered to the marble floor.

I heard my mother whisper, "Oh, Bridget," as she walked away.

"I forgot to tell you something," I said.

Nick arched a brow, the smallest tremor of worry on his lips. "What?"

"I forgot to tell you that I'm in love with you too."

His smile spread, but he pretended to think that over. "Did you?"

"Mm-hmm. And I am. I love you so much. Like, *stare at you while you're sleeping—text you a hundred times a day—miss you even when you're right beside me* love." I bit my bottom lip. "It might get weird."

Nick gave me his full picket-fence, truth-tooth grin. "I can't wait for your weird."

Epilogue

Brit

I woke up to the sun bearing down through the empty windowpanes of my new loft apartment. It bounced around the shiny surfaces, highlighting both its perfections and the multitude of things that still needed to be fixed.

Nick and I were working on the house bit by bit in between the weddings and photo-shoots I had bookings for and Nick's new position at his company. I spent a lot of time objectifying Nick in his tool-belt, hollering for him to take his shirt off, but I was also getting major muscles from my part in the manual labor. Nick and I were a good team—him head and me heart. Together I thought we could do anything. Except maybe catch a boat on time.

I felt stronger than ever, in more ways than one.

I'd been in Philly since the end of May. The day I'd graduated cosmetology school, Nick had driven to Boston for the little ceremony where I'd introduced him to Meri and Justin. We'd had a not-entirely-terrible dinner with my parents, then we'd loaded his truck with everything I owned and unloaded it here. I couldn't believe it was all mine, every chipped floorboard and uneven countertop. The non-working fireplace that I dreamed of hanging artwork over.

Speaking of art, Nick's beautiful body was splayed out beside me, face down on the air mattress that still served as my bed. We'd worn ourselves out last night, pulling down wallpaper and . . . other things. I'd still be comatose too if I wasn't so excited. ·

I watched his naked back rise and fall, the curve of his strong shoulders, and I felt a dizzying sense of joy at the idea of waking up like this again and again. Nick was moving in at the end of the month (another reason I hadn't bought a real bed yet, because of course he owned a real grown-up one and it was a dream). He was here every night anyway and he was rebuilding the place with his own two hands. It should be ours.

Besides, I wasn't meant to be alone—another thing I'd stopped feeling bad about—and I didn't think Nick was either. Every morning I woke up wrapped in his cocoon.

I slipped out of bed and pulled on a T-shirt. I couldn't help exploring the place again even though I'd memorized every floorboard by now. The apartment was bigger than the one in my original house, airy and bright with an open concept and vaulted ceilings, but the studio was smaller. It had room for four chairs, max. Which made more sense. I was just starting out.

I planned on opening the doors to Álainn in exactly twelve months. Nick and Tom had worked with me on my timetable, helping me break it down into manageable and affordable steps, and I'd hit the ground running. My blog was getting more traffic than ever, enough so that my name might actually be recognized by the time I started seeing clients here, and I'd picked up a steady job doing hair and makeup at the local theater. They liked my influencer background and paid me a bonus to cross-promote on my Instagram by recording tutorials on the actors and actresses. In addition to weddings and other events, I was booked nearly every weekend this summer.

After a few moments of internal squeeing over the new life that lay ahead of me, I felt Nick come up behind me. He pressed into my back, heat from his sleep still radiating off of him.

"You are gorgeous in the morning," he whispered.

I smiled, leaning back into his chest, and he wrapped his arms around me. "I can't believe this is real."

"I can't believe we found a place worse off than the first."

I pushed my elbow into his stomach, giggling. "We made it perfect."

I turned in his arms and pushed my hands into his sleep-wrecked hair. His eyes rolled closed and he pulled me closer. "Come back to bed."

"We have to go soon." We were meeting his cousins at the lake, a rare day off from renovations and work, and I needed to pack.

Nick ignored my warning and lifted me off of my toes, walking back to the mattress in the middle of the floor and dropping me onto it.

"We're going to pop this thing," I said as he stretched out over me.

"If we didn't pop it last night, I think it'll be fine. But we could christen a few other places around here if you want."

I giggled as he hooked my leg over his waist. "Whatever you say, *sweetheart.*"

Nick

Lake air would always smell like the best days of my childhood. I leaned my head back against the bench in my uncle's speedboat, letting the sun warm my face while I thought about all the times I'd spent out on this water. Me and Alex, and Tom and Drew, packing marshmallows and chocolate, then later, stolen beer. We'd hang out on that floating dock full of splinters, the four of us Callaway sons shooting the shit until we were pleasantly buzzed and unpleasantly sunburned.

I was an idiot for staying away from this place for so long.

Apparently Tom thought so too. "Figured you'd be seasick the first time we got you back out here." He handed me a beer, nearly toppling over as we bounced over the wake from a water-skier. Drew was driving today and I remembered why my uncle never wanted to let him take the boat out for a spin.

I tapped my beer to Tom's. "I'm just fine, dickhead. Thanks for your concern."

I glanced up the bow to make sure Brit was safe in her seat. She was, so I took a moment to appreciate her tan legs stretched out on the seat in front of her, the flamingo-print two-piece that matched the latest highlights in her hair. The huge smile on her pretty face.

Drew banked a hard right and Tom cursed. "Jesus, some things never change."

I laughed. A whole lot of shit had changed. I think that was why I was finally able to come back here.

Working on Brit's house woke some muscle memory in me. I'd forgotten how good it felt to put effort into something because I wanted to, not out of obligation. It didn't hurt that she was so easily impressed when it came to basic construction skills, and mine were more than basic. Making her smile by fixing a broken light fixture or laying down new tile in her studio was my favorite reward after the long days at work.

She was surprisingly into the grunt work herself, wanting to get her hands dirty as much as possible as if that gave her more of a claim on the place than just her name on the deed. I understood, and I only tried to talk her out of the most dangerous tasks. Jesus, I'd nearly pissed myself watching her run a wet saw.

"The girls love her," Tom said, pointing to the front of his boat where Brit sat in a captain's chair across from Kayla and Hannah.

I nodded. Tom and Drew's girlfriends had accepted Brit into their circle like she'd been there all along. It was less of a surprise to me than it had been to her. Anyone who didn't fall immediately in love with Bridget Donovan wasn't good enough to breathe her air. She just needed to find her people, and it turned out they were the very same people I needed to find my way back to.

I'd gone quiet and Tom looked at me pensively. "Is it weird? Being here without him?"

I chuckled, knowing he'd assumed my silence was brooding when it was the exact opposite. "Not as weird as I thought it would be."

He followed my gaze, still settled on Brit. "You're sprung, man."

"That's one way to put it." I sipped my bottle of beer and rested my elbows on my knees, lowering my voice. "I bought a ring."

Tom nearly choked, spraying beer onto his swim trunks. "Who are you right now?"

I laughed, grinning. Lately, I was no one I recognized, which was why I was happier than I'd ever been.

Tom shook his head, but he was smiling. "She says yes, prepare yourself for the kind of bachelor party Alex would have thrown. I consider it my duty."

That comment should have stung me in the little patches of

my heart that were still raw, but today it felt hopeful. That was how I knew I could offer her what she deserved.

Brit must have felt my eyes on her. She stood and made her way carefully toward me and Tom, while the boat rocked and jumped. She tumbled into her spot on my lap, wrapping her sun-warmed arms around my neck. I didn't care that Tom was still staring at me. I pressed my mouth to hers, thinking, not for the first time, that she *was* the sun.

"This is a lot more fun than my dad's boat," she said when I let go of her lip.

By that, she meant his stuffy yacht where we'd had to spend the Fourth of July docked in a marina. Let's just say there were no Rummy Bears. Her dad was coming around to me, but we were all very aware that I was never going to be Sean in his eyes.

My parents, on the other hand, had pretty much adopted Brit on first sight. My mother had just finished an eight-week out-patient program when I brought Brit over for dinner for the first time. My dad and I grilled some chicken, and Mom made potato salad and iced tea. We ate at the table in their backyard, and Brit seemed almost giddy to be a part of it.

By the end of the night, I saw the same awe in my mother's eyes that I knew shone in mine when I looked at Brit. Sometimes when we spent too much time with either one of our families, I thought of those bumper stickers people get when they rescue a dog from the shelter. The ones that say *Who saved who?*

"Where are we going?" she asked for the millionth time.

"You'll see when we get there. Just enjoy the ride."

She sighed dramatically. "This coming from the world's grumpiest road-trip partner."

*   *   *

The rope swing—Alex's rope swing—was exactly where it had been for the last twenty years. Drew docked the boat, and we climbed the small embankment on the east side of the lake. We'd replaced the rope twice since we were kids, when the frayed knots became less *part of the adventure* and more *someone could get seriously hurt*. I wouldn't have even shown it to Brit if I didn't know it was sturdy. Even so, I tested it a couple more times before helping her onto it.

"You know when to let go?"

Brit gave me her mock salute. "Yes, sir, Nicky, sir."

"At the top of the arc. Don't wait until you're on the backswing."

"Got it."

I held the swing with one hand and wrapped an arm around Brit's waist, lifting her enough for her to get her foot in the loop. "Hold on tight."

"Okay."

I plucked her sunglasses off of the top of her head and set them on her bag. I checked the tie on her swimsuit, bent over to make sure her foot wasn't going to slip off of the loop, then tugged the rope again a few more times.

"Let her try it, Nick!" Hannah groaned.

I waved her off. "You ready?"

Brit nodded, eyes wide with excitement and nerves. "Ready."

I pulled her back as far as I could, ready to launch her out over the water, but at the last minute I couldn't do it. Just before we lost the ground, I grabbed the knot above her head and hopped on.

In the three seconds it took to get out over the water she squealed and told me I was ridiculous and that she loved me. I told her when to let go, and we splashed into the lake like that, wrapped around each other. When we surfaced, Brit ran a hand over her hair and gave me The Look. She was treading water so she couldn't give me the hands-on-her-hips posture to go with it.

"I would have been fine, you stubborn mule."

"I know." I started to swim to shore and she wrapped her arms around my neck and climbed onto my back. "But it was way more fun together."

Acknowledgments

Authors often talk about how hard it is to write the "other" things that come along with getting a manuscript published—the query letter, the elevator pitch, the dreaded synopsis—but for me it's this: The acknowledgments. I'm desperately afraid that I'll forget someone this time in particular, because this moment feels like cresting a mountain I've been climbing for years, and you certainly don't climb a damn mountain without a LOT of help.

This book is *different* for me in that I remember every single moment of its creation, from the hatching of the idea to the tweaking of individual lines. I could probably recite every iteration of this text to you from memory. Brit and Nick have become living breathing people in my world and they've helped me accomplish something I've always dreamed of—having a book traditionally published. For that, I will always love them best.

To my agents Kimberly and Joy—"Sign with Brower Literary" was one of the first things I wrote in my manifesting notebook when I set out to query this book. You were the first query I sent and the last call I took, and a lot of things happened in the six months in between, making it even more incredible that it actually came true. Thank you, truly, for making this book so much better than when you found it. Thank you for helping me "kill my darlings" humanely and with the least amount of pain, and for understanding what I really wanted to do with these characters and helping me achieve it.

Thank you to Kate Byrne from Headline Eternal. The first email I received from you told me that this book had found the right champion. I knew immediately that you saw exactly what I'd hoped readers would see in these two characters. To Jill Cole, we've not had the pleasure of meeting, but thank you for teaching me how to spell buses and, you know, general comma usage. And to all of the Headline Eternal family who I haven't met yet, thank you for working on this dream with me.

To my CPs: The inspirational Wesley Parker, I still remember every comment you made on this manuscript—especially the one that referenced a Cardi B song and Nick not knowing how to act after. Thank you for feeling everything I felt along with these characters and especially thank you for your contributions to the playlist. Melissa Grace, your enthusiasm for Nick and Brit kept me going through numerous "wtf did I get myself into" moments. I can't wait until you get in those trenches so I can cheer you on. Mia Heintzelman, we could probably conquer the world in one of our brainstorming Zooms. Thank you for always being up for that.

To my beta readers: Cecile, Michelle, Andree, and Brooke—your early reads were immeasurably helpful and I can't wait for you to see what the book formerly known as Cruise Control has become. And to all of the readers, Bookstagrammers, bloggers and reviewers who have helped me build a brand and grow my career, I cannot overstate your part in making this happen. I'll be forever grateful.

Sophia, your insta game was on point for these two, from Nick's fake IG name to the COVID spin we had to put on the captions. You KNOW that foolishness is integral to my process. So are you.

Cici, your prompts in the writing chat are always great, but per the dedication of this book, this one was your best yet. When you told us the story of your co-worker getting stranded by a cruise ship, I yelled "DIBS" immediately because I knew . . . I KNEW you had just given me the key to getting to this place right here. I will never forget that moment or the Bryce (I mean Bruce) face that followed when I announced my signature Lauren twist.

Nat, Jordyn, and Demi, thank you for always supporting me. The Andy chat is my happy place.

To the village, and Jack and Michelle, thank you for celebrating every win with me. I know this business is weird and confusing from the outside but it didn't matter to you. If I was cheering, you were cheering even louder and that means the world.

Finally, to my husband. TJ, thank you for never even considering the possibility that this wouldn't happen. You were so sure, and as always, you were right.

HEADLINE
ETERNAL

FIND YOUR HEART'S DESIRE...

VISIT OUR WEBSITE: www.headlineeternal.com
FIND US ON FACEBOOK: facebook.com/eternalromance
CONNECT WITH US ON TWITTER: @eternal_books
FOLLOW US ON INSTAGRAM: @headlineeternal
EMAIL US: eternalromance@headline.co.uk